A Far-flung Life

Western Australia, 1958.
A truck rumbles along a lonely outback road.
A moment's inattention, and in a few muddled seconds the lives of the MacBride family are shattered.

But instead of leaving them to heal, fate comes back for them in a twist of consequences that will cause one of them to lose their life, and another to sacrifice theirs for the sake of an innocent child.

Set in the imposing expanse of Western Australia, where the weather is a capricious god and a million-acre sheep station is barely a dot on the map, *A Far-flung Life* explores the hearts of a handful of isolated souls and the secrets they shield in order to survive.

Capturing a family, a community, a generation, it tells of the many ways humans can do each other wrong and how we can go on when things can't be put right. With shimmering prose and warm wit, the mysteries of being human are laid bare in this meditation on time and resilience and the lengths we go to to protect what we love.

Coming 26th February 2026
In hardback, trade paperback, ebook and audio

For publicity enquiries please contact Alison Barrow:
abarrow@penguinrandomhouse.co.uk

M L STEDMAN

was born and raised in Western Australia and now lives in London. Her first novel, *The Light Between Oceans*, was a *Sunday Times*, *New York Times* and international bestseller and won the Goodreads Choice Best Historical Novel Award and the HWA Goldsboro Crown Debut. It was also longlisted for the Women's Prize and the Walter Scott Prize for Historical Fiction, nominated for the International IMPAC Dublin literary award voted for by librarians, and shortlisted as an Amazon Rising Star. In Australia, it won the Indie Best Debut and Indie Best Book Awards, and was longlisted for the Miles Franklin Award and the Literary Society Gold Medal. It also won the Australian Book Industry Awards for Best Newcomer, Best Literary Fiction and Book of the Year. *The Light Between Oceans* has been published in around forty-five languages and has sold nearly five million copies worldwide. It was made into a Dreamworks film starring Michael Fassbender and Alicia Vikander, produced by Heyday Films. *A Far-flung Life* is M L Stedman's second novel, to be published worldwide.

Also by M. L. *Stedman*

The Light Between Oceans

A Far-flung Life

M. L. Stedman

doubleday

TRANSWORLD PUBLISHERS
Penguin Random House, One Embassy Gardens,
8 Viaduct Gardens, London SW11 7BW
www.penguin.co.uk

Transworld is part of the Penguin Random House group of companies
whose addresses can be found at global.penguinrandomhouse.com

Penguin
Random House
UK

First published in Great Britain in 2026 by Doubleday
an imprint of Transworld Publishers

A CIP catalogue record for this book
is available from the British Library.

ISBNs
9781529965308 (hb)
9781529965346 (tpb)

Typeset in 12/16pt Goudy Old Style BT by Jouve (UK), Milton Keynes
Printed and bound in Great Britain by Clays Ltd, Elcograf S.p.A.

The authorized representative in the EEA is Penguin Random House Ireland,
Morrison Chambers, 32 Nassau Street, Dublin D02 YH68.

Dedication To Come

Epigraphs To Come

PART I

Image To Come

1

Western Australia

Friday, 10th January 1958

OUT HERE, IT'S red earth for as far as the eye can see. Overhead, the sun ploughs an unending blue sky. Under dust-green mulga, a lizard seeks shade and shadow; ants engineer heat-defying nests; kangaroos suck moisture from tender leaves, ears swivelling to locate a distant rumble: on the straight vermilion line that cleaves the sparse trees, a lone truck is approaching.

Strung along the seat of the Bedford, the three MacBride men sit, like unpacked Russian dolls. Phil's straight, dark hair and oval face is repeated in Warren, his eldest son, and echoed in Matt, his youngest. Like peas in a pod – same story for generations. Everyone reckons even Rosie, the daughter back at the homestead, born between the brothers, is the spitting image, too. The mother, Lorna, doesn't get a look-in. You can tell a MacBride a mile off.

Warren punched his little brother's arm. 'God, you come out with some bulldust!'

'No! Sailing around the world. Discovering uninhabited islands . . .' Matt said. 'It'd be great!'

'Well, unless you put in the elbow grease, the damned boat'll be eaten by white ants, so you'd sink as soon as you hit the water,' said their father. He gave the gearstick a shove, coaxing the truck over the coming rise. From the back, the few dozen sheep *baa*'d.

The fact that the MacBrides had a boat on their sheep station might have been unremarkable if their property bordered the state's six-thousand-mile coast. But Meredith Downs, nearly a million arid acres, is far inland, fringing into desert country in places.

'What was the bet about again?' Matt asked.

The discussion had begun when they passed a towering, solitary shape in the distance: 'Monty's shed'. Named for Phil's uncle, Montgomery MacBride, it was the most outlandish structure for hundreds of miles. The legend of how Meredith Downs – a property with twenty thousand sheep and an average annual rainfall of eight inches – came to be home to a fully rigged pearling lugger had been much embellished over time, but the essentials remained: a debt from an old mate of Monty's, settled in kind; towed behind a camel team by some Afghans; a dream that one day Monty would sail it himself, perhaps off the continent's south coast, despite the absence of pearls in the freezing Southern Ocean. It had come with the name *Alpha Crucis*, the brightest star in the Southern Cross. When Monty marched off to the Somme in 1915 to do his duty, his father promised to keep it in good order. He built the shed around it with money from the wool clip, and kept the vessel's timber oiled, and the spiders and termites at bay.

But when Monty came back gassed, all he was good for was to hunker in the boat in the blinding heat of the shed, and sail away to some safer shore in his imagination. When he died not long afterwards, his boat bone-dry and his dreams unlived, they stowed his ashes in the bow along with a compass and a bottle of beer, and a promise that one day they'd get the lugger in the water, to scatter his ashes in the Indian Ocean. Phil MacBride still kept up the ritual: varnishing the timber; replacing frayed lines; bringing Monty a beer every birthday. A man not given to whimsy, Phil made this exception: 'It's tradition,' was all he'd say, placing the bottle reverently in the bow.

Now, he answered his youngest son's question: 'Monty reckoned he could find water on his friend's property up north using just a divining rod: if he did, he'd get the boat. Sure enough, he turned up fresh water at thirty feet, and they never looked back. So the mate made good on the promise. Took the better part of a year to tow it here.'

The truck grumbled along, the sun stalking it more greedily with every hour. The orange gravel road was riven with parched gulleys from recent unseasonal rain. 'Better get the grader out here, Warren, see if we can iron out this stretch,' Phil said as they shuddered over a badly corrugated patch which sent the sheep stumbling. 'Get Miles to give you a hand,' and they went on to discuss how the Pommy trainee overseer, Miles Beaumont, had done, now that his stint with them was nearly over.

Saltbush began to give way to spinifex in places, and six black swans glided onto the massive salt lake, its border crystalled white. The lofty metal windmills in the paddocks turned gently in the breeze, pumping up the precious underground water. Now and then a few sheep scattered at the sight of the truck.

Wedged between his father and brother, Matt watched as a pair of emus darted out at the side of the road and for a moment kept pace with them before bolting back into cover. Daft buggers. But fast. Faster than the bungarras that would be there somewhere too? Countless animals, disguised by the scrubby bush: the Brown snakes and the redbacks; the little skinks; the ants in their millions. Camels, too, roaming wild after the era of cameleers: right now, somewhere on the property, there'd be one kneeling on a fence to break it and get to water. But they weren't nearly as bad as the dingoes, wary of traps and waiting for night to get at some poor sheep. And the roos. Bloody thousands of them, despite the best efforts of Pete Peachey, their roo shooter.

Matt's eyes began to close, weighed down with the early start, and yesterday's excitement of the telegram from Perth announcing his outstanding Leaving and Matric results: the end of school forever.

He'd lain awake most of the night, thinking about what he would do next. Warren, more like forty-two than his actual twenty-two years, would take over Meredith Downs when their father retired – that was set in stone. Matt would have to do something else. And right this minute, two days short of his eighteenth birthday, it felt like he could do anything at all: go to university, become an engineer or a scientist – or a cartographer – he loved a good map . . . Or, with his parents' help, buy a station of his own. Get married even? One day. He conjured the pale green eyes of Pattie Gosden who, his sister Rose had promised him, would be at his Young Pastoralists' meeting in town today . . .

After hours rattling along flat dirt roads, stopping to swing open and close the broad gate of each paddock, they reached the boundary of Meredith Downs. The truck, with three men and the load of sheep, was no more than a grain of living sand in the landscape.

* * *

The MacBrides took up country in Western Australia a few decades after the Swan River Colony was settled in 1829. Lyle MacBride and his brother Lachlan left behind their father's modest sheep farm, braving the gruelling voyage from England with wives in tow, and over a couple of generations, their families fanned out across the west, as land opened up for grazing. As years went on, the Crown Lands maps showed block after block leased to 'MacBride' in red cursive ink.

The MacBride name also began to turn up in all the other records you'd expect: Registers of Births, Deaths and Marriages, and the minutes of meetings of Vermin Boards and Roads Boards. In Bureau of Meteorology logs, which sent weather observations back to Perth and Melbourne, you'd also find mention of a MacBride or two. They were there in the Pastoralists' and Graziers' Association minutes and the Royal Agricultural Society ledgers and much else besides.

The MacBrides had the touch, it was said: sensible but shrewd, careful but not mean. When fortunes allowed, they were ready donors to good causes both religious and secular. They made ideal neighbours: fair in disputes, practical in disasters; good husbanders of land who followed the best practice of the day. Whilst Lachlan's lot drifted up north, descendants of Lyle stayed put on Meredith Downs and eventually increased its boundaries to just shy of a million acres, the maximum extent then allowed by law. But a million acres barely registers as a dot on the map of Western Australia, the million square miles that makes up a third of the continent.

The MacBride men were handsome fellows, and had the knack of attracting debutantes to join them in their bush life. These wives sometimes came with dowries bestowed by stockbroker fathers or gold-mining grandfathers, which meant there was usually the wherewithal to tide the station over the tough times that came often enough.

It's hard country, out this way. Back in England, a farm might support two or three sheep per acre. Here, with the lack of rainfall, you need more like forty acres per sheep. There is heat. There is sun. But on winter nights the water in the tanks will freeze over. The searing light that coaxes life into being here will bleach it out of existence with the same indifferent shrug, leaving blanched trees, and rusted corrugated iron on the roofs of abandoned homesteads. The wind that brings the rain can bring floods and flatten shearing sheds. Everything that can do you good can also do you harm here – that's just the way of it.

This land has seen improbable things: the evolution of marsupials and monotremes; of flightless birds and animals that fly. It's seen continents split and islands arise. It's seen oceans turn to desert and desert turn to glaciers. And it's watched people drag their little lives across its surface, flat and unforgiving.

As for drought . . . Well, that's like the bad relation you know will turn up sooner or later – it's not a question of whether but when. That's another reason properties have to be big out here: to spread the weather. At least on some part of the million acres you might get a bit of a shower and be able to move your stock to the green feed that springs up in the paddocks or around the clay pans that fill with water. If it looks like you're heading into a perish, you destock as quickly as you can, cut the staff numbers, and wait out the eerie silence that comes when no sheep bleats, no bird flies, and no leaf rustles in the wind because there are no leaves.

On the day of that drive to Wanderrie Creek in January 1958, as Phil and Warren chatted about fence repairs, and Matt daydreamed about his future, about seeing Pattie Gosden, the MacBrides' luck changed, and they headed into an altogether different kind of perish.

Phil MacBride had been able to drive since he was seven years old – as soon as he could reach the pedals. He'd taught his sons at about that age, too. And one of the main rules he'd impressed on them was this: never swerve to avoid hitting a roo. There was no telling which way it'd jump, so you were better off taking your chances of a busted radiator than to risk skidding out of control and rolling.

Perhaps it was the heat mirage, then, that made Matt's father, for less than a second, register the six-foot upright figure on the road in front of him as a man instead of a red kangaroo buck. By the time Phil's feet had moved to slam on the brakes, his head had told him his mistake, but by then the truck had ploughed into the treacherous soft gravel shoulder, and twisted onto its side in a snarl of metal and force, flinging one of his sons through the windscreen, and impaling the other on the gearstick.

Phil had just enough strength to pull Warren from the cab, and drag him clear. He could make out Matt, further from the truck, head bleeding, limbs sprawled. Then he saw nothing more.

Petrol fumes doused the tang of the saltbush, and the thrum of the nearby windmill died under the frantic bleating of the sheep as the truck's wheels spun in mid-air, flicking fuel like a Catherine wheel. Within minutes, the vapour had ignited in the heat and drowned the vehicle in an orange roar of flames, black smoke from the melting tyres sketching a ladder to the boundless, empty sky.

Peas in a pod, the MacBride men were, strung along the dusty road in blood that welled and eddied and banded into a single scarlet pool.

2

When Sneaky Snook in his mail truck happened upon the wreckage near the boundary of Meredith Downs, sheep were scattered along the roadside and the fence, bleating, dazed. Anyone approaching the scene could be forgiven for thinking they'd stumbled on a grisly barbecue. The bars of the truck had caged in a dozen wethers as their wool was singed away and they gradually burned to death: distressed, sacrificial, but smelling just as delicious as a grilled lamb chop ever had. So the barking of the mailman's dog, Lightning, could have been consternation, or merely appetite.

Fortunately, this was a relatively busy road for the area – usually at least one vehicle came along it each day. In fact, it was not even an hour before Sneaky found them, alerted by the smoke. Warren was bleeding but conscious, propped on an elbow, ordering Sneaky to get the sheep back, swearing when the man tried to move him. Matt, as still as a rock on the gravel – like his father not far away – was dead, Sneaky assumed: his leg was gashed, and blood crusted his ears. So the mailman concentrated on the one still talking. Save the life he could save, and so forth . . . Turned out later Warren's liver had been leaking blood, letting him swear and curse all the way to oblivion. The three men were just far enough from the truck to avoid being incinerated – 'At least we'll have the bodies,' Lorna would say later. 'At least we can bury them.'

Wheezing with the heat, the mailman hauled Warren into his truck cab, then dragged Phil's body over, letting out a grunt as he hoisted it into the back. Lightning, nobly forgoing the chance of a mutton lunch, was standing over Matt's chest, growling, when Sneaky returned.

'Get out of it!'

The dog ignored him, and licked the boy's face. An eyelid twitched.

'Crikey, Lightning!' Sneaky bent down to reassess the corpse. Detecting a faint pulse, he turned to the dog. 'Clever boy!' To Matt, he said, 'Hang on there, son. Don't you go anywhere, now.' He shoved aside parcels and mail sacks and crates of groceries to make room for him beside his father. 'Right. Keep an eye on him, fella,' he said, waggling his dog's snout, 'and yell out if he gets worse.' With that, he squeezed himself back behind the steering wheel and drove hell for leather to the nearest roadhouse, twenty miles away, where they had a pedal radio and bandages and an airstrip for the Flying Doctor.

When he landed his plane, Dr Finbar Rafferty, the normally unflappable Irishman who'd known the MacBrides for years, flinched at the sight that greeted him. 'Mother of God!'

Then he rubbed a hand across his face to collect himself, and began assessing the figures as patients rather than old friends; followed the clinical steps that led his thoughts onto safer ground.

On the morning that the lives of her menfolk were being haggled over by Life and Death, Lorna MacBride was in her kitchen, moving with her usual brisk efficiency as she made the fruitcake for her youngest son's approaching birthday.

The sprawling kitchen was the heart of the old stone homestead, which in turn was the heart of Meredith Downs. Its immaculately neat pantry, which Lorna provisioned on an industrial scale, held enough supplies to get them through months of being cut off by fires or cyclones. In addition to her own preserves and Vacola'd produce, shelves were stacked with cans of fruit and packets of dry biscuits, great hessian sacks of rice and flour and jumbo tins of powdered milk.

The kitchen had fuelled generations of MacBrides when they set off before dawn for a muster or came home thick with dust and grime after putting up a fence or repairing a bore. Its long jarrah table was the construction site for hearty lunches for neighbours who came to help erect a mill or for a cricket match, and for visitors calling in on their way to or from Perth. Sporting victories were celebrated here, floods and droughts lamented.

This morning the room was filled with the wafting aroma of the bread Lorna had put in to bake in the enormous wood-fired Metters: the only electricity in the homestead came from the thirty-two-volt generator, which provided a few hours of electric light in the evenings. Though the system managed only a dim glow, Lorna was still grateful for the flick of a switch rather than the toil of refilling oil lamps and trimming candles.

Like many stations out this way, there was no telephone either. Instead, beside the cooling rack that stood ready to receive the scorching hot loaf tins, sat the ped set, the pedal-operated transceiver that was the MacBrides' lifeline to the outside world.

It was not from the wireless, however, but from a knock on the front door, that Lorna learned of the crash. She had just put Matt's cake in to bake when two policemen from Wanderrie Creek, sixty miles away, hats in hand, guided her back through the house to sit at her own table before breaking the news.

Like rain running off a greasy fleece, their words barely touched her with meaning. Then, as they sank in, Lorna was aware of a strange, sick sensation: her family, the world – reality itself – had been destroyed, but every cup on every shelf, instead of falling to the floor to smash into a shattered mess as it surely should, sat, unmoved: unimpressed to be handled, at last, by Sergeant Wisheart, who made tea and put three sugars in it for her and for her daughter Rose. The girl, full of excitement just moments before as she recounted her ride to the old mine on their property with Miles that morning, now stood speechless and deathly white with shock.

All their men gone. The phrase echoed in Lorna's mind as she put her floury fingers to the cup handle, but couldn't remember how to lift it.

The crash that claimed those MacBride lives was not an extraordinary event. A light coating of death dusts any scene you care to observe in the bush: the desiccated tree weathered into twisted stone, the rams' horns flaking in the dirt, the insects banked up against the flywire of a homestead window in a snowdrift of wings and legs. Death twinkles in this landscape like mineral sand.

In any given year, you'll know someone fatally thrown from a horse, or killed when their car ran off the road, or bitten by a snake, too far from help. Mineshafts are a popular haunt for death too. As well as the miners who get lashed by a snapped steel cable, or whose heads are crushed when the operator absentmindedly hoists them up instead of down, there are plenty of people desperate for somewhere to jump from, in a largely flat landscape with no tall buildings. The mineshafts oblige them generously, particularly after a bender or a jilting. And an abandoned shaft can keep this a secret for months or years.

So you can't survive out here without the invisible network that spreads across stations and towns, like veins in a body, sending vital support to victims of calamity and carnage. After the radio call to the Flying Doctor, word flowed like water over the Sched, the cockies' name for 'the Schedule' on which the various stations were allotted time to use the shortwave radio frequency run by the Flying Doctor.

Everyone knew where Meredith Downs was on its yearly schedule of lambing and mustering and shearing. And everyone knew that if they were in the same Godforsaken straits, they'd want their neighbours to appear on their doorstep to help. At least it was January, the quietest month of the year, when you mostly just kept your head down and waited for the sapping heat to lose interest and move on.

Rose had insisted on following Matt straight to the hospital, many hundreds of miles away in Perth. 'Someone should be there when he wakes up. Or if he—' The two women had looked at each other across the table in silence. Though Lorna couldn't bear to part with her last healthy child, she yielded. She herself would get there as soon as things were under control at the station.

Maudie Knapp from Deep Springs station, fifty miles to the north, was the first to turn up after hearing about it on the Sched. She bustled in with a hastily packed suitcase, a big tin of her famous shortbread and the pot of stew that she'd had on the stove when the news came through.

'Oh, Lorna!' The sight of her dear friend, grey eyes gazing blankly, barely able to stand, robbed her of words for a moment, and she took a deep breath. 'Right. I'm here now, love. And Charlie's on his way. Bob Sowerby and some of his boys'll be coming from next door at Maundy Creek. Just tell us which paddocks the stock are in and what the hands are due to be doing.' She opened and closed cupboards until she found what she was looking for. 'Here. Drink some brandy.'

If you'd asked Lorna MacBride exactly how the time passed after that terrible event, she couldn't have told you. That first day, it was a matter of getting through a breath at a time, as though she might actually forget to take in air if she didn't make the effort.

She found herself obsessing about funerals. The undertakers

could wait a few days, but she knew they didn't have a cool room, and the Wanderrie Creek hospital morgue would accommodate 'guests' for only so long. But it might be bad luck to plan funerals before she knew whether there would be two or three?

Her thoughts were interrupted by Maudie, who was saying gently, 'I know you'll want to get to Perth to see Matt . . .'

'Mattie . . . Yes, of course.' But just in that moment, Lorna couldn't for the life of her remember whether that particular child was dead or alive. She knew– yes, she knew her Rosie had survived. Which of the boys, though?

3

THE SLIM WOMAN with the greying hair and trembling hands who took the glass of brandy was almost unrecognisable, her old friend thought. It was as if she, too, had been hit by a truck. For a few seconds after he came in, Charlie Knapp, Maudie's husband, didn't recognise Lorna either. Her usually ruddy cheeks were waxy, her shoulders stooped, and her warm, clear voice a timorous whisper.

Yet this was the same Lorna MacBride, daughter of an Adelaide stockbroker, who had been swept off her feet by Phil at the Shell Ball in Perth in 1933, and had come to Meredith Downs armed with humour and common sense and fuelled by the certainty that she had married the love of her life. She had swiftly taken root in the homestead, and settled so well into the district that she was soon known and admired for hundreds of miles.

Lorna could fix the generator and get the car out of a bog. She made the best Victoria sponge known to any branch of the Country Women's Association, and when word got around that she'd bottled her annual batch of tomato chutney, people made excuses to 'drop by' and pick up a jar while they were 'passing'.

Some stations sent their women to Perth for the summer. Suburbs like Peppermint Grove were dotted with cool limestone houses sheltering ladies with powder and blue-rinse perms who occupied themselves with tennis and bridge until the heat eased off sufficiently to return inland or up north. So the women like Lorna MacBride and Maudie Knapp, who stayed behind, were bonded by hardships big and small: like not being able to wash your hair for weeks on end because there was too little water, or what water there was was so hard that your hair stuck out like a scarecrow's. They lamented the difficulty of keeping food from going off in smoky kerosene fridges that half the time ended up covered in slime inside and out, or, worse, caught fire. These women reached for the rifle to shoot the snake that slithered into their kitchen, then chalked it up on the blackboard, comparing this year's tally with the last. They cooked and cleaned and tended to wounds and taught the kids their correspondence-school syllabus in temperatures that took your breath away. They plucked chickens and gutted them, seared the hair off the pork rind of the pig their littlies raised as a pet and that their husband killed in their slaughterhouse. They comforted those same husbands when the bank threatened foreclosure or rain refused to fall or the government announced some new tariff that would cripple them.

And they passed these abilities onto their daughters.

In the case of Lorna MacBride, that was Rose, the other person to receive the terrible news in the kitchen over Sergeant Wisheart's sweet tea.

Rose wasn't a beauty like her mother, but she had a winning smile, and radiated health and vigour. Her stocky build and determination suited her to station life: she could wrestle a ram down the drafting race, and change a flat tyre as easily as her brothers. Rose had none of Warren's cockiness, nor the easy-going charm of Matt, but she was quick and tenacious and a good sport. Perhaps naturally, everyone assumed she would be a chip off the old block, and would, in time, marry a decent chap from a good property and go on to forge a family under another name.

'It's funny,' Lorna would say. 'You feed them the same. You love them the same. But every child's its own country.'

It was Lorna who had the first inkling that the happy wedding and the quiet, motherly life might *not* be the path for her daughter; just as it was Lorna who first noticed that from an early age Rose was occasionally a stranger to the truth. Lorna MacBride, for whom there was black and white and right and wrong and not much in between, was uneasy that Rose's account of events did not always tally with fact.

As a kid, if Warren smashed a cup or hit a ball through a window pane, he'd take pride in claiming responsibility: Phil had told him that 'that's what blokes do – take your punishment like a man'. So he'd get his wallop, or go without his rifle for a week, and life would go on. Matthew was still too little then to be getting up to anything you could really call mischief. He adored his older brother and sister, and would often be their unwitting stooge, fetching things for Warren, or sitting still while Rose, almost three years older, dressed him as a princess. Rose developed a habit, if items were broken or missing, of saying it was 'Bubba's fault', then rushing to add, 'But he's only little. He couldn't help it,' and Lorna would invariably let it go. Until one day she found one of her few hats, a toque with a net veil, covered in dirt and its netting torn. The hat was kept in the top of the linen press, which Lorna had to stand on tiptoes to reach. She had sometimes caught Warren and Rose clambering up the shelves like monkeys, perching inside the cupboard while Mattie watched with frustrated admiration.

Phil had bought the hat on their honeymoon. When he put it on her head, he let out a whistle of admiration: 'Like they say, "There's nothing as beautiful as a woman who is loved."' It was the most romantic thing he had ever said, and the hat had been a talisman of those words, and of that time.

Things changed after kids, of course. Then war came. So, with Phil's battalion posted to North Africa in 1942, something in Lorna gave way at the sight of the damaged hat, and she didn't try to keep the crossness from her face when she marched into the lounge room, where the children sat playing. She held up the offending object. 'Right. Anyone have anything to say about this?'

'Mumma hat!' chirruped Matt.

Warren had a *Search me!* expression. Rose went a dark shade of pink, eyes darting from one brother to the other.

'Rosie?' asked Lorna.

'It's a hat. *Your* hat.'

'Any idea how it got dirty?'

Rose minutely inspected a piece of Meccano.

'Well?'

'I think Warre—' She saw Lorna's eyebrows shoot up. 'I mean Bubba – I think Bubba did it.'

The lie was so bold, and the performance so earnest, that Lorna had to suppress a laugh. 'Go to your room, and have a ponder. Then come and tell me whether that's right. I won't be cross. But I *will* want to know the proper truth.'

Lorna mentioned the episode in a letter to Phil, and, sitting in the kitchen late one night, she could almost hear his laugh when he wrote back, 'She's quick on her feet, I'll give her that!' He'd added, 'She'll grow out of it.'

Though Lorna smiled, a worry lingered that Rose might not grow out of it. And she wished Phil were there, to take her hand across the table. She said a silent prayer for his safety, and one of gratitude for the miracle of having met him in this big world.

4

THE NUMBERS OF kangaroos out here skyrocketed with the coming of the whitefella and his quest to bring enough water to the surface to support his stock. Roos relished the same young grasses and shoots as the sheep and cattle; they thirsted for the same sweet water that surged up from bores or shimmered invitingly in dams and troughs. That meant there was a decent living to be had roo shooting, travelling from one property to another, by arrangement with the owner, killing for skins or sometimes for pet meat, depending on the market and the weather. Some properties were big enough to keep a roo shooter busy all year.

Pete Peachey was the roo shooter for Meredith Downs, a lanky bloke with thinning hair neatly oiled back, and grey eyes that took in you and the horizon and everything in between with the same sharp gaze that seemed to see right into whatever he beheld. His face was as tanned as the roo hides he gathered, not so much lined as deeply guttered by the sun. He came around like a comet: who knew where he was or what he did when he drove off the property. Once a year he'd turn up to the district Vermin Board meeting, at the same time as he came to the police station to renew his annual shooter's licence for two pounds.

Silent as the grave, was Peachey. The only things generally

known about him were that he was a crack shot, having won the King's Medal, the Armed Forces' coveted shooting prize, a month after joining up in the war. This was all the more remarkable because he'd been born left-handed but had been forced as a child to become right-handed, so was ambidextrous and equally deadly either way. The other known fact was that he'd been taken prisoner by the Japs. Details were sketchy after that.

Peachey never mentioned family. Folks didn't think it polite to ask him outright, so rumours just blew about like grass seed, until no one rightly knew what his story was.

Despite his line of business, as long as he had access to water, he was always scrupulously clean and perfectly shaved with a cut-throat razor. He'd start work in the evening with his hair brushed, but by the end of it would be flecked with the blood that caked his clothes, so that he'd turn creeks red when he bathed in them. Once, during a cyclone that made the roads impassable, he'd pitched tent near the homestead and, in his camp oven, baked a ginger cake that Lorna had to concede was better than her own. Full of surprises, was Pete Peachey.

One evening in 1947, more than a decade before the accident, and about a year into his time working Meredith Downs, the roo shooter was lying on a groundsheet outside his tent, knees cricked into spindly twin peaks. Through binoculars, he took in the glow of the waxing gibbous moon, its magnified ashy craters clear and monochrome. The calm autumn night was too chilly for mosquitos and sand flies. 'Clear as day, fella,' he said; then, to the silence, 'Oh.' He was still getting used to the absence of the roo dog he'd lost to a strychnine bait, days before.

At the hiss of dried grass, he turned, quickly swapping binoculars for a rifle, scanning the halo of the campfire's light until the barrel was pointing at a scrawny pair of legs, which rose to join a child's torso and a head of long, unkempt hair.

'Rosie?' Pete exclaimed, lowering the gun. 'What the hell—'

'What were you watching?' the little girl asked.

'How the devil did you get here? Where's your mum and dad?'

She shuffled forward, and dropped the canvas bag from her shoulder. 'Warren's a worm. He gave me a Chinese burn and said I'd have to leave the station when I grow up, so I might as well go now.' She drew back one side of her mouth. 'He caught me playing with his Meccano.'

'Did he hurt you?'

'Nah.' Her small hand shoved the thicket of hair from her eyes. 'So I smashed his Meccano Sydney Harbour Bridge. He doesn't know yet.' She folded her arms. 'I've left home.'

'Come here. Let's have a look at you.' Pete turned her this way and that in the light: nothing amiss that a hairbrush and a bath wouldn't fix. 'Come and sit by the fire.' He pulled in an upturned crate, then fetched a scratchy grey blanket and draped it over her shoulders.

When he asked again how she got there, she just pursed her lips.

He put the billy on. 'Remind me . . . you're about how old these days?'

'Ten. Nearly . . .'

Peachey gave a grave nod. 'And Warren's been rotten.'

'Yeah.'

'So you decided to shoot through . . .'

The child gave a nonchalant shrug, but there was just the hint of a wobble in her chin.

'Fair enough.' He filled a tin mug with tea, stirring in some sugar for her. 'We're a decent gallop from the homestead. How long have you been walking?'

She looked at him as though he were very dim. 'I came with you,' she said, pointing to his empty trailer, its tarpaulin hanging open. 'I climbed in. When you stopped to open the gate at the house.'

'Ah.' Pete let out a breath and put his hands on his hips. 'Where are you headed?'

'Wanderrie Creek?' Rose flicked the tip of her pink tongue into the sweet liquid. 'Anywhere away from Warren.'

'Right,' said Pete, pulling up a crate beside her and drinking his tea. 'Anyone know you were going?'

She raised her bottom lip and shook her head.

'I see.'

The girl held out a hand, palm flat.

'What, you want something to eat?'

'It's for my smack. For being bad. I'll take it like a man.'

'No smacks from Old Pete, love.'

She left her hand there. 'Dad'll give me a smack.'

'That's up to him. My dad would've given me a smack too.' He put a fingertip to her palm to lower it. 'Can't say I've ever seen it do much good.'

They sat for a while, the little girl licking her tea like a lizard, while the crickets echoed the fire's crackles. She interrogated his camp with her eyes, sniffing the air now and then to get a better sense of it – the smoke, the gun oil, the whiff of kero.

Eventually, Pete took her cold mug. 'Right-oh. What's say I take you back to your mum and dad? They'll be worried.'

'What were you looking at, through the field glasses?'

'Just the moon.'

'What for?'

With a dip of the head as much as to say *See for yourself*, he picked up the binoculars and handed them to her.

Rose's mouth opened. 'But there are – there are holes and stuff.'

'Craters.'

'And a darker bit at the side.'

'Yep. Waxing gibbous moon tonight, so the dark bit's small.'

'Waxy gibbons?'

Pete emptied the dregs of tea. 'Let's make a deal. I'll tell you about the moon if you promise we'll take you back straight after. And that there'll be no more leaving home until you're . . .' He considered something, then touched his shoulder. 'Until you're this tall. OK?'

And so Pete explained to the little girl the phases of the moon, its waxing and waning, and the fact that on earth, because the time of its rotation is roughly the same as its orbit around the earth, we only ever see one side of it.

'But what's on the *other* side?'

He thought for a moment. 'I reckon that's the moon's business, Rosie. Makes no difference to how well she shines on us.'

On a hot December night, Pete Peachey goes down to the creek and washes the blood off his hands. The water's as cold as the dead, and as still. Once absolved of the thick red stains, his fingers move to the buttons of his flannel shirt, caked with dust and pungent with roo's blood and his own sweat and three days of travelling out here, alone.

He feels each button, counts them silently as they surrender, and finally sheds the shirt altogether. His boots come off with a *ffft*, then the thick wool socks. His buckle clinks as he undoes his belt and leaves it in the loops of his strides as they fall from his narrow hips. His underpants are more rust red than white, but still catch the moon's glow until they, too, are sloughed off. The hurricane lamp now hosts moths and beetles, flinging themselves at the scorching glass. He reaches into a tobacco tin for a bar of Sunlight soap, and wades into the creek.

He eases the soap into the water, and begins not the vigorous, harsh scrubbing with which he washes his hands at the homestead, but more tender, contemplative strokes. Accompanied by the insistent rasp of crickets, he covers every inch of himself with lather. With each stroke he rinses away the look in the roo's eyes, the quick rip as skin is torn away from muscle, the loud *crack* as he breaks the inside of the legs so they take up less space; the sight of the joey lying translucent blue, no fur yet, pulled from its dead mother's pouch.

He sinks to a sitting position to wash his feet, still feeling the weight of the tiny creature as he dashed its head against the rocky ground. Scenes of other blood, other torn skin, from long ago flicker and subside in memory. 'Forgive . . . forget,' he breathes.

As he rubs the soap across the contours of his nose, his forehead, his whiskery chin, he reads his own features like Braille. What would he feel like to a woman now? His thin hair is stiff with dust and sweat, and he ducks his head under the icy water that has him shivering and goosebumped. He washes away the miles and the hours with strong, skilled fingers. He is cleansed.

Emerging from the water, he dries himself and slips his boots back on, then stirs the fire, where the billy's just about ready for a brew. His dirty clothes are folded neatly beside the campstool; his rifles stand alert against the tent. He empties a tin of beans into his battle-scarred saucepan, and sets it to warm while he makes his tea. He's in no hurry. He eyes the kitbag just on the edge of the darkness, looks back at the beans, stirs them. He savours the feel of the air on his clean skin.

His meal finished, he sets up the ancient gramophone that has been waiting for him in the shadows, and blows the dust off a shellac disc, one of many he's accumulated over the years from station people discarding them in the rush to radiograms and LPs. He winds it up. As the clear, slender voice of Nellie Melba begins 'Il dolce suono', he reaches for the bag. Sitting naked, he'd not given a thought to looking around him – there's no one for God knows how many miles. But now, as he starts to undo the rope that fastens it, he looks furtively, strains for any human sound. Nothing. He reaches inside and retrieves a mirror. He gazes for a moment, taking in the greying stubble, the scar on his top lip pale with time.

His cheekbones angle sharply beneath the lines that cross them. He rests the mirror on his lap and takes out a pair of hairbrushes; guides his damp hair back off his face. Next, he snakes his hand blindly into the bag until it finds its target. He looks around him again, and draws out something crimson, as the long-dead singer promises him 'Del ciel clemente un riso la vita a noi sarà' – 'From clement heaven, life will be a smile to us.'

'Us' is an ever-changing thing, he thinks, and strokes the silk in his hands.

5

THE MAIL TRUCK that had happened upon the crash only came out to Meredith Downs every week or so; less often if a fire or a flood cut off the roads. Sneaky Snook had been the mail contractor on the route since 1950. Christened William, he was called Billy until an incident with some fire crackers at the age of seven, after which he was known to the world, his mother included, as Sneaky. His dog, Lightning, accompanied him on his mail run – it was good to have someone to talk to on a round trip of four hundred miles. The blue heeler was impeccably behaved – better table manners than his owner, people said – and was handy if a snake got too near when they occasionally camped along the way. A dingo trap had claimed one of the dog's legs when he was still a pup, but by then Sneaky had got used to the name, and couldn't bring himself to change it.

Sneaky had straight, sandy hair, and lizard-dry hands with cuticles that grew up the nail. His nose was bulbous, his leathery cheeks threaded with a fine purple lacework, and he wheezed when he laughed, especially if he was smoking. One of his legs was an inch shorter than the other, so he wore what he referred to as his 'dancing shoes'– one sole built up to stop the limp.

His appetite for bread and dripping meant that he had quite a belly to fit behind the steering wheel, and his fondness for Swan

Lager didn't help. His shirts were always straining at the buttons because, all in all, Sneaky was an optimist and believed heartily that next week, or next month, or next year, he'd cut down on the grog and see his knees again, and on that basis there was no reason to throw away a perfectly good flannel shirt. After many, many drinks, he could occasionally be persuaded to tap out the William Tell Overture on his teeth using a pencil or a .303 round, depending what was to hand. Not often, mind. And only if he liked you.

Sneaky was often people's first and last point of contact with Meredith Downs. Wherever possible, new station hands hitched a ride on the mail truck, as did staff who'd been given the push and were heading back to town. He could strike up a conversation with anyone about anything, and his passengers usually arrived at their destinations feeling a shade taller and more important thanks to all his 'You don't say?'s and 'You're a full bottle on that, aren't you, mate?'s.

In that respect, Sneaky and Pete Peachey the roo shooter were polar opposites: Peachey – as expert at avoiding conversation as Sneaky was at starting it – could go for days without talking. But on the occasions when their paths crossed, they got on well, Sneaky happy to chat away and Pete Peachey happy to let him.

Sneaky carried all sorts *On His* (and then *Her*) *Majesty's Service* – that phrase found on envelopes from the government – and felt a personal obligation to his Sovereign to treat in confidence the communications entrusted to him in their name. So while he'd talk in generalities about who he'd come across on his travels, or whether the new baby had arrived at the next station along, how many points of rain they'd had, or the state of the road, that's as far as it went: he never passed on tittle-tattle. That's not to say he didn't take it all in. He might chat about it to Lightning as they drove, the dog listening attentively, panting here and there or putting a paw on his shoulder by way of response. Then Sneaky would return to his reveries about steak and kidney pudding, or golden syrup dumplings, and his stomach would start to rumble as on they'd go.

It was for simple convenience that Pete Peachey got his mail sent to Meredith Downs. He didn't seem to have an address anywhere else. His tobacco and other supplies he got from the main stores on the property. They let him keep a running account, like the regular hands, which he settled up when it was time to be paid for the skins. But there were other things he could get only by mail order. Every few months, Sneaky would deliver a parcel or two for him from Boans or Ahern's or Bates Saddlery in Perth. The roo shooter said he got his work clothes cheaper there. Packages also arrived from further away – as far as Sydney or Melbourne sometimes. Once he even got a box from France. When Rose asked what was in the parcel that had come all the way from Europe he just said, 'I'll steam the stamps off for you and bring them next time I'm coming through.'

Perhaps it was that first, bold visit by the little renegade and her demand to understand the moon that meant that, ever after, Pete Peachey had a particular soft spot for Rose MacBride. For her part, she looked forward to his visits, and the chats with him that made her feel grown up. He would explain how to track animals; how to tell a dingo from a wild dog; where to spot the constellations and the Milky Way. But as well as showing her how to strip down a .25/20, he would describe the difference between shantung silk and taffeta, and how to distinguish a contralto from a soprano on the shellac 78s on his wind-up gramophone, even giving her records sometimes. He would bring her an exquisite feather, shed by a rare parrot, or an unusual flower. He would buy her hair ribbons, which she'd add to the collection in the china dish on her dressing table. In blues and scarlets and greens, satin or velvet or grosgrain, they glowed when the sun caught them. 'Keep a place in your heart for things that are beautiful,' Pete would say to her. 'Beauty'll help you get through dark times.'

When Lorna made a comment to Phil, early on, about whether they should be letting Rose spend time with a grown man, and such a loner at that, Phil said simply, 'I'd trust Pete Peachey with my life,' and the matter was never raised again.

Though Phil and Lorna, and even Warren, soon forgot about the 'Great Sydney Harbour Bridge Bombing', it continued to rankle with Rose, who had been dealt a smack on the bottom and had had to hand over some birthday money to her elder brother as 'war reparations'.

It was all very well taking your medicine, but it wasn't fair, she thought. It wasn't fair that Warren was always in charge. It wasn't fair that he had a whole Meccano set to himself in the first place. It wasn't fair that he got to go off shooting with Pete Peachey and she wasn't allowed.

And what was the point in owning up to smashing his stupid bridge if you just got punished anyway? She stewed over it for weeks, gradually resolving never to take the blame for anything again.

This was how she came to devise a special ritual, a ceremony she would use for the rest of her life.

She'd been perfecting it for some months when she decided to let Matt, about seven, in on the secret.

'You just write it down, and light it with a match, and it goes away. It's magic!'

'But', Matt said, 'you still did it. You still broke Mum's necklace.'

'*Did I*, but? She won't know. You don't have to tell her. You *mustn't* tell her. And now, I've owned up *under magic* and it's all gone. All flown away in the wind.'

If there was something to understand here, he couldn't see it. He squinted a little to sharpen his focus. Beside him on the old lemon gum branch Rosie swung her legs, making the whole bough sway precariously.

'It's a fact. When you're grown up, you'll understand.'

When he called her dumb because it was *not* a fact, and she *did so* break the necklace, and *would so* get into trouble, she teased a knot from her long, straight hair and said, 'I won't.'

'How come?'

'Cos you're not going to tell. I always stick up for you. And I didn't tell Warren when you wet your pants.'

Matt's face burned and she told him he was too young to understand about truth. 'It's not forever if you don't want it to be. It's just until you make it go away.'

'Are you sick or something? That's just words. Doesn't mean anything.'

'If you don't believe me, try it. Write down a thing you want to make go away.' She unhooked the small notepad strung around her neck and passed it to him, along with the pencil stub.

'You're a twerp,' said Matt.

'You're *scared*!'

'Am not! I'm just not a twerp.'

'Bet you're too scared to write down what you did.' Rosie started a sing-song 'Mattie is a scaredy-cat, Mattie is a scaredy-cat . . .'

He punched her shoulder. She punched him harder. There was a silence, and she put out her hand for the return of the notepad. 'You're too little still.'

Matt eyed the paper. 'Promise I'll feel better?'

'I always do,' she said. 'Always.'

And so Matt wrote, in the tiniest, neatest printing he could manage halfway up a swaying tree, 'Wet my pants when I got scared.'

'Now sign it.' Her sharp nudge made him grab the branch. 'You have to!'

He signed.

She passed him the brass cigarette lighter that had come into her possession a while back (at about the same time as one of the shearers had mysteriously lost his and accused a rouseabout of 'alf-inching it). 'Now, as you light it, you say "*Yawa, yawa, yawa*", then you send it off into the air.

'*What?*'

She sighed. 'It's "Away, away, away" backwards, drongo.'

'What if it starts a fire?'

'Then no one will remember you wet your pants anyway.'

Setting the paper aflame, Matt felt lightened. His shame at the memory turned to a laugh, as though it had been a deliberate joke he'd played, and for a moment he felt nothing – the same way he felt nothing when he said the eight times table.

Girls were strange. Or maybe it was just Rosie: he didn't know any others. *Yawa, yawa, yawa* . . . The words rolled around in his mind, and he tucked them away, ready to use another day.

6

MEREDITH DOWNS WAS full of places for MacBride kids to play. The old swing-set out the back of the homestead kept them happy when they were littlies, and as they grew, there were any number of disused sheds they could turn into cubbies. Old, abandoned cottages and rusting wagons yielded all sorts of games of 'olden days', and waterholes and creeks were favourite destinations – when they actually had water in them. The favourite spot of Lorna's three, though, was the old Proserpine mineshaft.

From the surface it seemed harmless enough: just a slit in the rocky ground, ringed at a distance by rusty barbed wire, though these days the four slack strands were more a memorial of a fence than a practical barrier. In the dirt lay a dilapidated sign on which, years back, a slapdash hand had daubed 'Danger. Keep Out', and which the sun had just about licked blank since. Generations of MacBride offspring, warned away from the mine by parents, had cheerfully ignored the instruction, until in time they'd grown old enough to issue the same edict to their own children, who ignored it in turn.

It was Herbert, the youngest of old Alfred MacBride's sons, who'd pegged claims and established the Proserpine tantalite mine in the late 1800s. He put up a mine head, a manager's cottage and a few tin shacks and camps for workers. But the yield quickly thinned out and the price of tantalite crashed, so that decades later, the stone outlines of floors and one or two crumbling chimney stacks were all that remained above ground.

The kids would ride out there on their horses and clamber down the shaft, using the timber sleepers as footholds, shining their torches and yelling and singing to get the thrill of the echo. Sometimes Warren would scare them with stories of evil spirits that lived deep in the furthest reaches, or ghosts of miners trapped under rockfalls.

This dark, cool space was Aladdin's cave, a trench on the Somme, Bluebeard's Castle, a distant planet. Games about cowboys or attacking Germans usually involved hand-to-hand combat: at eleven, Rose could easily beat Matt at wrestling, but Warren was too strong. It was around this time that he bestowed on her the nickname 'Bliss', which she was quite pleased with, until he sniggered that it was short for 'ugly blister', rhyming slang for 'sister'. Still, 'Bliss' stuck.

There was one cast-iron rule: Rose always had to play a boy. (On *no account* did her brothers ever have to be girls.) If she suggested she might be a princess or a fairy, Warren would make vomiting noises, and then go back to machine-gunning her with a stick. Sometimes she would take revenge by planting a kiss on his face and chanting, 'Girl germs! You've go-ot girl germs!' causing Warren to chase after her, pinning her down and letting spit drip from his mouth until it almost touched her face, then sucking it back up again. If Rose tried to give Matt girl germs, he would just wipe his cheek in disgust, then tickle her into saying sorry.

The three MacBride kids played and fought and grew until, almost overnight, 1948 came around and Warren, on the cusp of thirteen, left for Scotch College, the boarding school in Perth his father and grandfather had attended. Most of the station owners' children went to boarding schools in the city: it was that or correspondence school – few lived close enough to towns to be 'day bugs'.

Two years later, at the same age, Rose made the journey to St Margaret's Ladies' College. She had begun to develop what her mother called 'a nice figure', and when they were back for the months of Christmas holidays, Warren took to making comments about how Rose should wear her hair and whether a dress made her look 'cheap' or 'tarty'.

Things came to a head on New Year's Eve in 1951, a rare evening on which Lorna and Phil were away for the night at a party at Charlie and Maudie Knapp's. Rose had spent the afternoon dancing to her one Patti Page record while Matt built Warren's old Meccano on the lounge-room floor, once in a while being hauled to his feet by his sister to help her practise her twirls. Ignoring Warren's hollering from his room, when she started singing along, to '*bloody shut up*', she turned up the volume and sang louder. 'Practising for the boarders' social next term,' she shouted to Matt, inches away. As Rose intended, Warren stormed in, but instead of just yelling, he yanked the record from the turntable and held it high above her reach. 'You can have it back when you go back to school. If you try to take it before then, I'll shove it in the septic tank.'

An hour later, she appeared in the kitchen wearing lipstick and mascara, and a bustline not so subtly enhanced by a pair of socks. 'How do I look, Bubba?' she asked, turning her back to Warren.

She almost grinned as her older brother railed, 'What the hell do you think you look like in that get-up?'

'I'll dress however I like!'

'Yeah, well if you want to get a reputation as a trollop, go ahead. And don't blame me for what happens to you.'

And though she kicked and bit him, Warren dragged her to the bathroom and held her over the sink as he scrubbed the makeup off with a flannel. 'No sister of mine's going to dress like a tart! Talk about leading fellows on!'

She whacked his stomach as hard as she could. He clamped his hands on her biceps and said through curled lips, 'You should hear what they say about you at Scotch . . .'

Later, Matt, who had watched the fight, unsure of whether to step in or how, appeared in her bedroom. 'You all right, Bliss?'

'Yeah.'

'Wanna game of doogs?' He held out his bag of marbles. 'I've got two new tombowlers.'

'Nah. Thanks though, Bubba.'

'What did he do that for?'

Rose looked at her little brother, his arms and legs still spindly, swimming in a hand-me-down shirt of Warren's. 'It's just – just grown-ups' stuff. You wouldn't understand.'

'Oh.' Matt put a hand to his other elbow. 'Don't worry. If he throws your record in the septic tank, I'll get it out for you.'

In the lounge room, he sat in front of the grandfather clock they called Old Wally, trying to remember as many New Year's Eves as he could. He was always allowed to stay up till midnight at New Year, but usually had to be woken on the couch by the others just before twelve. As the clock finished chiming 9 p.m., he tracked down Warren in the kitchen, reading a Dick Tracy comic.

Matt folded his arms. 'Warren, what do they say about Rosie at Scotch?'

Warren gave him a steely look. Then he closed his comic and slid it across the table. 'Here you go. Late Christmas present.'

Matt arrived at Scotch College in 1953, aged thirteen, the year after Warren had finished school, so was left to sink or swim.

For Matt, being surrounded by hundreds of other kids was

overwhelming. It wasn't so bad for boys from the wheat-belt or down south, who lived close to towns. For station lads, the more remote their property, the harder it was to get used to so many boys.

Matt's friendship with Hughie 'Humpty' Dumpton, whose family owned one of the biggest sheep stations out Nullarbor way, began when they separately developed a strategy of wandering to the far end of the oval during breaks, to escape the avalanche of social interaction. Gradually, they got to talking to each other: a few words about wool clips or mustering. Comparing notes on the horses and dogs they'd had to leave behind, there was no need to explain how much it hurt not to see them every day. Their shared love of cricket cemented the bond, and they were soon inseparable.

Humpty owed his name to his habit of referring to his mother as 'the old chook', which, Matt pointed out, must make him an egg. So he was 'Egg' for a while, before the nursery rhyme inevitably turned him into 'Humpty' Dumpton. Not remotely ovoid, he was a streak of lightning on the cricket pitch – the fastest bowler anyone at school could remember.

In November 1953, Matt and Humpty were allowed to travel to the WACA to watch WA play South Australia in the Sheffield Shield match. On the old green MTT bus that chuntered back from the cricket ground on the Sunday afternoon, it was stinking hot and stuffy and sweat stuck their shirts to their backs, but they were still buzzing with excitement. As they rounded the Swan River, Humpty announced, 'I've got my life all planned out, you know. From now till I'm ninety. Just like dominoes.'

Matt laughed.

'No, listen.' Humpty's tone was not boastful, just sure. 'I go for the captain of the school team when I'm sixteen—'

'Sixteen? And the rest!'

'Barny Jackson was captain at sixteen—'

'In 1907!' Matt pointed out. 'And besides, he went on to captain WA . . .'

'Which brings me to my next step: WA Team. Sheffield Shield. Then Australia, then win the Ashes.' Humpty's grin was growing.

'That all? Jeez, you're full of bull.'

'Then I retire from cricket just as Dad's about to hand me the reins on Corella Ridge, and I settle down to the life of a Gentleman Pastoralist, and kick the bucket when I'm ninety-four years and three months old.'

'Three months?'

'A month more than my great-grandpa. A man should have something to aim for.'

They looked at each other for a moment, then Matt slapped the back of Humpty's head. 'You know you're a dag, don't you?'

There was no pause before the reply, or the pinch on the back of Matt's neck that came with it. 'Why else would I be friends with you?'

Of all their conversations, it was that one on the bus that sprang to Matt's mind two years later, in 1955, as he sat for the first time in Shenton Park Hospital for patients with head and spinal injuries. It was just after Christmas holidays, three months since landing chest-first in a dive for a catch crushed Humpty's spinal cord. Just a dive. Just a catch. And just like that, Humpty's map of his road to ninety-four years and three months lay in ashes.

'I – I brought you some of Mum's honeycomb,' said Matt, and thrust a waxed paper bundle at him. 'Got a bit sticky.' He took in the blank, white walls as he searched for something to say – normally, his opening comment would be about cricket.

'Humpty Dumpty had a pretty big fucken' fall, eh!' his friend exclaimed, and gave a half-laugh. 'See? Beat you to it.'

Matt was shocked. By the swearing – they didn't much go in for that; by the sound of his voice, which had a new, bitter edge; and by the fact that – all of a sudden – Hughie Dumpton was a grown-up. Not a kid any more. He found himself just staring at his friend, eyes filling with tears.

'I get a lot of that,' Humpty said. 'You should see my mum. Even my dad. Evie's the worst, though.'

'She's only six.' Matt felt his own words come out as though far away.

'You wanna ask stuff? Wanna know the gory details?'

Not with this tone of fake bravado. 'Nah. You're right, Egg,' he said, and wiped his eyes and nose on his sleeve.

'Dad reckons they're going to sell the station. Evie can't take it over – she's a girl. And the quacks here say I'll need years of physio or basket weaving or some crap, so I have to be near the hospital. Nothing like this out our way.'

'Oh.'

'Well,' said Humpty, unwrapping the honeycomb, pincering its sticky sides with his fingers to crunch a mouthful, 'tell us what I've been missing out on. How were the holidays? Warren and Rosie still picking on you?'

Matt attempted a smile. 'No more than usual. You hear we had the fires?'

'Yeah. You lose much?'

This exchange between the boys mimicked the conversations of all the adults they'd heard in the weeks following the bushfires that had raged over the summer. 'We lost a few wethers,' said Matt. 'Some of the fences were a write-off . . . The Sowerbys next door at Maundy Creek lost a hundred rams. They'd been loaded onto the truck to get away from the fire, but the wind picked up – changed direction. Whole truck – *poof*!' He added, 'Poor bastards,' because those were the words he'd heard his father use when recounting the story.

As the clock edged towards four, Humpty said, 'Visiting time's nearly over. Good to see you but.'

'You, too.'

'You think you might – you might come again?'

'Yeah, sure.'

Humpty nodded to himself, and inspected the wheel of his chair, tracing a finger along the tread. 'Reckon you could do me a – a sort of favour? Bring me something?'

'Course. Anything.'

'Good. Good, yeah.'

'What do you want?'

'My .22.'

'*What?*'

'Doesn't *have* to be mine. You can bring one from your place. Maybe if you go home at Easter. Doesn't have to be a .22 either. Just thought that'd be lighter than a .303.'

'Why do you want a rifle?'

'What, have you got a pistol? Your dad's old service revolver? That'd be better, yeah.'

'No, you spastic. What do you want a *gun* for?'

'What do you *think* I want a gun for, spastic yourself?'

'Target practice? To shoot something?'

'Not some*thing*. Some*one*.'

'Who?'

'*Me*, you moron! It's to shoot *me*.' Humpty moved his wheelchair closer to his friend, and stared up at him, opening his arms. 'Look at me! Crippling my way around and crapping into a bag. What sort of bloody life's that supposed to be?' His face was deep red, and his cheeks wet with tears. 'You're my friend. Help me.'

'If you don't come with a gun, don't come again. Ever,' Humpty had said to Matt at the door. After a day of agonising, Matt had reported the conversation in a letter to his mother, who reported it to Humpty's mother, who reported it to the hospital. He'd done it because he couldn't be sure that Humpty wouldn't ask someone else. Someone who cared less about him. Or who cared more.

7

IN THE HOMESTEAD at Meredith Downs, silence is a canvas on which each sound trails like a colour. The wind; a single fly; the clatter of a pan; the distant barking of a kelpie; the banging of a flywire door. There is no continuous murmur of traffic. No vague stream of voices. Each sound emerges for its solo, then fades into stillness, into a silence so complete it makes music of your heartbeat in your ears.

Beneath it all – constant, steady, infinitely patient – is the deep ticking of the ornate longcase clock in the lounge room, shipped out from Hewish & Sons of Clerkenwell in the days when the wool clip was sold direct to London and the station was starting to show a healthy return.

For reasons long since lost, upon its arrival the grandfather clock acquired the name 'Old Wally', and was often addressed directly by those passing it: 'Night, Wally', 'Happy Christmas, Wally'. The MacBride men would pour an extra drink 'for Old Wally', then declare that since it didn't look like he was going to touch it, they'd help him out.

The first Mrs MacBride to live in the homestead, Matilda, wife of Albert, was greatly relieved when the clock arrived, for it civilised time: put a yoke on its shoulders and drove it in an orderly, predictable fashion. The bush had its own, wild rules of chronometry: some days the wind seemed to push minutes along in a stampede that left her breathless and exhausted. On others, time stretched like a goanna in the sun, unable to creep forward even an inch. No more such disorder with the arrival of Old Wally, which rewarded her for making it through another sixty gruelling minutes by ringing out a delicate, elaborate chime, like the tinkling of fine china tea cups, before a sonorous bass declaration of the hour. Though adjusting a lever could allow these milestones to pass silently at night, Matilda wouldn't have a bar of it, and slept all the more soundly for being briefly woken by their reassurance, as if a servant had murmured gently, 'All is well, ma'am.'

After her death, though, the nocturnal chimes were silenced, and would remain so for decades until Lorna, in her lonely despair, reinstated the night-time strike.

While in the homestead it was Old Wally's deep *tick, tick* that unfurled the MacBride lives, in the paddocks the passing of time was measured by the growth of wool on the sheep's back, the gradual curl of a ram's horns, the stretching and the shrinking of the light that conspired to carry the years away. By late 1955, Warren had been helping his father for nearly three years after leaving school. The wool price was still booming, and he butted heads with Phil occasionally, urging him to up the stock numbers to boost the wool yield. His father would humour him up to a point, listening, nodding, but would eventually declare, 'Pull your head in. As long as I'm in charge, we'll take things steady. This country can only carry so much.'

After one such exchange, Phil said to Lorna, 'He's as hot-headed as his sister, that kid. At least *she's* your department. Let's hope she's pulled her socks up in time for Leaving.' Rose had failed her Junior Certificate exams first time around and had had to repeat the year, her report card diagnosing 'no shortage of intelligence, but a marked lack of application'.

Now, Lorna gave a rueful laugh. 'Kids. Who'd have 'em, eh?'

She hadn't mentioned the letter that had come from Rose's school the week before, reporting a week's detention for going into town on a Saturday without permission. Lorna had written an apologetic reply to the headmistress, and a stern warning to her daughter. Phil had his work cut out managing Warren, she told herself. She'd tell him later, when it had all blown over.

But before she'd found the right moment, an even bigger storm was to dump Rose back at the homestead, leaving Lorna sick at heart as she tortured herself for not having seen it coming.

'Do you have any idea of the trouble you've caused?' Lorna demanded of her daughter, a month later.

Rose sat on her bed, chin defiant save for the slightest flickering of a muscle.

'Oh, you think you're so modern, you and your city schoolfriends!' Lorna shook her head. 'Do you have any idea of the shame?' Rose's silence fuelled her mother's rage. 'You betrayed our trust. And the school's. You let *yourself* down.'

Her daughter had been dispatched from St Margaret's Ladies' College with such speed that November day in 1955 that she was still in her school uniform: navy skirt and white blouse, and the striped tie in her hands that she now kept rolling and unrolling as Lorna demanded how she could have done such a thing. And on school property.

Rose said nothing.

'Who is this "Derek", anyway?'

'He goes to Wesley. His cousin's in my class.'

These faint words, the first her daughter had uttered, tripped Lorna; halted the stampede of her anger.

'It'll be a miracle if they let you sit your final exams, you realise that?' She turned away. 'Your father's—well, I've never seen him so furious. He'll be after the boy's parents.'

'Dad doesn't own me,' said Rose, but her words sounded fragile.

'Well, *you're* certainly not in control of yourself! This is how girls' lives are ruined . . . This'll be all round the boarding house at Scotch, too. Imagine what it'll be like for Matt!'

She turned to face Rose. 'You think you're so independent, but you're not. You're a part of this family and this family is part of this district and your behaviour taints every single one of us.'

'He– he said he loved me . . .'

'Pardon?' Lorna genuinely hadn't heard the whisper.

'He said he loved me,' Rose went on, barely louder. 'And that if I loved him, I would. And if I didn't then he'd find someone who really *did* love him and who'd . . . who'd show it . . .'

For goodness' sake! Surely you didn't fall for that twaddle?' The heat had gone out of her tone now, and she sat down beside her daughter, brushing the blonde hair from her eyes.

'He said I was special . . .'

'Oh, Rose, Rose . . .' Lorna took a deep breath. 'Change out of your uniform and I'll make you something to eat. And go and apologise to your father.'

'He never wants me in his sight again.'

'Give him time to cool off.' She took the tie from her daughter's hand and hung it with the blazer she picked up off the floor. How many fleeces had it taken to pay for them, let alone the school fees? She felt a twinge as she remembered Phil's beaming smile the day Rosie had first shown off the uniform. 'He's a proud man, and you've hurt him dreadfully.'

For days, an electric current of tension arced about in the homestead. Warren refused to be in the same room as Rose. Phil drove to Wanderrie Creek to make telephone calls – first to the boy's parents, who were appalled that Rose had 'led the poor boy on' and 'flirted and teased until he didn't know what he was doing'. He was a chorister, a *prefect*, for goodness' sake. And now he'd been expelled! Phil negotiated for Rose to be allowed to sit her Leaving examinations at the Claremont Showgrounds, where the government held the exams for subjects too sparsely studied to warrant invigilation at each school. They also accommodated the handful of tearaways that schools had refused to have on their premises any longer.

For the week of the exams Rose was to be released into the custody of the Drebbings, whose daughter Lucy was a day girl in Rose's class. Keith Drebbing was an old army mate of Phil's, and had one or two events in his past which meant that Phil knew he wouldn't be looked down on for asking the favour.

Before Rose left for Perth, Lorna sat her down in the lounge room, while Old Wally ticked away. 'It's not just *your* life, Rose. Shame's like a disease. It blights the whole flock.'

Rose kept her eye on Wally's ornate black minute hand.

'It'll be a long time before I trust you again,' her mother was saying. 'You can look at the clock all you like, but there are things that have to be said. Don't think I'm enjoying this any more than you are! . . . You seem to think you can behave however you like. So let me make it clear that if anything like this ever happens again, you're on your own. We won't be there to smooth things over or pull strings.' She couldn't keep the anguish from her voice. 'Clontarf Orphanage is full of babies whose mothers gave in to the first boy who took a bit of notice of them. And those girls are ruined.'

The quarter-hour chime prompted Lorna to her feet. 'No one in this house will mention it again, and by the grace of God, it'll be forgotten.'

That night, Rose gathered her lighter and the folded-up note she'd written for her ritual. She sat in the lemon gum, listening to the crickets, flicking the brass lighter on and off. '*Yawa, yawa, yawa,*' she whispered, as she watched the flame lick and shred the paper, turning it into embers then ash, which floated into nothing.

When Matt gets home for the summer holidays a few weeks later, as always, the first place he visits is Wallaby Ridge, out at the breakaways. Like a set of spines on a crocodile's back that crop up and disappear, they sit between paddocks, fenced off to stop stock wandering up the steep slope and falling off the blind cliff on the other side. If you make the climb to the top, you can see for miles.

He loves the spot not just for the view, but for its stand of beautiful trees, and their story. These eucalypts, which produce delicate yellow flowers every March, are found nowhere else on the property, or in the district, for that matter. It was Jemima MacBride, Matilda's daughter, who first noticed them, and showed them to a Mr Sampson, a botanist passing through on an expedition east, cataloguing plants that were 'new to science'. Jemima had even come up with a name for them: *Eucalyptus vigilans*, because they seemed to keep watch over the place. There was some talk of sending the samples and drawings to Melbourne, or even to Kew Gardens, but nothing seemed to have come of it. No one quite knew what had become of Mr Sampson, or of the samples Jemima had given him, and her later correspondence with Kew to find out proved fruitless. Jemima's delicate watercolour pictures of them and other native plants were pressed in a book somewhere in the homestead. Jemima herself was in the very trees, now, her ashes long scattered on Wallaby Ridge to be reabsorbed into the earth. The family still called them 'Jemima's trees', preferring to remember the girl rather than the Latin she'd coined.

From here, the land for miles around is an ocean, flat and inscrutable. Matt imagines sailing over it in the *Alpha Crucis*, taking

Monty's boat far, far away, steering not by the North Star he reads so much about in English books, but by the Southern Cross, that constellation in his sky and on his flag and on the flour sacks in the storeroom.

He narrows his eyes, seeing it as land again, and watches the distant sheep, no more than dusty dots, chewing away at the saltbush. If Jemima's trees had once grown outside the breakaways, the stock would long ago have made short work of them.

Matt hasn't told his parents about the fight at school last week. A kid made a crack about Rose being a tart, and Matt punched him, giving him a blood nose. First time he'd ever been in a real fight. But family's family.

He pushes away the memory of the boy's taunts, and returns to the *Alpha Crucis*, and what it would feel like to steer a course of his own. What it would feel like to leave this land, this family, behind.

8

It took a good while, and a great deal of diplomacy on Lorna's part, to get Phil and Rose back on amicable terms. Rose had scraped through her Leaving exams after the scandal, though her marks wouldn't have got her into university. Nonetheless, Phil had a grudging admiration for his daughter's practicality and gumption. Strong-willed she might be, but stupid she was not, and he began to appreciate her help as he showed her the ropes of writing up the station diary and keeping on top of the other, voluminous, records.

One day in 1957, scouring *The Countryman* for a new pump, his eye was caught by an advertisement urging parents to consider 'A business career for your daughter!' from City Commercial College in Perth. Such ads were common enough, but this was the first time Phil had paid them any attention. It was about time they considered finding a match for Rose . . . A secretarial course would be an investment: quite the selling point that she could help a husband with the paperwork when she was raising a family on a station somewhere. As he sat with Lorna on the verandah that night, he announced his plan, his mind made up: 'We'll make a catch of her for someone yet.' He duly made arrangements for Rose to take a course the following year – even paid in advance to get the discount. An aptitude for administration was indeed a useful skill: life wasn't just about keeping your sheep watered and your fences strong.

For all that station land is wild and remote, life on Meredith Downs, as on all Western Australian stations, is meticulously documented, in a different book for every task. The older the station, the bigger the book. There are the ledgers; the wool returns; the vermin records; the *Field Book of Meteorological Observations* for the Bureau of Meteorology in Melbourne; the cricket score books; and the little greasy shearing tally books stained with lanolin from pulling them in and out of a shirt pocket as you count the wool clip run by run, shed by shed, day by day.

And there are the diaries. Every station, every day, writes down its activities and events. Who has come, who has gone; who has been born, who has died. They record when sheep were bought or sold or moved paddock. They reveal when times are good, with the mention of new motor vehicles or lighting plant or a swimming pool being put in. In bad times they'll chronicle a flood, or a property destocked in the teeth of an impending drought.

You keep these books in case the tax man wants proof of who's been doing what, or the Lands Department wants evidence of expenditure on improvements when it comes time to file your annual return, or the Undersecretary for Lands wants you to back up your claim for rent relief in a drought. Above all, you keep them because, a day at a time, they help you make sense of the world; add shape and meaning to a life as subject to chance as any roll of the dice.

A ration sheep killed to feed the hands; a shearer's strike; the declaration of wet sheep, when any blind bastard could see there was barely a cloud in the sky – all will be mentioned. Which hands were shifting stock in which paddock; who was out repairing a fence. You'll find entries about police calling at 5 a.m. because of a crash down on the public road, and asking for help and machinery to clear it. Mulesing and maiming will be described in the same dry, dispassionate style. But after a week, its importance fades a little, and after a month, begins its slide to the past in earnest.

Once in a while, there's a glimpse of the personal: a kid heading off to boarding school, or winning a scholarship. Phil MacBride's father, Ted, had a habit of switching from his cursive scrawl to capitals to report particularly momentous events: 'TM ATTENDED RECEPTION AT GOVERNMENT HOUSE FOR HIS ROYAL HIGHNESS THE PRINCE OF WALES, or 'PM WON 5 RACES AT WANDERRIE CREEK ATHLETICS CARNIVAL.'

Generation after generation, the lives of station people are poured into the diaries, and the ink left to dry, the pages to dust over, and the individuals they recorded return to the earth from which they wrung their living.

Now, as her father trained her, Rosie MacBride's handwriting began to form part of that record (though departing from the noble tradition that it be as neat as dog's sick). 'PM and boys to Randwick for baits'; 'WM, PM, N. Tinnett to Joker to discuss new mill'. And it was Rose's writing that recorded, on the third of September 1957, four months before the crash, an astonishing event: the arrival at Meredith Downs of the Honourable Miles Beaumont.

Take your pick: beef, lamb, wool, gold, cotton: the Beaumont family had a slice of every market in the British Empire and beyond, stretching from Cape Town to Sydney to Buenos Aires. They owned several large cattle stations in western Queensland and the Northern Territory, but their wool ventures were limited to smaller, lusher properties in Victoria and New South Wales. Now, there were plans to branch out into large stations in the West, or in South Australia, or perhaps both.

When Cecil, Lord Beaumont, over lunch at his stately home in Buckinghamshire, asked the visiting Australian chairman of Dalgety's whether he could 'find a spot somewhere' for his son on a big sheep property, 'to learn the ropes and so forth', telegrams were sent and strings were effortlessly pulled and Neil Tinnett, the Dalgety's rep in Wanderrie Creek, duly arranged for the Honourable Miles Beaumont to do a stint at various places, starting with Meredith Downs.

On the day of the visitor's arrival, as Tinnett's familiar, battle-scarred Dodge drew up, Rose watched in amazement. There emerged from the passenger side the most handsome – and the cleanest – man she had ever seen. She blinked. Dark hair, subtly subdued with oil; a blindingly white shirt, brand new moleskins, and boots so polished they reflected the spring sun. Neil's appearance as he got out – the height of neatness in jacket, tie and hat – now looked scruffy by comparison.

Phil joined Rosie at the door, muttering, 'Like something from a blinking fashion parade!' before going out to greet him. 'Morning. Phil MacBride. Welcome to Meredith Downs.'

'How do you do? Miles. I gather you're expecting me?'

Neil Tinnett joined them. 'Gedday, Phil.'

Phil exchanged a brief look with Neil that Miles didn't catch. 'Come in!'

Lorna served tea and cake in the lounge room, as Neil confirmed arrangements: Miles would be shadowing Phil and Warren, to get a sense of station life. He'd had experience in some Beaumont ventures, but nothing on the scale of Meredith Downs. He would be with them till January, staying in the vacant overseer's house.

The luggage that later emerged from the car heightened Rosie's excitement: three pale green monogrammed suitcases; a tennis racquet in a frame; and a wooden crate which, it transpired, contained a croquet set.

Phil and Warren took Miles for a drive to see a bit of the property, leaving Rosie and Matt with their mother at the kitchen table.

'How old is he?' Rosie asked.

'Twenty-seven, I think your father said.'

'Is he married?'

'Not that I've been told.'

'And does his family really own Coolabah Plains *and* Salt Flats?' Rose asked, referring to two large, well-known Queensland cattle stations.

'Apparently.'

'Reckon he plays cricket?' asked Matt.

'Probably. Ask him yourself, dear.'

'He must be really, really rich,' Rosie said. 'I bet he's got a butler!'

'Who cares?' said Matt.

'And that aftershave! Like – lemon leaves or something.'

Matt started a sing-song 'Bliss is i-in lo-ove, Bliss is i-in lo-ove . . .'

'Oh, for Pete's sake, grow up!' exclaimed their mother. 'Rosie, start peeling the apples while I make the pastry.'

9

When Lorna sent Rose to Miles's house the next day, she covered the five hundred yards to his verandah at an impressive lick with her cargo: extra blankets, for the chilly snap.

With her free hand, Rose tucked her hair behind her ear, straightened the collar of her blouse, undoing a button, and was about to knock, when she realised that the bars of the Moonlight Sonata drifting out weren't coming from the old gramophone, but the piano. She stood transfixed by the playing: soulful – almost sorrowful; note-perfect except where a couple of keys didn't strike. She dared a peek through the window. There was Miles, eyes closed, long, elegant fingers gliding over the occasionally missing ivories. He seemed in a trance, the notes floating about him of their own accord.

The flywire door she'd been propping open slipped and banged, and she ducked back as the music halted mid-phrase. Rose knocked, and as he opened the door, Miles's expression was still far away.

She leapt at his offer of a cup of tea, and took her time wandering down the passage to put the blankets in the cupboard, which now also held his suitcases – crocodile! Passing his bedroom, she was arrested by that wonderful lemon-leaf smell. The room was neat as a pin, with a few books on the bedside table, a paisley silk dressing gown draped over the foot of the bed, and a pair of slippers waiting soldier-straight beneath. Just like her dorm at boarding school – perfectly arranged, nothing to get you detention. *She'd* never had a silk dressing gown, though.

In the lounge room, they sat down by the fire, its flames skittering as the wind rumbled in the chimney.

'It was beautiful, the music,' said Rose.

'I'm awfully rusty.'

'So's the piano. Been here since the First World War – a manager got it for his wife. Hardly been played since.' She twisted the end of her jumper sleeve. 'Settled in all right?'

'Very well, thank you.' He poured her tea.

'Is it what you expected?'

Miles looked about. 'It's really very comfortable.'

'No, I mean the station; us . . .'

'Ah! To tell you the truth, I'd no idea what to expect. We have a number of farms dotted about, but I tend to stick to the money side of things. Then they—' An unreadable glimmer crossed his face. 'Well, my father, in his infinite wisdom, decided I should get a more practical grounding, starting with wool.'

'Oh?' Raising her cup, Rose decided to stick her little finger out, then her ring finger, for good measure.

'Our properties in the east of Australia are mostly cattle.' Miles stirred his tea. 'I'm due to go there, too, to see more farms, meet more farmers.'

'Probably better not let Dad hear you call him a farmer.'

'What's wrong with being a farmer?'

'Nothing,' said Rose. 'If you *are* one. But there's a big difference between a *farm*, and a station, like Meredith Downs is. Technically, we're *pastoralists*.'

'I see. And "pastoralists" are . . .?'

'Our land's mostly uncleared and uncultivated. Maybe in America they'd call us *ranchers*? In England – oh, I'm not sure there's such a thing.'

Miles smiled. 'Well, that's one faux pas avoided. Thank you.'

Rose tried to replace her cup like the Queen would. 'So how come you chose Meredith Downs?'

'*I* didn't. My father dispatched me, at rather short notice. And here I am.' Miles twitched the knee of his trousers, considering something. 'Can I let you into a secret, Rose?'

She nodded vigorously.

'I don't know the first thing about sheep. I can find my way around a balance sheet. I can say "Table for two" in quite a few languages, and I'm handy in a croquet match. But my usefulness to the MacBrides may have been somewhat exaggerated.'

'No one expects you to *run* the place.'

'Well, no. But I'd hate to be a hindrance.' He ran a hand through his hair. 'I'm used to sheep being white clouds of fluff in rolling, verdant fields: "Sheep May Safely Graze" and so forth . . . When I was driving with your father and Warren yesterday, I made the mistake of asking where the sheep were kept. All I could see was low bushes and red dirt.'

Rose laughed. 'Yep, well, that's where we "keep the sheep": you've got to find them, though.'

Miles coloured. 'Warren had a good laugh at me too. Can't say I blame him.'

Oh God. Warren would be absolutely unbearable if he got to lord it over Miles, show off his superior knowledge. But it wasn't just Miles who'd have to put up with his bloody smugness . . .

So it was as much to thwart Warren as it was to linger in Miles's company that Rose said, 'Tell you what, why don't I just give you a run-through: what we do, and when we do it. Enough so that Warren won't be a pain in the bu—' She stopped. 'In the behind. Where should I start?'

'Perhaps with the map your father gave me?'

They unrolled it on the table, anchored with the teapot and sugar bowl. When Miles's hand brushed hers in the process, though he seemed oblivious, it took Rose a moment to recover her train of thought.

'You've always got to know where your stock are. For most of the year, you keep the sheep separate. The rams and the wethers and the ewes and the weaners – weaners are the young ones just old enough to be taken from their mums – all in different paddocks. You keep the maiden ewes and the new rams separate too.' She showed him how the map was marked: Randwick had rams; Caulfield weaners . . . 'You put the ewes onto your pasture that has the best water, because they need to be in good condition to conceive, and they need lots of water so they can feed their lambs when they drop. Wethers don't need as much water, and can walk further to find it, so they're usually further away from the shearing sheds, too.'

Miles mused. 'It's a lot of land you own.'

'We don't actually *own* the land. We lease it from the Crown – the WA Government – for ninety-nine years at a time. No one owns their station outright. Our lease is nearly a million acres, but only about' – she pursed her lips – 'oh, seventy per cent or so of that's usable.' She pointed out salt lakes, breakaway country, claypans – the shallow wind-blown patches that fill with water after rain; she traced a finger over Lake MacBride, eight miles long, and five miles across in places. 'And if a paddock's been flogged too hard, we have to rest it for a year or two. A bit of rain might help it to come good.'

'Like letting a field lie fallow.'

'Yep.' Rose leaned back. 'We've got fifty-eight paddocks. Different sizes. The biggest one's forty thousand acres.'

Miles looked doubtful. 'But that would be . . . sixty square miles. That's bigger than Central London.'

Rose calculated. 'Could be . . .'

'My word!'

When he queried the names on the map – 'Pontoon', 'Blackjack', 'Flemington', and the like – Rose explained that the paddocks were mostly named after racecourses, the mills and bores mainly card games. Someone's idea of a joke, given it was as much of a gamble. She pointed out some self-explanatory exceptions: 'Misery', 'Hopeless Creek', 'Snake Bite'.

Miles frowned. 'So . . . Gosh, "Killer"?'

'That's the killer paddock.' Rose registered his alarm. '"Killers" are the ration sheep we're going to eat. Much smaller paddock. Close to the house, so quicker to reach.' They were usually older wethers, she said, or younger sheep with a fault, such as black in their wool, or a poor frame. You never killed a ewe unless she was very old or very naughty.

'And what qualifies as old?'

'More than about five or six. Their wool yield starts to drop, and the ewes' fertility, so we sell them off for meat or eat them. We might keep rams longer than that if they can still work.'

'Work? Oh . . .' Miles cleared his throat. 'I see.'

'Well, we run about four rams to every hundred ewes. We put them into the ewes' paddocks sometime after Christmas and take them out again in April when we muster for shearing. By that time, some of the rams have been so busy they can hardly walk. They're notoriously pathetic, and limp along at the back of the mob.'

Rose noticed a reddening in Miles's face, and she, too, began to blush. Her voice was higher and faster as she swerved to safer ground: their flock of roughly twenty thousand sheep had about nine thousand ewes, five thousand weaners, six thousand wethers, and four hundred rams. Roughly. She seized the next fact that came to mind. 'You know sheep don't have any top teeth?'

Miles laughed. 'And tell me about – oh, I don't know . . . about mustering.'

'Mustering. Well . . .' Rose could recite this stuff in her sleep, and began to wander about the room, curious for any clues about their guest. She explained how they'd started to use motorbikes, zigzagging from the back of a paddock to drive the stock until they eventually reached the holding paddocks in time for the arrival of the shearers. Sheepdogs helped keep them in line, making sure the mob didn't break up on the way, and got mobs to join together.

'The dogs don't actually touch the sheep, just give them the eye.' Her words petered out as she glimpsed a black leather writing compendium, and a piece of notepaper with a gold-embossed crest peeping out. She could read today's date and 'My beloved Sandy'. A fountain pen lay beside it.

Miles caught the direction of her gaze. 'And how long does mustering take? I imagine it's quite an undertaking.'

'Usually about eight weeks. Shearing takes about four or five weeks, and you're still mustering all that time, sending the sheep through the sheds gradually. Before we put them back in the paddocks, we cull for quality and cast for age – get rid of old or sick sheep, sell off any weaners whose wool's not good enough, and sell the older rams, and replace them later in the year. Then about five months after the rams have been joined with the ewes, the lambs start to drop, and lambing goes on for a couple of months.'

'Ah! Now I *do* know from home that farmers are run off their feet at lambing time, helping with delivery.'

'On stations, we just leave them to it. The mothers know what to do. Then, when lambing's over, we do lamb marking. Have you heard of that?'

'Enlighten me.'

'You do it in the ewes' paddocks – so not a big muster. You dock the lambs' tails; earmark them – you just chop a special shape out of the edge of the ear, like with a hole punch: our station mark and one for the year – the years go in six-year cycles. And we castrate the ram lambs. Then we put them back with their mums, till they're old enough to be weaned.'

Her face clouded. 'If there's a bad drought, though, you stop the whole show. You don't buy new rams; you don't put the ones you've got in with the ewes because the mums won't be able to feed lambs. You sell off the wethers if anyone'll buy them, otherwise you just have to let them die in the paddocks. If you can afford the bullets you can shoot them, but by that stage, you're probably too hard up. You always save your ewes if you can, because they're the ones that'll get your flock back up and running when the rain finally comes.'

She folded her arms. 'Right. That should help wipe the smile off Warren's face.'

'You're a marvel! Thank you, Rose. If you think of anything else . . .'

Glancing at the piano, she said, 'Actually, one thing. If Warren tries to tell you he can play Mozart, it means he knows "Twinkle, Twinkle, Little Star".'

When Rose had gone, Miles took up his pen and half-written letter. How could he describe the overwhelming scale of this place to Sandy? The distance; the effort everything seemed to take? London felt a world away. Many times since he'd arrived he'd already longed for his Mayfair flat, with its instant hot water and electricity and verdant, secluded garden. Here, if he wanted hot water, he had to light a fire under the donkey heater outside; the electricity from the generator ran for a few hours in the morning and the evening, though after that the batteries held enough charge to run a couple of dim electric lights. The Metters used wood, and had a knack to it.

What was on at Covent Garden tonight, he wondered . . . Blinking away the thought, he imagined Sandy's voice: 'Chin up, my darling. Make it an adventure!'

Meredith Downs had been hosting an annual Town vs Hands cricket match for donkeys' years. (And yes, there was some truth in the rumour that all you had to do to get a jackarooing job there was to bowl a lethal leg break, or have a killer cover drive.) So the thing that made the men on Meredith Downs overlook Miles Beaumont's plummy accent and forgive his occasionally highfalutin expressions was not the fact that he was a quick learner and a willing worker. It wasn't that he was an outstanding horseman, and worth his weight in gold on a motorbike when moving a mob of sheep. It sure as hell wasn't his title or his money. It was the fact that he had a Blue for cricket from Oxford. Blokes stopped referring to him as Little Lord Fauntleroy when they saw him hit his first six off a crafty spin delivery from a beefy mechanic on the town team one hot spring Sunday in 1957.

From the moment Miles walked to the crease, his bat never missed an opportunity to send the ball cracking out to the stony boundary, sometimes on the full. Having declared at five for 240, the station hands' team then sent him in to bowl, howling with glee as he delivered a hat trick in his first over.

At wicket, with his deep tan and pristine whites, Miles drew admiring looks from the women from town who'd come to watch, though none as ardent as those of Rosie MacBride.

When their sister applauded a six a little too enthusiastically, Matt and Warren would roll their eyes. It wasn't lost on them how weirdly Rose behaved around the trainee manager: finding excuses to run errands to his house, volunteering to make cakes and desserts if he was coming to visit, or showing off her riding skills.

'Ya gotta be kiddin' me!' one of the hands had declared when Miles first appeared in his spotless whites. ''Ave you been bloody *eating* the Omo?' Much beer was consumed to celebrate the station hands' eventual triumph, and the 'Omo' refrain was taken up in toast after toast until 'Omo' was bestowed as his nickname, someone eventually explaining to Miles that it was a brand of washing powder.

His reputation was enhanced even more when, next morning, he alone managed to surface at dawn to get things ready for the trip out to Pontoon to start putting up a new mill. Even Phil, who'd drunk only half as much as Miles, was unshaven and bleary-eyed when he finally emerged, to find the Englishman at the table, drinking tea with Lorna and Rose.

'Morning, Sunshine,' said Lorna.

Phil squinted a response, and shuffled to the stove to pour tea from the big iron pot.

'Good morning, Phil,' said Miles, keeping his volume low.

'With you in a minute,' Phil mumbled, and disappeared back down the passageway with his tea, muttering something about old age and foolishness.

Chewing her toast, Rose tried to act nonchalant. But as always in Miles's presence, her heart beat a little faster. He opened doors for her, held out a hand to help her over a fence, or knitted his fingers into a foothold for her to mount her horse. She was always left giddy by the way he seemed to look deep into her eyes when he asked her a question – about which shed an oil drum was in, or whether she needed help changing the brake fluid in the Land Rover. By the standards of Wanderrie Creek, this was courtly love.

'More tea, Miles?' asked Lorna.

He checked his watch, but Rose said, 'Dad won't leave without the boys, and they're not even up yet.'

'Right-oh. Then thank you, Lorna. Most kind.'

As Miles passed her his cup, Lorna took in the dark patch on the back of his hand. 'That's a nasty bruise.'

'War wound from yesterday. A bouncer.'

'Looks sore,' said Rose.

'What's that line from Keats? "Touch has a memory"? A day or two and it'll be fine.'

Keats! In that accent! Rose considered the bruise, and the smile, and locked away that phrase, 'Touch has a memory', determined to find out which poem it came from. And to find a place to use it.

A month later, as Rosie flicked through a dog-eared copy of *Country Life* magazine that had made its way to the dental surgery in Wanderrie Creek, a name caught her attention: it *did* say 'Lord Beaumont'.

In front of what looked like a castle, 'Lord Beaumont' was sitting with his gun dogs. The feature was about the forthcoming wedding of His Lordship's youngest daughter, the Honourable Alexandra ('the most sought-after debutante of her year, and sister of the dashing – and equally Honourable – Miles'), who was to marry the eldest son of a duke. A photographic portrait showed her in pearls and a satin gown by Christian Dior, with a diamond the size of a golf ball on her perfectly manicured hand. Rose checked the cover: three years old.

Turning back the page, she glimpsed her own stubby fingernails. She touched her hair: like mattress stuffing; looked at her gingham skirt. She thought of the boys she knew, the dances she'd been to – the shuffling feet and clumsy hands and drunken vomiting; remembered Derek and how he'd touched her like he owned her, without making eye contact.

'Touch has a memory.'

But now, the 'dashing Miles', who grew up in this stately home, was *here* on Meredith Downs. Maybe anything was possible? Imagine being *there* with him. She conjured the pearls, the satin; smelled the soft green rolling lawns; felt the cool, solid stone of the turrets. Imagine a conversation that wasn't about stock or drought, in a place that didn't reek of sheep, with a man who didn't spill beer down himself, and could ask for a table for two in umpteen languages . . .

The spell that took hold saw her drift through days and plan at night. But Miles seemed oblivious whenever she touched his arm as she made a point, or wore a top that showed cleavage. At the Wanderrie Creek Races, at the Knapps' anniversary party on Deep Springs Station, at the Young Pastoralists' Association picnic, Rose's attempts to get him on his own were met with his favourite phrase:

'Let's join the others.' His impeccable politeness never seemed at risk of blossoming into anything more.

The weeks passed. The grass dried and the heat grew. The rams were put into the ewes' paddocks to begin the next generation of the MacBrides' fortunes. Nineteen fifty-seven wandered lazily to its end in a string of days that passed the century mark. And all the while, silently, relentlessly, from time's endless ocean, the days hauled the tenth of January 1958 closer, like a shark on a hook.

10

On any old outback property, you can see them, the skeletons of dreams. Houses long abandoned, windmills rusting, fence posts splintered, tank stands collapsed: every one of them was once a hopeful beginning.

Sometimes, all that's left are the remnants of hopes and the bones of a rusting tin shack someone once called home. Occasionally, this shack now serves as a chook shed or a wood shed beside a sturdier house, and shows that luck was on their side. More often, there's just a crumbling chimneystack and fireplace, traces of brick foundations, or eaten-away timber frames. And not a living soul for miles.

Out here, whole towns go this way, where, once, shoals of hopes eddied around a mine site, or a port, or a rail siding, and flourished for a while, until circumstance and that old enemy, time, hounded them into a future that saw the mine exhausted, the port usurped by an airport, and the rail left behind by roads. The sheep and cattle stations they supported are battered by drought or banks or market collapses until they're nothing but a few strands of fence-wire trampled into the dirt, and the odd warped windmill groaning for grease.

But no one ever built a house out of despair; no one ever invested in a new wool press out of regret. Every wreck, every ruin is the relic of a shrivelled dream, lasting long after the body of its dreamer has been received back into the earth with love or remorse or indifference.

Our lives come and go like these gold-rush towns. We arrive, we grow, we thrive, then we're gone. Then the forgetting happens, and once-solid foundations are barely traces in the earth, from unguessable lives. Whole communities and the ties that bound them are blown away with the dust.

In the end, we're all looking for a place to ride out the storm of life. Among all these husks of houses and fossils of trees, we are like hermit crabs, borrowing a shelter for a time, and moving on. We relinquish who we were and strike on to our next moment, leaving an empty shell and a few traces: some letters, a wedding ring, a faithful pair of boots. Who can say what will last of us, and for how long?

We're all falling through space and time, but on the day of the truck crash in 1958, Matthew MacBride fell more suddenly and more spectacularly than most. When his body was thrown clear of the sheep truck and onto the stony road, his soul was flung clean out of his body, to a place outside time, exiled to a waiting room between life and death, between who he had been and who he might become.

It was almost a week before Matt opened his eyes after the crash, in Royal Perth Hospital. Rose had gone to get her mother a cup of tea, leaving Lorna alone with her younger – her only – son. When he blinked, she sprang up. 'Darling? Mattie?' But as she leant to kiss his cheek he lashed out with a grunt, hitting her face.

'It's me, Mum!'

He looked at her with terror. 'Off!' he snarled at the stranger. 'Get off!'

A nurse strode swiftly across the ward. 'Matthew! Finally! Welcome back!' She gestured to Lorna to keep her distance from him, enunciating slowly, 'I'm Nurse Raglan. You're in hospital. You had a road accident and you've been asleep for a few days . . . Can you hear me OK?'

'Piss off!' Spittle flew from Matt's mouth as he kicked at the bedclothes.

'Matthew!' exclaimed Lorna. 'What on—'

'Don't worry.' The nurse kept a cheerful tone, eyes still on Matt. 'He's not quite back with us yet . . . It'll take him a while.'

'I'm confident he'll live,' the neurologist, Dr Linto, said later that morning as Lorna and Rose sat in his office. 'But as to how *well* he'll live . . . that remains to be seen. Mercifully, there's no spinal damage; the broken ribs will mend by themselves. The gash in his thigh was nasty, but healing well. It's his head that's the worry.' The doctor explained the 'traumatic encephalopathy' caused by shearing forces moving the brain back and forward in the skull. His amnesia might pass, but it was too early to tell. He consulted his notes. 'You saw how his toes curled up, not down? And how his reflexes were very jerky? Indications that the brain's regressed to a – well, a more primitive state. Very common with head trauma.'

The general rule was that the sooner patients got better, the better they'd get, but that wasn't set in stone. As for the accident itself, 'It's not helpful to talk to him about it yet if he doesn't remember, other than in very general terms, *if* he asks. If you start loading up his mind with things that happened to him that he can't recall, it could make him paranoid, delusional . . . suicidal even. He's likely to be labile for quite some time. So . . . leave it a while before breaking the news about his brother and his father.'

Rose sat in silence, staring at her hands, as if the doctor might see through her, discover the whole story of what she'd done.

We think we know who we are: that each day, we'll wake up more or less the same person. But just as rocks are weathered, we are perpetually formed and changed by time and experience until we leave this world with not a single cell we came in with. As the ribbon of our life uncoils, the person who goes to sleep is imperceptibly different from the one who wakes up. Sometimes, instead of the gradual metamorphosis, a single event changes a life completely, and when it does, it changes everyone who has ever loved them.

Lorna MacBride fretted as her new son emerged from beneath the swelling and the sickening bruises: slow to speak; seething with frustration at his inability to understand what was going on; exhausted after a few moments' conversation; roaring at nurses. The child she had loved and nurtured was gone, and she had to come to terms with this stranger.

Dr Linto warned of confusion, aggression, anger, as well as speech problems and lack of dexterity; and no, he couldn't say how or when they'd improve. 'He'll have poor judgement for a while; trouble controlling his moods, his inhibitions. Don't be surprised if he swears a lot more, or exhibits . . . inappropriate behaviour.' He slipped some pages back into a folder. 'I have to warn you – it may be a new self he finds. There's no guarantee of anything. But pray, and hope . . .' He looked directly at Lorna. 'You go and see to things at home. We'll look after your boy, I promise.'

11

When Lorna wakes in the night she misses the breathing, the feel, the smell of Phil. She still expects to find his shirt in the laundry basket every morning; or his boots, like a cast of his feet, just inside the laundry door.

She remembers how, during the war, she used to hug his pillow and whisper news about the shearing or a thunderstorm, as if he could hear her over there in North Africa. When she mashed potatoes or bathed the kids, there was always that background thought: *He might be dead already – you won't know for weeks, months*. And her heart would hammer as she imagined breaking the news to her little ones. But she would not cry, just as Phil would not have cried – she wasn't about to let him down.

Then, home he had come, not a scratch on him, and, oh, the joy of being in his arms again, all set to carry on the long, contented life that war had nearly ended. But what the enemy couldn't achieve, a wretched kangaroo had managed with laughable ease.

She gazes at the porcelain shepherdess on the dressing table, a present from Phil when Warren was born, and her arms still flex to hold the infant, breathing in the milky warmth of his scalp. She recalls the morning of the crash and his casual 'Cheerio'. Phil's shadow, cut down before he had the chance to find his own shape.

He would have grown out of that arrogance, that cocksure way of his; found a nice girl who'd teach him that he didn't have to win every moment of life – that you had to let your guard down for love to really blossom.

Rolling onto her side, her thoughts turn to Mattie, her littlest, her cleverest, her little explorer, and her gut tenses. Will he ever even be able to feed himself again?

When morning bleaches away the edges of darkness, she pulls on a cotton shift, slips into her gardening scuffs. She goes out to the sweltering shed to start the generator, careful not to let the crank handle smash into her hand when it revs up. Beside the house she bends to light the fire under the donkey heater for hot water – not because she can be bothered to shower, but because this is the house of Phil MacBride, and she, and it, will carry on – rationally, efficiently, just as he would have demanded.

Lorna's first visitor when she got back from the hospital in Perth was Neil Tinnett, who had arranged Miles Beaumont's stint. One of Dalgety's most popular stock and station agents, he was a friendly chap, with a ready smile, genuinely interested in people – the life suited him down to the ground.

He had a gift for knowing exactly what his customers wanted to hear about, from the cricket score to news of a new Peppin stud just starting up. Always helpful, too: not just in getting your wool to auction or selling you some piping. He might know someone who knew someone with a few sheep they had to offload because it looked like their part of the country was heading for a drought. Or he could broker the sale of a block of land at the edge of a station on its uppers to a neighbour keen to expand. Swings and roundabouts, Neil would say: luck had two sides on its coin, and one man's bad luck was always someone else's good. He liked to make sure the coin toss was fair, though.

When he first came to Meredith Downs in 1946, Neil Tinnett had only just joined Dalgety's. After the war, the RSL (Returned Servicemen's League was a mouthful) was the one organisation that mattered: you got to know a bloke when you were both up against the Japs or the Germans. You knew who you could rely on; who'd had a rough trot and could do with a hand up. These bonds were carried back into offices and staffrooms and shops and farms across Australia. So when Neil looked up his old commanding officer, Phil MacBride, he got the Meredith Downs business on a handshake.

When the wool price went through the roof in the early fifties, Neil had more work than he knew what to do with. Sheepmen everywhere bought up big: new machinery, new plant – built new homesteads even, as wives rejoiced at the chance of indoor plumbing and walls that actually joined up with the windows.

The MacBrides were comfortably off – a solid family with a solid homestead and twenty-odd thousand solid-quality sheep. Not the sort to go mad on spending. Now, here was Lorna, like one of the war widows on Neil's beat, trying to keep hold of a property the size of a small country.

Maudie Knapp opened the door, and sent him through to Phil's study, where he sat with his hat on his lap.

He was taken aback when Lorna came in. Her greying hair was dragged back into a scruffy knot. Her cheeks were drawn and her eyes swollen: just about belonged in a coffin herself.

'Neil.' She didn't attempt a smile. He went to stand but she gestured to sit as she lowered herself, poker-straight, to the edge of the armchair opposite. 'Come to sell us up?'

He couldn't tell whether it was a question or a joke. 'Nothing like that, Lorna.'

'Just a pastoral visit then?'

Neil inhaled deeply. The familiar room, with the enamelled

brass plates from Egypt on the wall, and the army compass sitting on the desk, seemed almost to smell of Phil MacBride. He bet if he opened the drawer, his medals would be in there between the pencils and paper clips . . .

'To think of all he came through, then *this* . . .' Neil said. 'Phil was a fine CO and a good friend, Lorna.' He glanced at a photo on a table. 'And Warren – well, he was a beaut chap. Chip off the old block . . . There are things to sort out, in due course. But I'll keep everything ticking over for as long as I can.'

'How much do we owe?'

'You're in a lot better shape than some places. Phil had his head screwed on. Not too much to worry about, as long as the weather behaves itself.' He paused. 'And . . . young Matt? Any news about whether he'll . . .' He left the sentence hanging.

'Die?'

Neil's voice was gentle. 'Whether he'll recover soon.'

Lorna gazed out of the window at the frond of Palestine palm nodding in the breeze. 'I wanted to wait, until he could be at the funeral . . . Phil's and Warren's, I mean . . . But the doctors said best not.' She turned to him. ' "Best not"! What in God's name's that supposed to mean?'

'Means he's alive, Lorna.'

'At least they didn't suggest burying all three together.'

Neil cleared his throat. 'I wanted to talk to you about something. I know Phil was very impressed by Miles . . .'

Lorna's face fell. 'Oh – he'd been due to leave. I wasn't even thinking . . .'

'If it's all right with you, I'll have a word. See if he can stay on for the next few months – at least until Matt's – well, back on deck. You're three men down, Lorna. Even you can't manage this place on your own.'

* * *

It had been easier than Neil expected to get Miles to extend his stay. The Englishman had made a joke about being 'transported to penal servitude for life' that Neil didn't quite get.

'The MacBrides are a nice fam—*were* a nice family,' Miles said. 'Seemed so close-knit. We Beaumonts aren't as . . .' He left his sentence unfinished. 'Of course I'll stay on, till Matt's back on duty.' He gave a laugh at some private thought. 'It's nice to be wanted.'

Starting his car, Neil assessed the topaz sky. There had been precious little rain, and there were mutterings about a possible drought. Might need to destock before long. Better to sell what they could for what they could get than watch the sheep turn to bones in the paddocks. But one step at a time. He'd raise it next visit, perhaps, if necessary. But he couldn't help thinking that the coin of the MacBrides seemed to be bad luck these days, heads or tails.

12

As Dr Linto described it to Rose, the brain tiptoes up to memory of trauma from two directions. First, the patient gradually recovers the recent past, forming new short-term memories that build backwards in time from the present. So, a few days after regaining full consciousness, Matt could recall having breakfast, or being visited by a doctor that morning. Memory also grows forward, from the distant past towards the traumatic event. The old, long-reinforced memories – his name, who his mother was – tended to stay put once they came back. But new information could be as hard to catch hold of as clouds, and could come and go as freely.

He asked Rose more often about Phil and Warren, and about his mother, and why they weren't there. Matt would then forget he had asked, and ask again. When Dr Linto said she could break the news of the deaths, bafflement played across Matt's features. Then he became convinced that because Lorna wasn't there, she must have died too. And each night after Rose disappeared back to the hostel for patients' families, Matt would ask whether his sister was also dead.

The Wanderrie Creek police cleared the road of the blackened sheep carcasses and the mangled roo. They measured the skid tracks and towed the burnt-out wreck back inside the boundary of Meredith Downs.

Sergeant Wisheart, who had made sweet tea for Lorna in her kitchen on the day of the crash, went to Perth to interview Matt in hospital.

'Use short words,' Dr Linto warned. 'Simple sentences. He can't divide his attention between two things at once, so only ask one question at a time . . . Imagine you're trying to sit an exam when you're very, very drunk. That's what your questions will be like for him at the moment. So go gently . . . I doubt you'll get any sense out of him about the accident itself, though.'

Our memory reminds us what we like; prompts us about things to avoid. In its absence, Matthew MacBride, when offered a cigarette by a fellow patient with bandaged stumps instead of legs, accepted. From that day, he was a smoker. When asked if he spoke French, he said he didn't know.

Gradually, though, he recovered more snippets about his family, the station, the season. But he could remember nothing of the accident.

Or why he was ever in the truck in the first place.

On the last day of January, Matt sits on his hospital bed, knees hugged up to his chest. The hair still hasn't grown back over the white snake of flesh on his scalp from the stitches, but it will, the doctors say, it will . . . Just give it time . . . 'In cases like this, all we know is that the brain is sometimes – not often, but *sometimes* – capable of repairing itself in ways we can't even begin to understand. Pray that this will be a "sometimes",' Dr Linto tells Rose.

She longs for Matt to roll his eyes at something she said, tickle her in revenge for calling him a twerp . . . but he just sits, rocks. If she had a time machine she could change things, would do it all differently.

13

THE FRUIT CRATE room, on the western side of the homestead, stores things that are important but not official – keepsakes and so forth: an archive of happiness preserved in the boxes that give the space its name.

It's taken Lorna almost a month to bring herself to enter it again.

She drags the duster over the shelf where her wedding dress lies boxed in tissue paper. She remembers the thrill of slipping on the ivory duchesse satin at the dressmaker's for the final fitting; recalls how, as a child, Rosie was enchanted by the seed pearls and lace on its bodice. Perhaps Rose will wear it herself one day – the odd tuck and a stitch to the hem is all it would need.

Side by side in the jarrah cupboards are the 'Family Fruit Crates': pine crates in which apples or oranges were once delivered, and for which Lorna had sewn calico linings to hold the most special family memories. When she came up with the idea as a newlywed, she and Phil had just one crate between them: it seemed only natural to share. Layered carefully were things like their wedding invitation; a newspaper cutting with the rainfall report for the day (Phil's contribution); the long kid gloves she had worn just that once. There was the empty seed packet from the pumpkins she planted in her first act of taking over the Meredith Downs vegetable garden; a swatch of blue brocade from the curtains she had run up on the old treadle Singer; the menu from their twentieth-wedding-anniversary dinner in Perth. Dozens of treasures that took her, in the span of a few cubic feet, from the earliest days of their life together to the framed citation awarded to Phil on retiring as District President of the Pastoralists' and Graziers' Association just a few months before his death. Odd, how so much time could fit into such a tiny space.

Warren's crate had the little card from the hospital with his birth weight; his blanket, crocheted by Phil's mother, long dead. Crayon drawings; school projects in brown scrapbooks showing the different soil types of Western Australia and the effect of rainfall on the wool clip (complete with tufts glued to the pages now stained with wool grease). There were the articles from the *Wanderrie Creek Examiner* about his captaincy of this or that sports team at boarding school. His first tooth.

A numbness crept through Lorna: the crate was now complete. There would be no more treasures. Her own crate would have no additions either – what was the point, without Phil to share them?

Rose's Fruit Crate had a crimson satin bow – Phil's idea. It was 'just nice, seeing as she's a girl'. It had her best doll and her baby bonnet and the collection of eucalypt flowers she pressed when she was nine, when she heard the story of Jemima's trees. The lace handkerchief in it had been Lorna's grandmother's. A shooting trophy. A couple of old shellac discs.

She turned to Matt's, filled with essays and maps and a boat made of matches. His certificate for being Dux of the school, awarded weeks before the accident. Such an enquiring mind. Even as a littlie, he'd spin the globe on Phil's desk and tell her, 'I'll go there! And there!' prodding with an inky finger. She had always thought he was the one she'd have to give up; the one she'd have to learn to live without soonest.

For a while after the crash, Old Wally stopped working. It turned out that Lorna, taking over what had always been Phil's task, had overwound it. The clock was dismantled and dispatched to Wanderrie Creek in pieces, wrapped in pages of *The Countryman*.

Time regressed to its wild state, turning day into night if it wanted, so that Lorna found herself hardly sleeping during the darkness, then falling into little catnaps in the afternoon. Eventually, she recalled the story of Matilda, and, restoring the repaired clock to its position of authority over day *and* night, Lorna, too, found solace in the midnight chimes.

14

IN EARLY FEBRUARY, Matt is transferred to the Shenton Park Rehab centre, where years earlier he had once visited Humpty Dumpton, to begin intensive rehabilitation. It's less clinical than the surgical ward he was in, the air of urgency replaced by one of resignation. In its single storey, with wide, lino corridors, everything seems to be in slow motion as Parkinson's and stroke patients wade through empty space as though contending with a flood tide.

Doctors encourage him to wear his own clothes during the day. The rehab staff are friendly, and let Rose sit in on Matt's sessions, where the physiotherapist gets him to try to stand on one leg, walk with his eyes closed – things that now cost him effort. Matt, who just weeks ago could manoeuvre a horse in a stock yard with one hand, or balance on the rails in the shearing shed. When he fails some of the occupational therapy exercises Rose feels sick – tracing model letters on a page with a pencil; clipping pegs onto a string; putting a key into a lock. 'Fine dexterity movements,' the physio explains to Rose with a smile.

There's no telling how he'll react to her these days. Sometimes he sits like a grump. Then, without warning, he'll laugh hysterically at something mundane she's said – a report that they've had some rain, or that a foal has died. Then rage bursts out of nowhere and he shouts and sobs.

Rose gives him a hug, strokes his hair like when he was little, lets him rest his head on her shoulder – it seems to soothe him. She wonders what the hell he makes of it all.

A few weeks later, Sister Smiley, the fair-haired nurse Rose has got to know a little, laughs as she makes her usual joke: 'That's your smiley sister, and I'm Sister Smiley.' (Same joke for every patient with a visiting sister.) When the nurse tries to take his blood pressure, Matt puts a hand on her breast and squeezes. 'Enough of that, thank you!' she mutters, and swats it away. He looks at her sheepishly and then at Rose, who babbles apologies, but the nurse says matter-of-factly, 'Loss of inhibition – classic with head injuries. We get a lot worse, believe me. It'll pass . . . Or it should.'

Rose is still blushing when, at the door, Nurse Smiley turns to say, 'He's not doing too badly, given what he's been through. And he's actually getting better about the misbehaviour.' She puts a hand to her chest and, as though Matt were no more aware than the furniture, leans confidentially towards Rose: 'Last week he tried to get matron to touch his privates. She gave him short shrift, I can tell you.'

By early March, two months after the accident, Matt had a straggly beard: when a nurse had asked ages ago whether he wanted a shave, he'd given an indifferent shrug that was taken as a 'no', and it had been left to grow.

'You look like a real dag,' said Rose as she pushed a chair in front of the basin. 'Come on. Let's get the old Bubba back.'

From her bag, she produced shaving things from the chemist's, as well as a small portable transistor radio. At home, they'd be lucky to pick up the scratchiest short-wave signal of the ABC with a thing like that, but here it could get all the stations. She perched it on the window ledge, and tuned it until Marty Robbins began to sing about a white sport coat and a pink carnation.

'Right. Scissors first,' she said, laying pages of the *West Australian* on the floor to catch the hair, and began to snip. When she slipped a blade into the razor, Matt reached for it, but she held it away. 'Nu-uh. They reckon you're not up to this yet.'

'Cos I'm spastic . . .'

'Cos you need time. You can do your own shaving cream though – I'm not your maid.' She squeezed a dollop of minty cream onto his palm and frothed it, then handed him the wet brush. He hesitated, stumped for a moment by the task of co-ordinating with his mirror image.

'Just whack it on any old how.'

Once the shave was finished, Rose rolled up the used sheets of paper and stuffed them into the bin. Matt leaned down to pick up the clean outer pages, where the headline blared: 'QUEEN MOTHER VISIT TOMORROW'; then, 'Full motorcade route inside'.

'Who's the Queen Mother?' asked Matt.

Rose watched his face, waiting for more, but his expression returned to blankness as the thought slid from his mind and he shifted his gaze to the mirror again, as though trying to place his own face from somewhere.

A shiver went through her, but whether it was from relief or guilt, she couldn't tell.

Tuesday, 7th January 1958

Rose wiped her forehead with the back of her hand, then leaned on the handle of the rake, fanning herself with her hat. *Talk about glamour* . . . She imagined Miles's debutante sister, Alexandra, doing this job – spreading sheep manure on the rose bed – in twinset and pearls, her stilettos like cocktail sticks spiking the small round dags.

Flies crawled about Rose's eyes, and though she waved them away as she put her hat back on, they returned a second later. 'Get off, you bastards!' She swung the rake around her, but the flies just clung to her for the ride. 'Arrggh!' She hurled it down. 'Bugger bum blast damn bloody hell!'

It wasn't just the flies and manure, though. Lucy Drebbing, her friend from school days, had just returned from London with her parents, sailing on the *Aurora Queen* via Venice and Monaco and *blah blah bloody blah*. For months, Rose truly had tried to be happy for Lucy each time Sneaky Snook delivered a newsy letter, or a postcard of Buckingham Palace or Windsor Castle, but it had worn a bit thin.

She rested her chin on her hands, propped on the recovered rake handle, and surveyed the horizon beyond the neat rose garden. Yeah, she loved this place: it was where she was from; where she'd want her bones to crumble into the earth when she died at ninety, no matter where she lived in between. Maybe by then she'd have a husband and kids and grandkids . . . But *before* that . . .

She'd heard her dad talking to her mum about which families had sons who'd be a good match for her 'in due course'. His idea of a good match meant *How many acres? How many sheep? How many inches of rain? Sort of chap you'd be happy to have a beer with? A whizz with a bogged truck?*

This restlessness had started before Lucy's trip. It had been there ever since the gallant Englishman arrived. The Honourable Miles Beaumont . . . She watched him, sometimes, quietly reading a book on his verandah, like a beautiful statue. If he noticed her, he'd look up and always, *always*, smile as he said hello. So kind, so – *chivalrous*: that was a word that didn't get wheeled out much around Wanderrie Creek.

It had been lovely to daydream. But he'd end up marrying a

princess or something. She was aware of a sort of ache deep inside at the thought that he'd be leaving soon, heading over East.

But his tales of safaris and Scottish castles and South American jungles made her dare to believe there was a whole world to discover, where she could be not just *the MacBride girl*, but her actual self . . . whoever the hell that was . . .

She took a sip from her waterbag, then splashed some over her so that it cascaded off her hat brim. Lucy and her bloody postcards. If *Lucy* could get to London, there had to be a way Rose could do it. Today was the seventh of January . . . She calculated the number of days before Miles left, and let an idea peep out from the back of her mind. He always took her seriously. No one else had ever treated her quite like he did. Who better to ask about travel, and how to get a job in London? Hell, his family might even give her a job. She wasn't sure as what, but if she could wrangle a woolly ram and shoot a tiger snake, she could probably handle whatever the Poms could throw at her.

Of course, she'd have to convince her mum first, and let *her* work on Dad. It also meant not letting Warren know. She could just imagine him ragging her, putting on an English accent and holding out his little finger to mime drinking tea. As for Matt – he was hopeless at secrets.

At lunch a few days before, Miles had asked to see Proserpine Mine before he left, and Matt, so keen on geology, jumped at the chance to show him. They'd decided on the tenth of January. Phil and Warren would be busy taking some wethers to town, and would be dropping Rose at the Young Pastoralists' meeting (which she always referred to as the *Young Dags'* meeting). The Queen Mother was visiting Perth next March, and all the WA Young Dags' divisions would be sending representatives to the city to join the thousands lining the streets in the hope of a glimpse of the royal car.

Rose poked lazily at a few sheep droppings as a plan began to form. Her dad would have a fit if she just announced she wasn't going. But if Matt were to *ask* to go to the meeting instead of her . . . He was looking forward to showing Miles the mine, though. He wouldn't be breaking his neck to take her place . . . Then inspiration struck: Matt's secret crush.

Pattie Gosden had been captain of the St Hilda's debating team last year, when Matt captained Scotch. Debating being about the only activity where girls and boys were in the same competition, it was a hotbed of romance for the brainy kids and prefects. Matt had asked Pattie to the Scotch ball last November. The Gosdens had a station a bit west of Wanderrie Creek – mainly Collinsvilles, and some pretty good country, so Dad hadn't objected to the potential courtship. If Rose were to tell Matt that Pattie Gosden would be at the Young Dags' meeting . . . If she were to offer, as a favour, to show Miles the mine, and let Matt take her place . . .

Of course, Pattie *wouldn't* actually be there. Rose had got the letter with the list of attendees and the list of apologies: Pattie would be in Perth. Well, Rose would just say she'd forgotten. Matt'd get over it. And she'd make it up to him – do his next turn at putting the sheep dags on the roses, maybe. It was no big deal.

Still, she felt a twinge that night as she saw Matt trying to act natural when he told his dad about taking Rose's place at the meeting. When Warren eyed him suspiciously, Matt gave a shrug: 'You never know. I might get picked for the Perth trip to see the Queen Mother . . .' He didn't want Warren's ragging any more than Rose did. 'Bliss doesn't mind swapping,' Matt said, though his face coloured like sudden sunburn. Yep, hopeless with secrets.

So, at the same time as all the MacBride men set out for Wanderrie Creek on the tenth of January 1958, Rose rode out to Proserpine Mine with Miles. 'Last-minute change of guide,' she'd explained.

The morning was sparkling and fresh. There was an occasional jingle of a bridle from the tethered horses as Rose walked Miles around the ruins of the old mine manager's house, flicking up the odd rusted pot or fragment of violet glass with the toe of her boot.

'All those lives, and all that's left is some bits of metal and a hole in the ground.'

'"Look on my works, ye Mighty, and despair!"' mused Miles.

'Shelley! We had to learn 'Ozymandias' by heart for English. Sounds better when you say it, though.'

At the edge of the mineshaft, Miles peered into the gloom, but Rose put a hand on his arm. 'Watch it! That's a straight drop.' She shone her torch down the sides, lined with splintering wood. 'Just follow exactly where I go.'

As they clambered down the sleepers, which Rose's feet knew by heart, Miles called out questions about the construction, yield, operations. He in turn told her the story of Tantalus, who gave his name to the tantalite in the mine, and his punishment of never getting hold of the fruit and the water that seemed within easy reach. 'I know how he feels,' said Rose.

'Me too!' Rose thought she could see something pass across Miles's face, but he went on, 'And of course Proserpine is the Roman version of the Greek goddess Persephone.' He recounted the tale of her exile to the underworld for half the year.

They felt their way along the low, narrow passageways, the torch sometimes exposing an animal bone, or some miner's relic: a tobacco tin, a buckle. Miles knelt to pick up something that glinted. 'It's – a toy car.'

'That's Warren's!'

'Shall we take it back to him?'

'Nah. I hid it here when I was about seven. He can have it back when he gets a bit nicer.'

Back above ground, covered in dust and soon sweating with the heat, they sat on either side of the old chimney stack, resting against the warm bricks as Rose poured tea from a thermos. She'd played here all her life, but she'd seen it through new eyes today: Tantalus. Persephone . . .

She gathered her courage and confided, on a *completely* secret basis, her dream of travelling to England. Miles listened courteously, gave encouragement, said he'd still be in Australia, but would be delighted to put her in touch with friends. As for a job, though, he said his family could be a tricky lot, but his sister Alexandra was a good sport and would probably be happy to help find her something.

As they mounted to leave, Miles gave his horse's mane a gentle stroke. 'I'm going to miss this corner of the world, and I'll miss you' – her heart bumped, but he went on – 'all of you MacBrides. You've been very kind to me.' He gave a gentle kick to get his horse walking but Rose waited, taking in a deep breath. On the brink of her grand, secret adventure, she had an almost solid sense of happiness. She would make her own life, climb her own mountains, fix her own mistakes.

The shoe of her horse clanged as it stepped on the flattened 'Danger. Keep Out' sign, and she smiled at the thought that her years of playing there, being whoever Warren said she had to be, were finally coming to an end.

15

PREVAILING MEDICAL WISDOM favoured getting head injury patients back to familiar turf, where family and friends could visit more easily. So in mid-March, two months after the crash, Matt waved goodbye to Sister Smiley, and was transferred to Wanderrie Creek Regional Hospital, the nearest major medical base to Meredith Downs that had a consultant physician and rehabilitation facilities.

That consultant, Dr Donald Fairchild, ran through his patient's condition with Lorna, glancing occasionally at the notes on his desk. Matt still suffered 'some neurological deficits'. His balance could be iffy, and he occasionally struggled to get words out if he was tired or upset. His memory, though miles better, remained a patchwork, with some things perfectly preserved, and others still far beyond reach.

'So? What happens now?' asked Lorna.

'We step up his occupational therapy, sharpening his motor skills and so forth. He's in his own clothes, getting used to everyday living. I think he might be ready for a short trip home.'

Lorna fought a tear. 'When?'

He could see her struggling with the emotion. How had this woman, still fit and handsome, even managed to put one foot in front of the other? 'He could have a weekend visit, say. Just as an experiment.' He consulted the calendar on his desk. 'No risky activities of course: no riding, no driving. Absolutely no drinking at all: one drink will have the same effect as about five . . . Are there people who can help you?'

'My daughter Rose. And our trainee manager. Some of our other hands if need be.'

'Coming home for the first time can be very confronting for patients, Mrs MacBride, so go very, very gently. I'll sort out the details for . . . let's say Friday the twenty-eighth of March. It'll give him something to work towards.'

That last Friday in March started off hot, with only the softening of the light betraying the arrival of autumn. Rose fidgeted on the verandah as she watched her brother emerge from the car and wave away the offer of a strong, friendly hand from Miles.

Assailed by sights and smells both familiar and foreign, colours and sounds that had been with him only in his hallucinations, Matt wondered whether this 'return home' was just another bout of unconsciousness. He gripped Lorna's arms and looked into her eyes for a long time, half expecting her to vanish, but she gripped him back, and said, 'Welcome home, darling.'

Rose came and grabbed him fiercely. 'About bloody time, Bubba!' she said, a tear running down her cheek.

Matt brushed it away. 'Gedday, Bliss.' He stepped back. 'Where are Dad and Warren?' Then he grabbed the car roof as his knees buckled.

That evening, Miles joined them for dinner, and Rose was grateful for the skill with which he smoothed the conversation, subtly guiding Matt onto topics that put him at ease, waiting politely while he searched for a word. She loved the gallant Englishman for providing a kind of anaesthetic for this first gathering of her shrunken family, where the two gaping empty chairs made loss feel final, now; solid.

The talk was about the welcome boost in wool price; the broken leg of Bob Sowerby, next door on Maundy Creek station; a couple of hands who had left and some who had joined; how WA had done in the Sheffield Shield. No mention of Phil or Warren. No mention of hospitals. Matt ventured the occasional question, but mostly let the conversation flow around him, like a faintly familiar river.

As the evening wore on, his speech slowed, and his control of his cutlery became clumsy. When he fell asleep at the table, Lorna's heart melted. 'The poor kid's exhausted.'

'Right-ho. Let's get you to your cot, Matthew MacBride,' Miles said, and guided him down the hall to his room, where he helped him into pyjamas and into a bed which Matt eyed with a frown. He couldn't remember this ward, or this English doctor who was wishing him good-night. A joke about smiley sister and Sister Smiley echoed somewhere in his brain. But he was too tired. And he slid into a deep sleep.

* * *

It was decided that Matt should have a tour of the property the next day. Rose had volunteered to take charge, assuring Lorna that she was twenty years old, and had been bossing Matt around since she was three, so was perfectly capable.

'They've been talking about rain,' Lorna muttered as Rose headed to join her brother in the car, 'but I can't see much sign of it.' She searched the uninterrupted blue. 'Still . . . Watch out for the roads.' She bobbed down to speak through the driver's window. 'Maybe you shouldn't go . . . Just to be on the safe side . . .'

'The whole point of the trip is to remind him of stuff, Mum. See familiar places. Why even bother coming home if he just stays in his room?'

Rose had an itinerary planned that would include spots with

happy memories: a look at Lake MacBride; a visit to the Top Shed, the bigger of the two shearing sheds; maybe a dip in Blackjack waterhole. Lorna had put her foot down at the suggestion of Wallaby Ridge – far too tricky for him to negotiate the climb on rocky terrain, not to mention the drop on the other side. Perhaps on his next visit.

By the time they reached the Top Shed a couple of hours later, the emphatic blue of their starting point thirty miles away had been transformed, with isolated thunderstorms skirting the horizon.

Bugger. It was good to have rain, but not today. Not this far from the homestead. The empty shearers' quarters lay a hundred yards away. 'Right, Bubba, out you get. Picnic better be in the shed.' She passed him the blankets and the Esky and gathered up the cardboard box packed higgledy-piggledy with picnic things. She heaved at the wide corrugated iron door, making it screech and rumble on its rollers, and was hit by the familiar stink – of the dags and the lanolin and the ammonia of sheep piss; the machine oil and the diesel of the engine that powered the handpieces; and, today, the rich, herby smell of approaching rain.

'Welcome to Restaurant Le Top Shed!' Rose declared.

Matt explored the space warily, taking in the stands, tracing his hand down the tubes that dangled from the shearing plant, free of their usual combs and cutters; examining the thick red dust they left in the whorls of his fingertips. Words ambled into his mind: 'Expert'. 'Stencil'. 'Smoko'. It took him a while to retrieve their meanings. He picked up a tuft of fleece, touched it to his cheek, stretched out the crimps, then rolled it between his fingers and held it to his nose. The smell, the greasy feel; the way the daylight sliced upwards between the floor slats . . . Without warning, he burst into tears.

'Hey! Bubba! What's wrong?'

He turned away to hide his face. He'd told himself that it would all be different when he got home – he couldn't forget *home*. But here he was, lost and bawling.

The clang of the first few raindrops like gravel on the shed roof made Matt jump.

'It's all right,' said Rose, her mind half measuring the quickening of the rain.

The vastness of his loss – of his father and brother; of his old life – surged through him. 'It's *not* all bloody right! Nothing's right any more!'

It was going to be a tricky afternoon. Rose put an arm around his shoulder, and he rested his head against hers, an old gesture between them. The rain began to plummet like darts, and she pulled together a few half-empty bales of dirty wool tailings and threw a blanket over them. 'Here you go, a couch.' She took the foil-wrapped sandwiches from the Esky, then spiked open a can of lemonade, and handed it to Matt.

'Welcome back, Bubba.'

As they chewed their sandwiches, Rose tried to come up with old stories that might cheer him up: safe stuff, from long before the crash. All three of them riding an old mare called Buttercup. 'You always used to say "Cutterbup".'

'If you say so.'

'And remember Bex, your first pup? Dad got him from Termite Plains for you.'

'Where is he?'

Rose frowned. 'Well, he's dead, Bubba. Snake bite. Years ago.' She hoisted herself off the bales and pushed open one of the tin shutters. 'God, it's like bloody Noah out there.'

'Should we head back?'

'Too late. The road'll be a lake by now.'

Matt joined Rose at the window to watch the sky unload its enormous burden of water.

Rose, one hand on her hip and the other on top of her head, calculated. 'We're better off waiting it out here for the night. We can sleep in the shearers' quarters if we make a run for it later. It'll probably stop before long and run off into the creeks. Should be OK in the morning.'

'Won't Mum worry?'

'There's not much choice. She'll know we've been caught in the storm.' Rose blew air from her cheeks. 'Should be some lanterns and stuff in the cupboards. Check that side.' She smiled. 'I found a game of draughts once – shearers need something to do when the sheep are wet.'

They started opening the row of small, dusty cupboards lined along two walls. 'Empty beetroot tin,' reported Rose. 'A racing guide from 1953 . . . Ah, here we go – lamps and matches. Still got kero in them. What about your side?'

'A horseshoe. Half a tin of powdered milk . . . Pack of cards . . . Torch . . .'

'Torch and cards are handy. Anything else?'

'An old book,' said Matt. 'The Commonwealth Pastoralists' Almanac 1913.' He pulled out the heavy volume and rested it on the floor. Hidden behind it were two cans of Emu Export beer and, beside them, a bottle. He took it out and gave it a wipe on his jeans to get the dust off. 'Corio Whisky!' He checked the cap. 'Never opened.' The bottle glinted in the light of the lamps Rose had lit.

They sat back down on the blanket, and Rose began to shuffle the cards. 'Let's play Fish.' They'd played the game since they were tiny, but, just in case, she said, 'You know how it goes: five cards each. You ask me for a type of card – like "Any fives?" – and I have to give them to you, or if I haven't got any, I say "Fish" and you take a card from the pile. Whoever makes the most pairs wins.'

'And the loser skulls a beer,' said Matt, apparently surprised to hear the words come out of his mouth.

'What?'

'Didn't we do that?'

'You did it with Warren,' Rose said, then felt like she'd poked a bruise.

'Oh,' said Matt. Then, with a sudden grin, 'I can do it with you, then.' And before she could stop him, he had spiked open both cans of beer and was handing her one.

'Hey!' Rose exclaimed. 'Mum'll get cross.'

'Gonna tell on me?'

'No, but—'

'I'm bloody sick of it!'

Rose watched his cheeks suddenly redden, the vein pulse more visibly on his temple, like when he was about to cry as a baby. A thought came tapping on some window of her memory: her lie that meant it was Matt in the truck, instead of her. Her expedition to the mine with Miles, her dreams of exotic travels all seemed pathetic now. Shameful.

She eyed the can . . . One beer wasn't going to hurt him. 'OK, you're on. Loser skulls a beer.'

Losing the first hand, Matt downed his drink in one. 'Again!' he said, and Rose shuffled and dealt, drinking her beer quickly, in case he lost.

The rain hammered the roof, and an occasional flashbulb of lightning went off, leaving a snapshot in front of Matt's eyes – the wood, the bed, the bottle with its boast of 'Australia's Champion Whisky'.

'It's good, being back,' he said as the alcohol made his shoulders loosen, his jaw relax. He emptied the tea from their mugs and it sloshed through the floor slats. 'Celebration!' He reached for the whisky.

'No you don't!' Rose tried to grab it, but Matt snatched it back with a cheeky grin.

He splashed some into each cup. 'Cheers! Come on, down in one,' he said, and skulled. 'Huh! Too strong for you!' but Rose said, 'As if!' and followed suit.

When Matt poured another slug, Rose snatched the bottle. 'I'll keep the rest for when you're properly home.'

Matt skulled again, and started tickling her to release the bottle. 'Surrender!'

'Stop! OK!' she said, giggling in spite of herself as they tumbled on the wool, and she finally released her grip, her head already woozy. This was the little brother she remembered, happy for the first time in months. She planted a kiss on his cheek. 'Girl germs! Gotcha!' she said; then, more softly, 'You *are* back, after all. Yeah, I'll drink to that.'

They settled back down to the game. When Matt tried to match a king with a jack Rose smacked his hand. He frowned at the cards, then laughed. 'Penalty for cheating! Gotta drink again.'

'Go easy, Bubba,' his sister said, and poured more into her cup. At least if she drank it, he couldn't.

Eventually, she was declared the winner, and they both toasted her victory.

'Right, I'm bursting for a wee,' said Rose, and looked worriedly through the window. 'I'll get washed away out there . . .' She glanced at the slatted floor. 'No looking,' she said, as she withdrew unsteadily to the dark corner, hoisted up her skirt and manoeuvred her undies, squatting with relief and re-emerging from the shadows..

Matt, too, had a cloudy notion of wanting to piss. 'Back in a minute,' he said, and stumbled to the door.

'You'll get soaked!'

'It's only rain.'

When he came back, Rose said, 'You look like a drowned rat!'

He surveyed his soaked clothes and giggled.

'Yeah, hilarious, but *I'll* get it in the neck if you get pneu—pneu—Oh, you know.' She handed him the other blanket. 'Hang your stuff to dry on the rail and put this around you.'

Matt removed his boots and socks, then pulled off his shirt and jeans and flung them over the wooden rails. In his underpants, he wrapped the blanket around himself as Rose got a tea towel to rub some of the water out of his hair, trying to avoid his scar.

'Ow! Not so hard.'

'Right. There you go, you dill.' She gave him a tap on the nose. 'Now stay in-bloody-side!'

He poked out his tongue, and she rolled her eyes. 'So grown up!'

The clouds had sucked the light from the dusk, dousing the ends of the shearing shed in a thick dimness. Lamplight flickered around the walls, throwing shadows where the draught through the battens made the flames dance. It was like playing cubbies down the mine as kids – little outlaws in a pretend world made from contraband snuck out under their parents' noses: matches and candles; fruit cake and cordial; Dad's medals so they could be soldiers; a silk petticoat of Mum's so that Rose could be a bride (though that always got vetoed). She smiled dreamily at the memory of those days, and at seeing Matt become his old self again. A hazy warmth was washing through her. Who cared if it was only the booze? Who cared if all this was only pretend? Tomorrow would come soon enough.

They ate the last of the oranges and called it dinner, as they lay side by side, playing I Spy, the gaps getting longer, the guesses often not even starting with the right letter.

Matt tried to pick up his cup but kept missing. 'Bastard won't keep still.' He pointed sternly. 'Stay! Heel!' He wished his bed would stop floating up towards the ceiling. He stared at the metal roof. Never noticed it before. Everything was different tonight . . . 'No ward round yet?'

'What?'

He squeezed his eyes shut, then opened them wide. 'It's dark. Doctor's usually here by now, Matron . . . Sister . . .' He laughed. 'Sister Smiley!'

'Oh, ha bloody ha!'

Matt felt pleased at remembering this nurse's name. Then he remembered that feeling, when he'd reached out and touched her.

'I'm Matt. I think . . .'

A muffled buzz of anxiety shot through Rose. Somewhere far, far away, the last vestiges of logic wondered whether she should try to get him home, rain or no rain.

'Definitely no more of this for you,' she said, and skulled the last of the whisky. She vaguely recalled some plan about the shearers' quarters, but they seemed an ocean away now. At least here she was dry, and there was something like a mattress. She sank further into the warm, comforting blur of the drink, and the fuzziness that, just for the moment, made the real world feel like another planet. Playing cubbies. Warm and safe.

For Matt, the shed was rotating slowly; the rain was deafening, and the thunder stopped his heart for a moment in this strange hospital that stank of sheep. A woman's hand touched his chest, causing a thin electric jolt. 'OK. Time to sleep.' As she pulled a blanket over him, her skin brushed his shoulder, sending another jolt crackling through his body, and a sob burst from him.

He was drifting away from any familiar moorings, slipping into a foreign current. The hand stroked his hair and the woman's voice spoke to him quietly, words he couldn't make out. She was wiping the tears from his eyes, holding him tight, cradling him. 'Sorry,' she was saying. 'I'm so sorry,' leaving a kiss on his forehead that made his whole scalp tingle. And the feel of her, the touch of her fingers on his skin, the smell of her hair, made him fold into her, fold into the softness of whoever this was. If he closed his eyes the bed spun less. His blind mouth found her neck, hands circled her back, and, driven by the confusion, by the sheer frustration that had been building up so long in the wreckage of his old self, something in him broke loose: some instinct – suddenly free of its safe enclosure – that now followed a path as surely as a river seeks the sea. And in this twilight moment of the twilight world he'd come to fear since he'd lost himself, he felt freedom flood his veins.

16

THE LAST OF the darkness still clung around Rose as she woke. The thudding in her skull might crack it in two; her sandpaper throat might choke her. Focus slowly revealed the shearing shed. Something about rain – ferocious rain. There was silence now, but for the occasional heavy dripping from gaps in the iron roof. A weight on her chest gradually resolved into an arm. She tried to raise it, then realised it was not her own. A bolt of horror streaked through her and some strange sense, a fragment of a dream, scoured her gut. She needed to vomit. She needed the toilet.

As if repelled by a magnet, she jumped off the bales, where Matt lay on his belly like a corpse, mouth open, legs flung wide. A memory flashed like lightning and was gone. She felt for the torch and trained it on the body: a trickle of sick ran from the side of his mouth to a trail down through the shed floor, but he was breathing, pale and sweaty in the jaundiced beam. Her mind slammed the door on whatever her body remembered, and scrambled to the safety of here and now. Summoning her St John's Ambulance training, she felt the pulse at his wrist; checked his airway; then rolled him onto his side into the recovery position and pulled the blanket up, before slipping outside. She slapped her bare feet into a chilly puddle, sobriety wicking up through her from the earth as the raw air of dawn splashed her face. *Think! Think, you idiot!* Then, beneath that, *Keep your mind on* now.

She managed to pull his jocks up and get his shirt on, and threw a blanket over him in the back seat of the Land Rover. Dragging him down the ramp to the car was like hauling a stubborn wether. She doubled over to vomit again, and wiped her mouth with water from a pool at her toes. The sun was up now and skewered her eyes as she did her reckoning. It would take twice as long to get him to hospital if she tried to reach the homestead first. 'God, make the roads not be washed away,' she muttered, and headed off.

Half a mile down a track she realised she'd turned the wrong way. 'Bloody stupid bastard of a road!' she shouted, slapping the steering wheel as she spun it around. Whenever she hit puddles, she knew to drive straight through rather than try to skirt them. The dirt on the tracks was hard and compacted with years of use, and would see you safely across. The ground to the sides, even though it looked drier, would be soft and hopeless, leaving you bogged and buggered.

The treacherous road kept her mind occupied. She glanced in the rear-view mirror, checking for signs of consciousness in her brother. Occasionally the thought would come to her: *He's just asleep*; then the counterpunch: *But what if he's not?* would swing in, and she'd imagine him in a coffin, like her father and Warren.

'Whisky, for God's sake! If your father were alive he'd give you such a hiding, twenty years old or not!' In the days afterwards, Rose was almost grateful for the harshness in Lorna's voice as she called her an irresponsible idiot.

'The poor kid doesn't remember a thing! Doesn't remember being home at all. When he came round in hospital he asked Dr Fairchild what day his visit was going to happen.'

'It – I didn't mean to—'

'You were supposed to be looking after him! But trust you to lead him into trouble.'

'I didn't lead him – *he* found the bottle: he wouldn't stop drinking.'

'Don't you *dare* try and blame him, Rose MacBride! At least have the decency to take responsibility for what happened. Dr Fairchild says it's set him back weeks – months even.'

Rose reeled at this rare, unleashed fury of her mother.

'I didn't mean it to happen.'

'Just how many chances do you think you deserve?'

Lorna willed her breathing to slow. *I still have two children. Two living children* . . . At least Rose had had the sense to get him to hospital . . . 'Let this be the last time you bring trouble to this house, Rose MacBride. I don't think I can take much more.'

Rose was only vaguely aware that her mother had left her bedroom. She tried to press down the patchwork of sensations that kept surfacing. The rain, the booze, the blur. How at first, she couldn't believe what was happening, thought the whisky was making her imagine things, so she didn't even try to push him away. She could have. Easily. Then suddenly it was too late. Memories were just splinters: a touch here, a sound there. There had been no force at all: just a sort of clumsy need, like a little kid, who barely knew who he was, let alone who she was and what he was doing. So quick, so – so *nothing*. A handful of muddled seconds.

Later, the relentless conviction that *she* had caused the damage which meant he didn't know what he was doing, brought up the memory of other refrains she'd heard so often: *'led him on'*, *'been a tease'*, *'asking for it'*. Would anyone believe her?

Since childhood, Rose had convinced herself that she was never to blame for anything. Nothing at all: off it drifted with her smoke and incantation. But the crash had changed that. The crash, Matt's head; now this: everything – *everything* was her fault.

17

THERE'S A RHYTHM to the year here as strong as any lunar tide. Set by the sun and its limitless power, the rhythm carries on now without the MacBride men. Troughs wouldn't clean themselves; sheep wouldn't turn up of their own accord to be shorn. The station kept a few permanent hands and boundary riders for fencing and mill runs – trips to inspect the windmills to check they were in good order – and watching out for dog tracks (fencing being as much about what you keep out as what you keep in). At mustering time, more hands usually came from the towns and the local mission, camping out for the duration as they moved the sheep toward the holding paddocks around the shearing sheds. Then the shearing team would turn up – the shearers and the cook and the expert and the wool classer and various shed-hands, and for weeks the sheds would be a potent brew of muscle and banter and beer, until the shorn sheep were driven back to the wilderness and the clip was loaded onto trucks and sent for sale and everyone dispersed again, leaving the sheds to creak their corrugated laments, the ghosts of the men's sweat and swearing still floating in the air with the smell of the wool.

There were a few outcamps on the property – rough and ready places far from the homestead – to even up access to the stock. One had been staffed for years by Colin Dunleavy, an ancient Irishman who'd once taught about Yeats at Trinity College in Dublin before his fondness for drink proved his undoing. At another, Jackson and Daisy lived in the old shack they'd moved into when they got married decades ago. They still took off for ceremonies in due season, or for the occasional big funeral, but their kids had grown up and moved away, so it was a quieter place now. The MacBrides hadn't always won friends by their support of any natives who worked for them. But long ago, Augustus MacBride had declared, 'Anyone who calls themselves a Christian has a duty to help his fellow man, black, white or brindle. I treat any man who works for me fairly and with respect.'

Hiring and firing had always been Phil's domain. Miles was doing a wonderful job of helping to hold the fort, but Lorna knew they needed more station hands given the crash had left them three men down. She re-read the letter: '. . . I am nineteen and a half. I am six foot two and weigh eleven stone. I did my junior certificate at Esperance High School. I have had some experience with merinos on my uncle's farm at Fortitude Gulley. I have my own dog.'

Written on lined exercise paper, with no spelling mistakes, it was like so many others she received seeking work. And like the others, it was accompanied by a letter from the boy's former headmaster, and one from his parish priest, both confirming that he was an honest lad who came from good people and that they heartily recommended him for any position working on the land. She smiled, and added it to the pile to her left.

Lorna opened the next envelope, this one from a widow and her seventeen-year-old son: the husband had managed a big property in the Northern Territory before his recent death. Candidates for another of the outcamps, perhaps . . . She was about to take it to Rose, ask her opinion, but tutted to herself. The girl walked around in a complete dream lately: you could hardly get a sensible word out of her. Had she been too harsh on her about the state Matt had got into? But Rose never seemed to listen unless she read her the riot act.

Rose had no words since – since what? She couldn't speak to her mother about it. And she couldn't bear the thought of being near Matt, so hadn't argued when Lorna said she'd take over the hospital visits.

Rose's one island of comfort was Miles – kind, friendly, understanding. She could barely remember the version of herself who had confessed her secret travel plans, and she was grateful that, with his typical tact, he'd never mentioned them again.

In late April, he offered to teach her to play croquet, and she arrived at his house on a Sunday afternoon. 'Come through to the "croquet lawn". I've set up the hoops. Lemonade?'

'Everything all right?' asked Miles, when they reached the back verandah.

'Yes.' Rose sat down in the canvas steamer chair he dusted off for her.

'Now, how much do you know about croquet?'

'Nothing, except that it's very genteel,' she said vaguely.

'There are few more ruthless endeavours, I assure you.'

He explained the rules, and the tactic of using your shot to knock the opponent's ball off course.

'Sabotage . . .' murmured Rose.

'You seem a little distracted. Sure you're all right?'

She stood up. 'Let's start.'

He handed her a mallet and a ball, and showed her the various shots, getting her to copy him.

'Gently, Rosie,' he said when her ball raced off into the geraniums. 'It's more about strategy than might.'

She was just here. Just now. There was only *this*. When he put his fingers over hers to correct her grip on the mallet, she felt again the flutter of old daydreams – stately homes and rolling lawns. When his hands touched her shoulders to line up her side swing, she wished he would leave them there forever.

'You let me win, didn't you?' she asked as her ball hit the peg after her first circuit. She was aware of two completely different layers of herself, like oil floating on water: she smiled, and watched herself smile.

Then the fantasy evaporated. All that she'd driven from her mind came crashing back, and she let out a howl of tears.

'Rose, what's the matter?'

'Everything!'

He handed her a monogrammed handkerchief. 'You've been through – such a lot.'

'You've got no idea what I've been through . . . If you did, you'd have nothing to do with me.'

He searched her face, trying to decipher her meaning.

Against his instincts, against his better judgement, he leaned down to give her a light kiss, as though he might kiss things better. But when she responded urgently, fiercely, holding his head as she kissed him back, he pulled away.

'I shouldn't have done that,' he said. 'Please forgive me.'

It wasn't the first time Miles had been in a situation like this, and it probably wouldn't be the last, he supposed, but he knew there was no point in trying to explain. 'You're a . . . a lovely girl, and I'm . . . well, I'm very flattered. But . . .' He fiddled with a cuff. 'I'm not the right sort of chap for you.'

'Oh, I know! "Out of my league." Warren told me that to my face once.'

'Goodness, no! That's not it at all. You're – you're clever and you're funny and you're excellent company . . . But after all that's happened to you . . . One's emotions, well – they can leave one very vulnerable. Really: all my fault. I can't apologise enough.' He racked his brains for an excuse. 'I'm afraid I have to be going. I promised your mother I'd check on the stores – see what we're running low on. Please forgive me for not seeing you out.'

18

TWO DAYS AFTER the humiliation of the croquet afternoon, Rose stood beside her mother, chooks clucking loudly as she opened the wire gate to their yard.

'But why now, for goodness' sake, just before muster?' Lorna's tone was exasperated.

'Miles is still here. The new hands have started. Matt's coming home,' said Rose, following her in, armed with the basket. 'You'll manage.'

The discussion was about the secretarial course Phil had wanted Rose to do. Lorna was nonplussed by Rose's announcement that she wanted to start it now.

'I've been trying to ask you for ages but you're always too busy to talk. Dad already paid for it.' She took more eggs from Lorna. 'It's only till the end of the year.'

'Matt's back in two days. Wait till after that, and we can talk about it again. Surely you can wait two days.'

'You don't give a damn about me!'

Lorna took a step back.

'It's true! No one in this family ever has! I'm sick of being treated like a – like a—' Rose hurled the basket to the ground.

'What— Rose—' Lorna stared in disbelief as Rose ran off,

leaving the shattered eggs in her wake. She picked up the basket, and stroked the one intact egg with a thumb, thinking. Matt was the priority right now. Rose would cool off. Lord, that girl had a wild streak, though.

* * *

'*Matt's back in two days.*' Lorna's words were like a knife to Rose, still desperate to keep distance from her brother.

She had to get away. She dug out the old forms from her father's desk, and wiped the tears from the pages that he had completed in what seemed a different lifetime now.

The following day, Sneaky Snook the mailman took another bite of one of the sausage rolls Lorna had packed for him. 'Just to tide you over till lunch,' she'd said, passing the tinfoil package through the window of his truck. They were still warm, and the aroma that filled the cabin had Lightning drooling too. Sneaky had stopped halfway to the first gate, a mile down from the homestead, and tucked in, feeding one to his dog because 'fair's fair'. He pulled his hanky from his pocket and wiped the sweat from his forehead, then wiped the grease from his mouth, and finally his hands, ready to put them back on the steering wheel.

'Righty-oh, Lightning,' he said. 'Next stop, *déjeuner!*' and put the truck into gear, whistling the opening bars of 'The Queensland Drover'. Nearing the gate, he blinked at a figure. A girl. She waved an arm.

'That's Rosie MacBride, isn't it, mate?'

The dog looked ahead, then turned to his master, panting in vigorous agreement.

Rose had already swung the gate wide, and was standing by the window.

'Gedday, Rosie. What are you doing out h—'

'Can I get a lift with you? To town?'

'Course. I've just come from the house. Could have saved you the walk.'

'Go through and I'll close the gate.' She replaced the chain, then hoisted a duffle bag from behind the gatepost and slung it into the footwell before sliding onto the seat.

'Off on a jaunt?'

'Sort of.'

'Your mum didn't say anything.'

'It's . . . a surprise.'

Sneaky risked taking his eyes off the bumpy gravel long enough to study her. Away from the glare, her face was red and her eyes swollen.

'Everything OK?'

'Yep.' She turned to gaze out of the window.

'You sure?' pressed Sneaky, giving a brief pat to his dog, sitting between them on the front seat.

'Sure as eggs.'

Sneaky wiped his forehead again. 'How are you getting back?'

Rose turned and cupped the dog's head in her hands, leaning into its face. 'I'm fine. Tell your boss that, would you, Lightning? And tell him I don't feel like talking any more. Didn't sleep well.'

The dog nuzzled into her neck, the nub of his missing leg nudging her. 'Good boy,' she said, 'gooood boy,' and rested an arm around him.

They drove the rest of the way in silence, Sneaky speaking only to Lightning while Rose dozed.

Funny lot, the MacBrides . . . Everything they'd been through . . . Rosie could be a handful – always had been. Well, she was grown up now. None of his business what she was up to with her 'surprise' for her mother.

'Wakey wakey.' said Sneaky when the truck finally shuddered to a halt in town. 'Last stop.'

Rose's eyes shot open and she glanced around. For a moment the mailman saw a look of dread cross her features.

She got out. 'Thanks for the lift.'

'Where did you say you were going?'

'Just the bank, then the train station.' She gave Lightning a farewell pat. 'Bye.'

He watched her wipe her nose on the back of her hand and wipe her eyes with the heel of her palms. 'Right, Lightning. Let's go and see old Elsie Twitchen back at headquarters.'

At about the time Rose was climbing out of the mail truck, Lorna was pacing her daughter's bedroom, clasping a piece of paper. An empty envelope, addressed to 'Mum', lay on the bed. On the page, torn from an exercise book, jumbled words and phrases passed in and out of focus. 'Going to Perth'; 'knew you'd try to stop me'; 'promise I'll be fine'. The ink was smudged in places, and made reading all the harder.

This was well beyond Rose's usual shenanigans. Lorna turned it over in her mind: the drifting about in a daze since Matt's visit; then the rush to get away before he came home . . . There'd been a thought niggling somewhere at the back of her mind, but she'd ignored it. Something about Pattie Gosden, and Rose's mention that she would be at that Young Pastoralists' meeting. At the time, she had smiled to herself: no wonder Matt was willing to go in Rose's place. Then something Pattie Gosden's father had said at Phil and Warren's funeral made her think there had been a muddle, and she'd given it no further thought. But later, tidying Rose's room when she was away at the hospital in Perth, Lorna had glimpsed a YPA letter about it, which had Pattie down under 'Apologies'. With a sick feeling, she had to admit the likelihood that Rose had deliberately lied. Not for the first time. But Lorna had kept it to herself.

And now Rose – maddening, fiery, mercurial Rosie – had left. If she tried to force her to come back, she might lose her altogether. Rose was nearly twenty-one. She had plenty of old school friends in Perth: Lorna had to use all her self-restraint to resist telegraphing each of them to track her down. She thought through a hundred strategies. Most of all, she wanted to talk it over with Phil.

Lorna MacBride, until recently a woman of such competence and decisiveness, could now only sit numbly and let the phrases tumble in her head. *Oh, Lord, Phil! What should I do?* The immediate task still was getting Matt safely home – he needed her the most right now. Rose was more than capable of taking care of herself for a few days.

Two days later, Lorna was both greatly relieved and deeply hurt to receive a telegram. 'In Perth STOP OK STOP Will write soon STOP Love Rose STOP'.

It's possible that Lorna's hurt might have passed; that her wish to forgive her daughter could have survived the next communication, but not the one that followed it. Sneaky Snook delivered them both on the same trip, about two weeks later, and she waited till he'd gone before looking at them.

What she read first was the postcard showing the sweep of the Swan River taken from King's Park.

Dear Mum,

I've decided to skip the course and go travelling around WA. I'll get work as a temp or fruit picking, etc. I'll be back in time for Christmas. If you don't hear from me, no news is good news.

Rosie the Prodigal

Next, she opened a letter addressed to Phil, from the secretarial college.

Dear Mr MacBride,

Thank you for your letter of 29th April 1958 requesting a refund of course fees. As per your written instructions, we have issued the cheque directly to your daughter, Rose.

Enclosed please find your copies of the relevant forms. Please acknowledge safe receipt in due course.

Yours sincerely,
Ethel Stilly,
Administrative Director

There on the page was Phil's signature, dated months after his death.

That Rose had tricked Matt into taking her place, had let him get blackout drunk; that she had walked out on them just before the muster; that she'd stolen the course fees: these didn't entirely surprise her. But to sign her dead father's name . . . That was a calculated desecration, and something in Lorna hardened that day.

This time it would have to be Rose who offered the olive branch; Rose who finally faced up to what she had done, and how she had to change.

19

ERNESTINE BOBANAC WORE her hair in a dyed black perm that could, rumour had it, withstand the forces of the tropical cyclones that tore through Port Grace in the wet season. The whites of her slate-grey eyes were subtly tinged with pink, perhaps a reaction to the thick black eyeliner that made Nefertiti's look restrained, or to the constant shroud of smoke from her forty Rothmans a day. She wore sling-backs with kitten heels, and tight-fitting frocks invariably adorned with a large sparkly brooch, matched by voluminous earrings. And there was lipstick, a good deal of it, in a red which matched the blood of the slaughterhouse she ran.

The Port Grace meatworks funnelled in livestock from the northern parts of Western Australia. The town sat at the delta of five mighty rivers which entwined to shed their load where the animals shed their lives. In the old days it would take a month or more of droving for the stock to arrive at the abattoir, a few miles short of the coast. These days, they arrived by road trains on graded roads, having made the trip from even the furthest station in under a week. Like in the old times, though, the meatworks killed only in the Dry season, twenty-odd weeks from May to September. Only a madman would try getting beasts there in the sweltering Wet, when cyclones could wash away roads with a foot of rain in a day, or nonchalantly unroof houses and flatten fences and anything else that dared stand up to them.

Ernestine Bobanac eyed the girl in the chair across from her desk: she looked nervous. Tidy, though. Sturdily built. The older woman dipped her ash. '"Rose Smith." Good start: easy to pronounce. Easy to spell. Not exactly a lot of scholars around here. Got your Leaving in maths?'

'Yes.'

'Done bookkeeping before?'

'Yes, for our sta—for our farm.'

Rose explained she was from a sheep farm down south; wanted to travel, see a bit more of WA; decided to stop in Port Grace to save a bit of money.

'Family or friends up this way?' Ernestine asked, slotting her cigarette back between pursed lips.

'No.'

Port Grace was as far away from the run of family and friends as Rose had been able to think of, or afford, at short notice.

'How'd you'd hear about the job again?'

'The sign – in the window of Elders GM.'

The woman gave a sharp laugh. 'See? Who needs to splash out on newspaper ads when a bit of paper, a pen and a drawing pin'll do the trick?' She stubbed out the cigarette and immediately dosed herself another from the navy and white box. 'Any references?'

'Not with me, no. But I – I . . .'

The woman, who could calculate by eye the weight of a steer to within a pound, cast the same professional glance over Rose. Finally, with a wave of her hand, she said, 'I can always tell the wrong'uns. Half the time they forge their references anyway. You've got an honest face.' A cough rumbled deep in her lungs. 'Any questions?'

'The ad mentioned accommodation?'

'House comes with the job.' The unlit cigarette jiggled on Ernestine's lips. 'Nothing flash, but it's clean, give or take a few spiders. It's usually upwind of the killing yard, so a bit easier on the old schnozz.' She thought. 'And on the ears, for that matter. I'll do you cash in hand seeing as you're moving around. What you decide to tell the tax man's up to you.' She scrabbled about in a drawer and pulled out a heavy iron key. 'Front door. No idea if the lock works, mind you – not really much need for it. Power's still connected. Water, too.' She handed it to Rose. 'Come and I'll show you around the works. You'll be here in the office, but you might as well know what all the numbers are about.'

So began the tour of the enormous enterprise – three storeys of corrugated iron, starting with the steel race to the killing yard, full of a mob of Poll Shorthorns from the far north today, waiting their turn for the bolt pistol. The stench was overwhelming. Rose had been used to the smell of the slaughter room on Meredith Downs, but here, the dung and the blood melded with the reek of the guts and the rendered fat and the skins hung out to dry, not to mention the marrow extracted and the bones ground to meal. Without warning she turned toward the tin wall and vomited explosively.

'Jock! Get us a drink of water over here, will you?' Ernestine shouted over the growl of machines and bellowing of beasts to a dungaree-clad man twenty feet away, and turned back to Rose. 'Takes a while to get used to.'

'I'm so sorry.'

'Oh, don't worry about it. If I had a guinea for everyone who'd done that on their first day, I could retire.'

* * *

Within a few weeks, Rose had drifted into a world of tenuous safety. The pay was reasonable. The work was easy. The nausea from the stench was largely relieved by the jar of Vick's which Mrs Bobanac presented to her on her second day. A dab in each nostril worked wonders.

She didn't have to talk, tucked away in her little office out the back. Her mind was occupied every minute of the day with the digits that had to be mustered and wrangled and subdued into an order that was reassuringly solvable. There was always a right answer if you just followed the rules. At night she was dead tired, all the concentration leaving her exhausted and hungry.

She read more than she ever had before, working her way through the shelf of volumes left by the last bookkeeper, who had run off with the daughter of the licensee of the Drover's Reward Hotel. Rose's evenings were filled with the *Reader's Digest*, *Wisden*, and the *Cattleman's Bible*, punctuated by Dickens and Stephenson, a Brontë or two, and an inordinate amount of Mark Twain. None of them brought her much pleasure, but they did bring her sleep – black, dreamless sleep, into which she would escape until the town's roosters crowed her into the following morning.

After a month, Ernestine gave her a pay rise ('I don't see why you shouldn't get as much as a bloke'), a better chair, and a brand-new adding machine. 'I want you to feel at home,' she said as she brought in a turquoise vase made of anodised aluminium, and filled with vivid scarlet roses, in plastic.

'Thanks, Mrs Bobanac,' said Rose, almost tearful at the gesture.

'Call me Ernie,' the woman tossed over her shoulder as her heels clacked towards the door, bracelets jingling, earrings bobbing, hair rock-still.

Ernestine Bobanac, General Manager, saw in Rose a version of her own younger self – a girl who was bright and capable and who, though she wouldn't admit it, was seeking refuge from something. If Ernestine had had someone to help her stand on her own two feet, she wouldn't have had to marry Ivan and go through all that that entailed before the release of widowhood granted by the war, losing a husband but gaining his meatworks. Besides, she told herself, it was nice to have an employee who didn't drink or smell or try to touch her behind. That the girl was good at her job was a bonus.

* * *

Sometimes, a thought of home – home in the old days – would creep into Rose's mind and she would ache with the missing of it: the late afternoon light slanting through the orange dust that the mustered sheep always trailed in their wake; the view from the verandah, strung with waterbags on a hot summer's morning; swimming in the dead cold of a creek in early spring. But those thoughts led inevitably to her family, now shrunken, and to the fragments of that night of rain, which made it impossible to return. So she would fix her mind again on the numbers, on the plastic flowers, till she was safely back in her suspended animation, immune to the distressed bellowing of the cattle, the snarl of the bone saws and the reek of the renderings.

When Matt came home from hospital, much of the practical burden of getting him back to normal fell on Miles Beaumont, who had kept his promise to stay until Matt was back on deck. More than once, Miles had to smooth over situations, both with the station hands, when Matt would muddle instructions about which paddock to muster or which fence to repair, and in town, where he could fly off the handle about a spilt cup of tea or giving the wrong money for a newspaper.

The two had never spent much time alone together – Miles was a good ten years older than Matt, and had tended to keep company with Phil or Warren. But he liked the kid, and a friendship grew between them as Matt learned to depend on Miles, and Miles grew to admire Matt's determination to get on with life.

It was Miles who suggested they resume the tradition of maintaining Monty's pearling lugger. 'Good exercise for you, co-ordination and so forth,' he'd said. 'But no climbing the mast just yet, methinks.' He noticed how it seemed to soothe Matt – undertaking simple, repetitive tasks, even if he had to be reminded of the basics now and then. And Miles enjoyed the Quixotic endeavour: no chance it would ever see the ocean again, but it tickled him to imagine it might.

As they worked, they chatted about cricket, about sailing, Miles gently enquiring how Matt was getting along.

'I feel like a two-year-old,' Matt confessed as they sat mending a sail chewed by mice. 'People come up to me and act like they know me, and sometimes I can't tell if they do. It's worse if I get worked up: then it's like . . . like falling down a well with no sides, and no way back up. I can't tell if people are telling me the truth: not about *them* but about *me*!'

Miles shook his head as he pierced the canvas patch with his thick needle. 'I can't imagine what that's like.'

'And I keep finding out stuff. Things people say I said or did. Like when Mum had to remind me I was Dux of the school.' He levered the lid off a tin of varnish. 'It's as if I'm not really a person – I'm just a story, that someone else has to tell me.'

Miles knotted and cut the thread. 'Maybe we're all just stories, in the end . . . My family's version of my story isn't much like mine.'

'Huh?'

'Let's just say you and I both have lives that have been edited, one way or another.'

'I'll swap places if you like. You've got a brain that works, and the girls all throw themselves at you . . .'

'That doesn't necessarily mean I catch them.'

Matt's face reddened. 'I don't even know if I've ever – well, ever even kissed a girl.' Remembering faces laughing at him in town, he said, 'Don't tell anyone.'

'Of course I won't.'

So much for 'touch has a memory' . . . Miles tried to imagine what it must be like not to know something so fundamental: all the kisses and naked skin and the passion he had known. He thought of Sandy – those eyes, those lips – and longed for them. 'Don't give it a second thought. I'm rather good at keeping secrets, as it happens. Occupational hazard.'

Matt nodded, relieved. And rising like a bubble from deep in an underwater cave there appeared to him a picture that made his gut stir: flickering lamplight, a shadow on a wall. And rain. So much rain. But he couldn't tell if it was a fragment of a memory or a fragment of a dream.

In early August, Lorna's heart raced as she saw Rose's writing on an envelope. In it was a card.

Dear Mum,

I'm well and enjoying life. I've been up north and am just posting this while I pass through Port Grace. I'm actually saving lots of money because I get paid casual rates and it's cash in hand, so no tax. Say hi to everyone for me. Still planning to be back for Christmas.

Rosie x

It enclosed a bank cheque, drawn on the ES&A bank in Port Grace, repaying half the course fees.

Whatever else Rose was, as the cheque reminded Lorna, she was resourceful. Perhaps the time away was actually making her grow up. Repaying some of the money had to be a good sign, surely? Lorna pictured her as a little one, feeding an abandoned lamb, and a for a moment she longed to hold her, stroke her hair. Then she remembered Phil's signature, and was torn again between hurt and anger.

Four months into her job, Rose fainted at her desk, nicking her forehead on the handle of the adding machine. 'Might need a stitch or two,' Ernestine said, dabbing the wound with a tea towel. 'Better get you to Doc Daulby. You all right to stand up?'

'Of course,' said Rose. 'I feel so stupid! I've never fainted in my life.' She noticed Ernestine glancing at her ankles as she rose.

'Hardly worth the drive,' said Ernestine as she parked her Buick outside the surgery. 'But I couldn't take the chance of you fainting on me again.' She opened her door and dipped a foot out, then turned back, quickly tugging off her wedding ring and handing it to Rose. 'Here, pet. Why don't you slip this on, just for the visit?'

'What for?' A low warning hum arced through Rose.

Ernestine gave a *hmmph*. 'Pompous old bugger, Daulby can be. Used to make my blood boil. Less likely to talk down to a married woman, that's all.'

* * *

Dr Daulby's pepper-coloured hair was glued with oil into stripes that began from a parting just above his right ear.

'"Common misconceptions about conception", I like to call them,' he said as he washed his hands after examining Rose. 'Menstruation, or something like it, doesn't always stop. And you tell me your cycle's always been erratic . . . You're about five months, I'd say,' he said, sitting and leaning his elbows on his desk. 'First baby: such a blessing.'

Rose's face burned. 'But it's a mistake, I'm telling you! You're just wrong.'

'No chance of that, I'm afraid.'

'But I – It was only . . . It can't be!'

'It can take a while to digest the news when you find out late like this. On the bright side, though, most of the waiting's over. Junior's going to be here before you know it.'

Revulsion swirled in Rose's belly, in her throat, behind her eyes.

The doctor was peering into her face, tapping her cheeks. 'Back with us, then?' It took her a moment to realise that she was lying on the bed in the consulting room. And another moment to remember what she'd just been told.

'Take a few good deep breaths . . . That's right,' said Daulby. 'Here – have some water. Easy does it.' He helped her sit up, swinging her legs over the side of the bed. 'Better now?' He went back to his chair to make some notes. 'Your blood pressure's a little on the low side, so we'll want to keep an eye on that. Nice healthy diet, plenty of rest, plenty of sleep. I can explain all this to your husband if you like.'

'If I—' Rose stopped, searched her palms, trying to find the words. 'If I wanted – *not* to have the baby . . . what would I do?'

'Not have the baby here in Port Grace? Well, I can make arrange—'

'No. If I wanted to *not have* the baby . . .'

His smile vanished 'Are you talking about an abortion, Mrs—' He flicked a glance at his appointment sheet, and gave a slower blink. 'Mrs Smith?'

'I can't have this baby, doctor. It's – it's not possible.'

'Well, it's not possible to kill it, either. I'm sure you're aware that abortion is and always has been a crime, for doctor and patient alike, and one this late, where there's a perfectly healthy mother and baby, is . . .' He paused, and shook his head. 'Utterly unthinkable.'

* * *

'If you've got one, love, now's the time for family,' Ernestine said when Rose sat beside her in the car afterwards, the girl's tears and snot and hair mingling as she caged her face in her hands. 'I can write to them for you—'

'No! They mustn't know! Please don't make me!'

Ernestine put a hand on Rose's forearm. 'Pet, I'm not going to make you do anything. *No one's* going to make you do anything. And if anyone tries, you just let me know. Takes a brave man to tangle with Old Ernie these days.'

'But what am I going to do? How am I going to survive?'

'Exactly the same way you do now. Your story's *your* business, but you don't have to marry some brute just to keep a roof over your head. You've got a house – it's not Buckingham Palace, but it's free and it's yours; and you'll keep coming to work and doing the books, and when it's time, you can have the baby here, and then you can take your time to sort out what's next. Sufficient unto the day is the evil thereof.' She snorted. 'Stupid bloody expression, but it's true.'

It was late November when Miles approached Matt one afternoon as he was clearing out the old stables. The MacBrides had never got around to throwing out the old carthorses' harnesses from the early days, and they hung on the walls, furred with red dust, shedding stuffing and sheltering insects. Time to fling them on a bonfire, Lorna had said.

'Need a hand?' Miles asked.

'Wouldn't say no.'

'Your mother tells me she's expecting Rose back soon.'

'Apparently.' Matt heaved one of the collars onto a fire outside the stable.

'And you got the all-clear from the doctors, I understand?'

'More or less. And I'm OK to drive again. They call me *a miracle*. Not as though I can turn water into wine . . .'

'Have you tried?'

When Matt laughed, Miles said, 'But you're up to taking over the reins, you think? With your mother and Rosie?'

'We'll – we'll be right. Eventually.'

Miles picked up some carthorse reins cracked with age. 'These for the pyre?'

'Chuck 'em on.'

When Miles flung them into the flames, a shower of sparks erupted. 'Then, if things are back on an even keel, I've come for my Nunc Dimittis.'

Matt narrowed his eyes as he searched his memory for the phrase. Something from chapel at school. 'You're leaving?'

'If you can cope, yes.'

Matt pulled one end of the shaft from an old cart. 'I suppose your family are keen to get you back.'

'Ha! I'm a black sheep remittance man, and proud of it,' said Miles. His smile slipped for a moment. 'No, I'll travel around a bit . . . Visit some of our other properties . . . They're in no hurry to have me home.'

'Have you told Mum you're going?'

'I wanted to ask you first.'

That night, Matt sat on his mother's bed while she was at her dressing table, slipping hairpins from her bun. 'I'm only eighteen. I wouldn't have a clue how to run this place, Mum.'

'But *I* have, darling.' She reached out a hand to him. 'It'll be all right. Rosie'll be back. And Neil Tinnett'll always help.' She touched his cheek. 'You know more than you think you do.'

'Do I?'

'You were born here. You've been handling sheep since you could walk. Not like Miles, having to learn it from scratch. I'm sorry to see him go, but he's already stayed much longer than we had any right to hope.' She dropped the last hairpin into the crystal dish. 'You'll do a fine job, Mattie. Just wait and see.'

* * *

Two weeks later, Matt helped Miles load the last of his things onto the back of the mail truck. Lightning was sniffing around the cases, the smell of old crocodile skin a welcome curiosity. The only item left on the ground was the wooden crate which had arrived with Miles.

'Don't forget your croquet set,' said Matt.

'Actually, that's for you.'

'Me?'

'A souvenir of the mad Pom you had to put up with.'

Lorna emerged from the house with Sneaky, who was wearing the smile of a man carrying freshly made sausage rolls.

'Righty-ho, Lightning!' he declared. 'Lead the way!' and the dog jumped into the cab of the truck.

'Thanks for being such a godsend, Miles,' Lorna said, taking his hands in hers. She held his gaze in silence. 'I . . . we couldn't have coped without you.'

'I've felt very much at home here, Mrs MacBride.' He took one last look at the homestead. There was a crack in his voice as he said, 'Better not keep Her Majesty's mail waiting. Cheerio.'

Then he was gone, as dazzlingly clean on his departure as on his arrival over a year ago.

Later that evening, Matt was about to store the box on a shelf in the shed. On a whim, he opened the crate, and took out a mallet; felt the weight of one of the wooden balls – exactly a pound, according to Miles. A smile came to his lips as he recaptured the picture of the day Miles got the Omo nickname. Replacing the ball, he glimpsed something red at the bottom of the crate, and slipped a hand down for it: a greeting card featuring a Grenadier Guard in a sentry box. He read inside:

My darling Miles,

Something to keep you entertained during your exile in the Colonies, and to remind you of our games together. They can't keep us apart forever.

All my love,
Sandy.

Hmph. Dark horse, thought Matt, and imagined a reunion on a train platform somewhere, Miles sweeping this mystery woman up in his arms and whirling her around like they did in films. Maybe Meredith Downs's loss was Sandy's gain. He put the lid back on. Once Rosie got home, they could work out between them how to play the game.

When Rose went into labour while Ernestine was visiting her a week before Christmas, the older woman was unflustered. 'Right-oh. About time we sent for Doc Daulby, I reckon.'

'No!' Rose snapped. 'I don't want him anywhere near me!'

'I know he's an old so-and-so, but you need someone who knows what they're doing, pet.'

'Not him! Anyone but him!'

Ernestine sat on the bed and brushed the girl's hair from her eyes. 'I wouldn't want the old bastard either.' She screwed up her lips as she pondered. 'Let me pop home quickly to make a telephone call,' she said, and dug about in her handbag for her address book with the numbers written on the inside front cover under 'Emergency'.

She was soon on the telephone to the Flying Doctor base in town. 'Yes, I know you're not here for us townies, June, but the poor lass got on the wrong side of Dauntless Daulby from the off . . . Too true,' she replied to some comment. 'You know what the old coot's like. So I wondered if one of your medics might do a mercy dash.'

When the nurse hesitated, Ernestine reminded her that she had donated the money for their new transceiver system last year.

'It's her first, and she's young . . .'

After some discussion in the background on the two-way radio about who was available, the nurse said, 'We've got a fellow from another district covering for Dr Appledore. Nice bloke. Very good. He says he'll come.'

An hour later, Rose paid scant attention to the man with the black bag who appeared in the doorway of her bedroom. It was all she could do to remember to breathe, as urged by Ernestine.

'Afternoon, Mrs Smith. How are you doing?' the doctor asked with a smile, dropping his bag. 'I'm Dr—' He blinked at the patient. 'Rose?' he ventured. 'Rosie MacBride?'

20

FOR A MOMENT, Matt thought he was seeing a ghost. As Rose walked through the front door of the homestead just after Christmas, she looked haggard and wretched and not quite of this world. Lorna had collected her from the 'drome, together with the baby and Dr Finbar Rafferty.

Though Lorna carried the infant, and Dr Rafferty held Rose's few belongings, the girl seemed more burdened than either of them. Like a child herself, she was lost and frail in a way she had never been. When Matt went to give her a kiss on the cheek, she recoiled so violently that Dr Rafferty said, 'Let her get her bearings. She's still a bit topsy-turvy . . . You're doing a grand job, Rosie. A really grand job.' When she made no response, he rubbed his palms together. 'Could you rustle up a cup of tea for us, do you suppose?'

'Of course!' said Lorna; then to Rose, 'Important to keep your fluids up while you're nursing.' Since she'd heard the news a week ago, Lorna had teetered between outrage and sorrow and overwhelming shame. She tried again to build a bridge to her daughter, this stiff stranger. 'I remember I always had a drink on the go – tea, or barley water or' – she forced a laugh – 'a dose of medicinal stout come sundown.' The doctor caught her eye and gave a quick warning shake of the head.

'And I'm sure your mam won't mind making up some formula for the little man in a bit.'

Lorna was about to query this, but at Rafferty's glance said, 'Right. Tea. You all go through to the lounge room.'

She tried to hand the infant to Rose, but when her daughter's face clouded, Lorna thrust the swaddled bundle at Matt, who held it to his chest as if he'd just marked a football.

Rose led the doctor into the lounge room, gazing as though she'd never before seen the dark wooden furniture, the photographs in their frames, the heavy curtains. She sat beside the longcase clock, and was surprised as its name, 'Old Wally', appeared silently in her mouth. Its ticking felt loud, reproachful, and for a moment conjured the voice of her father. How many times had it ticked and chimed, ticked and chimed, since she'd left? Strange to think that time had been passing here at exactly the same rate as it had for her in Port Grace. It was stupid, time. Only brought trouble. Only told lies: one minute didn't have the same length as another. A handful of seconds could wreck your whole life. Forever.

She brought her attention back to Dr Rafferty, who was examining with exaggerated interest the chess board on the table beside his chair.

'I shouldn't have come back.'

'Port Grace was no place for you, Rose. You belong with your family.'

Standing in the hallway with his charge, Matt stroked the downy scalp that fitted neatly in his palm; took in its mysterious smell. He inspected the tiny face, its skin with a few minuscule pimples, mouth sucking even in deep slumber. It was the youngest baby Matt had ever seen. Reminded him of a joey before it got its fur, all translucent skin and heat and heartbeat. For a while he simply stared at it: this little creature that had ripped apart the few remaining threads of his already torn family, rending mother from daughter. It was past mending now.

For Matt, the time since the crash was often a slippery skein of impressions and half-memories and hypotheses and jagged feelings. He could remember the exact moment Lorna had told him about the baby, but the information had been so bizarre that he couldn't quite believe it wasn't another of his brain's tricks. Fin Rafferty had sent a cryptic telegram from Port Grace and Lorna had driven into town to telephone him, receiving word of Rose's true whereabouts, and of the baby's birth. Fin had urged Lorna to take her daughter in until a decision was made about what to do with the child. There had been shock, then terrible anguish in his mother's eyes when she broke the news. Matt recalled Lorna's bewildered face as she murmured, 'Who's on earth's the father?', a grey veil of shame descending on her.

Now there was the feel of this new body in his arms – lighter than a fleece, a whole life set ticking all on its own, with a future he couldn't imagine, and a past that baffled him. 'Bloody hell,' he muttered.

The child opened his eyes and fixed Matt with a look of such stern intensity that he felt naked, defenceless. The baby blinked, and stared again, this time giving the slightest of frowns, as if demanding something.

Matt touched a finger to the tiny cheek. 'Gedday,' he whispered, and carried him into the lounge room. 'Has he got a name yet?'

Rose gazed at her brother. 'MacBride, I suppose.'

'Oh! I didn't mean . . . I wasn't asking—'

'He means a Christian name, Rosie, love,' said Rafferty. 'And I think the answer to that, Matthew, is "not yet".'

From the moment Rosie set foot in the door with the carrycot three days earlier, she had remained tight-lipped and stony-faced on the subject of the baby's father. No matter how gently Lorna tried to broach the subject, her daughter simply would not be drawn. A grim, icy silence would descend on her, and without closing her eyes, Rose made it clear she no longer saw her.

Lord knows what Phil would have done if he'd got his hands on the boy. Or the man? As Lorna hung out washing or fed the pigs, she racked her brains. Could that Derek fellow have come back into the picture somehow? Or a boy from the Young Pastoralists? Someone in Wanderrie Creek? Or there was no telling who she might have met at the hospital in Perth. But the girl was barely hanging on. She dared not push her too far.

Until Rose would talk, Lorna simply had to carry on: going through Flintgrave's latest bumph on this year's stud rams; answering Odlum & Chopping about their shearing contract. And, of course, writing up the station diary.

She looked at her entry for 27th December 1958 and considered her decision to omit any reference to the baby in the mention of Rose's return. If the plan she was nursing worked, the whole episode would fade into the past, as such stories, mercifully, often did.

She found her hands, of their own accord, paging their way back to just over nine months ago, interrogating the entries for clues.

For years, most of the diary was in Phil's handwriting; occasionally hers or, later, one of the children's; and once in a blue moon that of a manager or a jackaroo: when, say, Phil had gone to collect her and each newborn from hospital. Later, more entries were by Rose. After the crash, though, it erupted into a kaleidoscope of penmanship. Some she recognised – Miles Beaumont's, Maudie Knapp's – and some she didn't. As for the comings and goings, the extraordinary – the names of the police, or the undertakers – rubbed shoulders with the mundane: the arrival of some well-sinkers; agriculture boffins from the CSIRO; a few stray Seventh Day Adventist missionaries. Lorna tried to call to mind the faces of the men who featured in the diaries around that time. Such memories were hazy at best.

As she noticed more and more entries in the graceful copperplate of Miles, the tiniest thought prickled: no more than a needle poised to pierce a veil. Then, for reasons she couldn't explain, it was followed by an image of the Annunciation: the Angel Gabriel, wings spread wide, delivering his news to the Virgin Mary.

She noticed it was Rose who had written 'RM and MB to outcamp' on 25 March, just before Matt's visit, and the Angel Gabriel drifted back into her mind's eye at this mention of her trip with Miles Beaumont. The words were neat, the pen not pressed with any particular force . . . but in contrast with the plainly written sentences that followed, about which of the hands were dummying a boundary fence out at Joker, and which laying concrete for the new shower block for the shearers' quarters at the Home Shed, there was a little flourish to 'MB'. She flicked back over the pages. There it was again, each time Rosie had written Miles's initials.

She closed the book abruptly.

* * *

In bed that night, the little needle thought of the Annunciation came back to her. She got up and went to check, tracking her fingers down the relevant Gospel verses by torchlight. Her memory hadn't failed her: the Virgin Mary didn't seem to have told a soul who the father was, not even Joseph – that was left to the angel.

Lorna considered Mary's silence, borne of some deeper wisdom – telling not even her mother – and her heart softened.

21

FOR MATT, THE sudden appearance of this baby at Meredith Downs was just another of the ruptures in the laws of nature that had surrounded him since the kangaroo had bounded in front of the truck and turned the world haywire. It took a lot to surprise him these days.

Watching Rose with the baby reminded him how she used to bring in newborn, motherless lambs. But she'd been more loving to the orphaned lambs. With the baby, she was almost businesslike – just keeping him fed and clean. It was Lorna who rocked him and jiggled his rattle; Matt himself who carried him about the house and out to the garden to hear the parrots and smell the tang of eucalyptus and saltbush on the evening air.

The baby never left the homestead, let alone the property. There was no showing him off to neighbours, or parading him around town. Any attempt to raise the question of the father was met with such wild panic in Rose's eyes that Lorna genuinely feared what might happen if she pressed for details. She would give her daughter a few more days before addressing the other inevitable issue with her – having the child adopted.

Ever since Rose got back, Matt had noticed her watching him. She seemed to peer warily from some inner den, a wounded animal checking the air for safety. One afternoon, as he fixed a kitchen tap, he turned to find her behind him.

'How long have you been there?' he asked.

'A while.'

'You must be *really* bored.'

Rose ignored the joke, and slid down the wall to sit on the floor. 'How come you can remember how to replace a washer?'

Matt was putting all his force into unscrewing a nut with a wrench. 'Different bit of my brain. Motor memory.' Dr Fairchild had explained that it wasn't at all surprising that Matt could still remember perfectly well how to perform some general manual tasks but had occasional holes in his memory for facts and events.

'There's stuff you still really don't remember, isn't there?'

Matt unscrewed a pipe under the sink. 'Like what?' Rose's silence drew him back out into the light. 'Are you crying?'

'No.' She wiped her nose with the heel of her hand.

Some instinct made Matt avert his eyes. He turned on the tap, now fixed, and poured himself some water. Through the window, the rusty old swing-set whined in the breeze. He could remember that well enough: hours and hours of playing on it. Without turning around, he said, 'I'm glad you're back.'

Rose didn't reply.

A thought had been worming away at him for days: a thought he barely had words for in his own head, let alone to speak aloud. He'd say it, just once, in case. Eyes firmly on a rag as he washed it in the sink, he said, 'Bliss, if anyone – if anyone made you do anything . . . If you want me to sort someone out for you, you know you just need to say.' In uttering the unutterable, the implications grew on him, and he said more urgently, 'God, if it's anyone from around here, anyone I *know* . . .' He stopped when he caught the look on her face.

'Sorry,' he said. 'None of my business.'

*

Once he'd gone, Rose sat rocking, rocking. She was tired, so tired, but sleep was impossible. Staring at the wall, it changed colour – the whole room seemed to take on a greenish tinge. She screwed up her eyes and rubbed them, then looked again, forcing the colours back into reality.

The late night was starry-cold when, navigating each familiar floorboard to ensure she made no sound, Rose crept out of the house to sit silently on the verandah.

The knowing, the remembering, was like a cancer that would spread. For so long, it had been her constant fear, a dread that sucked all future from the world. But surely Matt's comments that afternoon meant that what had happened had not only fallen through one of the holes in his memory, but that it was safely stuck beyond reach forever, like the moment of the crash itself. Perhaps the knowing might only ever be *hers*.

For the first time in months, Rose dared to feel a glimmer of safety.

She thought back to all the MacBrides who must have sat on this verandah before her: their triumphs and disasters. She barely remembered their names. Who knew what secrets had gone to the grave with them? If there was no one to force the truth on her, maybe she could survive. Once the baby had gone.

In the distance she could just make out a pale glow: it would be Pete Peachey, back from a kill. Night was his time, and for a moment she was comforted by a vague sense he was keeping vigil with her, this man who by all accounts had lived through things beyond imagining.

From her pocket, she pulled her old brass lighter, flicked it open and closed, relishing the cold, soothing touch of it.

22

The day Mrs Blencombe visited, remarkably few words were spoken beyond light pleasantries. A sturdy matron from the Anglican Society for the Australian Family, she briefly inspected the baby in his carry basket. 'Such a bonny little chap. The couple I've lined up are overjoyed.' She slipped a fallen dummy back into his mouth. 'Naturally, I can't say much more – we have strict confidentiality for both the unmarried mother and the adoptive parents. But they're a lovely young pair. The house is very modern, and she keeps it spotless. Regular church-goers. He's got an excellent job – a professional gentleman. Poor lass had to have a hysterectomy after some surgical complications.'

She gave Rose a sympathetic glance. 'I can promise that your baby will have a much better life than you could give him . . . in your situation. An illegitimate child has a very hard road to hoe, I'm afraid.' To Lorna, she said, 'You were quite right to get in touch.'

As Lorna poured tea, Rose asked, '"Strict confidentiality". Does that mean it will never be able to find me?'

Taking just a moment to understand the 'it', Mrs Blencombe said, 'Not in the ordinary course of things, no, he wouldn't, dear,' and stirred in a sugar lump thoughtfully.

'You can promise?'

The woman replaced her teaspoon and turned the roses on the cup to face those on the saucer as she considered. 'There have been instances – *very* rare – where a child, once he's old enough, has gone in search of his original parents, and found them. Generally just the mother. But it's *very* unusual. *We* certainly don't pass on information. But sometimes they manage to piece together dates, or snippets from here or there. It can be a family likeness that gives the game away. But we strongly discourage that sort of investigation. People rarely want to be reminded of terrible mistakes they've made. And as for the child, well, you know the saying: "Where ignorance is bliss, 'tis folly to be wise."' She sipped her tea.

At this qualification to confidentiality Rose's cheeks had paled, but Lorna took the pallor for something else. 'It really is the best solution, Rosie darling. A good home. A happy life. And you can put all the . . . shame . . . behind you.'

She turned to Mrs Blencombe. 'What happens next?'

The visitor ran through the paperwork. When she mentioned registering the birth, Rose interrupted.

'Does it have to be registered? Does *my* name have to be on the birth certificate?'

'Well, yes, it does. But that's just a formality.'

'And you don't – you don't have to put the name of – the father?'

'No, dear, we don't have to do that. Frankly, many girls just can't say for sure who the father is . . .'

'But *my* name would be there forever, if it ever looked for it?'

'I suppose so, yes.'

A silence fell. Neither Rose nor Lorna touched their tea. Outside, one of the dogs barked. A crow cawed. Eventually Old Wally chimed the hour, and Mrs Blencombe put down her cup. 'Well, I'd better be off. Long drive ahead. I'll stay in Wanderrie Creek tonight, then head back down to Perth tomorrow.' She put on her hat and gloves. 'I'll be back soon to bring the forms and collect the little chap.' She looked earnestly at mother and daughter. 'You're doing the right thing. You'd be surprised how often this happens. And how completely it's forgotten, given time.'

That evening, when Matt came home from a mill run, Lorna intercepted him on the verandah. 'It's all arranged.' To herself she murmured, 'The only people who have any idea are Maudie Knapp, Dr Rafferty and Pete. A couple of the hands . . . but they know not to talk.' Turning back to Matt, she said, 'The poor love can get on with her life.'

The next day, late afternoon sun spills onto Rose's dressing table through a gap in the curtains, splashing heat onto the hand that holds the pen. The snuffles from the basket behind her are occasionally joined by the vibrant song of a butcherbird outside and, somewhere closer, the buzzing of an insect that has found a way in despite the flywire.

She tears a blank page from an old exercise book of her grade four notes about the inundation of the Nile and the tapping of rubber plants in Malaya. She applies the tip of the pen and watches each word as it forms on the paper. She knows she has to set down everything she can remember, everything she could say out loud if she had the courage. Because that's how the magic works.

A wasp lands on the dish of coloured ribbons close by, and the buzzing intensifies as it patrols their bright satin for pollen. She shoos it off with a violent slap.

Her hand is shaking. If she can force the words outside of her, like squeezing out a sting, she can make it all disappear. The hardest thing isn't the writing of the words themselves, but overcoming the urge to change the story. Time and again, she hears a voice – her own – saying *but surely you could have . . . you should have . . . why didn't you just . . .?* In that shadowy memory, she is horrified by the look on Matt's face; the tears that dissolved into something foreign, then an expression she was never meant to see; the touch that made her freeze, unable to move because she was unable to believe her senses. Beside his body, in that brief instant she was in a separate world, distant, cold.

'It's all my fault,' she writes. Because the one thing she's sure of is that it's not her baby brother's fault. It's not *his* fault he was mental. It's not *his* fault he didn't know what he was doing. And it's a short, downhill tumble from 'All my fault' to 'Serves me right.' And even that hurts less than writing 'Matt is the father.' This, she prints, line after line, in capital letters.

She reaches into the hiding place and draws out the brass lighter, itself the subject of its own note when she first 'disappeared' it from the pocket of a shearer's dungarees years back when he'd gone for a shower.

She will make this go away. Matt will never regain the memory. The baby will live far away in a *modern, spotless house*.

She folds the paper over and over – it hurts her eyes to see any of the words. '*Yawa, yawa, yawa,*' she whispers, flicking the lighter on and off.

A piercing scream comes from the bassinet, and Rose twists to see the wasp on the baby's arm, withdrawing its sting and flying off. She hears her mother running.

'Rose! What in God's name—?'

She stuffs the note and lighter into the hiding place, and picks up the baby but Lorna rushes in and snatches him from her arms and starts soothing and shooshing. 'What did you do?'

'It was a wasp. Stung its arm.'

'Oh, you poor soul,' Lorna tells the baby. 'Poor, poor little thing. Come on, let's get a cold compress for you. Shh, shh, little one.' She gives a brief shake of the head, and her look accuses Rose of incompetence more eloquently than any words.

The spell of the ritual is broken, its promise of erasure lost.

A twenty-eight parrot is singing to itself in the big lemon gum out the back, and Matt listens, caught by the intricacy of the notes – these birds will sit for hours on end, constructing elaborate songs as bright as their green feathers. He and Rose are sitting on the back verandah, wound together in the song. It's the first time since Rose came home a week ago that she hasn't made an excuse to move away from him.

She and the baby seem to spend a lot of time sleeping. Matt sometimes sees her surfacing from her bedroom late in the afternoon, still in pyjamas; or sitting at the kitchen table at three in the morning, joylessly feeding the baby his bottle, gazing at the ceiling while the baby stares at her.

Matt rolls a cigarette, lights it.

'You smoke like a kerosene fridge these days. It stinks.'

'The nurses said doing rollies counted as therapy – manual dexterity. Practically good for me. Do you ever smoke?'

'No.'

'Did I? You know . . . before?'

'I've told you: you started in hospital.'

Taking up the sandpaper, Matt started again on the old cot Lorna had asked him to repaint for the baby when it had first arrived. The flywire that protected the wooden frame was still intact, and the hinges on the top had responded well to a drop of oil, so that it lifted up and folded back easily.

'Do you remember being in this cot?'

'Course not,' said Rose, and Matt wondered if her irritation was because she felt stupid for not remembering, as he so often did.

Matt's memory had grown back like a mesh. To fill the holes about the crash, he had to rely on others. Lorna had seemed resistant at first, changing the subject or saying she was busy. Only gradually had he worked out that, for her, answering his questions meant disturbing a terrible wound, like picking out shards of glass. They required her to relive a time that had taken away her husband and her eldest son.

As for other events in his life: for bare facts and the like, he could ask Pete Peachey; or Neil Tinnett, maybe. But there was other territory – private territory – that he wanted to recover. He sometimes wished he could ask Humpty Dumpton, but any attempt to contact him since that day in the hospital years ago had been met with silence. That left Rose.

Applying the paint with care, he said, 'Can I ask you a question?'

'What about?'

'Me.'

Her features hardened a fraction. 'OK.'

'When I was in the hospital, in the beginning . . . Did you – did you, well, think I'd gone nuts?'

'How would I be able to tell the difference?'

The parrot had fallen silent, and the only sound, other than the clacking of its beak as it plucked buds off the branches, was the soft *swish, swish* of Matt's paintbrush.

'I didn't know whether I was Arthur or Martha for a while. Sometimes I . . . I used to wish they'd just up the morphine and let it all be over.'

'I know the feeling.'

Matt turned, but Rose wasn't smiling.

'Last check-up, Dr Fairchild said I'll probably never remember some of the stuff. Says it's the brain's way of protecting us from trauma.'

'Lucky you.' Her gaze drifted. 'Gonna rain, you reckon?'

'Nah. We had some good falls while you were – while you were away, though. Nearly two inches at Canasta for July.' At the talk of rain, something stirred in his belly. 'I keep having this dream about rain. At least, I think it's a dream.'

Rose's cup jolted against its saucer. 'What?'

'Really heavy rain on a tin roof – like someone's chucking gravel on it. And it's dark. Don't know if I'm even *in* the dream, or if it's someone else. And there's . . . a girl? No idea what it's supposed to mean . . .'

'Probably means you're still nuts.' She clenched her jaw.

Matt pressed on to what he wanted to know: 'Did I have a – you know – a girlfriend? Before the crash?'

'*You* tell *me*.'

'That's the point. I *can't* bloody tell you! Can you imagine what that feels like?'

Rose picked up her cup, trying to keep her hand steady. 'You were pretty keen on Pattie Gosden.'

'Pattie Gosden?' Matt searched, and finally managed to retrieve an image of a girl with red hair. 'Was she – you know – keen on me too?'

'As far as I know. That's why you were in the truck – you were going to meet her at Young Dags.'

'Why?'

The urge to tell him about her lie rose in her throat. But the words simply would not form themselves. 'Search me. She sent you a get-well card after the crash.'

'Oh.'

He tried to trace the fine wire of feeling that made his gut tighten. 'Do you reckon *she's* the girl in my dream?'

'How would I know?' Rose stood up abruptly, and went inside without another word.

Rose couldn't think. She couldn't breathe.

She stood over the cot, watching the baby, the puffiness of birth having left its face, revealing hints of what its features would be. She was grateful for the few feet's distance. Grateful to be beyond reach of its milky smell, of the terrifying, intimate sound of each breath. Moonlight glistened on the saliva on its dusty pink bow of a mouth. Inside her, the loathing of it and the yearning for it did battle.

As she bent to touch one of its miniature fingers, already growing a healthy, pure white crescent of a nail, the sickening realisation struck her that it would get bigger and bigger. Even if it went to *a spotless, modern house*; even if Matt remembered nothing – this creature would just continue to grow and be in the world and one day it could hunt her down and interrogate her and there would be nowhere to hide. She could fend off the questions of a child, but this thing would one day be a man, with all the irresistible wiles and force that entailed. The world could not protect the both of them.

A thought crept up stealthily in her sleep-starved mind: it would take so little – just a pillow held gently, painlessly, over the tiny features, and they would all be free. Her belly loosened and her heart slowed at the imagined peace that would follow.

Then logic set in and her heart raced at the certainty that she would be shackled even more tightly by what she'd done.

She pulled the curtain closed, leaving the baby in darkness, and went to pace the verandah.

She needed a surer way.

23

THE RUMBLE OF an approaching car drew Pete Peachey warily to the flap of his tent, still holding the rifle he'd been oiling. It was Lorna's station wagon, but the silhouette at the wheel told him even from this distance that she wasn't the driver. Squinting into the brightness, he made out the fair ponytail of Rosie MacBride. He emerged from the tent to fetch the billycan, which was on the fire by the time the car came to a halt behind his camp.

He waited to hear the car door shut, but the only sound was Strife, barking his hello, paws pressed on the window of the familiar vehicle. 'Get out of it, Strife!' Pete growled, and the dog regretfully lowered his front legs. There was still no movement, so Pete put the mugs down and approached the Holden with his usual unhurried strides. With a half-wave he nodded to Rose, who attempted a smile from her side of the open window.

'Rosie,' he said, the single word charged with tenderness.

She looked up at him, her hands still gripping the steering wheel. 'Pete.'

'Long time.'

'Yeah,' she said, 'long time.'

He touched the window frame. 'You – ah – you planning to get out?'

She was about to reply when a burbling from the shadowed seat beside her erupted into a full-throated scream, a baby announcing its presence by flinging its arms out in fury.

The sound, the sight, startled him, sending a bolt of sensation through his chest. His face, however, betrayed no more than a long blink. His eyes resisted the basket, and he focused instead on Rosie, waiting for her to attend to the cries. But she kept her hands on the wheel and her eyes straight ahead. His attention flicked from mother to baby and back as the cries intensified and Strife whined in alarm and confusion.

'Rose?'

The deep lines on his forehead buckled briefly downward and, looking past the girl, he said, 'Hey, hey, hey. Steady on there, fella . . .' After glancing about as if for help, he finally hitched up the waist of his trousers a fraction, walked around to the other door and opened it to extract the basket with one hand. Above the screams he said to Rose, 'I'll take care of this bloke. You just . . . just join us when you're ready.' He returned at the same lanky pace to the tent, where he laid the basket on the long rickety trestle outside it that served as kitchen and writing desk and workbench.

As the child roared at the world, face flushed, tight and hard like a tomato, Peachey lifted him to slot the hot little head into his own neck, rubbing his back softly as he held him against his chest. 'Yeah, yeah, you let 'em have it, mate. You bloody well let 'em have it,' he murmured. The smell of the baby's scalp, the lightness of the tiny body: muscles and heart would no longer be denied their memories, and for a moment the roo shooter's breath failed him.

Then he said, 'Thaaat's the way, mate,' stroking the baby's cheek lightly as he rocked him. 'Tell Old Pete all about it, while he makes us a cup of tea . . .'

The deep voice, the strong heartbeat, the now steady breath of the man, gradually worked their spell on the baby, whose cries softened to yowls and then intermittent grizzles, and Peachey transferred him to the crook of one arm, so they could get a better look at each other. He picked up the bottle of milk he'd noticed in the basket, and touched it to the baby's lips.

After a few minutes of sucking furiously, the child was sated, and thrust up a hand to explore the stubble on the man's chin, scowling at the prickles. 'Well, I wasn't expecting visitors,' Pete said, and set about pouring the tea with one hand. He glanced at the baby every now and then – at the glistening lips, the piercing stare, the long eyelashes, still clumped into points by teardrops. 'No bloody wonder, mate. No bloody wonder . . .'

He was so engrossed that he didn't notice Rose standing a few feet away, watching with puffy eyes. Pete took in her drawn face, her greasy hair. Must have lost at least a stone.

'It's good to see you,' he said.

'You too.'

He stirred sugar into the tin mug and handed it to her. 'Have a seat.'

'Do you want to put him in his basket?'

'Nah. He can perch on me and I can perch on this.' He dragged over an upturned fruit crate. 'Got a name?'

Rose shook her head, and he turned to the baby. 'Well, I'll just call you "Sir". But you can call me Pete.'

Strife came to sit with his paws out in front, resting his chin on his master's boots. Every now and then, a breath of breeze made the leaves of the desert violets shiver into silvery ripples. Then stillness.

When Rose glanced over at Pete he'd closed his eyes, and was holding the baby lightly to his chest, lulling him and nodding slowly. The infant gave a few groggy blinks before surrendering to sleep with a heavy sigh.

'It's fine to put him in the cot,' said Rose.

'He's not hurting anyone.' Pete moved him onto his lap.

'Good tally lately?'

'Not bad.'

'Mum says we've been having a bugger of a time with the dingoes.'

'Yeah. More dogs . . . More roos . . . Sheep aren't the only things that like the water those bores pump up.'

A heavy silence settled on them. Then Rose frowned, and in a sob exclaimed, 'Oh, Pete!'

He gave her a sideways glance.

Whatever that thought had been, she wiped it away with the back of her hand. 'Do you think it's fair, all the roos you kill?'

His neck stiffened as if at a rifle shot. She was all over the shop, and he knew better than to attempt an answer.

'They never did anything to hurt you.'

He stayed silent.

'Do you think it's ever right, killing something?'

Pete pulled up the edge of the baby's cotton rug to shade its face. 'They don't suffer, the roos. Kill 'em quick, kill 'em clean. Make good use of the skins, of the carcasses.' He squeezed the baby's foot. 'They're here, then they're not. Free until their last breath. There are worse ways of dying. And of living.'

'Worse ways of living . . .'

Pete gave Strife's head a scratch. 'Getting any sleep?'

Rose made no response.

'It's hard, at first – bad enough when there are *two* parents trying to manage.' He rubbed his stubble where the baby had touched it. 'Gets easier . . .'

'How would *you* know?'

'Wasn't always just a roo shooter, Rosie . . .' He stood up, and flicked the dregs onto the ground. 'Have another cuppa,' he said, ignoring the question in her eyes, and reached for her mug. 'Shall I give you this bloke while I sort out the billy?'

'He'll be all right in his basket,' she said, and Peachey placed the little body expertly in the wicker carrycot.

'Sure you're right to drive home?'

'Just needed to get out of the house for a bit.'

'Stay as long as you like. Strife likes having company, don't you, mate?' The dog pricked up his ears, ready for conversation. 'I've got some biscuits here somewhere. You could do with feeding up.'

'Don't you want to know?' asked Rose suddenly.

'Know?'

'Whose it is . . .'

Peachey continued to look under this and that, finally rattling a tin. 'Makes no difference to me, Rosie love.' He emptied the few biscuits onto a chipped saucer for her.

'It would, you know.'

'Is that a fact,' he said, packing a few loose rounds back into their box. He ran his fingers along the torpedo-shaped brass of a bullet. 'No sleep . . . I've seen blokes turned to gibbering wrecks from that. Couldn't remember their own names.'

He rested a hand on her shoulder. 'You need a decent sleep, girlie. You can't see the world straight, the state you're in. And you're in no shape to drive home. I'll take you. When you're ready . . .'

Her eyes drifted to the basket. 'I'll never be ready, Pete.'

'I used to think that . . .' He scratched his head. 'It passes. Time'll get you through anything, in the end. *Old Bugger Time* . . .' He followed her gaze to the sleeping baby. 'Hardly seems a minute since you turned up here when you stowed away in my trailer . . . The secret's time, Rosie love. Give it time.'

And he looked at her with such kindness that for a moment Rose felt bathed in something like hope. Then words came out of her mouth before she even knew it: 'Can I leave him here? With you?'

'Is he a good shot?'

'He will be if he hangs around you long enough.'

He picked up the basket. 'Come on, girlie. Let's get you and Sir back to the homestead. Where you both belong.'

'For better or for worse, eh?'

'Oh, for better, I reckon. Always for better . . . Eventually.'

After the birth of her son, Rose MacBride's mind reached places which, if we are lucky, we will never know. As night gave way to dawn she watched this little baby: perfect, without guile, without sin, and was engulfed by the certainty that he was not and never could be safe from his invisible birthmark.

Since Matt's questions about his 'dream' of rain, her hope that that memory had gone forever had crumbled. Something about another mind holding the knowledge completed an electrical circuit – brought the truth to life in a way that was utterly impossible to bear. This baby who gazed back at her with neither judgement nor understanding would one day be stripped and judged and hounded. Always and forever.

Rose's father had drummed into her from childhood that it was wrong to let an animal suffer. No matter how valuable, if it faced terrible, enduring pain, it had to be 'put out of its misery'. The ewe whose labour had gone wrong; the ram savaged by a dingo; the horse crippled by a dog trap. 'You don't just wait and hope for the best,' he would say. '"Wait and see" is the coward's way.'

For the first time, Rose truly understood what her father meant. In whatever forests of distortion her mind had wandered to, she lighted upon this single memory as a crumb trail of logic. She had cost Matt his right mind, had caused all that flowed from that, and had no right to live – that was unarguable. And she could see now that the baby, still unnamed, didn't deserve to be condemned to a life that was cursed. She had to put it out of its misery.

From the moment the thought came to her, she felt an unexpected lightness.

She turned her mind to death and how it danced around her, slipped through the rocks and the trees, slithered through dust and waterhole alike, bringing the release of ending.

The sound of the infant sucking at its fist in the cot beside her spurred her back to the present – it would soon be hungry and start to cry. Her thoughts twisted and swirled.

Sitting at the dinner table, Lorna recalled the rule about a woman being a bride for the first year of her marriage, and thereafter, a wife. She wondered whether there was some sort of equivalent for widowhood – would she become a relict, perhaps? Tomorrow would be the tenth of January. She tried to remember sitting in this chair the night before the crash – was it savoury mince on toast she'd made for dinner? The talk about the trip to town the following day . . . As if it were any old meal on any old night. How could she not have known?

This evening, the sombreness was lightened by a single glimmer of hope: Rose had stopped spending all day in her pyjamas; had washed her hair and brushed it neatly. She had even volunteered to make dinner. The calm that seemed to have descended on her daughter Lorna put down to the approaching adoption, the relief it promised.

After serving roast hogget and a trifle, Rose insisted on clearing away the dishes herself. When Rose returned to the table, Lorna gathered her courage. 'We didn't celebrate a single birthday in this house last year. Matt, your birthday's in three days. We're going to have a nice dinner, just like we used to. And I'm going to make you a cake. And, Rosie, I wanted to ask you about something, too . . .' Her daughter stiffened, but Lorna put a hand on her forearm. 'What would you like to do for your twenty-first? I know it was in June, but better late than never . . .'

Rose threw her mother such an odd look that Lorna frowned. 'I . . . Yes' – she counted on her fingers – 'it was definitely your twenty-first, darling. You probably don't want a big do like Warren's . . . Perhaps a holiday somewhere? Once you've . . .' Here she came to a complete stop. 'Once everything's finalised with the little one. Mrs Blencombe's coming the day after tomorrow. A change of scene after that'll do you good.'

Rising from her chair, Rose said, 'Thanks for thinking of it.' At the door, she turned to Matt. 'You're—' She glanced at a nappy pin on the sideboard. 'You're all right, you know, Bubba. You're a good kid.' She gave him a brief, radiant smile that found a mirror in his face. No dig, no sarcastic remark to undercut it: just a moment of undefended fondness between them.

'Goodnight. Both of you. Sleep well.'

* * *

In the hours that followed, Old Wally chimed away 10 p.m., then eleven, then, as Rose stood in front of the clock, midnight, pushing her into the tenth of January. The baby squirmed in her arms, and for a moment she allowed herself to imagine it growing with each chime: crawling then toddling then striding past Old Wally and raising a glass to him at Christmas as MacBride men always had. But the moment's warmth turned to ice in her belly: that could never be.

The smell of wood polish, the ticking of the seconds, the waft of the crickets' chirrup through the flywire – they were as much a part of her as her heartbeat, there beneath all the moments of her existence, even when she'd been away from them. Strange, that it could all fit within this space, her life. Rocking the baby gently, she walked soundlessly through the other empty rooms one last time, whispering their names to him.

The baby snuffled, and she squeezed her eyes shut, then opened them wide, as if to sober up. From the hook in the kitchen, she lifted the keys to her mother's Holden, before closing the back door behind her with a soft, familiar click.

Outside, she approached the dogs, chained at their shed, and patted and shushed them. 'Good boys. You stay quiet, now.'

The night was warm and the scent of the mulga and the eucalypts eddied about her. Gazing at the Southern Cross, for the first time in months she allowed herself the thought she'd pushed from her mind: *If I could just undo it all – go back in time . . .* She whispered uncertainly to a God who'd always seemed stand-offish, and in the past year completely absent: 'If you can do everything, then make the day of the crash go away, that first day. Just change those few moments. Then I'd have my whole family, and everything would be normal. Please?' The words, murmured aloud, dissolved as tears channelled down her cheeks.

The stars said nothing. The baby opened his eyes and regarded her, taking in every inch of her face in respectful silence. The dogs clinked their chains.

Looking up at her beloved moon, she felt its old comfort harden into something colder. 'Come on,' she said to the baby. 'Time to go. Before it's too late.'

She drove at a snail's pace away from the house, the engine barely turning over, tyres almost inaudible on the gravel. The white of the verandah was picked up by the moonlight; the silhouette of the mill stood sentinel; beside her in its basket, the baby began to doze, lulled by the car's purr. Regret and relief, longing and despair swirled through her body as, in the rear-view mirror, the homestead sank into blackness.

24

As Pete Peachey neared the Proserpine Mine just before dawn that January Saturday, a parked car caught his eye. 'What the hell would Lorna be doing out here at this hour?' he asked Strife, beside him in the Jeep. He'd had a rotten night's shooting, so had taken the shortcut across this paddock; empty, there wasn't much chance of his trailer getting bogged.

The world was just on the cusp of surrendering its monochrome to colour, a transition that always absorbed him. But the sight of the station wagon sent a wiry unease through him, and he pulled up. 'Back in a minute,' he said, and grabbed his torch. 'No. You stay put.

'Mrs M.?' he called into the stillness, but his voice disappeared over the distance. 'Lorna?' He shone the light through the window: a baby's bassinet lay on the front seat, empty, save for a bottle of milk that glowed in the beam. He scanned the surrounding area again with, then without, the torch, but it revealed nothing.

Perhaps Rosie had had trouble getting the baby to sleep? He remembered how the car engine could sometimes quieten little ones down. But this was a bloody strange place for a lullaby. He recalled her weary, haggard features. Now, the look reminded him of how he himself had felt, standing at this place not long after the war, when the dark pit had beguiled him with the neatness of its solution. He broke into a sprint towards the old shaft, hurdling the tangled wires of the fence.

'Rosie? Rose, are you there? It's me, Pete.' At the mouth of the mine, his torch illuminated the rocky sides below, sending a couple of lizards slithering away from the dazzle. His eyes took time to adjust to the darkness, to the depth. His focus slid down the rows of wooden sleepers, and the jagged walls beyond them, to something that made his gut churn: fuchsia wasn't a colour that belonged there. Fuchsia polka dots. 'Rosie!' he yelled, this time hit by the echo that bounced straight back at him, so that for an instant he took it for the girl's reply. 'Oh Christ . . .'

The dawn was intensifying, drenching the surroundings in oranges and dusty greens. In the few short moments he had been there, ants had begun their morning work, and he absently brushed dozens of them off his legs, ignoring their burning bites.

Pete knew the way down the mine; Phil MacBride had shown him where the footholds and handholds were along the way. He'd returned several times on his own, but not since that last one, when it had taken him all his strength to walk away from the edge.

He felt for the rungs offered by the sleepers. Sometimes the ancient wood would splinter under his weight and he would plummet to the next one, only just managing to dig his fingers in to stop himself tumbling into freefall. The deeper he went, the more musty and damp the air grew, untouched by the now piercing sun above.

'Rosie?'

The torch's batteries were nearly spent, and offered only a dim, buttery circle. It took a moment for him to piece together the fragments: a slippered foot; an outstretched hand. Face down, she was as still as the rocks around her. 'Rosie! Oh, sweetheart!'

Her cotton pyjamas were ridiculously clean, and it was only when Pete turned her over that he saw the sticky blood pooled beneath. Her face had been bashed against a jagged piece of granite, staving in her cheek and nose. 'Oh, little one, no . . .'

As he touched her shoulder, of all the thoughts that crowded his mind, one came to the fore: *I've seen worse*. And it was true. If anyone had to find her in this state, it might as well be him. He brushed the matted hair from her eyes. 'Let's get you home, love,' he said, and shone the torch upwards. He willed his thoughts back to the practical, and began calculating weight, and angle, and depth, reaching out his arms to estimate the clearance, and whether he could do it alone.

He could almost have missed it. Something yellow. Pete shone the failing torchlight on it, and at first struggled to make out the shape. In a yellow smock, there was Rosie's little lad, on a nest of fallen leaves and dirt, a trickle of blood coming from a small cut near his eye. Thrown clear from her arms upon landing, he supposed. Christ. Never even had a bloody name . . . At least he'd be able to retrieve one corpse, he thought grimly, and went to pick it up.

But whereas Rose was cold to the touch, this little body was still warm. He looked again, and put his ear to the baby's chest, touched the fontanelles. The face was faintly blue, the translucent eyelids unmoving, but there was a heartbeat. He picked him up and held him tightly to his chest as the child let out a cry. 'That's the way . . .' He rocked him gently, kissing the downy scalp. 'Remember me? It's Pete. We're old mates.' Now there was fury in the child's screams. 'You just keep those lungs working, Sir, and Old Pete'll do the rest.' Baby cradled in one arm, with renewed urgency, he began his ascent to the light.

Fin Rafferty knew, of course. He was the one who flew out to check on the baby. Completed the details for the death certificate, too. Pete Peachey – well, he'd found the poor girl, so he knew. Lorna and Matt, of course. The other person who knew was Sergeant Wisheart. It was routine for the police to come out and have a word about deaths on a property. There were enough of them, God knew.

Making his way into Lorna's kitchen again, a year to the very day since he'd announced her widowhood to her, Wisheart was struck by the unfairness of being back there. If he had more families as law-abiding as the MacBrides on his beat he reckoned he'd be out of a job.

Arriving by car, he got there a good while after the Flying Doctor, who confirmed that Rose's fatal injuries were consistent with a fall.

'Fall . . . or jump, would you say?' he asked Fin, out at the airstrip later.

The doctor thought carefully. 'A fractured skull's a fractured skull . . . "Fall or jump" is your department.' He bunched his lips, remembering his landing on the Meredith Downs airstrip just after Christmas. 'Rose had had a hard time of it with the baby. A lot of shame. Knew what it must have done to her mother.' He gave a grunt as he heaved his bag into the plane, then folded down the step to the cockpit. 'Do you think there's any good to be done by dragging them all through the mud now?'

Wisheart took a deep breath as he put his notebook back in his pocket. 'Let me have a death certificate, and I'll see about the rest.'

Sergeant Wisheart took the view that it was his place to investigate wrongdoing, and ensure it was punished. He wouldn't put up with wife beaters or cattle rustlers. He came down like a ton of bricks on rapists and thieves. All in all, it kept him pretty well occupied. But there were cases, he believed, in which there was clear daylight between what the law demanded, and what justice called for.

The policeman was not inclined to punish Rose MacBride. A suicide would mean an inquest, which would mean a sideshow. It wouldn't be Rose who was punished anyway – it would be her poor bloody mother and brother, and that innocent baby, who surely deserved a chance at least?

He quizzed Pete Peachey about the circumstances in which

he'd found the body. He inspected the scene. He spoke to Matt and Lorna, who said it was all their fault: if a girl does something like that, then surely it's only because you failed to notice something? Failed to stop her?

In his cells back in Wanderrie Creek, Wisheart had a bloke who'd been stealing gold from the mint, another who'd tried to chop off his wife's head with an axe, and a woman who'd put her little boy into scalding water to teach him not to wet the bed. He was buggered if he was going to spend time and money on a circus about suicide when it should be spent on punishing the wicked and trying to set the damaged on the right track.

Would anything be put right by reporting it as suicide, holding an inquest? Would justice be served? Anyone's life improved? The hell it would. So Rosie MacBride died in a fall. A tragedy. Full stop.

Nothing too hot. That was the phrase which kept running through Lorna's mind as she looked through the things hanging in the wardrobe. It was important to choose something comfortable, light. There wouldn't be much shade – just that sun blazing down mercilessly.

She pulled out a dress at random, and held it to her. In a daze, she drifted to the bed, and sat hugging it. Through the window, a crow barked its disgust at the heat, or maybe just its despair – long, guttural syllables as black as its feathers. Lorna stroked the sleeve's cuff and noticed a button missing. Too late to sew it back on now. Her mind knifed back to the previous January, and the frayed cuff on Phil's shirt. He never cared about clothes. 'Still plenty of wear in this,' he'd say, if she suggested a new one. A new bore, a new ram – well, that was different. That was an *investment*. That would *make* you money, not fritter it away. It had been right – the frayed cuff, the mended tear in the knee of the trousers where he'd snagged them on fence-wire freeing a ewe that had got her head stuck. She had put them with the tweed jacket, the sturdy woollen socks, the R. M. Williams boots that had been resoled and restitched umpteen times. That was the man. Those were his clothes.

Rose chose Warren's clothes that day. Cricket whites. He'd always looked so dashing in them.

Washing. Sewing. Caring for her men and what they wore. Lorna remembered how it had suddenly all seemed so trivial. Not nearly enough, surely? She would have done more. There should have been time for *more*.

You always assume there's going to be more time. Now, when Lorna's thoughts return to Rose, she's almost startled by how she failed to know that her daughter's, too, would be a life cut short. All those things she thought would come to Rose later in life; even the forgiveness and reconciliation she thought might somehow come about, over the baby. In hindsight these hopes seemed ridiculous. 'Such a *little* life,' Lorna had whispered when she'd heard the news of her death.

In her daughter's room now, the faint trace of Rose's scent almost overwhelmed her, but she pressed on, pulling at a few blouses, some checked shirts, skirts and, finally, a mint-green sleeveless dress with tiny pink roses around the neck that Lorna had sewn for her. She picked out some sandals, and laid them beside the dress.

'You'll never be hot in that, will you, love?' she murmured. Then she gathered the clothes to wrap, for Pete Peachey to take to Gribbles', the funeral directors in town.

As she left, her eye strayed to the corner of the room, where, deep in oblivion, her nameless grandson lay in his cot. In light of events, Mrs Blencombe's visit had had to be postponed, and the baby slept on, in limbo.

When he woke on the morning of Rose's funeral, it took Matt a moment or two to find his way back to reality. Since helping to haul Rose's body from the mine a week ago, it was hard to distinguish dream from day and fear from wishful thinking. Just when his mind had finally begun to trust its grip on the world, he had to factor in yet another unfathomable absence.

Stretching the skin on his prickled jaw to smooth the path of his razor took him back to that day when Rose shaved off his beard in hospital. Now, Old Wally's chime drifted down the passage, and a word came to him. 'Untimely'. He'd heard it used a lot about Rosie's death. As he turned it over in his mind – 'un time' – it reflected new angles of meaning. Not just 'premature', but 'existing outside time' like 'unworldly'. As if life had escaped the limits and laws of time, and events years apart now bled into and over one another.

He recalled Rose's lifeless body; imagined her, heading to the mine that night. He could feel the bumps under her tyres and the stones under her feet; the dark, damp smell of it, cold and mysterious, like the breath of the underworld spirits Warren used to scare them with.

He was in a dim inner vision, replaying their underground games. And over and over, he saw his sister's corpse come tumbling down on the three of them – grown-up Rose and her baby falling past them or even landing on them mid-swordfight, mid-treasure hunt – as though she had always been going to tumble down that mine. He felt a sharp pain and blinked at his reflection, the razor in his hand. Maybe the roo was always going to bound in front of the truck; was still bounding in some eternal present. He splashed away the last of the foam on his face, and dabbed at a nick with the corner of a flannel.

Walking past Rose's room, he heard the baby gurgling and sucking at nothing. *Who was his father?* So far, he looked like any MacBride baby in family photos. Matt wasn't sure he could cope with knowing any more, yet. There'd be time to find out. Or to get comfortable with not knowing, once Mrs Blencombe had taken him.

Back in his room, Lorna had left one of Warren's suits for him to wear. He braced himself for how Rose would rag him about it, then remembered.

'Sorry,' he said, in apology for the forgetting.

As funeral proceedings drew to a close, Matt glanced at his mother, dry-eyed beside him. She looked so *old*. She'd always seemed ageless, but today she seemed to stoop, facial muscles grim beneath papery skin, and she walked with a perceptible hesitation at each step.

Matt and Pete Peachey took up position as the lead pallbearers. Wasn't all that heavy, the coffin. As they carried it from the church, Matt was vividly aware that his face and Rose's were inches apart, divided by a mere polished plank. If he turned his head, he could talk to her; look into her eyes, almost . . . get her to change her mind. Then he remembered the shattered face. He concentrated on keeping the steady pace.

At the wake, a girl with short red hair approached Matt and, when it was clear he had no idea who she was, said, 'It's *me* . . . Pattie . . .'

'Pattie?'

'Pattie *Gosden*.'

That name . . . And yes, the face . . . Matt remembered Rose's words, the girl in the dream: *'You were pretty keen on Pattie Gosden.'*

She was good-looking, but he felt . . . nothing. A sick niggle emerged. 'Pattie. Of course . . .'

'Are you all right?'

Matt's hand strayed to the scar under his hair.

'You never got in touch,' she said.

'I was in a road accident last year. Hurt my head.'

'I *know* . . . I waited so long to hear from you after the school dance . . .'

There was something about her – her lips, the way she shrugged her shoulders . . . Like jumping over a crevasse, his memory tumbled onto a feeling: he'd kissed those lips, he was almost sure of it. He'd put his arms around that waist. What else had he done?

Glimpsing the memory through a dense fog, Matt squinted as his own words laid the path back to that time. 'You were going to be in town . . . That's why I was in the truck. I was going to see you at the YPA meeting.'

'Must have your wires crossed. I was in Perth. I thought Rose would have told you.'

Pattie touched his forearm. 'You still here?'

'Sorry. Miles away. So what are you up to these days? It would be good to see you. I could drive over . . .'

She explained she was at uni now, in Perth. The conversation stumbled to a halt, and she had walked a few paces when Matt called, 'Wait!' He caught her wrist. 'Did I ever – do anything to you? Go too far? Hurt you?'

'Apart from forgetting I existed?'

'Apart from that, yeah.'

'No. You broke my heart for a while. But I'm fine.' She touched a dainty silver ring on her right hand. 'I'm going round with Greg now. He's in my chemistry tute . . .' She kissed his cheek, and her hand lingered a moment on his shoulder. 'You take good care of yourself.'

She gave him a sudden, tight hug, her skin brushing his neck, and as he brought his arms up to her back, his body took the measure of her, then let go.

He imagined her in his dream, but the feel was wrong, the smell. He was interrupted by a gnarled hand that sought his. 'Matthew. Glen Chiselhurst, old mate of your dad's from army days.' And for the moment, Matt returned to the room, to the present, leaving the dream to rain its rain in some deep cavern of his mind.

25

LATE THAT NIGHT, by torchlight, Lorna drifted to the station diary almost in a trance. She reached into the desk drawer and took out Phil's old Conway Stewart fountain pen and the bottle of midnight-blue ink. Unscrewing the barrel of the pen, she squeezed the bladder to empty the last few drops back into the bottle, before dipping the nib in and pressing the rubber again, this time to suck in the blue, like sucking in the breath needed to say what she had to.

She wrote: 'Rose funeral.' There it was. Up there on the first line for 16 January 1959. The nib rested on the page; then she saw that the ink had escaped the confines of its full stop. She took a piece of blotting paper and soaked up the mistake.

She couldn't bear to see the words all alone like that, and searched for other things to write: '5 pts Top Shed.' 'Muggy.' There wasn't much else to report for that day: the station had come to a standstill for the funeral, with just Maudie Knapp staying behind to look after the baby.

Lorna found herself flicking back, a few weeks at a time, and soon stumbled upon the writing of Miles Beaumont, and of Rosie. The sight of her daughter's handwriting stabbed her; flung at her the flat, unarguable fact of death. And the gnawing question.

She stood up and rubbed the small of her back, that niggling ache that had started when she was pregnant with Warren, growing more pronounced with each child until it had eventually become a permanent companion. Tomorrow. She would deal with things tomorrow. Padding back down the passage, she looked in on the baby in his cot, breathing easily, arms flung wide, one thumb meeting an index finger with perfect poise. A snatch of song drifted into memory – a piece from a school carol concert: 'O magnum mysterium' . . . 'Oh, great mystery', then something about 'lying in a crib'.

The child took a deep, world-weary breath. He'd be awake and wanting his bottle soon. Lorna continued to the kitchen and warmed the milk, still by torchlight, taking consolation in the brilliant stars through the window.

Telegrams went back and forth with Mrs Blencombe, postponing appointment dates, and with each delay, Lorna sensed the change within her deepening. *Magnum mysterium.* The mysterious baby lying in a manger, come to redeem the world. In spite of herself, since Rose's death she had found that the tiny, warm body brought her a visceral comfort; the way he gazed at her, free of sorrow, wanting to be touched and held and sung to. Day by day, he was taking root in her heart – for good or ill, she couldn't say.

She'd consulted Matt only briefly on her decision, worried in case he objected, but he gave the same shrug he gave so often these days. 'If you think it's what we should do . . .'

So Lorna MacBride eventually set off to Perth to register the birth of her only grandson, on the same day as she registered the death of her only daughter. A hint of concern crossed the face of the young man behind the counter at Births, Deaths and Marriages, but she eyed him fiercely, daring him to pity her. He cleared his throat and pointed to the boxes relating to 'Father'. 'You don't seem to have filled these in, Mrs MacBride.'

'No.'

'It's – ah – not an oversight, then?'

'No.'

He gave a nod that segued into a shake of the head – very slight, and he exhaled as he considered something.

To pre-empt any challenge Lorna said, 'I understood it could be left blank. I did telegraph to ask.' She undid the clasp on her handbag. 'I can show you the reply they sent—'

The clerk waved her hand down gently. 'You're right. That box isn't always filled in. As long as we've got the mother's details, the birth can be registered.' He slid the forms back, with precisely pencilled 'x's showing where to sign.

Within the armour of her brittle manner, Lorna felt melted. She was even ashamed of how she had chosen the child's name. Rose had referred to him at best only as 'the baby', and at worst 'it', and had resisted all urgings to think of what to call him. So, after Rose's death, Lorna had opened the book of names Phil had bought for her when she was expecting Warren, but didn't get further than Andrew. It would do. For his middle name – Ross, same as all the eldest MacBride sons for generations. There was no other surname but MacBride to give her grandson, so he might as well have the middle name that went with it.

The clerk signed something with carbon paper under it, and tore along the perforation to produce Lorna's receipt for the application for the death certificate. He repeated the procedure for the birth certificate, and handed them to her.

She opened her handbag and slipped into it the documentary remains of her daughter, and the beginnings of her grandson. A brief sense of comfort ran through her as she thought of the two of them together for a moment, enclosed in that safe space, enfolded and carried by her, as was only right.

Lorna MacBride thought about it. She thought about it as she watered her roses. She thought about it as she tallied the cash book; as she fed her grandson his bottle and burped and changed him; and as she put him in his cot, washed and content and blinking drunkenly to sleep. It crossed her mind to mention it to Matt, but what was there to say yet? She would dare this one approach, and if nothing came of it, well, that would be that.

She went through the ritual of filling Phil's pen and took a sheet of the thick cream writing paper that she saved for her most special correspondence.

30th January 1959

Dear Miles,

I trust this letter finds you well. I am not sure where you are these days, so I hope you will forgive my writing to you 'at the office', so to speak.

I have such fond memories of the time you spent here, and, later, such gratitude for the kindness and support you gave Meredith Downs at such a difficult time.

It is because I think you made good friends here that I felt you would want to know that our beloved Rosie died suddenly three weeks ago, in a fall at the old Proserpine Mine. I should also tell you that she is survived by a son, who was born on 18th December last year. He is a fine, healthy boy, who is the image of my own MacBride babies.

Matt has made a wonderful recovery, and continues to confound his doctors.

If you ever wanted to visit, and perhaps meet Rosie's son, I would welcome you. You know where to find us, and that no appointment is necessary. Of course, you must be very busy, and I realise we are very far flung.

With fond wishes,
Lorna

She read it over briefly, then addressed the envelope care of Beaumont Enterprises Australia in Sydney, printing in the top left corner: 'Private and Personal. Please Forward'. Adding the stamp, she took it to the kitchen and slipped it into the post to be collected by Sneaky.

She had sent the signal. Who knew whether it would reach Miles, and whether it would shed any more light?

26

THE DISTRICT WAS still agog at the latest MacBride death. Of course, the old timers could dredge up stories of worse calamities – entire families burnt to cinders in a bushfire; three generations blown up on the same night shift at a gold mine – but even *they* conceded that Lorna had had a pretty rough trot.

People's solemnity turned to confused amazement however, when, a few weeks after burying her daughter, Lorna MacBride, jaw firm, eyes set straight ahead, appeared in the main street of Wanderrie Creek wheeling . . . a pram. Whether it was just the heat that made her face flushed, who could say? But, hat and gloves in place, she walked with measured paces into Spearritt's the Mercer's (who prided themselves on selling 'everything you can think of and a few you can't') and bought dummies, nappies and pins, and a Wendy Boston teddy bear. She added sheets for the cot, and a fine silver napkin ring, which she had them engrave then and there with 'A.R.M.'.

Lorna had been on the point of 'consulting' Phil about it all, but some deep knowing silenced her, and instead she confided her decision, and then her plan, to Maudie Knapp from Deep Springs station. 'But, Lorna, are you sure?' Maudie had asked.

'Of course I'm not sure.'

'It's not too late to go through with the adoption,' her friend had said.

After long thought, Lorna said softly, 'He's all I've got left of Rosie . . . I was too harsh. Too hard on her. Always held her to a higher standard than the boys – thought it was for her own good. Maudie, this is the only chance I'll ever have of making things up to her.'

The words silenced her friend, and Maudie made the pact to be in Wanderrie Creek at the appointed time today, to meet Lorna in the tea rooms and, baby in the pram beside them, have a cup of tea. In public. In broad daylight.

As Maudie refreshed the pot with hot water, she muttered through a clenched smile, 'They'll stop staring eventually, dear. Just look like I'm saying something terribly interesting.'

On the day Lorna went to buy baby things and let her grandson be seen in town, Matt set about redecorating Rose's room for the baby, as his mother had asked. His sister's bed was still made up, with Ramsey the old knitted sheep still guarding her pillow. As he leaned forward to strip the bed, he was taken aback. Everything still smelled of Blue Grass, Rose's perfume. He wrestled his attention back to the task, removing the bedsteads from the wire frame beneath the single mattress and resting them in the hallway.

It was late afternoon by the time he finished returning the tarpaulins and paint tins to the shed. He carted out the bedsteads, then last of all the mattress. Turning it lengthwise to stand it against the shed wall, one of the handles came away, revealing a neat slit in the fabric.

In the dim light, he pressed his fingers against the ticking to explore it. Something was buried in the horsehair and the wool. Reaching in, he pulled out a small, cold object – Rose's brass lighter.

Delving further, he found a sheet of paper, folded over and over. He held it to the light, and read 'Yawa yawa yawa'. He smiled at the memory of his sister's daggy ritual, and his own initiation into it on the tree branch as a child.

He hesitated, torn between respect for the dead and the urge to do what he knew full well she'd have done in his place. He could almost hear her: *Come on, Bubba, what are you waiting for? Have a sticky-beak!*

He pushed the lighter back into the mattress, and carefully unfolded the paper, wondering what childish confession she had stashed years ago, ready to burn. But it soon became clear that this was something recent – something he was never meant to see.

The words on the page melded with the smell of the mattress, and a kaleidoscope of events, of dreams, of sensations and puzzles whirred and pulsed and rattled and finally clicked into place, ripping into his insides.

His dog Trooper came into the shed and gave a thin whine at the sight of his master, now curled on the floor, eyes wild, gasping for breath from the blow of Rose's words.

There is a time when anything is possible: a time when we could be whoever we dream of being. Then life gets in the way, and our existence shrinks to a single moment. So the man who cracks his head on the corner of the bar in a stoush, whose brains and life leak out there and then, well, gradually he's boiled down to 'Jimmy who died in that brawl'. People use hindsight to map the road to his demise, bestowing retrospective significance on points along the way. Just as Jesus was always going to die on the Cross, they prune and shape their memory of a fellow's life so that it always led up to this inevitable event.

The same goes for Burt, the one who punched Jimmy so hard his head cracked against the bar. Burt who spent the next ten years in prison; who, until the second before the fight, was 'a decent bloke'. But after . . . he's only ever 'Burt who killed that bloke', because of this one moment into which, it turns out, every day of his life was being funnelled all along.

There are some events you can't come back from. Some gates close off every other path you could possibly take. A single moment in your past denies you a future: condemning you to a death in life. And in that moment, as he read those words, Matthew MacBride stepped through just such a gate.

Though Matthew MacBride's life is changed irrevocably in the moment he reads Rose's note, the landscape gives no hint of it. It remains unmoved by his shaking terror, his vomiting, his endless nights without sleep. At sunset on Wallaby Ridge, where he sprawls helpless and exhausted, the earth accepts him. The trees shadow him, unmoved; the rocks stand steadfast, unjudging. The sky remains implacable, undented by his transgression. Nature's response is silence: a refusal to be appalled or impressed.

It is Lorna who notices the difference, from the moment she gets back from Wanderrie Creek, when he disappears for hours and comes back drunk. Lorna who is confounded by his relapse into anger and rudeness like after the crash, picking fights with staff, botching basic jobs so that she has to get station hands to do them again. And he won't even stay in the same room as baby Andrew these days.

She is so worried that it's some sort of flare-up of his old head injury, brought on by news of the baby becoming public, that she even persuades Fin Rafferty to fly in, under the pretence, for the purposes of the radio call, that the child is unwell.

Back at the airstrip, having seen Matt, the doctor tells Lorna, 'Cognition, movement – all seem OK. But I agree, something's off.

I'd call it a depression. Keep an eye on him, Lorna. Time may sort it out. If he gets worse, get in touch with Dr Fairchild.'

It's all Matt can do to string a sentence together these days. As for Fin Rafferty's visit: he was a nice enough bloke, but he had no bloody idea. No one did.

Whenever the squalling comes from Rose's old bedroom, Matt goes to the doorway and stares at the cot, watching as, wet or hungry or colicky, the baby stiffens and shrieks. It takes all Matt's control not to shriek too. Once, he gets as far as standing beside the sleeping baby and touching its cheek. The creature gives a slight wriggle and smacks his lips, then goes back to his dream.

Now, in the shade of Jemima's trees, Matt considers the doctor's words of encouragement – setbacks happen, still miles ahead of where he was after the crash – but they mean nothing. He's spent the morning repairing the fence around the old mine and nailing up a new sign painted by one of the hands, saying 'Danger. Keep Out'.

A familiar urge rises in Matt – he has to get away. Then he thinks of his mother: he can't leave her to carry on alone. He imagines a life for them in the city, where no one knows who they are.

He will bide his time. *Time. Patience.* These are the words that come silently to his mouth over the weeks that follow. Silence itself becomes a balm: a soft, absent touch that gives him at least a glimmer of peace. The rocks *are*. The sky *is*. The trees grow on regardless, some of their branches dying, but not because of him. This country, unflinching, timeless, might save him.

In the days and weeks after the revelation of the MacBride baby, webs of opinion spread out across the wires and the airwaves and along the dusty roads. Station people disliked uncertainty. There were enough imponderables in life, what with the weather and the wool price. So in answer to the inevitable question – *Who the hell's the father?* – everyone formed a theory. Not the same theory, but a theory, nonetheless, which took the burden off the question mark, and allowed a sense of satisfaction in their own powers of deduction.

They proposed a range of candidates: one of the shearers; or a regular visitor to the property – that roped in Sneaky Snook and Pete Peachey and Neil Tinnett (these were rejected by those who knew the men); someone from Perth, perhaps – after all, she'd been at boarding school there. And, more recently, she'd spent a lot of time hanging around her brother's doctors, for that matter. Or another patient? The front runner, from a crowded field, however, was that posh manager they'd had in, Miles of Money: he showed a clean pair of heels before the girl came home . . . Each person would say, 'Of course I can't be sure, but I reckon it's . . .'

The thing that stopped it becoming an open sport was that the girl was dead. Made it less fit for entertainment somehow. The MacBrides had been through the mill. So, people might have looked surreptitiously at the baby when it turned up in public with Lorna or Matt, but they kept any wisecracks about the family being taken down a peg or two till they were out of earshot.

And so, from birth, a layer of invisible information draped over the MacBride baby like a caul, to which it remained oblivious.

27

FLIES SWARMED OVER the feast of roo meat that Matt and Pete Peachey had cut up and laid on the bait racks, ready to inject with ten-eighty poison. Though dingoes weren't the roo shooter's domain, he was happy enough to help out.

Whilst a kangaroo would drink your sheep's water and eat their feed, the damage it did was nothing compared with a wild dog. That animal could rip the heart out of a hundred sheep in a single night, often not bothering to eat them: it hunted just out of instinct.

In the old days it was strychnine they'd have laced the meat with before scattering it around empty paddocks. Of late, the Agriculture Protection Board was experimenting with ten-eighty because, since the poison occurred naturally in some West Australian plants, it was less likely to kill native animals which had built up an immunity to it over thousands of years. Feral cats, dogs and rabbits, though, didn't stand a chance. Nor did people, for that matter.

The signs on the racks said, 'Danger! Poison!' The labels on the bottles and the boxes sported a skull and crossbones. Pete Peachey wasn't one to make a song and dance about things, but even he saw the wisdom in wearing the thick rubber gauntlets that made your hands sweat like hell.

Matt took one last drag on his cigarette and squashed it, swiped his hair back off his forehead, then scratched his nose for good measure.

'Let's start this end,' said Peachey, and they took opposite sides of the bait rack – a long, home-made frame about waist height built from old drill pipe, strung across with fencing wire to make a netting table top of sorts, four feet by twenty feet. Four racks stood side by side, each with fist-size lumps of roo meat.

Matt passed Peachey a poison bottle with a large syringe attached, then picked up his own. The gloves made his hands clumsy, and he pushed the plunger down so hard that the liquid squirted back out from the meat.

'Easy does it,' said Pete, injecting pieces with unhurried efficiency. When Matt botched the next chunk, Peachey said, 'A little goes a long way, remember. One push'll do you, nice and slow.'

'I know that!'

A thought of the baby broke Matt's concentration yet again: the future seemed to stretch before him like a prison. He kept wishing the needle he held was going not into the meat but into his own arm.

Head down, Pete watched. 'Keep an eye on him, will you, Pete?' Lorna had said. 'There's something not right with him, but for the life of me I don't know what.'

'In some ways, strychnine's the better way to go,' mused Peachey.

'What?' Matt wondered whether his thoughts were that obvious.

'In the overall scheme of things . . .' Pete kept his steady rhythm. 'Ten-eighty takes a fair while to work. Slow and painful . . . but with a dose of strychnine, it's lights out, instantly.' He spiked another piece. 'If I were a dog, I'd prefer that.'

'Good to know.'

As they made their way along the rack, Matt continued to fumble.

'Everything all right?' Pete asked.

'Mind your own business.'

Peachey let the remark pass, but when Matt spilled some of the poison, just missing his feet, he grabbed the bottle. 'It's not cordial, son. Here, let me do it.'

'I'd be better off drinking it.' Matt's voice threatened to crack. He took a frustrated swipe at the open container, which toppled, drenching his shirt and jeans, and he couldn't keep the despair from his face.

'Right, that'll do, soldier,' said Pete. 'Get your gear off and we'll wash you down.' He strode to the car for the jerry can of water, but when he got back, Matt was still standing there, now without gloves, soaked in poison.

In an anguished, almost dreamy voice, Matt said, 'It's all shit. Life's turned into one big shithole.'

'It'll get a bloody side worse if you don't get out of those clothes.'

Still Matt remained frozen.

'Let's get this off you,' Pete said, and with fingers hampered by gloves, undid Matt's shirt.

'Lean on my shoulder and lift your foot,' he instructed, bending down to heave off Matt's boots and socks. 'Right, can you manage your strides?'

Matt fumbled with his flies, and gradually struggled free of the drenched fabric, one leg at a time. 'I'd be better off dead,' he said, as though it had taken him all that time to work out the thought.

'Well you don't get to be dead today, mate.' Peachey doused him with swills of water. 'Keep your eyes closed,' he said at one point, but remained otherwise silent as he wiped him down, reminded of times years ago when he'd dry the little boy and his brother after an afternoon's swimming in a waterhole. The arms and legs he towelled now had hair and were taut with muscle, yet at this moment, it was the child he seemed to be touching, not the man.

They drove back to Peachey's camp in silence. It was dusk, and Pete found Matt some trousers and a shirt, then lit the fire and made tea. Strife, banned from the dog-bait expedition, welcomed the arrivals and licked Matt's hand, though he received only a distracted pat in response.

Pete studied the boy's face: weary and shadowed, a line etched between his brows. 'Don't worry about the baits. There's plenty of time to put them out.'

After a long lull, Matt burst out, 'How come *I'm* the one who still has to live?'

He was not much of a one for touching people, Pete Peachey. If he let Lorna kiss his cheek at Christmas that was news. But now, he reached a gangly arm around Matt and drew him in to his side. Matt allowed his head to touch Peachey's shoulder, then leaned away again, tears running down his face.

'That's the way, boy,' said Pete, and patted Matt's arm.

'What's the bloody point, Pete? It's all – God, one big bloody mess.'

'Messes have a way of sorting themselves out . . . in the end.'

'You don't know that. You don't know anything!'

'I know what it's like when you can't . . . see a way out.'

'Not like this you don't. And it's only going to get worse.'

Peachey looked at the boy and took a breath. 'I'll tell you this. For what it's worth. When you spend time as a POW, things happen that you couldn't begin to imagine. Things get done to you . . .' He paused at some thought that seemed to get stuck in transit. '. . . that you think you'll never survive. And you end up doing things to other people just to keep existing one minute more . . . The trick is to keep living, Matt: carry on one breath at a time, one day at a time.'

There was silence, punctuated only by the spit and fizzle of the fire.

'But how do you get over it? The . . . stuff that happened?'

Peachey rose to feed the fire another few bits of branch, and poked the red coals until flames licked the dry bark. 'You don't. It's part of you. Never goes away . . . But if you're lucky, it loses its hold over you . . .' He turned, took in the boy. 'Matt, you go on because the world's interesting, and the ticket out of here's one-way. Living is your one chance of revenge on life.' He threw his cigarette butt into the flames. 'How old are you now?'

'Nineteen.'

He eyed the trees, reduced to outlines in the distance. 'I wasn't so much older than that when I started ripping blokes' guts out with bayonets. You don't always get a say in how life turns out.'

Pete poured some of his tea into the bowl beside his chair for Strife, weighing up the things he knew – about life, about Meredith Downs, about Matt and all he'd been through. 'Your mum's not getting any younger – she can't run this place without you . . . And as for Rosie's baby – he's your family.' If he saw Matt flinch, he didn't remark upon it. 'In my book, if you've got responsibilities, you may as well shoulder them willingly. Some things, the more you run from them, the harder they hunt you down.'

Matt hugged his own arm, and shifted in his seat.

'That business today . . .' Peachey said. 'If you want to drown yourself in poison or some bloody thing, I can't stop you – you'll find a way. But if you do . . . you'll never know what you missed out on.' He poked the fire again. 'You'll never know how the kid turned out. You'll never see your future, Matt. You'll just have been buried by your past.' He lit another cigarette for them both and gazed out to where the moon was starting its climb into the sky – a fat, ivory harvest moon held up by the silhouette of some elderly gum trees. 'Full moon.' He drew on his cigarette. 'Rosie always loved the full moon, didn't she?'

Matt nodded.

'Well, stick around to tell her little boy that. Show him the full moon. Show him what she loved.'

Days pass, and weeks, as Matt tries to make sense of his life. When he can, towards sunset, he comes to Wallaby Ridge, in breakaway country, where he can catch the last trace of the sun as the dust quiets and the animals still themselves for a while.

From here you can just make out the scar that appeared one day in 1947 when the earth got restless and shrugged, creating a three-foot ridge for twenty miles across the property. It's a reminder that solid ground, unchanged for millions of years, can rearrange itself without warning or permission. You just have to live with the new terrain. Repair what roads and fences you can. Start from scratch for the rest of it.

Matt contemplates the setting sun – this moment that turns his mind to life and the death it promises. He can sit all afternoon watching a tree: watching the light slowly carve into it, and show him every piece of its bark, every notch where an insect has burrowed under its defences and started up a wound that's never going to heal, even though the tree stays standing. He can see the start of its buds, the scars where a branch has been torn off by the wind or sawn off for a fencepost. But if he watches long enough – if he just sits there, facing the western sky – everything he thought he knew about that tree will start to dissolve. The details go first, then the colours, then before long he's left with just a lacy black tracery of leaves and branches – a flat black skeleton propped up by the last of the sky. When Matthew MacBride looks at the evening sky, he knows he, too, is a skeleton waiting to happen. Time will not be denied its due.

This evening, Matt eyes the witnessing moon, ponders its one side, always concealed. He pulls the folded note from his pocket and strikes a match, scrunching his eyes to clear tears that blur the flame on the paper as it completes the magic that Rose had begun.

The borders of the paper etch an illuminated lacework as the fire eats its way inwards, turning up the edges in pure orange flame. He holds it until it is barely a corner, lambent flames licking his thumb and forefinger, which protect the word 'rain'. When he is sure that it, too, will be consumed, he frees it, and it flakes upwards into the evening sky.

He is drawn back to that moment on the lemon gum branch with his sister as a seven-year-old – to how every part of him felt lighter once the words on that first, long-ago page had floated out of existence. '*Yawa, yawa, yawa.*' He mouths the words silently now, and waits, alert for any physical change that might come over him.

Perhaps the magic left this world with his sister.

He is still here, unconsoled, unforgiven . . . He gives in to tears and sinks to the ground. A lone boobook calls above the click of the crickets.

He thinks about Pete's words. '*If you've got responsibilities, you may as well shoulder them willingly.*' If he keeps his mind on the tasks of each day, he'll survive, maybe. Before it ultimately takes him from this world, time will build him shelter.

PART II

Image To Come

28

Friday, 10th January 1969

On Meredith Downs, out towards the boundary fence, hours from the homestead, you can see the blackened hulk of a truck, a Bedford in its day, rooted into the tall grass that grows up around its wheels. The bare metal pedals – clutch, accelerator, brake – seem lonely for a foot to give them purpose. In the air around float many ghosts, which never quite leave, despite the breeze that blows through time, in this graveyard of abandoned things.

A dark-haired boy drives the truck far out into the desert, or sometimes to the ocean, though its wheels stay anchored in the dirt. The two station hands who have brought him today dump broken pump jacks and an old fridge next to the other scrap metal that lies about. They are oblivious to the child's imaginary journey, and to the array of special places he has on the station. Just past his tenth birthday, this is one he cannot reach on his own. Most, he visits on foot or by bicycle, more rarely by horse; almost always with his kelpie, Rascal, whose eyes have the mischievous look that gives him his name.

The boy haunts the station like a spirit reacquainting itself with once-familiar territory, drifting through creeks and paddocks and rock-holes. He explores. He collects. He imagines. He gathers objects, and builds them into stories: the casing of a brass army compass; the bolt from a .303 rifle; a field telescope; a broken sextant – these speak of the war, of his grandfather; or of Pete Peachey, the roo shooter. He seeks out rocks with brilliant colours or uncannily strict angles to add to his precious collection.

In his world of fragments, knowledge comes in pieces rather than as a smooth entirety, so this MacBride boy mixes and melds and adds whatever is required to create a whole. Nowhere is this more necessary than with his mother, and he invents details, about the shape of her fingernails, how she sounds when she sings, her favourite foods. Today, when he gets back from the truck and rides out to the Home shearing shed, he cooks with her, concocting potions in bottles the colours of stained glass, discarded over decades: dirt and a dash of engine oil; iodine and a splash of friar's balsam; washing powder and a Bex and Mercurochrome. She tells him it will be delicious and gives him a proud smile.

He wipes his hands on his jeans and drops to his haunches to haul Rascal into a hug and a pat for watching patiently and not trying to eat the cooking. Slinging an arm over the dog, he peers into the distance and says a prayer for his future. Then he wonders whether God can even see him, just a dot in all this space. He wonders whether God's ever been out this way at all. It's not easy to reach.

* * *

In Lorna MacBride's kitchen, on the wall calendar the tenth of January is unmarked, but glows with menace. She commemorates the date with no religious service; no graveside visit. She and Matt make no mention of its significance in front of the boy. But the child notices, over the years, that she spends a little time at the piano on that day, playing the same three pieces. For her husband, it's 'Pack Up Your Troubles', for Warren, 'The Wild Colonial Boy', and for Rose, 'My Love Is Like a Red, Red Rose'. In the evening, she sits on the verandah and takes in the waft of the gardenias, their scent full of memories of long ago happiness. Then she prays for the strength not to miss the blessings life may bring, still; prays for her surviving son, and for Rose's boy, sprung up like wild green wheat in the desert.

* * *

Distance and time. These are the elements that have rewoven the fabric of life on Meredith Downs after Rosie MacBride's death. Matt never forgets the date: of the crash that flung his life off its axis; of the night a year later when his sister broke under the weight of what followed. When he can, he spends the anniversary here in Monty's shed, sanding, planing, varnishing the pearling lugger.

He wonders where his great-uncle might have sailed to, given enough life. Maybe one day Matt will take the voyage for him, scatter his ashes in the ocean. One day soon . . . Then he remembers Pete Peachey's words from a decade ago: '*Stick around . . Show Rosie's baby the full moon. Show him what she loved.*'

He dusts the urn that holds Monty's ashes, and promises to return with a beer on his birthday, then climbs down from the boat and heads out into the blinding light.

The Meredith Downs that Matt oversaw was a leaner affair than his father would have imagined. The wool price was a quarter of what it had been in its heyday, and the money from the latest wool clip was a far cry from Phil MacBride's final wool cheque.

In the 1950s, Australia was said to 'ride on the sheep's back' thanks to the boom caused in part by America's demand for wool to clothe its army in the Korean War. When the federal government snubbed America's offer to buy the entire national clip, the price hit a pound a pound. Suddenly, wool, the staple of garments since the Dark Ages, became too costly for others *not* to have a crack at replacing. Only a madman would have predicted that its competitor would come not from an animal or a plant, but from a viscous liquid deep within the earth: oil.

Converted into fibres with names like Nylon, synthetics promised *convenience* and *economy*. Impervious to drought, disease and death, oil was turned into cheaper fabrics, which could be chucked into a washing machine with water as hot as you liked without shrinkage, liberating housewives from the tyranny of hand washing.

In consequence, by 1969 the MacBrides had had to tighten their belts. They replaced the ageing ex-army motorbikes, which cost a fortune to maintain, with zippy Kawasakis. They made do with fewer permanent hands, bringing in seasonal help for musters and lamb marking.

That January, going over the books with Matt, Neil Tinnett reassured him: 'There's still a healthy living to be made, as long as you don't get a drought. Just keep your head down, and take things a season at a time . . . You MacBrides have always adapted to fortune.'

But oil wasn't the only threat to Meredith Downs that Mother Earth had up her sleeve. The economy of Western Australia had always see-sawed between agriculture and mining. The colony's early days had been dominated by livestock and crops. Then the 1890s ushered in the Gold Rush, bringing new mining laws that trumped earlier land laws when it came to who could do what on the Crown land occupied by pastoralists.

When the easy gold soon dwindled, most of the grand towns it paid for withered away, leaving the pastoralists once again with the upper hand in the fight for survival. Until, in 1960, the see-saw swung again when the Federal Government loosened its export ban on iron ore. Suddenly, the state's immense unmined iron deposits beneath Crown land were worth staggering money in foreign markets hungry for steel. The starter's pistol had been fired.

Within the million square miles of Western Australia lay

unguessed-at mineral treasuries, and miners turned fresh eyes to the outback, scouring it all over again. As well as iron ore, claims were being staked for bauxite, molybdenum, nickel, copper, mineral sands – just about whatever the geologists could imagine. From as far away as Switzerland and America, companies came to explore, and every day seemed to bring news of a new find, of nickel or alumina, even uranium. Drill a hole practically anywhere in this state and you'd find something worth a bob.

The miners had the power now. And the pastoralists, for all that their Crown leases were vast, were being reminded, often painfully, that they were merely temporary holders of the *surface* of the earth, at the mercy of those wanting what lay *under* it.

29

On the tenth of January 1969, Bonnie Edquist casts her eye over the open country soaked pink by the setting sun, and gives a snort. This certainly qualifies as the middle of bloody nowhere. Just what she'd begged her uncle for.

As she runs her fingers through her hair, they rasp with the dust that's already got every-bloody-where: in the creases of her elbows; grinding between her teeth, even though she only got here today. Her gaze turns to the welcome sight of the bush shower – a giant canvas bag rigged up to a tree hanging over the creek. She'll shower with her clothes on, and strip them off when she gets back to her caravan. She's the only woman on this geology survey team, and all in all, the blokes behave. But still.

The crew set up camp a couple of days ago, so are happy to get her precious contribution of fresh milk and bread. Bonnie's worked with all these boys before, and as they sit around the campfire that evening, it's the usual chat: the heat; the ants; the rock samples they've started to collect and map; how the hell anyone can get the stuff out of the ground if it's there. Merv Sempton, older than the rest by twenty years, reminds them that's not *their* problem. They just have to find it. Tony Criddles, who used to copy her geology notes at uni, passes her the Aerogard spray, and she douses herself in it in an effort to ward off the squadrons of mosquitoes.

Mick, the youngest field assistant, hands out more cans of beer. As Bonnie takes hers, she asks, 'By the way, how did it go with the owners?'

'Haven't called in on them yet. Wanted to get properly set up first,' says Tony.

She stops her beer halfway to her lips. 'You're kidding! Ever heard of manners?'

'They can't stop us being here, can they? Manners is all it is,' says Mick.

'Manners and common sense,' she says. 'This far from anywhere you need all the friends you can get . . . I'll go myself tomorrow.'

Before Bonnie turns in, she sits on the step of her caravan, cooling her face with a wet flannel, lights out so as not to attract insects. The night is alive with their trilling and clicking and croaking. Looking up, she is dazzled by the wide bright wash of the Milky Way, unfaded by city lights. For a moment, her heart contracts at a memory of dancing under moonlight, Stewart's smooth cheek touching hers, the feel of his arms on her back. She shakes her head. 'New start,' she whispers. 'Get thee to bed, Edquist . . .'

The next day, the thermometer Bonnie carries in her Land Rover tells her it's 115 degrees: she can feel every one of them, dry air burning her nostrils.

She walks along the edge of the dam, bigger than an Olympic pool dug into the earth; through binoculars she surveys the sparse, flat saltbush country all around. There isn't a breath of wind, so the mill stands silent, gasping for breeze to pump the water into the tanks and troughs, as evaporation inches the waterline downwards. The sheep that ran off at her arrival are once again dotted around the dam's edges, thirst overcoming fear. On top of the tank beside the mill, a butcherbird is perched, on the lookout for any lizard foolish enough to break cover at the hottest point of the day.

She got through the morning's search earlier than planned: the area she'd chosen was a dead loss: not a promising rock in sight. She's taken plenty of photos anyway – at least she can rule that place out. It'll be as hot as hell in her caravan, with no breeze, just the flies getting into her eyes . . . Better go and call in on the owners, let them know what's going on.

But . . . in front of her, the glistening surface of the dam is irresistible.

She ventures a few steps down the slanting side and scoops water to splash her face. Unlacing one dusty Kodiak boot, then the other, she peels off her sturdy black woollen socks. She unbuckles her old khaki army surplus shorts and lets them drop, already undoing her checked shirt as she steps out of them. Sweat trickles down her face, her neck, and she blinks it from her eyes. Gingerly, because the side of the dam is barbecue-hot and treacherously sloping, she edges down into the water, then lets herself drop into the delicious cool. The sheep *baa* in consternation, some trotting off in protest.

She somersaults, over and over, and swims around the boundary of the dam, grimacing at the sheep dags that have rolled down the sides, and here and there a ram's skull or a few bones where an animal has fallen when the water was too low to reach but too tempting to resist. She begins her old game of seeing how long she can swim underwater, then repeats the exercise over and over.

By the time she surfaces for the last time, the dam is echoing with the urgent bleating of sheep and she sees the butcherbird flee its post with a single flap of its wings, alarmed by some threat out of Bonnie's view.

30

MEREDITH DOWNS HAD inched its way through the decade after the crash, the new, strangely shaped MacBride family growing in the shadow of the one shattered by a lightning strike.

Matt's health recovered. The past receded. Over the years, he regained some sort of equilibrium. As though dumped by a giant wave, he gradually struggled to his feet. Matthew MacBride emerged as a quiet, introspective man, though friendly enough towards the station hands and people in town. He took over some of the roles on committees that Phil or Warren once held, which stopped him from becoming a complete hermit. A good bloke, people would tell you, though to guess his age from his manner, you might add ten years.

For Matt, there were still dark times. Still, sometimes, the poisonous knowing would race through his veins and he would feel sick and cold from his tingling scalp to the ends of his toes. He would shake with the nausea of it, at night, in his narrow bed.

But he wouldn't run away. This was the life he was in: an innocent boy depended on him. He knew, too, that Lorna's love for Andy, and Andy's love for them both, needed the special oxygen of ignorance to survive.

As for the boy who is beginning to stack up his little pile of years: during that decade, distance and isolation weave him a cocoon even more dense than that of other kids born onto remote stations. The few people who do cross the borders of Meredith Downs are kind to Andy MacBride. The paediatric nurses who fly in twice a year to check on him on their rounds are cheerful and encouraging; boundary riders bring him bilbies or baby quolls orphaned by dingoes.

By the time Andy's four, shearers let him flop onto the feathery fleeces piled up in the bins after classing, waiting to be pressed. On his mail round, Sneaky Snook starts to deliver him comics, and for his fifth birthday Pete Peachey fashions him a toy rifle out of mulga, a beautifully hewn and polished thing that the child carts everywhere, even to bed. Noticing Andy's fascination with the colour and feel of the rocks he encounters, Matt saves him any interesting examples he comes across, and passes on his childhood copy of *Junior Geology*. He makes sure, too, that the boy knows how to hold a cricket bat, how to bowl overarm, and that he understands the basics of footy (though Andy's first attempt at the word, with a misplaced 's', gives rise to Matt's nickname for him: 'Sooty').

He lies with him at night under the stars, showing him through field glasses the pointer stars to the Southern Cross, helping him identify Sirius and the ancient constellations that glide soundlessly over their night. Matt thinks of Rose as he explains how the moon waxes and wanes; how it's the same moon Andy's mum loved when she was little; how there's a side of it we can never see.

Andy's life is a far cry from how Matt and Warren and Rose grew up. He's never been shoved just to see if he'll fall over. He's never had to fight for his toys or his toffees; never had to defend himself against teasing or ganging up. So on the rare occasions he does encounter other littlies, Lorna has to give him a gentle push to play with them. For years, Andy is oblivious to another difference in his situation. Yes, his story books feature mummies and daddies, but they also have goblins and bunyips, and it's only by accident that Lorna realises, when Andy is about three, that he believes parents are fictitious. So she gently introduces the idea that he, too, once had a mummy and daddy, but that 'they're not here any more'. Even that young, the child can detect a change in her voice, a tightening in her neck.

If you watch a bungarra, those huge, muscly lizards that can give a racehorse a run for its money, you'll notice how they take in their surroundings. They don't just see and hear: they *taste* the air around them, slithery pink tongue venturing to test the atmospheric pressure, sensing for danger. Andy MacBride develops a similar skill. Without being aware of it, the little boy learns to sense the difference between those things it's 'safe' to talk about, and those it's not. Grandpa Phil, for example – that's OK. Lorna and Matt will recall tales about a habit of his, or a funny episode. They talk about Uncle Warren, and how sporty he was.

He's allowed to ask about his mum – within limits. Was she a good rider? Was she brainy? It's 'very sad', how young she died, Lorna says, 'taken from us too soon'. Sometimes she says, 'When you're older, you'll understand better,' and sometimes, 'There's not much to tell. She was a lovely girl, and would have grown into a good mother . . .' A kiss is always bestowed on the top of his head at that point, like a full stop. Or a keep-out sign.

By the time Andy is seven, he knows it's all right to ask Nanna Lorna about the Crash, but not Matt. 'Too many bad memories for him,' his grandmother says. 'If there's something you want to know about it, ask me, Beetle.'

It's not that anyone would ever get cross with Andy about his questions. It's more like when the barometer in the lounge room's dropping before a cyclone, and you feel the air change. That's what it's like if Andy mentions his father. Lorna will say, 'We didn't meet your dad, love, so I can't tell you much about him. I can tell you, though, that I'm lucky to have such a lovely grandson.'

As for Matt, he'll just touch a finger to the scar under his hair and say, 'Can't help you there, Sooty.' Or, 'I'm the last person to ask: after the crash my memory packed up for a while. Now, brush your teeth before bed and I'll come and say goodnight.'

The correspondence schooling Matt did as a kid had been replaced by School of the Air, which broadcasts lessons to far-flung pupils over the Flying Doctor radio. Listening to the teacher, and speaking into the wireless microphone when it was his turn, Andy began to devour information – the more exotic, the better. In a social studies lesson once, he heard that you train elephants by starting them off with a big heavy chain around their ankle when they're young: they try to break it but can't. As the elephant grows, the big chain is replaced with a lighter one, then with a rope, then a thinner one, until eventually, the creature is so unused to being able to break free, it can be kept just by a piece of string. Even Andy didn't notice how he gave up asking questions that changed the air pressure.

It was like sealing off the room in Sleeping Beauty's tower, which eventually got so overgrown that no one remembered there was a whole castle behind all those thorns. A *whole castle.* Let alone a sleeping princess snoozing away inside it for a hundred years. How could everyone in the kingdom forget that? But they did.

In September 1966, the countryside was still ablaze with colour from the wildflowers that show up after the bite of winter – vast swathes of pinks and violets, reds and blues that burst onto the landscape like fireworks, and disappear after a few weeks, though the season was late this year. A couple of new jackaroos were due to start shortly, living in the old manager's house where Miles Beaumont had once stayed. Sprucing it up for their arrival, Matt was accompanied by seven-year-old Andy, who had begged to help.

'Watch out for snakes and spiders, Sooty. It's been empty a while. I'm going to start on that stuck kitchen window.'

'What's my job?'

Matt cast an eye about, and from beside the concrete laundry trough picked up a few rags. 'You can be chief duster.'

In the lounge room, Andy ran a finger over the table, furred with dust, and smiled at the gleaming stripe he'd made. But when he started polishing, the dust just settled straight back. He soon got fed up, and went to explore the other shadowy rooms.

In the bathroom, he stood on the bath to reach the cabinet, where he discovered a little blue bottle of Mercurochrome. Under the dressing table in a bedroom he found a box of matches and a tortoiseshell comb, and a florin wedged between two floorboards. His search for stray marbles or comics proved fruitless: anywhere grown-up hands could reach had been picked clean. Behind the heavy chest of drawers his little fingers made out something flat, and managed to winkle it out: a photograph portrait of a man, in a uniform like the Queen's soldiers with the big furry hat and sword and boots. The writing on the back was beyond him, so he skipped back to Matt.

'Look at the treasures I found! Can I keep them?'

Matt turned from sanding the window frame as the boy laid the booty on the table and thrust the photo at him. 'Who's this?'

'No idea . . . Looks like a Grenadier Guard.'

'What does the back say?'

Matt read aloud, '"I'll miss you terribly, darling. And I'll wait. All my love always, Sandy xx".'

Matt's memory stirred. Something about Miles . . . Something about a 'Sandy' . . .

Andy put out a hand for the picture, but Matt said, 'I'll hang onto that, actually . . . And the matches. You can keep the rest. Let me know when you've . . .' He studied the photo. '. . . umm . . . finished the dusting.'

*

That evening, Matt took the photograph to the shed. *Sandy* . . . His memory must be up to its old tricks. He blew thick dust off the croquet set. Inside, there it was: the card he remembered – not a photo, but a sketch, like a greeting card for tourists. Identical writing. Identical signature. 'My darling Miles, Something to keep you entertained during your exile in the Colonies, and to remind you of our games together. They can't keep us apart forever. All my love, Sandy'.

When Miles had called himself a 'black sheep', Matt had taken it as a joke. Now, shock streaked through his body, then a sick sense of betrayal, of having been deceived by this man he looked up to – God, envied. All that time they'd spent together and Matt had had no idea.

The face in the photograph was young, good-looking . . . Matt cast his mind back to a conversation with Miles – something about both their lives having been edited. He put a hand to his head as things fell into place.

God knew what would have happened if people here had found out. Out this way they liked the rules kept to. Only last year he'd heard about a well-sinker working on a station eighty miles away, who'd been caught with one of the young station hands during a party for the shearers cutting out. Both men had ended up in hospital. One lost an ear. And nothing more was ever said about it.

His fingers trembled as he rolled a cigarette and lit it, then set light to both cards, letting them burn on the concrete floor. '*Yawa, yawa, yawa*' – from nowhere, the words appeared on his tongue. He stamped out the ashes, and headed back to the house.

31

For all that the world was changing in 1966, life in Wanderrie Creek was much the same as ever. The Bachelors' and Spinsters' Ball was still on the same weekend every year; Queenie Podger was still president of the Country Women's Association; Sneaky Snook was still the mail contractor for Meredith Downs.

There was, however, a notable alteration in post office staffing. Around the time Andy was helping Matt prepare for the arrival of the new hands, a Mr Clive Eedle was transferred to the Wanderrie Creek Post Office to get things shipshape after Old Elsie Twitchen's son turned out to have been stealing postal orders from his postmistress mother. It wasn't Clive who caused raised eyebrows, but his wife, Myrtle. And the problem wasn't so much her zeal in helping her postmaster husband with his duties, as an unusual habit she had, which soon earned her the tag of 'the funeral fanatic'.

No one ever called her that to her face, of course. But over a few sherries at the Wanderrie Creek Races a year or so after her arrival, a gathering of district matrons tried in vain to recall a single funeral at which Myrtle had not turned up. Most of these women had attended some of the funerals – everyone's someone's great aunt or godmother or former governess around these parts. But between them they couldn't recall even one that Myrtle, born and bred in the

Perth suburb of Mount Pleasant, had missed. Life, for her, seemed just one long opportunity to mourn.

Ideally placed to hear about the demise of anyone within hundreds of miles – what with handling telegrams and running the party phone line for those who had it, as well as having the ability to listen in on the Sched – she possessed dour frocks for every weather. Nothing above the knee, no sleeve higher than two inches above the elbow (a necessary concession to avoid heat stroke during the service. Some of those bush churches were barely tin sheds).

As to *why* she attended them – less kind souls speculated it was a sort of wish fulfilment to get rid of her Clive, who wasn't the most exciting man God ever put breath into, and whose psoriasis made him very difficult to look at some days. Whatever the reason, everyone knew that funerals are the one social occasion a person can respectably attend uninvited.

What people didn't know was that, where an order of funeral service had been printed, she archived it in dedicated desk drawers. On each pamphlet, she wrote shorthand notes about the manner and circumstances of death. Where there was no official booklet, she would make the notes in a little black leather notebook and slot the page into the archive. A casual shuffle through her 'Drawers of Death', as Clive called them, would reveal annotations such as 'Heart failure. Aged 90 so house already passed to children', or 'Shot herself with husband's .22 (he carrying on with cook).' 'Car crash (his fault).' 'Car crash (not her fault).' 'Died in labour leaving three children under five.' 'Fell down pub stairs*.' 'Died in sleep*.' Asterisks marked Myrtle's private suspicions, where it seemed to her that the truth was being glossed over or downright suppressed. In these cases, she conducted her own further enquiries, sometimes over a period of years: patient questioning at morning teas; casual enquiries to anyone buying a stamp. She was in no hurry. The thing about truth is that it will always wait.

She would ponder her mysteries in her garden, taking tender

care of her Lorraine Lee rose bush. Divulging her suspicions in a whisper, she would ask the plant, 'What do *you* think, darling?'

The MacBrides, so garlanded with death, held a peculiar fascination for Myrtle, particularly the story of Rose. From the moment she'd heard it, there was something about it that drew her in. Like a jigsaw puzzle made mostly of sky, it would take patience and time and observation, and Myrtle Eedle possessed an abundance of all three.

32

BY THE TIME Andy turned nine in December 1967, the Department of Health had long since stopped sending birthday cards to check on his weight and number of teeth. Any post for him from School of the Air was addressed to Lorna; Pete Peachey gave him the exotic stamps from his own mail, as he had done with Rose. But in the same way that Andy had once believed that only other people had mums and dads, he took it without question that only other people got letters. When he mentioned this over a cup of Ovaltine at the kitchen table with Sneaky Snook, a few weeks after his ninth birthday, the mailman tousled the boy's hair and said, 'Nonsense! What you need is a pen pal!' and explained how the system, promoted in 'Junior Corner' of the *Countryman*, worked.

It was with a great sense of solemnity that on his next visit, Andy handed Sneaky the letter to 'Junior Corner'. When Matt showed him the published version weeks later, Andy was beside himself at reading his own words, officially typeset – somehow proof that he actually existed:

Dear Uncle Bert,

I would like to have a pen pal please. My name is Andrew MacBride and I am nine years old. I live on a sheep station called

Meredith Downs, near Wanderrie Creek. My hobbies are rock collecting, cricket and sheep. If anyone would like to be my pen pal, please write to me at Meredith Downs Station, Via Wanderrie Creek, W.A.

'You've got to give it a bit of time, son,' Sneaky said when Andy accosted him on the next mail run. The following time, he said, 'Just because you haven't heard yet doesn't mean you won't. There's probably a kid just breaking his neck to write to you, but it's shearing time where he is, or they're in the middle of sowing or harvesting. Just sit tight, young fella-me-lad.'

Andy gradually gave up rushing out to ask, 'Anything for me, Mr Snook?' In fact, he had put the whole episode behind him as 'stupid' when, after almost three months, Sneaky finally arrived flourishing an envelope for 'Master Andrew MacBride'. It was marbled red with dust, and Andy raced to his bedroom to open it.

17 Ore Street
Mount Halcyon
Western Australia
10th April 1968

Dear Andrew,

I would like to be your pen pal please. I am eleven years old in November so quite older than you. I like rocks, and have a very good collection. I also like sheep. There are some very big sheep stations near here and I visited one once which was quite interesting. The shearing shed smelt a lot. I live in Mount Halcyon. My father works on the mine. They mine crocidolite, which is Blue Asbestos. It is a very important product for Australia.

When I grow up I will be a geologist or maybe work in the asbestos mine with my father.

A list of my best rocks is on the back of this page. What rocks do you have?

Yours sincerely,
Harry Badger. (PTO)

Andy raced to the kitchen. 'I've got a pen pal, Nanna! I got a letter – look!' He thrust it almost into Lorna's face. 'He's got some turgite and red-banded jasper.'

The last time she had seen Andy this excited was when he got Rascal as a pup. As she watched him show the letter to his dog and warn him not to dribble on it, something in her heart gave way for a moment. It was impossible to overestimate the thrill of the outside world making its way into your life here. The thought that Andy might really have a friend – a boy who shared his interests, his hobbies, gave her the courage to hope.

33

Every day, Myrtle Eedle scours 'the local rag', as she calls the *Wanderrie Creek Examiner*, and the *West Australian* when it finally arrives from Perth, as well as any other newspapers that happen to come her way.

She always starts with the Deaths and Funeral Notices, marking her diary accordingly. She keeps on top of town matters, too: the election of a new mayor; a fancy-dress ball sponsored by the Rotary Club; the results of a cake-decorating competition. She revels in a royal tour – no matter how minor the royalty or how distant the visit – and reads with delight about every vice-regal reception, or road lined with flag-waving schoolchildren.

Myrtle is especially keen on the court reports. She follows criminal cases, studying the eventual verdict, then the sentence – seeing justice done. Something of a bush lawyer, she can recite the penalties meted out by the WA Criminal Code. Murder won't get you hanged these days: technically it still could, but in practice it's commuted. Manslaughter – that's imprisonment with hard labour for life; rape and carnal knowledge, too. Incest will also get you locked up for life (if you're a man. Only three years if you're a woman). Doesn't matter that there was consent. Same for 'unnatural offences': you could get fourteen years hard labour, with a whipping.

If she spots a judge in town, dining in starched solitude at the Grand Imperial Hotel, she tries to imagine how it feels to sit down to beef stew and dumplings, knowing that you've just sent a man to gaol for the rest of his days.

Sometimes she weeps over a baby found lifeless at the hands of its drunken father, or a girl's life blighted by a rape. There's a strange comfort to be had in the tumult of others' experience, which lets her count her own comparative blessings. Clive Eedle's not the greatest catch a girl ever had. But he's kind and he's fair, even if his skin is on the flaky side and his breath's not as fresh as in the adverts. And he lets her keep her little notebooks, and doesn't laugh at her when she cries at the beauty of the winter blooms of her Lorraine Lee rose bush. Any one of the women who ended up on one side or another of the criminal trials Myrtle follows would be grateful for a man like Clive Eedle.

And when her thoughts reach this point, she fetches the *Golden Wattle Cookery Book* to hunt out something really tasty for his dinner.

34

ANDY KNOWS WHERE he's allowed to go in the homestead and where he's not. Lorna's strict about privacy: if a door's closed, you knock. You stay out of her bedroom unless invited. You mustn't touch Grandpa Phil's books unless she's there to check your hands are clean. You keep away from the old station diaries because they're important business records. And you don't touch the Family Fruit Crates.

Andy obeys these rules to the letter. As long as someone else is around. But when he's alone – if Lorna's busy in the orchard and Matt is out with some of the hands somewhere, say – then the lure of Rose's Fruit Crate, the ultimate shrine of 'Mum things', becomes overwhelming.

It holds treasures like Ramsey, the knitted sheep that's a pyjama holder; two dolls with eyes that blink if you shake them; her merit award for a poem called 'Jemima's Trees', written when she was fourteen. There's an old shellac gramophone disc: 'My Love Is Like a Red, Red Rose'. Andy especially likes her bible, bearing an inscription from a godmother he's never heard of. He likes the whisper of its fine, rice-paper pages, edged in scarlet and cool under his fingertips. Sometimes he pretends he's a vicar, doing blessings. Sometimes he imagines he's Jesus the Good Shepherd, being very knowledgeable about merinos and flocks, though he can't help noticing that the actual Jesus doesn't seem to know much about sheep, and never mentions shearing or the wool price. He hasn't even got a sheepdog.

These are top-secret missions: Nanna Lorna would be dark about it if she caught him, or worse still *disappointed*, so he explores a little at a time, replacing things exactly. Like scouting the coastline, he first gets the general sense of an object – a book, a box of hair clasps, a bag of knitting – then decides what's worth deeper investigation next time.

14th June 1968

Dear Andy,

Thank you for your letter. It is good to have a pen pal. Your rock collection is very good also. Expecially your tektites.

In this parcel is some crocidolite. It is like the bit of wool you sent because it has skinny fibres that you can pull into strands with your fingers. Asbestos is very important because it makes the world safer. It is used to insalate houses and also on engines of ships and also by scientists for filters that acid can't spoil.

The town I live in is new. There are approx. 600 people. My family is my mum and dad, my sister who is a baby and me.

Our town is the Pride of the North West. It says on the sign. All the houses have water and electricity. They are asbestos. The school and library and hospital are also. There is a swimming pool. When it is more than 105 degrees at school we are allowed to go home. What is the biggest temperature you have ever had? How tall are your sheep? Do you go to school?

Who is in your family?

Yours sincerely,
Harry Badger.

* * *

29th June 1968

Dear Harry,

Thank you for your letter of the 14th *inst.* [Sneaky had assured him that this abbreviation would make him sound very businesslike.] *I have put your crocidolite in my collection.*

Your town sounds good. It would be good to have a swimming pool. We swim in the dams if it is very hot. Or also waterholes and creeks. If they are not dry. It is sometimes 120 degrees.

Our rams are approx. 3 feet high at the shoulder when they are in the wool and the ewes and wethers are a bit smaller. Each sheep has approx. seven pounds of wool when you shear it. We run Shawsdale merinos which are good in dry country. There used to be Belders but they can be bad mothers and sometimes leave their lambs if they are frightened. My nanna says they are flighty and not worth the trouble.

I have a lot of rams horns and skulls do you want one?

My family is me and my grandmother Mrs Lorna MacBride and my uncle who is her son Mr Matthew MacBride. The MacBrides have been pastoralists since olden days.

Did your family come to Western Australia in the olden days too?

Yours sincerely,
Andy MacBride

* * *

15th July 1968

Dear Andy,

Thank you for your letter. My family came to Western Australia two years before I was born from Italy. Our name before was

Baggio but people could not spell it or say it so they changed it to Badger which everyone can say. My Italian first name is Ercole which is Hercules but people cannot spell that so I am Harry.

My dad used to work on the marble quarries in Carrara in Italy. When I am a geologist I might go there but I would probably go to the King Leopold Ranges in the Kimberleys first because the rocks are so old that there are no fossils in them so they have existed before life on earth which is good.

Do you have a mum and dad as well as your grandmother and uncle or are they dead?

I would yes please like a sheep skull.

Yours sincerely,
Harry Badger.

It was a cool morning in September 1968, not long after lamb marking, as Matt and Andy did a mill run on horseback. The sheep were back in their separate paddocks, with just a few weaners left to be separated from their mothers.

Matt rarely rode these days: doctors had warned that he couldn't risk a fall, and that a gentle trot from time to time was his limit. So it always felt special to Andy when his uncle took him out riding. Lorna had taught her grandson to ride and given him his own horse – Caramel. He wasn't a bad seat for a kid of nine, though he didn't have that knack that hers had from spending so long in the saddle that it was just another set of legs they put on of a morning. But the days when horses kept the whole show going were long past, and only a few remained, more as a tribute to tradition. Motorbikes meant that a handful of stockmen could flick around the paddocks to muster: as Matt explained to Andy, their machines never needed food or rest, never needed hobbling at night to stop them wandering off. And now, light aircraft could spot the sheep 250 feet below them, knocking even more time off the muster.

When they reached Poker, Matt and Andy stopped to give the horses a drink and have a look around, check everything was all right. Matt turned the water from the bore back on, now that most of the winter rains were finished, but wasn't happy with the flow. He tethered the mill to bring the squeaking sails to a standstill, and the water trickled to a halt. He fiddled with the rods, daubing on grease.

Andy sat on a rusty oil drum, watching Matt intently as he worked on the giant metal structure, which dwarfed him. It blocked out the sky above him and made Andy's skin cold where it cast a shadow: a forty-foot tower topped with a steel sail fourteen feet across, each of its blades six feet long, and its tail, just like every other mill on the property, branded with 'Southern Cross'.

Caramel's bridle jingled as she tossed her head.

'Did you do all the mustering on horses in the olden days, Matt?'

Matt laughed at '*olden days*'. 'Yeah, it was mostly horses when I was little.' He climbed down, retrieved the scrubbing brush from his saddle pack, and set to scouring the trough. Andy fetched a brush from his own saddlebag and started on the other side, scrubbing out silt and dead beetles and a matted bundle of feathers.

'What's the first thing you ever remember?' Andy asked.

Matt let his brush hang in his hand as he thought about it. 'I don't know if it's the very first thing, but I remember Rosie got an orphaned lamb, and I fed it from a bottle. I dropped the bottle and it tried to eat my ear instead.'

Andy squinted at his brush. 'Matt?'

'Yep?'

'If the thing you remember is called a memory, what's the word for a thing you forget?'

Matt gave him a look, then turned skywards to consider. 'Never thought about it. I don't actually think there *is* a specific word for a thing you've forgotten.'

'Is that because you don't remember you've forgotten it?'

Matt had heard so many medical discussions about the nature of memory: what gets forgotten, how the memory recovers, and what it recovers. A sick feeling washed through him. There were some memories he would never get back. And some he didn't want to. 'Good question,' he said at last. 'Let me know when you've got the answer.'

'I reckon there should be a word. *Forgetment*, say. A *forgetment* is the opposite of a memory.'

Matt turned the word over in his mind, contemplating the time when his life had been one big forgetment.

Andy traced 'forgetment' in the dirt with a stick, and added a question mark. 'Everything turns into a forgetment eventually . . . It's sad.'

'Maybe.' Matt swatted the flies away, and checked his watch. 'Maybe not.'

Andy echoed his uncle's gesture, aware that he had probably taken his questions as far as he could for now. If he pushed too hard, the shutters would come down, and Matt's mood would darken. So he quit while he was ahead.

35

NEAR THE END of September 1968, at the Perth Royal Show with Matt, Andy is allowed to wander by himself around the exhibits of produce and machinery, history and handicrafts. He loves the vast Wool Pavilion, with open boxes of pillowy fleece as far as the eye can see, some awarded ribbons, all with dust clinging to the greasy ends, giving a clue to where they're from: the dark grey-brown dirt from down south to the ochres further up and inland and the brick red of up north. He feels at home with the sticky touch as he stretches out the staples with a snap to test their strength, counts the tight crimps that make the finer fibres so precious. Unlike the city kids, show-bags strung along each arm, traipsing after their parents, Andy hardly notices the whiff of sheep dags that still haunts the wool.

Next stop is the Sheep Pavilion, where he sizes up the various breeds that have come from hundreds or even a thousand miles away (merinos are best: he won't be persuaded otherwise). He parts the fleece of an enormous Peppin ram to feel the heat of the creamy white wool underneath, and carefully closes it over again so that the surface fibres stick to each other and seal the coat. He inspects the hooves, the big frame, the enormous pendulous testicles like a balloon filled with water, and the fat folds of wool cascading from the animal's chest, all of which features have earned it a bouquet of rosettes, including Grand Champion Ram.

He's looking forward to lunch with Matt in the Members' Pavilion, all starched tablecloths and silver cutlery and ladies in frocks, so he's been making a big effort not to wipe his hands on his trousers.

The Royal Show is a time for country kids – the ones who haven't started boarding school in Perth yet, or won't be going – to make new friends, or catch up with old ones. They might know each other from their regional cricket or tennis tournaments. Or they may have tuned into the same lessons on School of the Air. And station people tend to marry station people, so there are often relatives floating about. In fact, there's another MacBride at this gathering, a second cousin or something, still in his riding gear from the polocrosse display match he's just played – his team from the Kimberleys against one from the Goldfields. Sixteen, surrounded by his mates, he's older than Andy by seven years, and not interested in mixing with the 'little kids', as Andy's heard himself described just now when he said hello.

Andy tries to think of something to talk about: something that will sound grown up. 'Do you get many tektites up your way?'

'Who cares?' says the cousin, Johnno, and laughs with three or four older boys from his team.

'We get tons of them,' says Andy. 'They're really interesting. Don't you reckon? That they've probably been in actual outer space, and then they end up getting licked by sheep?' At the stony silence, he tries again. 'Do you get any fossils?'

'Well, Gran's pretty old,' cracks Johnno, and Andy gives the laugh that seems expected of him, though he doesn't think it's as funny as the others apparently do.

Andy offers his hand to the first of the other boys. 'I'm Andy MacBride. I'm a sort of cousin of Johnno.'

'"Sort of"' is right,' smirks Johnno, and gives a slight sideways nod towards Andy.

The friends look at Andy, then back at Johnno, and one of them laughs: 'So this is the one that buggered the MacBride pureblood lines.' The others chuckle.

'I don't get you,' says Andy.

The oldest of the group says, 'They always said you MacBrides could be bastards.'

When Johnno practically doubles over to show how funny this is, Andy says to the friend, 'We're not bastards. We're very friendly when you get to know us.'

He thinks he's pulled off the joke because the others laugh uproariously, but Johnno says, 'Get your granny to explain what a bastard is, mate.' Then, turning away slightly, 'You're going to need to understand.'

'I know what a bastard is,' Andy blurts. 'And an – an arsehole. And a . . . a shithead. I bloody swear all the bloody time!'

The older boy cackles. 'I never said you were a shithead, just a bastard. The MacBride bastard . . .'

None of the group had noticed Matt approaching.

'You right there are you?' Matt asked him, then turned to his cousin with a quick dip of the chin: 'Johnno . . . These kids giving you trouble, Andy?'

'Who's this?' the older one demanded.

With a slight squeak, Johnno replied, 'This is Matt, Andy's uncle.'

'That all right with you, son?' Matt asked. Without taking his eyes off the youth, he asked Johnno, 'What's his name?'

'Ah – this is Greg Crimp. He's from up—'

'Crimp,' Matt cut in. 'You'd be Geordy Crimp's kid, would you?'

'What if I am?'

'*Geordy Crimp* . . . Now, why do I remember that name?' Matt mused. 'What is it I heard about him not so long ago?'

A change came over the boy's face. Beneath his freckles, his face turned a scarlet you'd never have guessed it could manage, and Matt said, 'Glass houses and stones, Greg. And your aim's pretty shithouse.'

The others had now switched their attention from Andy, trying to decipher whatever it was that Matt and Greg Crimp held in the tense space between them.

Matt broke the silence. 'Right, Andy, time to head off. But before we go, Greg wants to apologise to you.'

Crimp's head jolted back.

'Don't you, Gregory . . .'

'Why?' asked Crimp.

'Because if you don't, my memory will get better. I'm pretty sure it was something really interesting that your dad had been up to.'

The boy looked at Matt, but couldn't hold his gaze, and turned his eyes to the dirt at his feet. 'Sorry.'

'That's OK,' said Andy with an innocence that made Matt's heart hurt. The little boy put out his hand to shake Crimp's. 'See you next year maybe.'

To Johnno, Matt said, 'You should be really proud of yourself.'

As they walked towards the car park, Matt braced himself for the inevitable question. 'Matt, isn't "bastard" just a swear word for a nasty bloke? Like, you know, "you bloody bastard"?'

'Well, yeah, in slang, Soot. But "bastard" actually means something else too. I'll explain later. But don't let the likes of Johnno get to you – they're just deadshits.'

That November, as Andy works through the sums in his CPM textbook, Lorna casts an occasional eye in his direction from Phil's old desk. The days when her kids' correspondence lessons used to arrive in a hefty bundle by post at the start of each term seem a lifetime away, along with the struggles to keep the children at their desks at mustering time, or when one of the sheepdogs had pups. Then, for a second, it's as though her three are still right there: happy, scruffy larrikins, with their lives ahead of them.

A few more years and Andy'll be off to boarding school at Scotch. He's quick and diligent – just like Matt was. Such a lovely little boy. When she gets to that point, the other feelings flood back, the other thoughts: it should be Rosie enjoying these moments with him. It should be Rose who's filled with pride at his report card, or at how he's mastered the art of casting Rascal out to the balance when they're working a mob of sheep. Rose is missing out on the loving of him, and he of her. Then Lorna strays further into darkness: how could her daughter have abandoned this little boy, who's rubbing an eye as he concentrates on a sum? But of course it wasn't just Rose: the boy's father had a lot to answer for, driving her daughter to do such a thing . . .

There had never been any reply from Miles. There are no answers to be had, probably never will be. She turns to her grandson. 'Right-oh, sixteen times tables, please, for ounces, then fourteen, for pounds. Off you go.'

Homework done, Andy comes to pore over his favourite things on Phil's desk: the bayonet that serves as a letter opener, the army compass as a paperweight. He lifts it, watches the little bubble float about in the liquid under the glass as the needle bobs giddily. About to put it down, he asks Lorna what the paper under it is.

'Just the brochure from Mr Flintgrave at Shawsdale Stud. You know, the chap we buy our rams from. Shows the dams and sires,' she says, and explains the importance of the bloodline in maintaining a consistent flock.

Like any bush kid, Andy knows the facts of life: they're hard to avoid in a world that depends on the arrival of lambs and calves and chook eggs at the right time, but he's never thought about it like this. He thinks back to his recent visit to the Show and the enormous grand champion ram he'd patted and inspected, with all its rosettes. A shadow crosses his face as he remembers Johnno's friend, and the crack about '*the MacBride pureblood line*'. When he'd asked Lorna whether he had to say he was a bastard, she'd told him just to say he was an orphan and leave it at that.

*

Lorna knows nothing of the project Andy starts that afternoon. So far it features just him and Rose, and Lorna and Phil, on the dam side, with all the spaces on the side of the sire blank. Whether he's colouring in rainfall maps for geography, or out exploring with Rascal, throughout the days his mind drifts to that blank space, and he works on his handwriting to make sure that when there is a name to put in, he will be able to write it beautifully, so that his father will be proud.

The early January trip to town had become something of a ritual for Lorna and Andy. When it came around in 1969, Matt, as always at that time of year, was busy with the hands getting the last of the rams into the ewes' paddocks. This left the coast clear to shop for Matt's approaching birthday on the twelfth. Lorna had bought him a new shirt, and Andy had chosen a bottle of aftershave for him on the basis that its plastic lid was in the shape of a cowboy's head, and therefore of indisputable quality. Lorna had kept to herself her opinion that it smelt like sheep dip.

'Right,' she said, 'see you at the library at two, Beetle,' and headed into the sparkling white CWA building, in time for the committee luncheon.

Flies droned in the heat, and Andy's palm sweated around the twenty-cent piece his grandmother had given him to buy an icy-pole before visiting the cool, jarrah-panelled municipal library. But today he was busy, and strode straight past the milk bar, resisting the clack of its doorway curtain of colourful plastic strips that kept the flies out. He hurried on to his destination near the town's edge.

The low iron gate of the graveyard squealed as he entered. Tombstones jutted from the bone-dry earth at drunken angles. Desiccated grass surrounded a few graves, and all were caked in red dust, their marble cracked, the inscriptions of many lost to the years. Even on blazing days like this, a breeze seemed to whisper amongst the headstones, above the criss-crossed lizard tracks and the shallow gulleys where thunderstorms had lashed the ground and left scars but no water.

A crow's mournful caw – like an *Ah, bugger it!* – ricocheted off the headstones into the barren paddock beyond. As Andy approached its gravestone perch and sat down, the bird flapped away.

At that moment in Wanderrie Creek, you could find people having a beer or a fight or both. You could find women laughing and men weeping, government clerks writing and bookkeepers adding. You could find an old woman dying while a daughter sat beside her reading a book; kids in back yards playing skippy and knucklebones and skittles. Miners washed the dirt from their backs while their wives scrubbed it from their dungarees; men argued over the price of a wool press or the pros and cons of mulesing. There was probably at least one proposal of marriage being made, and several more of a less permanent nature being accepted or rejected. But of all the activities being grappled with in that town on that day, no one could have guessed Andy MacBride's.

When a skink skittered out from behind the gravestone, Andy took it as a signal to finish his conversation with a Mr Bertram Culloch (1916–1960): '. . . so that's what I came to let you know,' he told the lichened granite slab.

He stepped over the low iron railing around the grave and cast a finger about the plots. 'Eenie, meenie, minie, mo . . .' The rhyme ended on a Mr Theodore Dearlove, another stranger, and Andy wandered over and sat cross-legged, facing the gravestone.

'Hello. There's something important I've got to tell you.' He was trying for a gravity somewhere between Sir Robert Menzies and the man on the Movietone newsreel. His heart beat faster as he said,

'You don't know me. But you knew my mum, Rose. She died just after I was born. Maybe you called her Rosie . . . Anyway. What I've come to say is: you're my dad.' He paused, to let his tongue taste saying '*you're my dad*' out loud – in broad daylight. It felt like running around with no clothes on. The feeling of it, the touch of the consonants on his tongue: these were not words he could speak in front of another living person. He had made sure not to sound sad. Or sissy. No one was going to want a son like that. 'Anyway, I just wanted to introduce myself. Very glad to meet you.' He left Theodore Dearlove (1934–1965) to his own devices, perhaps to swap glances of astonishment with his fellow grave dwellers.

At his mother's grave, he paused to pull a caterpillar off the angel. He wondered what she looked like now, there but gone. His mind turned to other people he'd known who disappeared – folks who drifted through, pitched camp for a while, or turned up as a bookkeeper or a shed hand or boundary rider and then vanished forever, without warning or trace. It was like that with his mum. She'd lived lots and lots of days, but there was nothing left of them; of her. It was all part of his theory of *forgetment*.

Looking it up after his talk with Matt, the dictionary told him there was no such word, as did his English teacher from School of the Air. Andy, however, was sure this was just an oversight, because forgetment was everywhere – you only had to think about it: all those ancient languages with funny writing no one could understand now, or civilisations people 'discovered'. They were just someone's everyday life once.

And maybe his dad didn't have to be a forgetment.

36

Saturday, 11th January 1969

ALL MORNING ON their mill run, Andy has been getting Matt to try to guess what he's giving his uncle for his birthday tomorrow. An elephant is Matt's latest suggestion.

'Too hard to wrap,' says Andy.

As their ute pulls up at the dam, the sheep scurry off like a school of fish, following their leader down the side and off into the scrub.

'Who the hell—?' Matt exclaims at the sight of a parked Land Rover.

Rascal leaps off the tray and dashes up the side of the dam, followed closely by Andy. By the time the boy reaches the top, the dog is sniffing a pile of folded clothes.

Andy is astonished: something's moving under the water. He's vaguely hoping *crocodile*, though he knows it can't be. The thing emerges to take a great gulp of air.

A lady.

With *no* clothes on. Not even undies.

He is transfixed.

She sees him and gasps. She tries to cover her body, but he watches her discover that if she does that, she can't tread water. Her face is as red as a Santa suit.

They stare at each other for a second.

'Uh, hello . . .' the lady calls.

It's Matt who responds, appearing over the dam's edge. He squints. 'You right there?' When he tells Andy to wait by the car, the kid throws him a look and scampers away.

'Hello . . .' the woman says.

'Um – afternoon.'

'I – didn't hear a car.'

Matt looks away, a flummoxed hand on his head. 'Mind telling me what you're doing in our dam, miss?'

'It was so hot . . . I—'

'Actually, better get dressed first. I'll just . . . Rascal! Come, boy.'

'I – They—' Before the woman can splutter an explanation, Matt has disappeared, leaving her to clamber out. She towels herself with her shirt, pulls her clothes on, and hurries down to her car.

'I'm *so* sorry,' the woman began. 'Are you one of the owners – the MacBrides?'

'Matt, yeah. You lost or something?'

'No.'

Matt frowned. 'Where are you headed?'

'Here. Meredith Downs.'

His fingers gripped a cigarette. Should he have been expecting a visit? He didn't recognise this woman – slim, blonde; hair in a ponytail and long tanned legs showing between her shorts and socks. 'Did you tell us you were coming?'

'Seems not. I was on my way to introduce myself, let you know where we'll be working. We've set up camp out near your eastern boundary fence.'

'You've what?'

'I should have explained. I'm with Hollamby Mining. Bonnie Edquist.' She held out a hand to shake.

He drew on his cigarette; tried to unjumble his thoughts. The occasional fossicker was one thing. Even a lone prospector didn't worry him too much. But Hollamby Mining was the big league.

Plenty of other properties in the district had been invaded by bloody miners. It had only been a matter of time before someone turned up here, but it was still a shock.

He asked to see her Miner's Right. If she had that, there was pretty much nothing he could do to stop her.

'I haven't got it on me, but the whole crew's covered by a consolidated Right.'

'"The whole crew"?'

'Just a small team of geologists at the moment.' She pulled a folded map from her pocket and pointed to the spot, assuring him she hadn't seen any stock in the paddock.

'That doesn't mean much – that paddock's twenty thousand acres. But as it happens, no, there shouldn't be any stock in it at the moment. What are you looking for, anyway?'

Bonnie shifted her weight to one hip. 'Won't know till we find it . . .'

'Well whatever it is, you're not going to find it in our dam, are you? Poor bloody kid didn't know where to look.'

'Sorry,' she said to Andy, then to Matt: 'But what are the chances of anyone coming out here?'

'Higher than you seem to think. It's a *dam*.' Matt glanced at the sun and checked his watch. There was nothing he could do about this right now. He needed time to think, talk to his mother. 'We're behind on the mill run. Andy,' he said, and gave a nod toward the windmill.

Rascal scrambled to the boy's flank, and Andy picked up the toolbox, mumbling a faint 'Bye . . .'

'Right.' Matt took a breath. 'Get your boss to call at the homestead and explain.'

She took off her sunglasses, squinting at the glare. 'Actually, I *am* the boss.'

*

As Andy tethered the sail, ready for Matt to climb the mill, Bonnie's Land Rover started with a growl and receded into the distance.

'Why were you so crabby to her, Matt?'

'She's bad news, Soot. She's a miner.'

'What's wrong with miners?'

Matt picked up the wrench. 'Miners and sheep don't mix.'

'How come?'

'Because any so-and-so can buy a licence called a Miner's Right for fifty cents and call themselves a miner. Then they can waltz onto our property, do a bit of paperwork, and start digging a bloody mine. Right in the middle of a paddock.'

'But this is *our* place. They can't do stuff without our permission, can they?'

'It's complicated, Soot. Basically, we lease our land from the government, and miners' rights to get what's *under* the ground beat ours to use the surface.'

Andy drew Rascal close to him, circling his arms around the dog's neck. 'But – but – fair go!'

'Nothing fair about it.' Matt rested on his haunches to explain to the boy how the rules were made for the goldrush days of small-time fossickers and prospectors. Nowadays, big mining companies hauled in drilling rigs and bulldozers that could leave the station's fragile roads unusable. 'And if they peg a claim on prime pasture, near good water, then our stock can't use it.'

'What's pegging a claim?'

'They hammer in posts and dig trenches at the corners to mark land they want to use. You hear about them chopping down trees; cutting fences that are in their way . . .'

'But the stock'd get out!'

'Exactly. And they buggerise around with water.'

The encounter with the stranger had rattled Matt, and his words tumbled out unchecked. 'Jack Birchmere from Quondong caught a mob of drillers doing their washing in one of his sheep troughs – water was undrinkable.'

Andy scowled.

Matt went on almost to himself, 'They put down bores, but sometimes move on without sealing them, so sheep can smell water they can't reach, and hang around and die.' He reconnected the rod that had become detached from the mill head. 'Or they can get stuck in the claim trenches if they're dug too deep. The miners can lodge as many three-hundred-acre claims as they want.'

The boy looked out to the horizon, doing the sums, then turned worried eyes on his uncle. 'They can't take our whole station, can they but?'

Matt thought of Termite Plains, where practically the entire place had been pegged for nickel a year ago, leaving the Brevany family with a homestead and a useless rump of salt lake and not a penny of compensation. He only said, 'Let's hope not.'

Andy turned the spanner in his hand over and over, torn between the excitement of having *actual geologists* on the property, and the fear they could destroy his home.

'Will I be able to watch them do their exploring and stuff?'

Matt's face darkened. 'Steer well clear.'

'Will they definitely start a mine here?'

Matt wiped sweat from his forehead. 'Not definitely.'

Sidling up to him, Andy put a hand on his shoulder. 'Nanna Lorna always says not to meet trouble halfway. And the lady seemed nice.' He passed him the spanner, and gave him the bravest smile he could manage.

A day later, Bonnie Edquist stood in the shade of the homestead verandah. Snatches of 'Daydream Believer' drifted out from a record player somewhere while she waited for her knock to be answered. She hoped the broad brim of her hat hid her blush at the memory of the episode at the dam.

Matt opened the door, his smile vanishing as he recognised her.

'Nice hat!' said Bonnie. 'Having a party?'

Matt snatched off the shiny cardboard party hat Andy had insisted he wear to blow out the candles on his birthday cake. He looked at it in surprise, then threw it behind him.

Seeing she wasn't going to get an answer, Bonnie said, 'As promised,' and from an envelope addressed to 'Miss Bonnie Edquist, Head Geologist', drew out a copy of the Miner's Right, bearing the seal of the Mines Department. Matt inspected it, checked it was current, and handed it back.

She tucked it into her pocket. 'Look. You must already know mining's going crazy. If it's not us, it'll be someone else turning up. We're local, but we're not running on the smell of an oily rag – we won't be cutting corners on the regs. And we like to be good neighbours.'

'What, by setting up camp without even coming to tell us you're here?'

Bonnie held up a hand. 'Bad start, I admit, but I've read the boys the riot act. We know you're running a business.'

'We're running our *home*.'

'Of course. I understand.'

'I doubt it . . .'

Matt recalled an old joke about the real money being not in *geol*ogy but '*near*ology': the best chance of finding a mineral was pegging a claim next to a known body of ore. If this lot found something, the world and his wife would pile in straight after them.

Beneath his anger, Matt sensed something else. How many years had it taken to build a safe, quiet life here again? How soon would this bloody woman wreck it?

'We'll respect your stock, your fences, your water points,' Bonnie was saying. 'The boys all know to leave gates as we find them. We've got a better track record with pastoralists than most other miners in the state.' She smiled. 'And yes, I've heard the stories . . . No washing our socks in your sheep troughs . . .'

Matt ignored the joke. 'And you're looking for what, exactly?'

Bonnie pushed her hat down a little. 'Hard to say.'

Matt gave her a look.

'Might be any number of things here. We've looked at the aerial photos and the aeromagnetics. The magnetometer map looks promising, but until we get our hands and knees dirty, we're just guessing. Galena, copper, manganese, columbite . . . You're probably outside nickel country, but you never know . . .'

Footsteps sounded from the hallway, and Lorna, also in a party hat, opened the flywire door. 'I *thought* I heard a car earlier . . .' She turned to Matt for an explanation.

'This', said Matt, 'is apparently the head geologist from Hollamby Mining. The ones who are looking to peg the place.'

'Did you say "*head* geologist"?'

'I'm Bonnie.' She extended a hand to shake Lorna's. 'Beautiful homestead.'

'It does for us,' said Lorna. She breathed in the burning air. 'You'd better come in . . . have a cup of tea.' As an afterthought, she added, 'And the bathroom's just at the end of the hall.' There were certain rules of bush hospitality, miner or no miner. 'Andy's disappeared to his cubby with Rascal, Matt. You coming in?'

'No. I'm off to check on that fence at Joker.' He grabbed a bunch of keys from the hall table. 'I'll get out to your camp after that, Miss Edquist: check the gates and fences. And the troughs.'

Heading off, he passed her parked Land Rover. Brand new and, under the dust, emblazoned with 'Hollamby Mining' and the logo of a wombat.

Bloody wombats. They'll dig under any fence out Nullarbor way. But it's the animals that follow them in through the holes that cause the real damage.

37

MYRTLE AND CLIVE Eedle at the post office weren't the only new faces in the officialdom of Wanderrie Creek. For some time, there had been rumblings from the higher-ups in Perth about Sergeant Wisheart, the town's senior police officer: running things his own way; turning a blind eye too often; not bringing in enough in speeding fines. So, at the end of 1968 they'd given Wisheart a gold watch and a pension, and imported from Subiaco Sergeant Benedict Rundle, complete with permanent-press shirts and a ginger moustache.

Benedict Rundle was never 'Ben', not even to his wife, Janine, who accompanied him with their son Gavin and daughter Pam in their brand-new Holden Premier station wagon with venetian blinds in the back, in time to enrol them in Wanderrie Creek Primary before the new school year started in February of 1969.

A year in the bush ('Rural Posting') was required for Rundle's CV on his way to the top, and he'd dodged it as long as he could. Armed with degrees in law and statistics from the University of Melbourne, he was the 'new face of policing': the WA government was keen to standardise the enforcement of law around the state. So, no more missed revenue opportunities by letting locals off a fine, or waving through a gun licence a few weeks after it should have been renewed. This place had been the Wild West for long enough.

'Statistics', Rundle likes to tell Gavin, 'are useful not just because they tell you what's there, but what's missing.' At this point, Gavin, who's heard this before, usually takes a break from the press-ups he's doing beside his father, who'll continue his speech without losing his own count. His dad won't notice that he's stopped, propped on outstretched arms, wrists tilted backwards.

'Sure,' Rundle continues, 'folks are different from one place to another . . . But fundamentally . . . people are people . . .' At each pause he's a few inches higher or lower. 'They don't change that much. So . . .' He takes a breath and squeezes out the next words: 'If you turn up in a town and find that no one is ever fined for, say, driving without a licence, what do you do?'

'You interrogate the numbers,' recites Gavin.

'Exactly. You interrogate the numbers . . . And if the rates of reported drink-driving are eighty per cent lower than in the last cop-shop you were at, what do you ask yourself?'

'What are the chances!'

This conversation had been carried out in one form or another since Gavin was old enough to count the peas on the tray of his high chair. A father should have an interest to share with his son, after all. And statistics were Benedict Rundle's interest. Within weeks of arriving in Wanderrie Creek, sifting through the old records, he found himself asking more and more frequently, 'What are the chances?' Speeding fines seemed virtually unknown in the shire during the reign of Sergeant Wisheart. And no one ever seemed to have driven without a licence in his time. A lot of the other paperwork was pretty sketchy, too.

Funny thing was, once Rundle set up his own speed trap, the numbers started to fall back into line with the average for country districts of WA. When, on two consecutive Tuesdays, he checked the licences of everyone driving down the main street, he discovered that fifteen per cent of them didn't actually have one. 'Things were a bit tight,' they'd mumble, and they had to save money somewhere, and Wisheart had always been a good sport on that score. But in Rundle's book, if they could afford a car, and the petrol to go in it, well . . .

People soon learned to be careful about what they let drop when the new cop was within earshot, including the fact that 'Sergeant Rundle' was swiftly contracted to the nick name 'Trundle'. They parked further from the police station if they had bald tyres or a broken indicator light. They took the back roads after a night on the turps. Nonetheless, arrests for being drunk and disorderly shot up, as did fines for selling liquor to minors.

One or two draft dodgers, mistakenly believing that fleeing to the arse end of nowhere would keep them safe from being called up for national service, fell into his net, and ended up shipped off to fight in the Vietnam War after all.

Even Benedict Rundle, however, knew he had to pick his battles, so he let the town's brothels tick along (a hundred years of mining tradition couldn't be undone overnight). Besides, they kept undesirables off the streets, and kept *respectable* women safer. Prosecutions for 'unnatural acts', however, soon saw an increase: he picked up men for carrying on with each other, or with sundry fauna (both crimes were covered by section 181 of the Criminal Code, he liked to point out), some instances being deemed so serious that they were tried in Perth, with the perpetrators ending up in Fremantle Gaol. Abortions, incest, bigamy, 'the whole moral sewer', as he put it to Janine over rissoles and mashed potato one evening, needed dredging. 'Just because these people live in Woop Woop, doesn't mean they can behave like savages.'

Late at night, he'd sit alone by the radiogram and listen to his classical records, reminiscing about his student days in the Melbourne University Choral Society and picnics on lush lawns and trips to concert halls. He just had to stick this place out for a year. Then he'd be back in the city. Only Perth, but that was just about a city, anyway. And he'd wipe the dust off the record cover that had settled just in the time since he'd taken it out, and take solace in the cello solo.

38

TWO WEEKS AFTER her arrival, Bonnie again braved a visit to the homestead, bringing the company's latest annual report, and some brochures for investors. Lorna thanked her, and laid them aside before pouring tea.

Perched on the edge of the sofa, Bonnie took in the lounge room: the family photos going back years, the big grandfather clock, the piano. She reached into her bag. 'I . . . also brought something our lawyers put together . . .'

Matt came in as she was speaking, and Lorna offered him tea.

'I'm right thanks, Mum.' He turned to Bonnie. 'Lawyers?'

'It's – it's just a sort of summary, about what we're allowed to do. So that there are no surprises. I don't know whether you've had much experience with mining companies . . .' She handed a thick letter to Lorna, but Matt intercepted it, and started to scan it.

He read the words "from the 1904 Mining Act" aloud. '"The holder of a miner's right shall, subject to this Act and the regulations, be entitled (except as against His Majesty) (1) to take possession of, mine, and occupy Crown land for mining purposes . . ."' He glared at Bonnie.

'It's best if we all know where we stand. Nothing personal.'

'This says you *can't* occupy land where there's a dam or a bore. Section 28 (4).'

Bonnie pursed her lips. 'Actually, if you read a bit further, you'll see we can't do it "without paying compensation".'

Lorna reached out a hand for the paper. 'We'll have a word with Neil Tinnett about it, Matt.' She turned to Bonnie. 'Was there anything else?'

'Actually, I was wondering if we might be able to come to some arrangement about supplies. Is there any chance you'd sell us some fuel? You've got better storage facilities than we have.'

'Why would we do that?' asked Matt.

'We'd pay you a premium. Say, ten per cent?'

'That's still less than you'd have to pay to get it to your camp,' he said.

'Fifteen per cent?'

Lorna said, 'I think we could arrange that . . .' Matt threw a dark glance at his mother, but she hadn't finished. '. . . with an agreed limit, and payment in advance.'

'Great.' Bonnie pushed on. 'And – would you consider selling us meat? We haven't got a fridge, so probably just some butchered cuts now and then.'

'The lawyers' letter doesn't mention any right to our sheep,' said Matt.

This time it was Lorna who frowned at Matt. Usually, they happily *gave* meat to visitors passing through. It wasn't as if they were short of it . . . 'We can probably work something out.'

'And if you give us a map of your tracks and paddocks, and mark where your stock are, I'll make sure we stay as far away from them as we can.'

Matt and Lorna exchanged a look.

'We don't keep spare maps just lying around,' said Matt.

'Actually, I brought one with me,' said Bonnie. 'Maybe you could just mark on that with a pencil?'

Lorna took it from her. 'Leave it with us.'

Driving back to her camp, Bonnie totted up the wins and losses. A yes on fuel (that was big), a maybe on meat, and an unlikely on ungazetted roads on the map. Damn: she'd meant to ask if they needed anything brought back from town tomorrow. 'Always make yourself useful if you can' was her philosophy. They must know a hundred ways to make her life difficult, Mining Act or no Mining Act. Her peace mission hadn't been an unqualified success, but they hadn't marched her out of the homestead at gunpoint, either. Could have been worse.

An uneasy truce developed on Meredith Downs. Other than to collect fuel or meat occasionally, the miners kept themselves to themselves. The paddock they were working in was being spelled. For weeks, Matt and the hands had been caught up repairing fences on the other side of the property, forty miles away, and contact had been limited.

Taking a shortcut back to the homestead one afternoon in early February, Matt did a double take and pressed on his brakes: there was the rangy figure of Bonnie Edquist, leaning against her Land Rover. Its front had been staved in by a tree, thanks, she explained, to a blown tyre on the ungraded dirt track that just about passed for a road.

'What the bloody hell were you doing here anyway?' demanded Matt.

'Just having a scout around.'

'Snooping for promising formations . . .'

'Well, it *is* my job.'

'You realise you could have been here for days, don't you? Could have died of heat stroke. If I hadn't taken this shortcut . . . It would have been *our* problem if something had happened to you.'

'I've got plenty of water, some food. The boys would have come looking eventually.'

But her voice was shaky, and Matt studied her more closely. 'You're bleeding.' He gestured to her neck. She reached a hand around and her fingers came back sticky red.

'Did you pass out?'

'I – I don't think so. But I didn't notice this,' she said, examining the blood. 'And I don't remember . . .' Her words trailed off as she slid downwards and Matt grasped her arm.

'You all right?'

She had already blacked out. Matt lowered her to the ground and slipped his hat under her head. 'Miss Edquist? Bonnie? Can you hear me? Oh, for Pete's sake!'

Fetching the first aid kit from his ute, he also grabbed a jerry can, and raised her feet on it. 'Come on. Back you come . . . Bonnie?' He put two fingers to her neck, and his gut relaxed as he felt a pulse, clear and strong. He brushed her hair back from her face and trickled some of the water from his waterbag onto her cheek, bringing her around with a start.

'That's better.' He was about to offer more encouragement when she turned and vomited on him, drenching his shirt and his jeans as he knelt. 'Bloody hell!' He surveyed the result with a grimace.

'Oh God!' Bonnie groaned.

He leaned in, observing her pupils; got her to follow his finger to her nose, wiggle her toes and fingers.

'It's just my neck . . . I can barely turn it.'

He dressed the cut, then held the waterbag to her lips. 'Drink some water.'

She took a few sips and pushed it away.

Matt splashed water down his shirt and jeans, wiping off vomit with an old towel.

'Better get you to our place. You all right to stand up?'

Bonnie pushed a hand on the ground to raise herself, but collapsed. Squatting down, Matt put an arm under her knees and shoulders and hoisted her up, carrying her the few steps to his ute, sliding her carefully onto the seat, then went to check her car. As well as the blown tyre, the radiator was buggered, and the front axle. He hauled out the water bottles and her shoulder bag and laid them by her feet. 'Right, let's get a move on.'

Turning the key, Matt's hands froze as splinters of a memory surfaced: a sunny morning; the smells of a fully laden sheep truck; a glimpse of the back of his father's neck, criss-crossed with deep lines from the sun. He gave a quick shake of his head, like a dog flicking off water.

They headed off down the red, red track, the car jolting on the stones and shuddering over the corrugations. 'I'll radio the Flying Doctor when we get back. You might be concussed.'

Bonnie protested, but she had grown paler. 'I feel a bit sick.'

Wary of a repeat, Matt touched the brakes a fraction. 'Shall I stop?'

'No. I think it's – oh, actually it's you. You smell of sick.'

Matt wound his window down further to let the smell out and the dust in. He fell into a silence, tapping the steering wheel with a finger now and then. Glancing over after a while, he saw Bonnie's eyelids were getting lazier with each blink. 'Right. Just talk – out loud, so I know you're still alive.'

'About what?'

'Anything . . . First thing a doctor would ask you: what's your name? What's your date of birth? What day is it today? Where are you? Who's the prime minister?'

'Uh-huh.' She closed her eyes, silent.

'Well, come on. Name.'

'For goodness' sake . . .'

'I'm serious. Full name.'

'Bonnie Elizabeth Edquist.'

'Date of birth?'

'Third of February.'

Matt glanced at her. 'No, the date's the *next* question. When's your birthday?'

'Third—yes, third of February.'

'Your birthday's today?'

'Is it?'

'Is what?' asked Matt, wondering who was more confused.

'Is today the third of February?'

'Was this morning.'

'Then it's my birthday.' Bonnie closed her eyes a moment, considering something. 'Ha! Yep. Definitely my birthday.'

'Happy birthday,' said Matt. 'Turning out beaut so far . . .'

'A real doozy. You haven't asked how old I am.'

'Not sure I'm supposed to ask girls how old they are. Anyway, don't want to strain your brain.'

Bonnie tried to turn to him, but couldn't. 'Is that an insult?'

'More what the medics call a cognition test. To see if you can tell it's an insult.' So? Keep talking. Miles to go yet.'

When she suggested he talk and she'd listen, he pointed out that that would only prove *he* was awake. He flicked a crusader bug off the window frame. He didn't want this bloody woman on his station, let alone in his car, but she'd be an even bigger problem dead. 'Tell us about – oh, anything. What you were looking for today.'

'Just getting to know the ground. Signs of what might be underneath.'

And so they drove on, mile after mile, surrounded by stunted trees, joined by the occasional fly or grasshopper that blew in, or splattered against the windscreen. Bonnie talked about her crew; her job at Hollamby Mining, whose owner, Sir Reginald Hollamby, Matt knew, was a millionaire with operations all over Western Australia. She told him about her geology degree; her family (omitting the fact that Sir Reginald was her uncle); how she lived with her parents in

Peppermint Grove; why she refused to learn how to sew. To all of these, Matt nodded, or gave an occasional 'uh-huh', until she said, 'I'll just grab a catnap.'

'No you don't.' Having run out of questions, he remembered something a nurse had once asked him in rehab therapy. 'What's your hidden talent?'

'What?'

'Like a party trick – something you can do that no one would expect.'

Bonnie thought about it. 'I can peel a banana with my toes. Does that count?'

Matt actually laughed, and gave her a sideways glance. 'Oh, that *definitely* counts.'

'What's *your* hidden talent?'

'The point is for *you* to talk, not me. Do your fourteen times tables for me.'

And so she began on that, faltering, it had to be said, until, as shadows stretched long in the thick honeyed light, they drove through the gates to the homestead.

When Bonnie woke the next morning, daylight was leaking through the curtains, and she gradually pieced together where she was: the previous day; the prang. She vaguely remembered Lorna, instructed over the wireless by the Flying Doctor, checking her for fractures, re-dressing her cut; asking about pain, whether she felt dizzy or sick. The advice had been to keep an eye on her overnight, in case of a mild concussion.

Bonnie screwed her eyes tight and opened them again: no, she hadn't imagined the figure of a boy sitting in an armchair on the other side of the room, staring at her. She stared back.

'That's Nanna Lorna's nightie.'

Bonnie checked. She was indeed wearing a nightie.

'I'm Andy. Matt's my uncle and Nanna Lorna's my grandma.' At the question on Bonnie's face, he said matter-of-factly, 'My mum was Matt's sister but I'm an orphan now.' He looked down at his bare feet. 'We—um – we met at the dam.'

'Oh God!' said Bonnie. 'How long have you been sitting there?'

'An hour and twelve minutes. Nanna and Matt took it in turns in the night. The doctor said you needed to be "observed" to make sure you didn't stop breathing or choke on your vomit and stuff. I took over so Nanna could cook breakfast.'

'Ah. Well, thanks.'

'*Are* you going to vomit? Or choke?'

'I hope not.'

'Good,' said Andy. He wiped his palms on his shorts. 'Head Quiz is a very unusual name.'

'Pardon?'

'I've heard of Bonnie before, but not Head Quiz.'

'Ah. It's *Edquist*, not Head Quiz . . . But that's not the strangest version I've ever heard.'

'Are you going to bulldoze our fences and take our best pasture?'

She blinked. 'Well, we won't bulldoze your fences. We might discuss putting in gates, maybe. As for your best pasture – minerals don't ask permission for where they turn up, I'm afraid.'

After a silence, Andy said, 'I've got a rock collection.' He folded his arms. At Bonnie's puzzled look, he repeated more clearly (perhaps the crash had made her deaf), '*I have got a rock collection.*'

'That's what I thought you said,' she replied, her fingers exploring the dressing at the back of her neck.

'Aren't you a geologist?'

'Yes.'

'Isn't that rocks and stuff?'

'Yes, that's rocks and stuff.'

The boy gave a short nod. 'So, have you got a rock collection?'

Bonnie thought for a moment. 'I collect rocks all the time – that's what I'm doing here.'

'I mean your *own* rock collection. Treasures and that.'

'Yeah. I've got treasures. Loads.'

'What sort?'

'Gosh. Where do I start?'

'Top three,' Andy shot back, as though it were a well-established convention.

Squinting with the effort, she nominated a piece of banded breccia, a sample of arsenopyrite in the middle of a quartz crystal, and a big piece of botryoidal chrysocolla with azurite.

Andy nodded approval, and asked how she decided what was a treasure.

'Hmm. Sometimes because they're rare. But sometimes because of where I found them or who I was with. Some are presents . . .'

'Huh,' said Andy, and it was impossible to tell whether he approved or not.

'What about yours?' Bonnie asked.

'Mine's mostly stuff from our station. But I've also got quartz and zircon and gold and a little emerald. I've got tektites. Wanna see them?'

'Sure.'

'I'll go and—'

'Um, maybe not right this minute . . .' Her head was killing her, and she was trying to figure out the ramifications of the prang and how the hell she was going to get anywhere.

'Oh,' Andy said, as grown up as he could. 'Another time . . . I'll go and tell the others you're not dead.'

39

SERGEANT RUNDLE HAD frequent cause to visit the post office, what with the summonses that had to go by registered post, or the telegrams to Perth.

'All quiet on the Western Front, sergeant?' Myrtle would ask, somehow reassured by his stern face.

'Satisfactory,' he would respond.

As the weeks went by, Myrtle's enquiries progressed to: 'Settling in well?'

'Satisfactorily.'

'And Janine and the youngsters?' She'd met the wife in the grocer's several times, and seen the children riding their Malvern Stars up and down the main street, gradually accumulating friends.

Rundle gave her a sharp glance, and a fine muscle in his cheek flickered. 'They're well, thank you.'

Myrtle beamed at the breakthrough.

'Starting to feel like a local?' Myrtle asked the sergeant one Thursday in early March.

'Still finding out who's who and what's what.'

She slid him a form to sign. 'Let me know if I can assist in any way on that score. Always happy to help.'

'I see.' He straightened the pen on the counter. 'Barry Hapwell, from Saltbush Gulley Station. You get much mail for him?'

'For Barry in particular?'

'In particular.'

'Well, I'd have to say no. He's one of those hippie types. Spends most of his time in Perth.'

'Never gets mail from the university? Nothing to indicate he's studying?'

'Not that comes to . . .' Myrtle worked out where this was going. '. . . mind.'

'Seen him recently?'

'No.'

'You know he's been called up though.'

'I'd gathered as much.' The mustard-coloured envelopes for National Service were unmissable, and she had indeed put one for Barry in the Saltbush Gulley mail bag a while back.

'His mother's claiming he's eligible for student deferment.' Rundle scratched a fly speck from the glass on the fading Annigoni portrait of Her Majesty on the wall beside him. 'Good sorts are they, the Hapwells?'

'As far as I know.' (No asterisks about them in the Drawers of Death.)

'Well. If you see Barry about, let him know I'm looking for him.' He slipped his letter into his pocket, then with a nod consulted his watch. 'Afternoon,' he said, and strode out into the street, the door swinging closed behind him.

That afternoon, Myrtle was manning the fort alone. Strictly speaking, she wasn't a PMG employee. But any wife worth her salt helps her husband where she can, and Myrtle could often be found minding the counter while Clive was at a Roads Board meeting, or out inspecting termite damage to telegraph poles.

Sitting in the back of the post office, sorting the mail, she tutted as she assessed the badly torn wrapping on some packages that had fallen off during unloading. She cast a glance at her great roll of brown paper and its sharp slicing edge: perhaps she should rewrap and relabel the worst of them? Getting a peek at the contents barely crossed her mind as she set to work.

So . . . Mrs Swincer was buying romantic novels again . . . Things must be bad out there on Bilby Rock. Young Rupert Threlkeld had got not one but *two* toy trains for his birthday. She felt a twinge as she imagined the little boy playing with them, and moved swiftly on: she quite liked this new frock of his mother's . . . Of course, she could run it up herself on her Singer for a fraction of the price: more money than sense, some people.

The final parcel intrigued her. Postmarked Melbourne – a flattish rectangle that would usually mean a dress or some such – but feather-light. It was upside down and the torn paper exposed a box with '*George's of Melbourne*' – the monogram of the famously swish department store. She checked the time. Another half an hour before Clive was due back. At two o'clock on such a hot afternoon, no one in their right mind would come to post a letter, and even if they did, they'd just ring the counter bell.

Moving of their own accord, Myrtle's hands opened the box to discover layers of tissue paper cradling something frothy in azure satin. A negligee of crêpe de Chine, with organdie silk across the bust, fastened by a cream satin ribbon. She gasped. Myrtle Eedle, wife of a postmaster, owner of nine different mourning dresses, had never in her life even seen such a delicate garment, let alone held one. She longed to put it to her cheeks, to her lips, but her powder and lipstick ruled that out.

Under another sheet of tissue lay a matching nightdress. She blushed. But those shoestring satin straps: surely they wouldn't last a single night's sleep? Useless . . .

In some far recess of memory or imagination, an old, deep sensation awoke in her, and she quickly banished it.

She turned the item this way and that; stroked it; sniffed it; ran it over her forearms, barely conscious of her rapid pulse. Only when she held it against herself did she discover it was for a much taller woman, with a bigger frame: more the size of the station women she served. *Strapping*, that was the word for them.

She checked the address label: 'Meredith Downs Station'. That Lorna MacBride! Too old for nonsense like this, surely . . . Myrtle recalled the wistful smile that came to Lorna's lips whenever she mentioned her late husband. She pictured Lorna's frocks, and imagined her in this. Impossible! But there again, Myrtle Eedle knew better than most people that you can't tell what's really going in someone's life from the outside. The thought stabbed her, and the texture of the delicate fabric took her fingers back to a long-ago touch of the softest lambs' wool bonnet, barely bigger than her hand, and the younger self that had crocheted it with such care. She shivered, and muttered aloud, 'Pull yourself together like a sensible girl!'

Folding the lingerie painstakingly back into its nest, something made her glance at the label again. Below the Meredith Downs address, in small print was: 'Attn P. Peachey Esq.'

Myrtle reached for her glasses, and read again, but the name remained the same. She polished the lenses, as if it would help her understand. And it did.

Good Lord! The dark horse . . . Her mind raced at the possibility, and she immediately recategorised Lorna's smile from the wistful to the illicit. Then she reconsidered: it wasn't *necessarily* Lorna MacBride he was carrying on with, but in all likelihood it must be a station-owner's wife. Or daughter. She conjured Peachey's image: lanky, athletic, quiet. He did have a certain – *magnetism* . . . Or could it be one of the girls in the brothels here in town? Much more their sort of work attire, after all, she said to herself, recovering her composure, and disconnected that thin electric current of memory that had made the back of her neck tingle. Mr Peachey . . . Well she never . . .

She considered the letters and money orders he occasionally sent to Queensland. Never seemed to get any replies. Didn't say much, Peachey. Rarely attended funerals, and didn't look like he'd be having one himself any time soon, so she'd never paid him much attention before: didn't know a thing about him. Now, she made a little note in her black book, and went about rewrapping the box.

40

ON THE NOTICEBOARD of the Wanderrie Creek Warden's Office, pages fluttered like butterflies trying to escape the drawing pins that anchored them against the March breeze. The requirements had long been the same: peg a claim in the ground in the country round about, fill out the form stating its exact location in degrees and minutes, and stake your claim for specified minerals. For decades there had been a handful of claims a week, but lately there were dozens a day, festooning the noticeboard and the walls beside it.

Once a claim was duly advertised in the newspaper, and the fees paid, unless an objection was lodged it would be granted, and marked on the district registry's map, which was periodically sent to Perth to update the central record. The job of mapping those rights fell to the Mines Department's busy cartographers, one of whom, a Lawrence Niblock (MSc (Geog.) UWA) now sharpened his pencil almost to a needle, which he rested on the thick paper in front of him while he consulted the date on his desk calendar, then printed it neatly: '3rd March 1969'.

He checked the claim at hand: an area in a paddock on a pastoral lease in the shire of Wanderrie Creek. He applied his pencil to the map.

When the English arrived, the Australian continent was already home to probably at least half a million people, spread across three-million-odd square miles. Classifying it as 'practically unoccupied', the colonists were apparently unable to detect an existing legal system, so declared the entire land mass *terra nullius*, and imported English law lock, stock and barrel. Rather like the illiterate, they could see, yet not interpret, what was in front of them. For the land, though not marked by man-made borders, was intricately bounded by law and custom and tradition, described in hundreds of complex unwritten languages by people belonging to highly evolved groupings with connections to specific areas: all of which facts were, in 1969, largely lost on the Mines Department, and indeed the Land Registry.

This piece of land under the pencil of Lawrence Niblock had, in the last century or so, magically become 'property', now owned by 'the Crown in right of the State of Western Australia', and leased to pastoralists for up to ninety-nine years at a time. Both immediately before and after this, the paddock itself looked not so different from how it had looked for thousands of years. Yet at this pencil stroke its very nature had changed. This wasn't achieved just by Lawrence's whim. He was the instrument of a legal mechanism that crossed oceans and millennia: rights in *real property*.

He checked a number on the memorandum, and drew a line. It always struck him as a kind of alchemy: by the precise application of graphite, without his leaving his padded leather drafting stool, hundreds of acres of bush had just changed their very nature.

The cartographer inspected the three-hundred-chains-to-an-inch cadastral map of the relevant pastoral lease – sheep, most probably, out that way – its paddocks entered in an elaborate hand on the map of the Department of Lands and Surveys. This was the information that was stored. Not the feel of the red, fine soil, the tang of the saltbush on the wind, the thin call of the wedge-tailed eagle high, high above as it carried a tiny joey to its nest for its chicks; not tales of how the constellations above it were birthed in the timeless Dreaming. Just the measurements, the water points, the names of the registered rights holders, and the fees they had to pay, on pain of forfeiture.

Leaning forward, he interrogated his handiwork under a magnifying glass: the land was captured.

He yawned, and transcribed the claim details into the register, complete with the folio reference, the date, the survey fee, the shire, the plan, and the exact location of the claim, checked it again, then put the map into the out tray, ready for dispatch to the Government Printer.

Just as the MacBrides' right to occupy Meredith Downs had once been conjured on the map, suddenly, a right to enter and explore beneath its surface had been granted to a mining company. Now, a mineral claim was granted to Hollamby Mining Ltd for cobalt, copper, nickel, molybdenum, rhodium, palladium, iridium, zinc, lead and asbestos. It was all settled.

41

In 1969 Wanderrie Creek is busier than it's been in years, thanks to the influx of mining companies from around the world, with outfits big and small pegging nickel claims. There are more men drinking in the pubs – the drillers who pull out the core samples and the truckies who haul up their equipment; the boffins who come and go, opining on whether what comes out of the ground is any good. Some top brass even swan in by helicopter. The only pastoralists not moaning about a mining boom exploding on their properties are the ones who were canny enough to peg the first claim. Shopkeepers and pubkeepers and petrol stations are happy enough at the turn of events, though.

'Rome wasn't built in a day, Bonbon,' Sir Reginald Hollamby said, when Bonnie apologised for initial poor assay results. 'You can't *put* the stuff in the ground. Just don't miss it if it *is* there. Wait too long to peg a claim and some other bugger will have beaten us to it.' And so, as the weeks passed after her prang, her team had carried on, with Bonnie occasionally returning to Perth to report in.

According to the locals who had dealings with her in town – at the assay office; at the Warden's Office; at the chemists' who sent off her pictures to be developed – Bonnie was a friendly type, smart, but easy to get along with. And it didn't take long for the grapevine to pass on the fact that she was Sir Reginald Hollamby's niece. This meant she was immediately accused of getting the Head Geologist job because of her connections: a woman really couldn't be up to it.

When Bonnie came to drop in a cheque for fuel in March, Matt was out, and it was Lorna who wrote her a receipt, and offered her a cup of tea. As she was finishing it, Andy appeared at the door to the lounge room, one hand holding the other elbow, silent.

'Hi,' Bonnie said.

'Hello. Nanna Lorna, can I show Miss Edquist my rock collection?'

'I'm sure she's very busy.'

'I'd love to see it,' Bonnie said. 'If it's all right with you, Mrs MacBride.'

Lorna was far from thrilled about the idea of the woman traipsing through the house, but the excitement on Andy's face pricked her. When else was the poor kid going to be able to show it to anyone?

'Please?' said Andy. 'At least some of it?'

Lorna yielded, and Andy led Bonnie down to his room, where he had already arranged his best samples on the floor, including a large array of tiny black specimens, some shaped like small marbles, some like buttons, and some like miniature dumbbells. None was bigger than an inch or two.

Bonnie reverently inspected each of them, before declaring, 'That is, by a country mile, the most impressive lot of tektites I've seen outside a museum, kiddo.'

Blushing, Andy evened up one of the rows. 'I like all the rocks, but tektites are the most exciting.'

'Are they from around here?'

He nodded, and she asked, 'And you know the name for Australian tektites, don't you?'

'Australites!'

'Yep.' Bonnie examined one with the magnifying glass. 'How did you get them?'

'People bring me them.'

'People don't usually just give away tektites.'

'Pete Peachey – he's our roo shooter – brings them. Or some of the hands. And neighbours and that.'

'Lucky you!'

Andy carefully wrapped another one back in cotton wool. 'It's cos they feel sorry for me.'

'Sorry for you?'

Andy's tale of his mother's fall at the mine, delivered in a matter-of-fact tone, left Bonnie floundering.

'I never really knew her, so I can't really miss her.' He went on packing away his collection. 'I sort of miss her a bit now, though . . .'

'Of course . . .' This was not Bonnie's domain. People didn't usually stray into the deeply personal when discussing their rock collections. And she discussed rock collections a lot. There'd been no mention of his father, though she recalled his saying he was an orphan . . . She steered onto safer ground, handing him the last sample. 'Tell you what, I'll make sure that if the boys turn up any tektites, we save them for you.'

Andy's face fell. 'Means you feel sorry for me too . . .'

'It means I *like* you. And I remember how much I loved it when my uncle's people would bring me finds. That's how I got my bit of arsenopyrite in the quartz crystal that I told you about. It's still the thing I'd save if my house were burning down. My *Prime Sample*. What about you? What would you save?'

Andy squeezed his eyes shut for a moment. 'It's not a rock. I'd save Ramsey. It's a toy sheep that's a pyjama holder. From my mum's

Fruit Crate.' He frowned. 'I'm not supposed to play with the stuff in the Fruit Crates, so don't tell Nanna Lorna.'

Though stumped at whatever his *'mum's fruit crate'* might be, Bonnie mimed zipping her lips. She smiled. 'You're a funny little bloke, aren't you? An old head on young shoulders.'

'Is that good or bad?'

'Oh, it's good, mate. Definitely good.' In the distance, Old Wally struck the hour. She held up fingers red with dirt. 'Better go and wash my mitts.'

Andy was left considering his collection with a renewed pride. This lady understood it, in a way that even Matt didn't. It was a funny feeling. There were so many more things he wanted to talk to her about.

As Bonnie was saying goodbye to Lorna, Matt came in, greeting her with a wordless frown.

'Just settling up for the fuel,' said Bonnie.

'Right.'

'And Andy's been showing me some of his rock collection. So impressive!'

Matt gave her a look. 'That's a bit low, isn't it?'

'What do you mean?'

'Trying to get information out of a little kid?'

'He was showing me tektites. We're not exactly going to start mining *them*!'

Matt felt the heat come to his cheeks at having jumped to the wrong conclusion, and mumbled an 'Oh . . . '.

That evening at the dinner table, Matt said, 'Soot, watch what you say to that Bonnie Edquist.'

'She's really nice.'

'For all I know, she is. But it's bad enough having her lot holding a rifle to our heads. Don't hand her the ammunition for it. Remember, she doesn't know nearly as much about this place as you do, so be careful what you tell her about which of your samples came from where.'

'I thought Andy was pulling my leg just now,' Bonnie told Matt a week later. 'He said I'd find you in "Monty's shed", and when I asked him what that was, he said "The one with the boat in it"!'

Matt clambered down the ladder from the deck. 'What can I do for you?'

'I went to see your mother. Thought maybe while we've got the drill rig here, you might want us to put down a bore or two for you. She said to check with . . .' Her words trailed off as she took in the line of the bow, the gaff-rigged sails, the height of the masts. 'Is that . . .' She turned to him. 'Is it a pearling lugger?'

'Yep,' said Matt, surprised at the accurate identification.

'A long way from Broome, isn't she?'

'Yep.'

When it was clear he wasn't going to elaborate, Bonnie said, 'Pretty shallow draught.'

'Big tides up that way – means she doesn't topple over when she's beached at low tide.'

Bonnie ran a hand along the varnished timber. 'Brings back memories.'

'Of your days as a Master Pearler?'

She coloured at the sarcasm. 'Of sailing – that smell . . . the varnish, the oil.'

'So, the map?'

Bonnie pulled it from the satchel slung over her shoulder.

He examined the pencil marks, and some printing he recognised as Lorna's. 'I'll look tonight.'

'Don't leave it too long.' Bonnie surveyed the boat again. 'Not bad condition, considering.' She rested a hand on the keel. 'Do you look after her yourself?'

'Yeah. Sort of a family tradition.'

She walked around to the other flank. 'You know I've got to ask. What the hell's she doing *here*?'

Matt gave her an abridged version of Monty, his bet, his fate.

'Ever think of sailing her?'

'One day, maybe . . . Her seams have split, being out of the water so long. She'd have to be recaulked; eased back into the water very gradually. Huge job . . .'

'Pretty landlocked here: do you know how to sail?' At Matt's expression, she asked, 'Where'd you learn?'

He told her about starting at school, eventually building up to ocean racing. 'Crewed on the Bunbury and Return once.'

At the mention of the gruelling 170-nautical-mile race, from Fremantle down the coast to Bunbury and back, Bonnie said, 'I've crewed for that on my uncle's boat.'

'I thought girls weren't allowed?'

'Technically. But my uncle tends to get his own way . . . I had to earn my place though – "No passengers", as he always says. I still remember the swish of the hull through the moonlight on the water . . . Getting a bit too close to breakers on reefs . . . Terrifying. But worth it.'

'Sounds about right.'

Bonnie tugged one of the ropes, working on a thought. 'Most people have to worry about protecting their boat from the salt and the wind and the waves – from *using* it. But *you* have to protect yours from *not* using it – dust and white ants; dried-out timber. Probably takes *more* effort.'

Matt lit a cigarette. 'Might as well do this now.' He checked the map again, then gave a nod. 'They look OK. Thanks.' He handed it back. 'If there's nothing else . . .'

'I'll get out of your hair.' Bonnie started to leave, but turned back. 'If you ever get her into the water, I volunteer to crew.'

'I wouldn't hold your breath.'

Grumpy sort of bugger, thought Bonnie as she drove away. Still, miners could hardly expect to be welcomed like Old Home Week. She watched the enormous shed dwindle in the distance, and shook her head. A pearling lugger! . . . You could hide just about anything on a place this big.

42

A WARM EASTERLY was gusting down the main street of Wanderrie Creek when Sneaky Snook parked his mail truck behind the post office. Clive Eedle had opened the big back doors, and gave a wave. As Sneaky hoisted the canvas cover of his truck, Lightning appeared at the tray, tongue stretched out.

'Out you get, old fella. Bar's already open,' said Clive, pointing to a basin of water by the door, and the old dog made his rickety three-legged landing to set about lapping noisily.

'I've got a couple of registered letters to sort out before you go, Sneak. Myrtle'll fix you up a cool drink. She's in the garden with Lorraine Lee,' Clive said, repeating an old joke, and headed back into the office while Sneaky arranged the load in delivery order of the properties along his route, pulled down the tarpaulin and went through to the back yard.

Myrtle turned from snipping a spent rose. 'Morning, Sneaky.' She threw the dead flower onto the compost heap and slid her secateurs into the basket by the door as she came in. 'Have a seat,' she said, fetching a jug from the fridge.

'Lorraine Lee thriving?'

Myrtle smiled. 'As ever.' She poured two glasses, and sat opposite him at the table. 'So . . . what news on the Rialto?'

Sneaky grinned at Myrtle's habitual question. 'You know: the usual.'

They chatted about the Millers' kids, just getting over chicken pox; about the state of the roads. When Sneaky mentioned that old Arthur Glew's funeral was planned for Tuesday, Myrtle jotted something on a notepad that materialised from her apron pocket then vanished.

The mailman's eyes wandered to a batch of biscuits cooling on a rack.

'Where are my manners?' Myrtle exclaimed. 'Shortbread?'

Sneaky patted his tummy. 'Won't say no.'

She slid a plateful in front of him. 'And how are things at Meredith Downs?'

'They actually had a decent shower or two a week ago. Country's looking good.'

'That reminds me: I popped a parcel for Mr Peachey into their bag. He's still out that way, isn't he?'

'Far as I know.'

Myrtle twiddled one of the little yellow pompoms that fringed the tablecloth. 'He's a dark horse, that one.'

Sneaky gave a look that neither agreed nor disagreed.

'I'd like to meet his wife . . .' said Myrtle.

Wiping his fingers on his trousers, Sneaky turned with an expression that invited more detail.

'Or perhaps it's a girlfriend . . .?' Sneaky said nothing. 'Girlfriend, then . . . Well . . . I can tell you, because you're really PMG too. Let's just say that some lucky lady's getting a very nice present.' At Sneaky's look, she added, 'His parcel came undone. I had to rewrap it.'

Sneaky sipped more squash.

'I was trying to work out who the lady might be. I can't think of any women out that way who aren't married.' She checked for any chink in Sneaky's expression. 'Unless of course . . . Well, none of the *girls* thereabouts would be old enough to be interested in a man Pete Peachey's age . . .' She looked directly at the mailman: 'Would they?'

'Search me.' Draining his drink, he slapped the glass on the table. 'Delicious. Thanks. I'll go through my day a happier man!'

When he was safely gone, Myrtle opened her notebook again, this time doodling all around the word 'Peachey' with question marks of various styles.

43

STANDING IN THE shade of the homestead verandah, Matt examined Bonnie's map. Marked in biro were two new bores, which would bring up precious water, sunk by Hollamby Mining, in return for not lodging an objection to their claim. In truth, Lorna and Matt hadn't had much choice, knowing Hollamby could outspend them in any fight in the Warden's Court.

'Glad we could help,' said Bonnie.

Matt couldn't quite bring himself to thank her, and just nodded. 'We'll start putting up the mills tomorrow.'

Old Wally's chime reminded him: better grab lunch. He had to join the boys fixing the lighting plant for the Home Shed. 'Goodby—'

He was interrupted by the loud rumble of Bonnie's stomach, and she reddened. 'Skipped breakfast.' The gurgling came again, louder.

Matt found himself saying, 'Stay for lunch if you want.'

Bonnie hesitated.

'It'll just be a sandwich. Mum and Andy are in town.'

They settled in the wicker chairs at the old table on the back verandah, enveloped in the solid silence that Bonnie still hadn't got used to, even after all these weeks.

She took a bite of the sandwich Matt had made her. 'So good to have a change from Spam and tinned stew.'

'You'd soon get just as sick of mutton and chutney sandwiches, I can tell you. When you're out on a muster and they've been in the sun, or warm from the horse, they turn to mush inside the foil.'

He answered Bonnie's questions about mustering, due to start in April, ready for shearing in May; explained how these days using a plane to spot the stock cut down on time. He couldn't tell whether she was genuinely interested, or just trying to steer him away from questions about Hollamby's plans.

He topped up her tea. 'Your brochure mentioned crocidolite. What's that?'

'You'd probably know it as blue asbestos.'

'Thought it rang a bell. Andy's got a pen pal in Mount Halcyon. Didn't know you found it anywhere else in WA.'

Bonnie gave a pout. 'Maybe no one's looked hard enough. Mount Halcyon's just about been worked out. And the price is in the doldrums.'

'And you reckon it's in this new claim you've pegged?' asked Matt.

'If we don't include it in the claim and it's there, someone else can bag it. But as for finding it – if you could tell from just the aerial geophys and a look at the surface, I'd be out of a job.'

She pushed her empty plate away and sat back, taking in the land that stretched before them. The expanse almost had a density to it. 'A million miles from how I grew up: the neat suburban block and all that. *You've* got to drive for hours just to get off the property . . . Must be a pretty hard life.' She crossed an ankle over a knee. 'Maybe it's different though, if you always knew you'd take over the station.'

'Wasn't supposed to be me. I thought you'd have heard about . . . There was – a crash . . .'

'I – I had heard: about your dad and your brother and sister—'

By reflex, Matt said, 'Rose didn't die in the crash.'

'Andy actually mentioned . . . a fall. Sorry. Didn't mean to get into . . .'

Matt gazed intently at the cigarette he was rolling, and when he finally spoke, it was more to himself. 'I was meant to be the one that got away . . . Go to uni, or build boats or make maps . . . Sail around the world . . .'

'You still could, couldn't you?'

'Not – not until Andy's old enough to take over, or to decide he doesn't want to. Mum couldn't run this place by herself – she's getting on. And she'd never leave . . .'

Bonnie stood and swept the crumbs off her shorts. As she pulled her car keys from her pocket, Matt said, 'Hang on.' Returning with the map, he sketched in a broken line to a road that came out near the Hollamby camp. 'That's a fairly reliable track. Only dirt, but it'll knock a few miles off your drive back.'

Bonnie thanked him, and chalked it up as progress.

As Matt watched the dust trail from her car, he was aware of an odd feeling. He wasn't used to talking about himself. And he couldn't quite work out why he had – to Bonnie Edquist of all people.

44

'NO, I WON'T reconsider it,' said Sergeant Rundle, arranging his police tunic on its cedar hanger and slotting it precisely into place on his side of the wardrobe.

'But the poor kid's heartbroken,' said Janine. 'Surely you can do something? You're his father, after all.'

'I *am* his father, yes.' Rundle buttoned the mustard permanent-press shirt that signalled his return to the domestic realm. 'But I made my decision in my capacity as his hockey coach. He's just not up to the standard of some of the other boys, Janine. He hasn't earned a place.'

'It's only a game, for goodness' sake.' His wife handed him his end-of-day glass of beer, but he put it on the bedside table and went on working away at some scuff marks on the shoes he'd just taken off. 'It's not as if he's a draft dodger or something,' she said.

'I thought *you* of all people would understand . . . This is exactly what I've been up against ever since I got here. That attitude: "The rules are for *other* people." Well, where would the world be if everyone thought like that?'

'You're making a mountain out of a molehill, darl,' said Janine.

'Molehills have a way of turning into mountains all by themselves.' He consulted his watch: time to attend to the stamps that had arrived in that day's post. One or two rather interesting South American ones would nicely fill a lacuna in his collection.

As Rundle marched to the lounge room, Janine processed behind with his beer, and sat opposite him at the table, where he laid out his album, magnifying glass and philatelic paraphernalia. She put the glass on a coaster and pushed it towards him with a fingertip. 'Come on, love. It hasn't been easy for Gavin: new town, new school. He's heartbroken not to be on the team.'

'For the last time, Janine: I don't *make* the rules, I *uphold* them. The only reason Gavin should be on the hockey team is merit. How much respect do you think he'll get – *I'll* get – if everyone can see that he's only there because he's my boy? If people know I'll bend the rules for my own family, they'll be quite entitled to want me to bend the rules for theirs. Barry Hapwell . . . that draft dodger . . . his mother was in tears – *hysterical* – when we arrested him. Called me an unfeeling brute. And worse.'

'I'd probably have done the same,' said Janine. 'Damned ridiculous system, the birthday ballot. How you can bring yourself to dob those poor kids in, I don't know.'

'Like Churchill said about democracy, "It's the worst system except for all the others." My brothers didn't get a choice about whether they went to fight in the war.' He glanced at a photo on the mantelpiece of three boys in army uniform. 'Keith didn't ask to die in El Alamein. They were called up and they went.'

'What's that got to do with the price of fish? I'm not asking you to fight a ruddy war for Gavin.'

Rundle slapped the album shut and stood up. 'It starts with one little thing like this. A little bending of the rules. A little favour. And before you know it, you owe someone something. You owe it to them *not* to do your job where it concerns *them* . . . We fought a war not so long ago so that you didn't get ahead just because you were a member of a particular party, and you didn't get gassed because of the particular way you prayed to God. For Pete's sake, we're fighting one right now so that we don't all have to become members of some communist collective and recite bits of Mao's Little Red Book! My part of this war is to enforce the rules that our *freely elected government'* – he jabbed the table with his finger at each of these words – 'has put in place. And that starts with . . .' He took a breath. 'With the Wanderrie Creek Under Fourteen B Hockey Team.'

After dinner that evening, Rundle knocked on his son's door, and proffered a tennis racket and ball. 'How about a hit against the garage wall before lights out, sport? Get some practice so you'll be ready when they pick the pennant teams for school. Give you a chance to really shine.'

45

THINGS WERE WINDING down at the Flying Doctor tennis fundraiser on Sturt Plains Station, forty miles down the road from Meredith Downs. Every year, locals gathered for the tournament on a March Sunday. As ever, Bill and Dorothy Harrop hosted the event with efficient good humour.

This year, the pairings in the mixed doubles had seen Finbar Rafferty, the senior Flying Doctor, teamed with Bonnie Edquist, who'd scored an invitation thanks to a sizeable donation by her uncle towards the new plane. They worked their way up the fixture ladder, finally taking on Dorothy Harrop and Matt MacBride. The deciding match was interrupted briefly by the presence on the court of a king brown snake. Time was lost not due to the snake itself, but because Dorothy had axed its head so forcefully with her racket that the wood had split.

When Matt hit a shot suspiciously far beyond the baseline, handing victory to his opponents, Bonnie protested. 'You did that on purpose!'

'Thank God he did!' shouted a voice, and a cheer erupted as someone speared a new keg.

'If you hadn't thrown the set, sure now I would have!' Dr Rafferty said to Matt. 'I'm too old to be running around like that.'

Matt turned to shake Bonnie's hand. 'That's quite a backhand you've got.'

'Years of Saturday mornings at Arthur Marshall's Tennis Academy.'

'*And* she fixed the generator when I couldn't get it to start earlier!' said Dorothy. 'Quite the all-rounder, this one. A real catch! Now, time for a drink. Beer or barley water?'

They headed back to the bough shed, where by now most of the food had been devoured, but the 'amber nectar' still flowed freely. Some of the older codgers sat in folding chairs and argued about the Wool Board. Grandmothers swapped war stories about invasions of ants or infestations of moths, while the younger men talked cricket scores, and who'd got how far with which bird.

The talk amongst some of the girls was of the Bachelors' and Spinsters' Ball, the annual mating ritual known to WA country towns as early as the 1920s.

'Are you going, Bonnie? To the B&S?' Dorothy Harrop asked. 'I won't be, of course – it's hardly for married folks. But *you* should. They're usually a hoot. And a good way to meet someone. If you're looking, of course . . .' She saw Bonnie's gaze drift to Matt in the distance. 'What have you got to lose? Ask him. But . . .' Leaning in a little, she said, 'Word to the wise, dear. You'll probably have to make the running with that one. A truly lovely fellow, but not exactly the forward type.'

It was dark by the time Matt was ready to leave. 'Sure you won't stay the night?' Bill Harrop asked.

'I'll be right.' Matt lit a cigarette and took a long draw on it. 'Early start tomorrow.'

'Give my regards to your mum, then . . . Night, Bonnie,' he called to a figure approaching the car beside Matt's.

Matt turned to her. 'Heading back to camp?'

'Yep.'

'You right finding your way in the dark?'

'Maybe I could follow you as far as the sealed road?'

'I'll be taking a shortcut actually, through a few back tracks. Just follow me, and we'll come out not far from your camp. I'll make a detour to make sure you get there OK. Just keep your eyes peeled for stray stock, and roos.'

There was just enough light from the homestead for Bonnie to make out the shadow of stubble on Matt's jaw, and the way his Adam's apple moved as he spoke. Beneath the cigarette smoke, he smelt of soap, and that unmistakeable smell of blokes – the smell that pervaded all her days at camp. 'Actually, I was wondering—' Without warning, she screamed and started flapping the hem of her shirt. 'Aagh! There's something up my top!' Then, 'God! It's on my back now!' By reflex, she grabbed Matt's arm. 'Get it off! Get rid of it!'

'Stay still!' Matt lifted her ponytail with one hand and stretched the collar of her shirt outward to check her back. Before Bonnie could say anything, he had put his other hand up the shirt and flicked off a huntsman spider four fingers wide. He brushed her damp skin again, picking off a detached spider leg, and stamped on the damaged creature.

'Ugh!' said Bonnie. 'I'm okay with snakes, but I hate bloody spiders!'

'That one wouldn't have done you much harm.' Matt set her ponytail back in place. 'You all right?'

'Yeah.'

'What were you about to say? Before the spider. You were wondering something.'

'Oh! Well, just . . . are you going to that thing?'

Matt looked at her, lowering his head.

'The Bachelors' and Spinsters' Ball they were talking about.'

'Oh, that . . . Nah.'

'Oh.'

'Why, are you?' Matt was looking at this girl now: her eyes; how her blonde hair picked up the light.

'I thought I might,' she said.

He took a moment. 'Good for you. Hope you enjoy it.'

'I probably won't know many people there. I – well, I wondered if you might want to come with me?'

Matt shifted his weight on his feet as he considered the invitation. 'Not really my cup of tea. If I want to drink myself unconscious I can do it at home – don't have to put on a dinner suit for it.'

'I just thought it might be fun. I bet you'd look good in a dinner jacket, conscious or unconscious.'

Matt took a last drag on his cigarette and stamped out the butt. 'I'm sure *you* would too . . . Look good – in a ball dress, I mean. Though somehow I doubt you'd be unconscious . . .'

Somewhere inside rose that feeling. Getting to the brink of something, and being yanked back, like a dog on a chain. *This isn't for you, this stuff. You lost the right a long time ago.*

He considered warning her off getting mixed up with a MacBride – how the bad luck might rub off. 'You can go by yourself, you know – that's the whole point of a B&S. But if you really want company . . . ask Steve Glew. From Friday River Station – that really tall guy over there. Great bloke.'

Despite the darkness, Matt saw Bonnie's face flush. He opened the door of her car for her. 'Just follow me, and blow your horn if anything's wrong.'

'On second thoughts, I can find my own way.'

Her car followed Matt's down the long driveway and out through the homestead gate, then the two of them turned in opposite directions, each threading their own fragile trail of light through an ocean of darkness.

46

MATT HADN'T SPOKEN to Humpty Dumpton for nearly fifteen years – not since the day he had refused to bring him a gun in hospital. The letters he'd written had been returned to sender, and Matt had finally given up. After the crash, for a while he'd forgotten that Humpty even existed.

Now, Matt greeted his old friend, helped out of the car in front of the homestead and into his wheelchair by a strikingly attractive redhead. Rascal and Trooper both strained on their chains, barking at the visitor and his strange contraption.

'Settle down!' Matt ordered, and they stood on full alert, hoping the guests might need rounding up.

'Sorry about the dogs,' said Matt. 'Gedday.'

'Matt, you old bastard! How the bloody hell are you?' Humpty grinned as he wheeled himself towards his friend. 'This is Coral. My missus.'

The pride in Humpty's face dissolved Matt's apprehension, and he felt a surge of happiness as old affection, walled off for years, washed through him.

Sixteen years, thought Matt as they sat in the lounge room and Lorna poured tea in the good china. Sixteen years since that bus ride after the cricket when Humpty had mapped out his life. Where the hell were those two kids now? How could life pull a vanishing trick like that?

'Hugh's always talked so fondly of the Meredith Downs mob,' Coral was saying. 'I've been on at him for years to be in touch, but' – she shrugged – 'you know how it is. Life gets in the way, doesn't it? But when I heard my cousin's wedding was going to be in Wanderrie Creek, I just bulldozed him into it.' She turned to her husband. 'Didn't I, sweetie? It's only a hop, skip and a jump away, after all . . .'

Humpty laughed. 'Unfortunate turn of phrase for me . . .' but his wife replied, 'You can cope,' and leaned over to squeeze his hand, throwing in a kiss on the cheek.

'See the sympathy I get?' said Humpty.

A figure whipped past the doorway.

'Andy?' called Lorna. Silence. 'I know you're there. Come and join us.'

Humpty's eyes widened as there materialised before him a replica of Matt and Warren as kids. 'Whoa! Talk about a MacBride!' For a moment, his voice caught in his throat, then he held out a hand. 'Gedday. I'm Humpty. Old mate of your uncle's.'

'Surely it was only yesterday you two were that size?' said Lorna.

Andy stepped forward to shake hands, then, armed with cake, settled cross-legged in an armchair. As the grown-ups chatted, he listened like a detective to what he classed as Intelligence – how Matt and Humpty knew each other, and their tales of their time at Scotch; Humpty's visits to Meredith Downs; cricket matches; mustering and camping and making an old bathtub into a boat during a flood one time. How he met Coral when she was working as a rehab nurse a few years after his accident.

'It wasn't quite love at first sight,' said Coral. 'More that he wouldn't take no for an answer. Said he needed someone to take him to watch cricket matches and I'd do.'

'I call her my silly mid-on,' Humpty said. 'Because you'd have to have rocks in your head to volunteer for her position,' and he looked into her eyes with such a deep passion that it threw Matt off balance. Just for a moment, he dared to pay attention to a sensation in his chest: a longing for something.

Humpty turned to Andy. 'Play cricket?'

'When there's enough people. Otherwise I just practise bowling against the stumps. And Rascal fields.'

'Rascal?'

'My dog.'

'I used to play a bit myself in the old days. How about a match?'

Andy couldn't help but stare at the wheelchair.

'Don't be fooled by the wheels!' said Coral. 'He's still a demon bowler. And I'm usually his runner when he bats.'

As if no time had passed at all since boyhood, they trailed out through the back of the homestead and along the path to what had once been the cricket pitch watered and mown in season by Warren and Matt, where Meredith Downs had seen matches between jackaroos and shearers and drovers and cockies from far and wide, and where Miles Beaumont had once turned so many heads.

Left alone after the match, Matt gathered the bails and stumps, Humpty the bats. Matt was pensive, wiping the wood to get the dirt off.

Humpty rubbed his jaw. 'I – well, I didn't like to say anything to your mum. But I know you've all had more than your fair share of strife since I last saw you. I was sorry to hear it.'

Matt shrugged, and put the stumps back into their old army duffle. The day was fading, throwing long shadows over the men, thickening the air so that the calls of the cockatoos seemed to echo off nothing. Matt was still holding one of the bails, turning it in his fingers, tracing his thumb over the letters 'MD' for 'Meredith Downs' he'd carved in it years ago, back when Humpty was going to captain Australia. Back when there was a future. Meredith Downs, for as long as he could remember, for as far as he could see. How could so much space feel so suffocating now? He pushed the thought away.

'Here you go. Souvenir,' he said. 'You can burn it and have your own Ashes.'

Humpty took the bail with a laugh. 'God, I was a dickhead back then.' He put it in his shirt pocket. 'Thanks, by the way. For telling on me. For telling your mum.'

After a silence, Matt said, 'The way things have turned out here – sometimes I know how you felt.'

'How I felt?'

'Like there's no way out. Like life's a – I don't know . . . a prison.'

'If you don't like it here, why don't you just walk away, literally?'

'Mum's entitled to at least one of her kids, I reckon.' Matt paused. 'And there's Andy . . .'

'What about girls?' asked Humpty. 'The birds must be queuing up to be Mrs MacBride Junior.'

'Oh bugger off.'

'You could do worse than get married and have some kids. That's . . . Well, nippers aren't on the cards for me and Coral. But we're going to try to adopt. "Give some kid a happy home" and all that.'

'I reckon you would,' said Matt.

'So what's stopping *you*?'

Matt gave him a clip on the back of the head, which Humpty automatically countered with a punch in the arm, in their old ritual. 'Come on,' said Matt. 'Time for tea.'

Finishing her cup, Coral gave a stretch. 'OK, Dumpton, we'd better get going if we're going to make it to Wanderrie Creek this side of Christmas.'

'Righto. You head out to the car and I'll be with you in two shakes. Just want to see the view from the back verandah one more time. Come on, Matt – a trip down memory lane,' and the two men headed out to the wide verandah and around to the other side of the house.

'Never changes, does it, this place?' mused Humpty.

'Not much to change.'

'That silence . . . That's what I miss most from Corella Ridge. Never get it in the city. Still, life works out in the end.'

'But don't you regret . . . you know . . .' Matt ventured, eyes on Humpty's legs.

'The accident? What'd be the bloody point? Besides, if all of that had to happen for me to meet Coral, I'd do it all over again.' Matt looked shocked, and Humpty said, 'Bloody oath . . .' He lifted each foot back onto the foot plates of his wheelchair, and cackled. 'It's the human bloody condition, mate. Life: bite the bastard. Chew off one day at a time. That's my eminently qualified philosophical advice.' He gripped Matt's arm with a force belied by the lightness with which he said, 'Nah, you'll be right. Eventually. None of that bullshit thinking . . . Beaut kid, by the way, that Andy. Got the makings of a decent spin bowler.' He paused. 'When you think about it, everyone's life's a prison – of days, sort of. The trick is to get comfortable in it, I reckon. Find your freedom *inside* whatever your prison is.'

47

BILBY ROCK STATION is a big property. Sixty thousand sheep in its heyday. Down to thirty thousand now. A shade under a million acres. Ten inches of rain a year if you're lucky. But plenty of space for a party.

Madge and Brian Swincer never mind hosting the Bachelors' and Spinsters' Ball there. After all, they met at one nineteen years ago, getting off to a rather over-enthusiastic start that saw them at the altar and the maternity ward in pretty short order. Four kids later, they tell themselves they've done all right, considering.

The sixteen-stand shearing shed, one of the biggest in the state, is decked out in crêpe-paper streamers and balloons, with only the occasional sheep dag clinging to the wooden slats of the floor. The early-autumn afternoon is hot, so the corrugated iron shutters are all propped open, and the big doors are flung wide to coax in any breeze.

All day, neighbours have been turning up with salads and trifles and grog in eskies. The pig's been roasting on the spit since dawn, the sheep since a little later. The Birchmeres are cattle people, so they've brought a steer, butchered and ready to barbecue on the halved forty-four-gallon drums.

Brian Swincer and Sally, their oldest, are set up at the property's main gate, about a fifteen-minute drive from the homestead. They greet the arrivals, check they've got a ticket, sell them one if they haven't, and direct them up the road according to whether they've brought a swag or a tent or have bagged a place in the shearers' quarters or the sleep-out in the house. Some will sleep in the back of their ute or in their car. Most won't sleep at all.

At about six, a blonde woman and a dark-haired man arrived, dressed in their finery.

'Gedday,' said Brian Swincer. He hoiked his glasses up onto his forehead to get a better view of the fellow behind the wheel. 'You're a Glew, aren't you?'

'Can't deny it, Mr Swincer.'

Brian scratched his ear as he calculated. 'So you'll be the youngest: Steve, right?' He peered into the car.

'Oh,' said Steve, 'and this is Bonnie. It's a double ticket.'

'Pleased to meet you, Bonnie.' Brian consulted his list. 'Now, Steve, I've got you down as a swag, and your lady friend's got a guernsey for the shearers' quarters. Just follow the dust trail up till you hit something.'

With a wave, they set off on the last stage of their gruelling drive, during which only an hour ago Steve had had to strip off to his undies to change a tyre. 'I wouldn't usually get my daks off in front of a bird,' he'd explained. After the time spent with her crew, Bonnie wasn't fazed, and concentrated on keeping her hem out of the dust as she paced behind the car.

The homestead on Bilby Rock was a rickety affair, the original walls built from local stone, but added onto all around with timber or corrugated iron or fibro or anything else that came to hand when it needed more rooms over the years. It wasn't grand, but it had a wide, closed-in verandah surrounded by bougainvilleas in a riot of orange and pink and crimson. Three date palms towered above the flat land, living monuments to three Swincer boys safely home from the Great War, the last one having died only four months ago at the age of seventy-nine.

They pulled into a cleared paddock where cars and trucks and utes caked in red dust were parked in more or less identifiable rows for hundreds of yards.

Bonnie inspected her long navy satin dress, retrieved on her last trip to Perth; checked her pearl ear studs were secure; touched the pearl collar around her neck. She felt a sinking in her stomach as she remembered the last time she'd arrived at a party in this dress – for her engagement. A different man, when she was a different person. She had hesitated over bringing it to wear this evening, but it was the only long dress she owned these days, and she was determined to put all that behind her. Yet the memory stung, even now. Her grandmother's words from back then rang in her ears: 'You'll just have to make the best of it, dear.' She took a deep breath, and smiled as brightly as she could as Steve opened her door.

* * *

A couple of hundred people had already gathered by the time Matt MacBride got to the shearing shed at Bilby Rock, having reluctantly answered Madge Swincer's plea delivered in person to come and help out. 'The Brinley boys have gone down with chicken pox or some wretched thing. You know what it's like, Matt – there's always some twit who impales himself on a keg spear or picks a fight about a girl or some damn nonsense.' So, despite his protests that he never went to these shows, Matt, dressed in black tie, freshly shaven and hair brushed, stepped into the shed, where, amid the racket of the jazz band and the roar of conversation, girls' heads turned discreetly as they scrutinised the handsome newcomer, and the shapely brunette on his arm.

'Can I get you a drink?' Matt asked her.

'I'll have a glass of champagne.' At the look on his face, she burst into laughter and poked his arm. 'Had you there for a minute! Punch'd be great, Mattie.'

Waiting for the drinks, he looked around the shed at the faces he knew and the faces he didn't. He still got called a snob occasionally when he looked straight through a bloke he'd maybe played cricket with, or a girl he'd debated at school. In fact, even when Madge Swincer had introduced them back at the homestead that afternoon, Matt had been at a momentary loss.

'Rhonda. *Kippin*,' the girl had added for emphasis. 'I used to – Warren and I—'

Madge intervened. 'You remember Rhonda. She and your brother were very close, weren't they?'

The words 'Were they?' had been on the tip of Matt's tongue. But yes, he gradually did remember something about a Rhonda. He tapped his temple with the heel of his hand.

'I barely recognised you either, to tell the truth,' she said. 'You certainly scrub up well!'

Madge put a hand on the shoulder of each of them. 'Matt, would you be a dear and drive Rhonda up to the dancing? It's all under control at this end now, I think.' She paused to inspect them. 'Nice,' she said, patting them both on an arm, and headed off to oversee the concoction of another massive drumful of punch.

Matt returned with Rhonda's drink and a beer for himself.

'Have a dance with me?' Rhonda asked.

'I'm not much of a one for dancing, Kippers,' Matt said, and they both laughed at the old nickname for her that had sprung out of some hidden compartment of his memory.

'Fair enough. But *I* am. Mind if I desert you?'

'Go for your life.' He raised his beer in salute.

Rhonda drifted off into the throng and was soon flinging her arms around a man she either knew very well or wanted to. 'Bloody *Kippers*,' he mused. 'Warren and bloody Kippers, thaaat's right . . .' and he laughed aloud as he lit a cigarette.

As the throng grew, the night got warmer. Long evening dresses were hoisted up and tucked into girdles at the hips, or gathered and tied in a knot at the side. If there were layers, they were shed. Mascara ran, lipstick smudged, bow ties hung loose on collars or found their way onto women's wrists or bare necks. Occasionally Matt was called on to carry a bare-footed girl over a patch of ground where a beer jug had shattered, or ferry some bottles of spirits safely to the bar. He was a popular point of call for rollies and his lighter. Once or twice he had to persuade a bloke to mind his manners, but managed with no more than an arm around the shoulder and a 'Come on, mate, time for a smoke, I reckon.'

He was leaning against the corrugated iron, taking in the crowd around him, when a woman with a familiar face approached. 'Matthew bloody MacBride!' she said. 'Lordie! Talk about a blast from the past!' The punch glass in the woman's hand was neither full nor steady, and she kissed Matt on the lips – a real smacker.

Matt untangled her arms from his neck and held her a little at a distance to get a better look. 'Angie? Angie Bellaqua, isn't it?' Another old girlfriend of Warren's.

'The one and only!'

A man's hand slid around her shoulder, and its owner said, 'That glass looks shockingly empty, Angie! Step this way and we'll correct that immediately.' As the anonymous hand steered her off towards the bar, it snaked down to squeeze her behind, and she returned the compliment.

Matt collected another beer and wandered out of the shed until he found an empty keg, which he claimed as a stool. He rolled a cigarette, and summoned again the feeling of Angie's kiss. Bloody Warren: two old flames at one party. Anyone would think he was Casanova. Not much family resemblance, then . . . Matt felt his cheeks redden: the handful of times he'd got near to going out with a girl it had quickly fizzled into a paralyzing awkwardness.

He flicked his lighter on and off several times before finally touching the flame to the paper. Would Warren have ended up with Kippers? he wondered. Would he have ditched her for someone better looking, maybe? In the space of a few seconds, he found himself constructing a whole unlived future: Warren's six kids, his father's retirement celebrations – the whole world that might have existed but for the crash. A wife for him, maybe . . . Rosie and – oh, Christ, Rosie . . .

In the silence that hung there after the end of a song, Matt's eye was drawn to a figure that cleared the treeline of dancers spilling out into the paddock. Steve Glew, as tall and thin as a telegraph pole, was instantly recognisable above the rest. The music started again, something slow and romantic, and the girl he was with put her arms on his shoulders and started to sway with the beat. It took a second to realise it was Bonnie, and a few more to recover from the gut punch of it: his body was cold, fingertips tingling with the adrenalin jolt that had ambushed him. She hung her head down, just swaying, swaying, and when she threw it back to laugh, the light caught the sweat on her chest and shoulders above her strapless gown. The more he watched Bonnie, the more he felt something shift inside him. He tried to identify the sensation. There was anger, maybe, or even jealousy? And then he placed it: it was what he'd felt when he'd seen the look that passed between Humpty and Coral. That deep longing. That knowledge of what he could never have.

And it could have been Humpty's words or it could have been the beers or the moonlight on Bonnie's shoulders – or it could have been just years of plain frustration that drove him to his feet, dropping his cigarette and navigating his way – stepping over a dead-drunk bloke still hugging a beer jug; past the barbecue where a last few pieces of steak had turned to cinders; fending off a stray hand from a girl trying to tug him into her orbit – finally making it across the paddock, to put a hand on Steve's shoulder in greeting, before turning to Bonnie and taking her hand to ask 'Wanna dance?'

48

MATT COULD PRACTICALLY do the drive back from Bilby Rock Station blindfold. It was flat and dusty and bumpy, and by the time you'd opened and shut all the gates along the way, took about three hours. This morning though, sometimes it felt as if it was taking all day, sometimes just five minutes.

It felt like seeing the landscape for the first time: the rusted orange of the dirt road; the dazzling aquamarine of the sky; the pair of falcons hunting in tandem, hundreds of feet above. What did the world look like from up there? What would they make of this bloke in his car who was singing under his breath and tapping his fingers in time on the steering wheel?

He slowed a little and steered with his knees as he pulled the stopper from his waterbag and took a swig. He splashed some on his face and threw the bag back onto the seat, beside a note scrawled on a woman's folded handkerchief: 'IOU 1 x dinner jacket – Quiz'

It had got chilly as they sat talking down by the creek just before dawn, and Matt had slipped his jacket over her shoulders, taking her hand in both of his to feel its texture – the whorls on her fingertips and the callouses she said were the geologist's occupational hazard. To be looked at like that – looked right into, without a trace of blame, as though she knew a part of him that he hadn't known himself . . .

Where had it come from: that dance? That kiss? How what came next needed no words, felt completely ordinary, as though he was just a normal bloke with a normal life after all?

A sentence formed in his mouth as if he were reading it on a passing road sign: 'Welcome to Hope'. He picked up the hanky. There was that perfume. Flowers; like the smell of her skin and her hair. There had been laughter – they had skated between shy giggles and embarrassed laughs as they'd been thrown off balance by the surprise of it all. Then the awkwardness had vanished like morning fog.

He slipped the handkerchief into his pocket and drove on.

A few miles inside the boundary of Meredith Downs, as Matt approached Two Up Bore, just before the Top Shed, he noticed sheep crowded around the empty trough. The pump might have packed it in. Might as well check now. He was still humming to himself as he got his toolbox; still smiling at the thought of the IOU in his pocket when he inspected the trough and cleared out three crow carcasses that had caused a blockage. He checked that the water was flowing, put his tools away. Then the shearing shed caught his eye, and his whole body clenched.

No clouds obscured the sunshine. The temperature didn't change. But as he drove the rest of the way home, now he could only see so far in any direction, the dirt and the sky assuming their familiar prison hues.

Coming in the front door, the silence struck Matt. Then he remembered: Lorna was taking Andy to the annual church fete for the missions. In his bedroom, he pulled off his boots and shirt and headed to the bathroom to get some Bex for his head. He leaned on the basin, waiting for the powder to dissolve in the beaker of water. Nothing had changed . . . He gulped down the liquid. This was his life.

As he passed Old Wally, he had a sudden urge to force the clock's hands backwards, around and around to undo the years. Back to the day of the crash, when everything lay open and possible before him.

On his way past Andy's room, once Rose's, Matt's toe smashed into a roller skate. *For God's sake, Andy!* Nursing his foot in his fingers, he felt the last dregs of that sense from the night before drain away. Who had he thought he was kidding? He flung the roller skate down the passageway and headed to the bathroom, stripping off the rest of his clothes. Bugger lighting the donkey heater. At first, he left the taps just barely on, as usual. But the drizzle that spilled down over his head hardly even got him wet, and suddenly infuriated him. *Stuff it!* He turned them on as far as they would go, making them gurgle and splutter with shock. Fingers cradling his scalp, face turned up to the chilly water, his sensations of Bonnie – the touch, the scent, the smile – were washed away, his tears drowned out and carried back into the earth of Meredith Downs.

49

Myrtle Eedle keeps a bowl of butterscotch toffees on the post office counter, 'For kiddies only', and glares at any adult who tries to swipe one. She usually pops out from behind her post to inspect any baby in its pram, or jiggle the foot of a toddler on its mother's hip. She even bumps down postage prices on Andy's heavy parcels to his pen pal.

She never demurs when people refer to her as 'childless': everyone has their cross to bear. But the older she gets, the more suffocating she finds the label. After all, a 'childless' woman of thirty might have four kids by the time she's forty. But when Myrtle turns fifty-one, the door on the prison cell of childlessness is finally slammed shut, and she feels its clang deep within.

Myrtle's fifty-second birthday falls on the same day as the funeral of Dorothy Borrett from Bettong Flats Station ('Heart failure, 83, widowed. 3 children,12 grandchildren'), so her morning begins in church. ('Presbyterian – born Methodist but married out.') Lorna MacBride is there, and Matthew. Myrtle draws immense comfort from their presence, and their apparent ability to withstand untold grief.

The tear in her eye is blinked back by doing the calculation in her head of how many funerals she has attended since that first one, for a neighbour, when she was eighteen. The relief that welled up in her on that long-ago November day in 1935 feels fresh this morning: that was the day she had sobbed uncontrollably at the requiem mass of a Mrs Spanney ('30, mother of young twins, drowned in boating accident'); shed tears and collapsed into her own loss, under camouflage of the death of a nice enough neighbour who, in all honesty, she barely knew, and no one had batted an eyelid. Myrtle's mother had put a consoling hand on her shoulder, and when they got home, her father had made her a polony and tomato sauce sandwich, the first time he'd done anything for her since she'd come home from Sydney.

By the time Myrtle met Clive, newly back on civvy street in 1946, she was twenty-eight and already an old hand at every aspect of funeral rites, the war having accelerated her experience considerably. At first, it hadn't felt safe to explain the reason to him – surely he would wash his hands of her? Then, by the time she realised that he would have loved her anyway, it felt too late: the failure to tell him this one – big – thing, might make him think there were others she had hidden. It would crack the foundation slab of the marriage that, if it wasn't the only thing she wanted, was at least the only thing she had. And the more that time passed, the more she couldn't bear the thought of the hurt that would come to Clive's watery eyes, his scaly cheeks, if he were to discover that every time she had planted a Lorraine Lee rosebush and he had watered and fed and pruned it with her, he was in fact toiling in a foreign land – a part of her past where he didn't speak the language.

Myrtle's thoughts were drawn back to the Borrett service now, as the final hymn floated into awareness, and she found she was already singing it. The coffin was carried out by sun-scarred men in rarely worn suits, and the light streamed onto the silk lilies on the altar. For a moment, Myrtle thought her knees might give way, and she wanted to fold over and collapse. She wished Clive were beside her to hold her up. 'The day thou gavest, Lord, is ended . . .' Oh, the *whole damned life* thou gavest . . . Fifty-two today . . . Her baby would be about twice the age, now, that Myrtle herself had been when she gave birth to her at seventeen.

She sat down in the pew and let others file past her. Looking up, Lorna MacBride's glance caught hers, and the woman gave her an understanding smile. Matt walked behind his mother, solemn, unreadable. The father, the brother and the sister, all taken before their time. And the sister torn from her newborn child. *Rose MacBride*, she thought to herself. *Am I luckier than you, still being on this earth?* She waited until the people milling about in front of the church would have dispersed to the wake, then picked up her handbag and left through the side door, the *clack-clack* of her heels the only sound.

50

A FEW DAYS after the ball, as Bonnie was going over the rock samples in front of her, tallying them with pencil marks on the map, her mind kept wandering to Matt MacBride. She'd been amazed to see him at the dance at all. She could still feel the tingling, the butterflies when he came to find her: how the rest of the world had fallen away. And he had seemed transformed somehow: unguarded, open.

He'd talked about Meredith Downs, called it 'pretty country', and said how hard it was to accept the idea of inflicting damage to get to what was below it. He'd asked about her life, about her job; had really listened when she'd tried to explain the challenge and the mystery of understanding the forces and the processes that moulded the earth they stood on; how time and crisis and weathering shaped and reshaped the wild, wide world. He'd laughed at Andy's name for her – called her 'Miss Head Quiz'. And when they'd danced, he'd held her as if he were afraid she might break in his arms.

She came back to his radio silence since that night. Maybe he'd been drunk? Woken up with a hangover and regrets? But that shy smile, the gentleness of his

touch . . .

She'd kept an ear out for any approaching vehicle at the camp, hoping Matt might come to reclaim his dinner jacket. Once or twice, when she was sure no one was around, she'd slipped it on, breathed in its smell. For days, she waited. Then Dorothy Harrop's words at the tennis tournament came back to her: '*You'll probably have to make the running with that one . . .*'

So it was that the following Sunday, Bonnie arrived at the homestead to return the jacket.

'Matt's not here. Nanna Lorna's in the orchard,' Andy said, eyeing the coat. 'Where'd you get that?'

'Oh, Matt – um, lent it to me.'

'At the ball?'

'That's right.' She felt suddenly ridiculous under the scrutiny of this ten-year-old. 'I'll just leave it with you, then—'

'No! You should stay! I'll get the new samples Harry Badger sent me!'

* * *

As he walked through the front door, Matt scarcely had time to take in the presence of Bonnie, and his jacket, before Andy ambushed him. 'I said you'd show her Wallaby Ridge. She's never seen it. She'll like the laterite structure. You should go now – you'll be there in time for sunset!'

'Oh, I don't know,' Matt said, his face suddenly hot. 'She probably doesn't want to see it this minute. She's pretty busy, you know.'

'Not *that* busy,' said Bonnie. 'Hello, by the way.'

'Hello.' Matt was thrown back into the turmoil he'd been in all week. He suddenly felt like a kid – torn between acting as though nothing had happened between them, and the urge to fold her into his chest. 'It's nothing special – compared to other places you'll have seen. It's hardly Ayers Rock.'

'Sure. No. I . . . understand if it's a bother,' Bonnie said, at which point Andy tugged at Matt's sleeve and gave him a meaningful look.

Up on the ridge, Bonnie scanned the horizon through field glasses. 'You can see for ever! Andy was right. It's magnificent!'

'I like it,' said Matt.

Bodily memories of the night of the ball hovered in the air between the two of them, trapped in a silence.

'Is this your "place"?' asked Bonnie after a while.

'My *place*?'

'Your special place. Where the world feels right.'

'I don't know about *right*, but – yeah, it's probably my place.'

'Mine's Cottesloe Beach.' Without noticing, she rested a hand on his shoulder. 'Indian Ocean as far as you can see.' The sun was low in the sky, and a breeze drifted up from the plain. 'Puts things into perspective, doesn't it, this much distance?'

'With any luck.'

'What are those trees?' Not sure I've ever seen them before.'

'A kind of eucalypt,' said Matt. 'Don't find them anywhere else on the property. We've never run sheep in this spot – too hard to get them in and out – so the trees have grown pretty much undisturbed. Beautiful yellow flowers in February. Apparently Jemima, one of the early MacBrides, even sent some samples and drawings of them off to Kew Gardens in the early days. Don't know their proper name. We just call them "Jemima's trees".'

'So beautiful. Thanks for letting me see.'

'Well, you asked.'

'But you didn't have to show me.'

There were a hundred and one reasons just to walk away at this point; to say, *Well, I said I'd show you the view and I have,* and send this girl, who didn't bloody belong here, back to her camp. And yet, the very person who made that essential – he was the one whose face had lit up when Matt had finally agreed to take Bonnie to the breakaways; he'd engineered it, for God's sake, crafty so-and-so.

What now? What next? The questions jabbed him. The feelings jabbed him – this sense of being . . . all right, normal . . . God, of being *happy*, beside her, when he had no right to be.

She might have been speaking, she might not have been. The voice Matt could hear was Rosie's. Rosie from before. *Go on, you dag! You're a long time dead. She's a nice girl. Live your bloody life for once!*

Bonnie was not speaking, as it happened. She was studying his face intently, waiting for an answer to a question she'd apparently asked. He took in her tanned skin, the small mole on her neck, then the blue of her eyes, turquoise like the beach she loved.

'You're not going to make me—' Bonnie stopped in mid-sentence.

'Make you what?'

'Make the running forever, are you? . . . Matt, if you don't like me like that, just say.' Her cheeks flushed. 'I can take it.'

And in this place, where Matt had howled and sobbed and cursed the world – in this place that had held him together – he put a hand to the nape of her neck and leaned down to kiss her, and kept kissing her as he lowered both of them onto the smooth stony ledge, just touched by the last red glow of day.

Lorna still keeps Phil's old wicker chair on the verandah. In the corner with the roll-down canvas shade, they would sit together as dusk surrendered to darkness, listening to the crickets and yarning about the day. The weathered blind has been patched and stitched over the years, and the wicker mended, but this is still Lorna's favourite spot. Even now, she comes here to chat to Phil: when you live long enough with someone, and know them well enough, you can still hear them.

This evening, Lorna thinks about Hughie Dumpton and his wife. Wonderful to see him so happy after all he went through. Perhaps there's hope for Matt yet . . . For all that she's a miner, Lorna has to admit that that Bonnie Edquist seems a nice girl. Good family. Lovely manners. Lorna is conversing silently with Phil – almost sees him nod. But then she's jolted back to an actual conversation she had with him, in these very chairs, not long before he died.

'What do you make of that Rhonda Kippin,' he'd asked. 'You know, the lassie Warren seems so friendly with?'

They'd chatted about her, her family . . . Phil thought she was a bit forward. Then he'd turned to the subject of a husband for Rose. When Lorna had said Rose was too young to be worried about marrying, Phil countered, 'She'll be twenty soon. Don't want her hanging around here and getting tangled up with the first bloke who looks sideways at her. God knows we've seen that happen enough around these parts.' He took a sip of his beer. 'Why not write to Joyce Munsie – see if her lads'll be in Perth for the Show. They're good sorts . . . and they've got three stations.'

'Before you know it, it'll be Matt we need to find someone for . . .'

'Oh, yes. Matthew,' said Phil, as if trying to put a face to a name. 'In due course . . . But Warren's the one we need to take care with. He'll be taking over this place.'

Now, sitting here years later in the pale orange twilight, Lorna raised her eyebrows at long-absent Phil. 'Turns out we were *both* wrong about that.'

Matt and Warren were chalk and cheese when it came to girls. Warren had always seemed to have someone in tow, whereas Matt . . . Lord knew she took every chance to throw him in the way of nice lasses . . . But she didn't like to pry. It was a part of his life that seemed just sealed off since the crash, and she respected that. But he was a handsome boy, everyone said: a wonderful son, and so kind to Andy. He'd make a fine husband and a good father. If only the right girl came along . . .

Bonnie *MacBride* . . . How good was she with sheep? Lorna enquired silently of the rising moon.

51

AUTUMN CONTINUED TO tiptoe in with its subtly cooler light, its thinner days, its occasionally crisp nights. On Meredith Downs, the muster got under way, as the hands on their motorbikes winkled the sheep out of their paddocks in a flurry of dust and the heavy patter of hooves that sounded like gloved applause, moving the dusty mobs a little closer every day to the holding paddocks, drafting off the rams, the dogs a whirlwind of sly efficiency as they corralled their quarry in readiness for the shearers.

The task was complicated this year by the presence in places of Hollamby Mining's claim trenches and trucks and equipment, but by and large Matt and his hands managed to navigate around them without damage to sheep or claim.

Whilst stations like Meredith Downs continued their old pattern of activities, in Wanderrie Creek things were changing, thanks to the new policeman. The more Benedict Rundle went through the old paperwork, the more statistical anomalies he discovered. And statistical anomalies made him itch. What if this was just the tip of the iceberg? When, in a neglected storeroom, he came across a cobwebbed filing cabinet labelled 'Misc. (Defunct)' – a title, for him, like fingernails down a blackboard – he hauled out the small handful of files it contained. And the file on the death of Bert Ashbrook was the first one he opened.

Had he consulted Myrtle Eedle on the matter, Sergeant Rundle would have found that her Drawers of Death recorded it thus: 'Bert Ashbrook. 42. Died of botulism*. Wife Betsy a cook. Four kiddies under ten.' Myrtle had gleaned the barest facts at the wake, which Betsy had been unable to attend at the last minute on account of her nerves playing up. Whenever Myrtle had seen her in her post office in those days, she'd wondered at the amount of slap the woman seemed to put on just to post a parcel.

Sergeant Wisheart would have found no mystery in that, though. More than once he'd had a sharp word with Bert about the bruises his wife tried so hard to cover. The policeman had done nothing more official only because Betsy begged him not to, 'for the kids' sake'. They wouldn't survive on just her cook's wage. Bert was a mean drunk, but usually only after pay day at the railyard. He hardly ever hit her when he was sober.

She hid it from the kids: 'Your dad and me were just messing around'; she hid it from her sister whenever she came to visit. But that didn't mean the fear wasn't there, always just below the surface. She carried on: scrubbing the kitchen floor with Tru-sol every day, doing the washing in the old copper, keeping the children spotless, wrapping the broken china in plenty of newspaper so that the bin men wouldn't notice the wreck of whatever Bert had thrown at her that week.

She carried on, too, making her admired preserves and pickles and Vacola'd fruit, even donating jams to the church fete. Whilst the kids knew not to touch her 'special batches' of preserved vegetables, Bert was oblivious to the separation of the sections in the cupboard. He never bothered to watch her make them. Never noticed that, whereas she heated other things until they were scalding hot, she let the jars destined for this section get barely more than tepid.

You couldn't guarantee that each under-sterilised jar would

have the botulinum spores in them to start with, so it was more like a game of Russian roulette. She'd think about that as she wrung out a bloody flannel after one of his goes at her. She'd think about it as he held her down and nearly strangled her. And she'd think, too, of the kids and their need for a mother at least.

When Bert died of botulism after a meal of corned beef and potatoes and preserved beans, at first, Betsy had only been aware of a sort of mathematical interest: how many jars of vegetables had it taken?

In due course, Wisheart asked her to show him where and how she kept the food that the autopsy said did for Bert. Opening the cupboard, she'd said, 'Help yourself.' And when he'd asked about the different sections in which the jars were kept, she just said, 'I used to make special batches for him. The kids wouldn't touch them with a bargepole.'

He looked at the cupboard, then at the woman, her hair unbrushed and her nails bitten to the quick. She limped a little these days, since what she'd told the doctor was a fall down the verandah steps, and Wisheart winced involuntarily at the pain that crossed her face as she sat down across the kitchen table from him. 'How are the little ones?' he asked.

'They're all I live for.'

'How will you manage, with just your wages?'

'I'll get some sort of widow's pension, the Railways say. Less than he earned, but enough to get by on, as long as I don't marry again.' She waited for the policeman to speak; then, into the silence, asked blankly, 'What will happen to me now?'

'Why should anything happen to you?'

'Well, I fed him and he died.'

Wisheart glanced again at the cupboard. Then two pairs of eyes peeped low down around the doorframe, before ducking quickly out of sight, followed by a scuttling down the passage. That would be the older two. He tugged at an earlobe as he chose his words. 'If I were you, I'd be thinking of a fresh start, Betsy. He's not coming back. Give his clothes to the church. Sign up the forms for the pension. And . . . chuck out all those jars. No point keeping his special stuff if he's not here to eat it.' He stood to leave. 'You won't be hearing from me again. I'll have a word with a few people about the official paperwork. You look after yourself, now.'

Benedict Rundle would go and meet her. If he was barking up the wrong tree, he'd soon know. Maybe Janine was right and he was imagining things. But he had pretty good instincts, and you ignored those at your peril.

When he knocked on her door, three peaceful, contented years collapsed in an instant like a bridge in a flood, built, as they were, on flimsy foundations. Rundle knew he had no way of proving his suspicions, and the crazy thing was that Betsy knew it too. If she'd kept her mouth shut he would have had to walk straight out of that door with nothing but a niggle at the back of his mind. But to his amazement, he'd barely sat down – in the same chair Wisheart had once occupied – when she said, 'I can guess why you're here.' And the whole story gushed out, like a dam finally bursting.

'So you took the law into your own hands?' was Rundle's response.

'I didn't know what else to do. I was . . .' she looked down at her neatly filed fingernails, '. . . too ashamed to tell anyone . . . what he'd been doing.'

'The penalty for hitting your wife isn't death, Mrs Ashbrook. It isn't now and it wasn't then. That's why the law doesn't leave it up to victims to decide what punishment gets meted out.'

A pimply boy walked into the kitchen holding an empty cup, but stopped at the sight of the visitor.

Betsy looked from one to the other. 'This is Robbie, my oldest. Robbie, this is . . . this is Sergeant Rundle.'

'Where are your other children, Mrs Ashbrook?'

'The little ones are out the back with the dog. Judy's doing homework.'

'Is there a neighbour who can take care of them?'

'I—But—'

'You're going to need to come with me now.' His voice was measured, not loud, not unkind. 'Pack a change of clothes and a toothbrush.' He looked again at Robbie. 'Your face is familiar. I don't think I've come across you in my work, though . . .'

The boy, still bewildered, instead of asking the hundreds of questions that whirled in his mind, could only mumble, 'Hockey. You stood in for Mr Drake as our hockey coach one day. Said I had potential.'

52

By May, shearing was in full swing, and Andy was keeping Bonnie company at the homestead as she waited for Matt, who was late for their meeting. 'The shearers' cook walked out this morning,' Andy had explained. 'He was a bit of a drinker. The shearers reckoned he was trying to poison them, but Matt says he probably put the metho in the stew by accident. Anyway, Matt had to talk to Mr Chopping out at the shed about a replacement and what they'll do in the meantime.'

The boy was showing her the photos on the piano – MacBrides through the ages. 'Well there's no mistaking *you're* one of this lot,' she said. 'Spitting image of Albert, except for the great big whiskers. And you've got the same mouth as that MacBride chap over there.'

'He's not a MacBride, he's a Catchlove. Nanna's grandad.'

Bonnie was fascinated to see resemblances popping up across the years and the generations. A person looks like so many different family members over time. 'Well, he's a very handsome fellow. And so are you. Especially with your duelling scar!'

'What's a duelling scar?'

'That little scar near your eyebrow. Looks like you got it in a sword fight.'

*

Andy had always taken for granted the tiny mark near the outside edge of his eyebrow – a pale ridge no longer than the width of his little fingernail. If you'd asked him to draw his face, the mark wouldn't be there, any more than the freckles on his nose. In the summer, when he tanned, the scar always remained unstained white.

That evening, Andy went out to the verandah, where Lorna was thumbing through the Yates seed catalogue, and Matt was reading his book on Gipsy Moth and the man who'd sailed it around the world.

'Nanna, how did I get this scar?'

'Which scar's that, dear?' Lorna asked, running her finger down a list.

'This one.' He leaned his face to her. 'See?'

Lorna pushed her reading glasses down her nose. 'Oh yes,' she said, peering. 'Yes, you *have* got a tiny scar there. I think you got that from . . . a fall. When you were very little.'

'When?' he asked. 'Where did I fall? What was I doing?'

Matt glanced up from his book, and Lorna cast her eyes upwards. 'Now, let me think . . . I can't really say what you were doing, Beetle. It was a long time ago. And it's well and truly healed. Does it bother you?'

'No. I just wondered. It's *my* scar on *my* face and I don't know how it got there.'

'I know the feeling! I sometimes walk into a room and don't know why I went there.'

'That's different, but. This was a thing that *happened* to *me*. I was *there*, but I don't remember anything.'

'Well, I'm not much use to you, I'm afraid,' said Lorna. 'I grow more addlepated by the day.'

'Nanna hasn't got a *memory* of how it got there,' Andy said to Matt. 'She's got a *forgetment* of it! Do *you* remember?'

'Put me down as a forgetment, too.'

In early June, Andy asked, 'What was your surname before you married Grandpa Phil?'

'Catchlove. I was born Lorna Faith Catchlove.' She sliced the block of butter in half. 'Pop the rest back in the fridge, would you, Beetle?'

'And what about your mum?'

'She was born Ethel Thaxted.'

'And what was *her* mum's name?'

Lorna stopped greasing the scone tray. 'I never knew her. But she was – Brookfield? Brookdale? . . . Glazebrook! That's it. Elizabeth Glazebrook.'

'And *her* mum?'

Pouring milk into the scone batter, Lorna said, 'Goodness, Andy. If I ever knew, I don't remember! Now, sago for dessert tonight, or peaches and custard?'

'Frogs' eggs!' Andy called over his shoulder, using the family nickname for the butterscotch dessert, as he scurried to his room.

Lorna smiled. Funny little monkey.

He reappeared just as the scones came out of the oven, their aroma filling the air. Lorna buttered one and put jam on it for him.

He handed her a page.

'What's that?'

'You have to read it!'

'I haven't got my glasses, dear.'

'It's our family tree!' he said, a little offended. 'Or the start of it.'

Lorna squinted. It did indeed look like a tree – there were leaves and roots, with words perched rather precariously in the branches. A few of the spellings looked a bit on the creative side. 'Lovely.' She put the jam back in the cupboard. 'What brought this on?'

'It's for the project.'

'What project?'

'The Pastoralists' Heritage Project.' Andy launched into a somewhat garbled explanation of the School of the Air project for the centenary of Wanderrie Creek, tracing the family trees of settlers since 1870. 'You got the thingumajig about it last week.'

'I can't say I paid all that much attention, dear. I'll dig it out later. Now, how about you grab a tea towel and practise drying up?'

'I'll get to find out all the olden days people. Not just olden days like you, but really, really olden!'

'Glad to know I'm not "*really, really* olden".'

It wasn't until two days later that Lorna read the letter, and realised what Andy had told her. That evening, Matt, back from helping repair a mill at the far side of the property, emerged from the shower, hair washed and clothes changed after the long, dusty trip, and was about to retrieve his dinner from the oven, where Lorna had left it warming between two plates, when she said, 'Let's pop out to the verandah a moment.'

Outside, she asked in a low voice, 'Did you know about Andy's project? The family tree?'

'Oh, that thing about old pastoralist families . . .'

'That's what I thought it was, too. I promised him I'd hunt out more information about the MacBrides for him.'

'And?'

'What's he going to say about his parents?'

'His par—What have his parents got to do with it?' Matt couldn't keep the shock from his voice. 'He said it was "olden days".'

'That's where it *starts*, yes, but I've just read the bumph properly, and it goes up to today. He's supposed to get his mum and dad to write a story for the last bit, about how they met, the day he was born . . .'

'Oh . . .' An old numbness spread through Matt.

'Then the whole jolly thing gets exhibited at the Town Hall next February.' Lorna folded her arms. 'What do you think we should do?'

Matt's fingers strayed instinctively to the scar under his hair. 'Does he have to do the last bit? If you explain to his teachers . . . No one would want to upset a little kid.'

'*He*'s not upset!' said Lorna. 'He thinks it's terrific! *Especially* the bit about his mum and dad.'

Matt took his pouch from his shirt pocket and stared at the tobacco strands, as Lorna went on, 'We hardly want to advertise about his father. And you've said yourself he's far too young to find out how Rose died. If he goes digging, who knows what'll come up?'

Matt put a hand over his face.

'I know, love. Brings everything back . . .' To push away the memories, she took in the night's sounds – its clicks and soft chirrups and croaks. 'Well, it's months before he has to hand it in.' She eyed the glowing moon. 'We'll think of something. I'm old enough to know that you pick your moment for these things. I'm off to bed. You should eat your dinner then get to sleep too. You don't look well.' She put a hand on her son's shoulder. 'Those cigarettes'll be the death of you one day, Matthew MacBride.'

'Serves me right,' he said, and took the first, long gasp of smoke into his lungs.

53

THE NEXT DAY, Andy watched Pete Peachey in fascination as he butchered the roo on the bench of the meat house. The roo shooter dropped in an offering of this sort now and then, which would go to feed the dogs or the pigs. Usually Pete left the skinned and gutted carcasses for Matt or one of the hands to butcher, but today they were busy putting up the new wireless aerial, so Andy couldn't 'attend' School of the Air.

The room, a stand-alone timber rectangle a short walk from the homestead, had a concrete floor for sluicing, and, at some stage after it was built, the godsend of flywire had been added to the open window frames. The morning was cool, and Peachey worked silently, with smooth, meditative movements that belied the potent force he brought to every stroke of the knife. Now and then, Andy threw a glance to Rascal outside, who was giving an occasional eager half-whine of appetite, while Strife sat in stoic silence.

A chirrup leaked down through the old wooden shingles.

'What kind of bird's that?' asked Andy.

'Butcherbird.'

'Huh,' the boy said. Perched at the other end of the bench, he picked up the black whetstone, and concentrated on the heavy, cold weight of it. 'Do you know your family tree?'

'I know the branch I sit on. Not much more than that.'

'I'm doing a project on mine, going back to the olden days.'

'Right.'

A different song drifted down through the shingles now. 'What kind of bird's that one?' asked Andy.

'A butcherbird,' said Pete, tossing the first of the large chunks of meat into the old tin tub on the floor.

'No, that was the other one.'

'Same bird, different song.'

Andy was dubious, but had other things on his mind. 'Did you know Grandpa Phil?'

'Yes.' Pete wiped his forehead, dripping some of the blood from his hand onto his shirt.

'And did you know my mum?'

'You know I did.'

'So you could help me with the family tree project, maybe. Tell me things about them . . .'

Peachey adjusted his grip on the knife. 'There's nothing I'd tell you that Matt or your nanna couldn't.' A new song started nearby. 'Now, what kind of bird's *that*?'

'A magpie?'

Pete stopped slicing, and turned to Andy. 'Nup. Same bird, son.'

'But it's completely different!'

Pete smiled. 'Yup. Good, isn't it?'

Andy touched a finger to his face, beside his eyebrow. 'Did you know I've got a scar?'

Pete glanced over, and the steady rhythm of the cutting faltered briefly as he registered its significance, recalling the feel of the featherlight baby as he had climbed from the mine. 'So you have.'

'It's a *forgetment*,' said Andy, who had already enlightened Peachey as to his theory. 'Unless' – his tone brightened – '*you* know how I got it?'

'Why would I know that?' Pete reached his hand out for the

whetstone, which the boy returned, and as he honed the knife, said, 'Sounds to me like a forgetment's a free pass, Andy. How would you *like* to have got it?'

The boy looked puzzled.

'Maybe it's your chance to make your *own* story about it. No one can say you're wrong . . . unless you get too far-fetched.'

A slight smile came to Andy's lips, as he imagined sword fights, or Apache arrows, or . . . The word 'far-fetched' brought him back to more likely encounters with barbed wire, or falling off his pony.

A new, high-pitched keening came from a tree. 'OK, and what's *that* bird?'

'Definitely not a butcherbird,' said Andy.

'Definitely *is*, young fella.' Pete wiped the knife methodically on a rag. 'A butcherbird has lots of songs, Andy. It's got its territorial song, and its mating call, its distress call, its warning cry. And sometimes, it just sings to itself, because it wants to; because it can.' He stored the blade in its leather sheath. 'Just because you've heard one song, doesn't mean you know the whole bird.' He turned to look at the boy. 'Good rule of thumb for life in general. No one's just one thing.' He lifted a bucket of water to the bench. 'Right. Off you get, unless you want a bath.'

Andy jumped down, and Pete proceeded to wash the wood, still scrubbing away long after the clots of blood were gone and the water ran clear.

15th June 1969

Dear Andy,

Thank you for the malachite sample. It is very good. Here is some galena on quartz. I like its cubic habitt.

I think I would not like a mine in my back yard. I hope you will not have one. It would probably annoy your sheep, and their wool would get very dirty.

Dad says this mine is not as prophetable as before, so they probably need to find another lot. If you have an asbestos mine my dad could work there and we could go prospecting together.

I am glad your family tree project is interesting. It is interesting to not have a dad because my dad has just always been here. He just works and sleeps. He was too puffed to do the dads egg and spoon race at sports day.

How many people are on your list for maybe being your dad so far?

I think it is very good that you have a friend who is an actual geologist, even if she is a lady one. She could help you find out about your dad if your nanna and uncle will not because she is a grown-up and is good at exploring.

Yours sincerely,
Harry (Badger)

The family tree project occupied the minds of each of the MacBrides, though for very different reasons. Andy felt a secret thrill at this chance to ask questions. But when he quizzed Lorna about anything recent, she fobbed him off with olden days stuff. Feeling thwarted, he began to look through the station diaries, forbidden though it was, to the year he was born, and to take notes of visitors he came across of, adding them to his List of Names. And Harry's idea of asking Bonnie to help secretly warmed him like a glowing ember.

54

IT WOULD TAKE a while, Myrtle knew: she couldn't expect an answer straight away. Still, since sending the parcel, she felt unaccountably nervy when the mail came in for sorting. Nearly three months had passed since she had sent it, on her birthday – the day of Dorothy Borrett's funeral.

She had sent a covering letter with the personal note, and the gift. It was a mad thing to do, but Myrtle often felt like she was going mad these days: her body heating like a combustion stove without warning; her rickety sleep a constant battle with bedclothes that left her too hot or too cold; irritation that would explode into fury at the least provocation, which she would then have to smother.

Myrtle had not taken a risk since she was seventeen, and though her sixth decade seemed rather late to start, she had taken the plunge.

She knew by heart the address of the private nursing home in Sydney, thousands of miles east of Perth, where she had had her baby. She had seen the infant, heard her squally newborn cries only briefly, before the child had been ferried from the room. But that had been long enough to hear it was a healthy girl, and to tell the nurse, 'Her name's Lorraine Lee. Please make sure she knows . . . Would have been Victor for a boy.' The nurse had given her a non-committal smile and a dip of the chin, and said, 'She'll be well cared for, don't worry.'

Myrtle's covering letter, addressed to 'Matron in Charge, Camperdown Nursing Home, 34 Sleet Road, Camperdown, Sydney', began:

Dear Madam,

I write on behalf of Miss Myrtle Keenan, who attended your establishment in March 1935 and was delivered of a baby girl, adopted through a private arrangement via your then medical director.

Miss Keenan would be grateful if you would contact her adopted child in order to deliver the enclosed gift and letter. Naturally, this matter is confidential, and any reply will also be treated in strict confidence.

Yours sincerely,
Mrs M Abernathy
Poste Restante
Wanderrie Creek
Western Australia

For thirty-four years, Myrtle had imagined her baby daughter: her smile, her velvet cheeks, her tiny fingers. Every baby she passed in the street, every illustration in an advert for baby formula – all triggered the image that was never far from her mind. And in the little vignette, she always pictured giving her daughter a doll – delicate porcelain, with eyes that opened and shut when you moved it. So, upon entering Spearritt's the Mercer's, that day in April, she had burbled something about a cousin in Melbourne who was expecting, and paid cash for just such a doll with wavy brown hair, who had come all the way from Germany and languished in a glass cabinet for years.

As for 'Mrs Abernathy', Clive would never know if someone of that name collected a poste restante reply while he was out . . . She thought about the doll; realised it was ridiculous to send it to a grown woman – to someone who in all likelihood had children of her own by now. But it had been in her heart so long, she couldn't *but* send it. As for the letter with it – she had agonised before setting pen to paper.

My dearest Lorraine Lee,

I wonder if you still have that name, which I gave you when you were born? It comes from my favourite rose (your grandmother's favourite, too), which blooms even in winter. Forgive me if you are called something else now.

I do not mean to intrude into what I hope is a very happy life. But I write just in case it is not. Just in case, for any reason, you may have thought that the woman – the girl – who bore you, did not love you; that you were given up for adoption because you were not loved.

Nothing could be further from the truth. I have thought of you every single day, and I have sung to you in my dreams and prayed for you so very often.

I also wanted to reassure you that there is no bad blood in you that you need to worry about. I know that sometimes children are given up for adoption because they are the product of something illegal or irredeemable. Your story is much more ordinary. Your father was the manager of the music shop where I worked as an assistant, serving customers and sight-reading sheet music for them on the piano when they wanted to choose a new tune. He was a very charming man, who, I discovered too late, had a wife and children who later joined him from Melbourne. I was seventeen, and could not have made a good life for you.

If you would like to know any more, write to Mrs Abernathy, and she will pass it on to me.

You are probably too old for dolls. But perhaps you have children who are not?

I wish you every good thing life can offer, my little one.

With fondest love,
Mother

55

By July, Bonnie was a familiar face at the homestead. Though it was winter, the cold nights could still deliver fine, mild days like this one, that saw her ready to set off with Andy.

'Right, Soot – got everything?' Matt put a hand on the boy's shoulder as Andy slid into Bonnie's front seat.

'Yep.'

'What time do you reckon you'll be back, Quiz?'

Bonnie checked her watch, then the sun, just edging over the horizon in a dazzle of yellow. 'Eleven? Twelve at the outside.'

'Keep an eye out, by the way – there'll still be lambs dropping in some of the paddocks you go through. The mums can get a bit upset if they're disturbed.' To Andy he said, 'Bring me back some gold.'

'I told you. We're not looking for gold. We're looking for tektites.'

'Well, *you're* looking for tektites,' Bonnie said. 'But just a tip: never turn up your nose if you *do* happen to trip over a gold nugget.'

Matt waved a salute as they headed towards the homestead gates, the dust clouds rising in their wake. At first, he had assumed Bonnie was just being polite when she let Andy buttonhole her about a rock he'd found, or a question about her work, but when she began visiting just to bring the kid some new sample or other, he realised she was genuine.

Andy couldn't help liking Bonnie, even though 'miners and sheep didn't mix'. He'd been angling for this trip ever since she'd mentioned that she would be heading out to Wordsworth paddock on some more searches. That was where three tektites had been found over the years. Now, as they drove, Bonnie tested Andy on crystalline formations; on whether basalt was igneous, metamorphic or sedimentary. In turn, he grilled her: how do you get to be a geologist? Was the study hard? What did she like best about it?

Then it was Bonnie's turn again. 'What was all that stuff taped to your wall? Looked like some sort of project.'

Andy seized his chance. 'That's the Rural Family Tree thing.'

'What's that when it's at home?'

He ran through the details, and mentioned some of the other names that belonged on the MacBride tree: Quortie, Skitch, Trellingham.

'One of my great-aunts married a Trellingham,' said Bonnie. 'Her name was Dora. Her father-in-law was shipped out as a convict when WA needed cheap labour in the 1850s. Is she on it?'

'I'll check,' said Andy, pleased with the connection.

'And what about the Brinleys? They had three or four stations out this way.'

'Yeah, I've got them.'

'I'm actually a Brinley,' Bonnie said. 'Nathanial Brinley, who came out on the *Parmelia* in 1829, was my great-great-great-grandfather.'

Andy frowned. 'Isn't your name Edquist?'

'Yeah. But it doesn't stop me from being a Brinley too.' Bonnie shook her head in mock despair. 'Typical. The women just vanish from the picture – they get married and lose their name, and become invisible . . . I bet you know all the old MacBride *men* on your family tree.'

'Yeah.'

'What about the MacBride *women*, who had to change to their husbands' names?'

'Oh . . .' Andy pondered the implications. 'So, do you know how to do family trees then?'

'A bit. From when my uncle got interested. He hired some researcher in London; traced us all the way back practically to the Middle Ages.'

Andy stared ahead, turning to survey an occasional sheep in the distance. 'If the women all lose their names, then I shouldn't really be Andy MacBride, should I?'

'Why's that?' The child's surname had simply never come up: he was just 'Andy'.

'Cos I should have my dad's name.'

'And what's that?'

Andy shifted in his seat. 'It's an ominous.'

'Anonymous?'

Bonnie stole a glance at him. Suddenly she had the impression of having wandered onto thin ice. She'd always assumed, from his declaration of orphanhood, that his father had died as well as Rose.

They continued in silence, Bonnie alive to a swarm of questions, Andy watching the red ants' nests, like miniature mountains. Eventually, he asked, 'Do you reckon he'd want to meet me?'

'Who?'

'My dad.'

'Umm . . .'

'Do you reckon he knows about me, and that he doesn't want to meet me? Or that he doesn't know about me, but would want to meet me? Or that he knows about me and wants to meet me? Or that—'

Bonnie felt a stab as this little boy went on to unburden himself as logically as he could. She had an urge to pull him towards her and plant a kiss on the top of his head.

'What does your nanna say? Or Matt?'

Andy pulled at a thread on the seam of his moleskins' pocket. 'I can't ask them.'

'Why not?'

'Well, it makes Nanna Lorna look like she's going to cry, and Matt gets grumpy, like he's bored.'

'Oh.'

'It's all right and everything . . . Nanna says that sometimes in life there just aren't answers, and part of growing up is getting used to that.'

'I see.'

He knitted his fingers tightly and blurted out, 'You could help me explore for him please.'

'Pardon?'

'Help me find my dad. Find out who he is. Or who he probably is.'

'Gosh . . . I'm not sure it's that simple, Andy.' Bonnie wiped each hand in turn on her jeans and returned it to the wheel.

'Who else can I ask?' He didn't take his eyes off her.

'Let's concentrate on your tektite hunt for the minute, and I'll come up with some ideas. I'll have a word to Matt.'

Horror shot across Andy's face. 'No! You can't talk to Matt about it. Or to Nanna Lorna.'

'Why not?'

'You just *can't*.'

She thought a moment. 'OK. Like I said. Leave it with me . . . Now, how much longer do you reckon it'll take us to get there?'

Bonnie agonised over what to tell Matt. When he walked her out to her car after she dropped Andy home, she said, 'Get in a minute, would you?'

'Sounds ominous,' said Matt, sliding into the passenger side.

'I thought I should tell you I . . . I know about Andy's father.' Matt froze, and she hurried on. 'Andy mentioned today how he doesn't know who it is.'

His adrenalin subsided and the muscles in his stomach loosened a fraction. 'Right.'

'You never told me,' said Bonnie.

He gripped the passenger strap above his window. 'It's not exactly something we shout about.'

She dared her question. 'Do *you* know? Who it is?'

Matt's breath slowed. 'I – don't think Rose ever told anyone.'

'I wonder . . .' Bonnie murmured. 'Whether he's still around somewhere . . .'

'If – if Andy's father could have claimed him, I'm pretty sure he would have . . . How did it come up, anyway?'

Bonnie recalled the boy's desperate '*No!*' 'Oh, he was just talking about his project.'

'That bloody family tree project! He's been driving us nuts with it. Once that kid gets the bit between his teeth . . .'

Bonnie leaned over and kissed him. 'I'm glad I know. And for the record, it doesn't make any difference to me.'

For a moment, Matt looked at her in the rear-view mirror in silence, then rubbed a hand over his face.

56

AFTER BETSY ASHBROOK'S arrest, the papers were full of stories about 'Botulinum Betsy'. With a mixture of sadness and fascination, Myrtle studied the charges and transfer to Perth to stand trial for murder; the defence of 'diminished responsibility'. And though she knew that the law would give no weight to what Betsy's husband had done to her, given she had carefully planned and intended to kill him, Myrtle couldn't help thinking he had it coming. A brute, by all accounts.

When Lorna MacBride read the first newspaper report in passing, she gave a concerned tut at the mention of Betsy's 'turbulent marriage'. Poor woman. Poor kids. All in children's homes now, it said. The article made no mention of what it was that caused Mrs Ashbrook to confess to the killing. Had Lorna known, she might have paid closer attention.

Betsy Ashbrook's was only the first of a number of old cases that Sergeant Rundle had reopened based on Misc. (Defunct) files. There was also Mr Jukes, for example. Seemed he'd been caught stealing from the collection plate, which wouldn't have been so bad had he not been the vicar. Johnny Sitterall – he married Sadie Binton and they were still married to this day, but she was only fourteen, and nine years his junior, on the wrong side of the legal line, when Cupid first shot his arrow. Then there was the small matter of the life insurance pay-out to the widow of Frank Chister when he seemed to have managed to crash his car into the only structure for miles. Policy wouldn't have paid out for suicide.

Rundle's investigations revealed that Reverend Jukes had given up the drink and the gambling and been promoted to bishop. The Sitteralls had six healthy kids, most of whom had already finished school and gone on to gainful employment, and the Chister family had managed to pay off the debts that threatened to hound them off their station, the oldest son taking over from his late father. That's how these stories had played out, in the fullness of time.

But that was Wisheart playing God, in Benedict Rundle's view. If you gave everyone a decade or so to see whether they made up for their crimes, gaols would be a darn sight emptier. And even though Wisheart did seem to have a knack for picking who would get back on the straight and narrow and stay there, that wasn't his prerogative.

Each of the handful of Misc. (Defunct) folders held a similar tale, and one by one, with no fanfare, Rundle was working his way through them, often in his own time. They were in no discernible order – date, alphabetical, nature of offence. So there was no telling when he would get to the file labelled 'MacBride: Rose Annabel'.

57

THE LAST OF winter passed quickly, with Bonnie away in Perth to report in about their disappointing results, and Matt taken up with lamb marking and drafting the weaners and buying in the new rams. Now, the September spring day was drenched in sharp light, hot in the sunshine and chilly in the shade. This picnic was the first real time they'd had alone in weeks.

'It's just the way I am. Don't take it personally,' said Matt.

'I'm the one who's asking, and I'm the one you're saying no to: how's that *not* personal?' Bonnie propped herself up on an elbow on the rug beside the creek, but Matt turned away for his tobacco.

He pinched the brown strands onto a paper. 'It's just – well, it's embarrassing: talking about myself – and about that sort of stuff.'

'What's so embarrassing about your first kiss?'

'Plenty . . .' He rolled the cigarette. 'She was still chewing gum . . . Her dad barged in on us . . . God!' The match shook a little. 'Can we just drop it?'

'Mine wasn't much better.' Bonnie gave a snort: 'Jeff! . . . We were twelve.' She took a sip of lemonade and rested the can back in the creek. 'Didn't count, really: he was my cousin. It was just sort of practice.' She noticed the tensing of Matt's neck, but was determined to keep going. 'So after – what was her name?'

'Julie.'

'So after Julie, who was your next girlfriend?'

He sat up. 'What is this? An interrogation?'

'Occupational habit – digging,' Bonnie said, and leaned to kiss him, sprinkling water from her fingertips in the neck of his shirt. 'So after Julie . . .'

'For God's sake . . .' He wiped off the water. 'You sound like that Sergeant bloody Rundle!'

Bonnie sat up and smoothed her T-shirt, then fixed her eyes on her knees as she slowly brushed the sand off. 'I . . . I have to tell you something.'

Matt looked doubtful.

'I *want* to . . . I was asking because . . . I – I don't want there to be surprises . . . or secrets between us.'

Matt drew smoke into his lungs, trying to steady his breathing. 'Bonnie, you don't have to—'

She cut him off. 'I was engaged. Before.'

Matt took another drag on his cigarette, letting the information sink in. It made him feel better somehow.

'Aren't you going to say anything?'

'What do you want me to say?'

'Aren't you going to ask me about it? Who he was?'

'No.'

'Or if we – how far we went?'

Matt stood up. 'How the hell's that my business? That's . . . It's private.'

'You've got a right to know.' Her voice dropped almost to a whisper. 'I thought he was going to marry me . . . So now I'm never exactly going to be the . . . well, the blushing bride . . .'

He knelt beside her, taking her hand in both of his. 'Let's both leave the past in the past, Quiz. Please.'

'Turned out he . . . he had another girlfriend all along. When I found out, and asked him how he could do it, how he could keep something like that secret from me . . . I'll never forget the look on his face: he seemed genuinely surprised. He said, "You never bothered to ask." ' She brushed an ant off and turned to face Matt. 'So I'm asking you. Straight out.'

Matt put his hand to the scar at the back of his head, touching the raised ridge under the hair as if it might guide him to a response. He looked her in the eye. 'Bonnie, I haven't got another girlfriend. I don't *want* another girlfriend.' He touched her cheek. 'And I swear on anything you like that I'd never cheat on you.'

She touched his hand. 'So, no secrets?'

The question pierced him. His heart sounded in his ears as he said, 'No secret girlfriends.'

58

CLIVE EEDLE WAS off at the Masonic Hall, getting things ready for his Lodge meeting. He'd left Myrtle to man the counter for the rest of the day, and cash up. Still, she had waited before she could safely pull down the blinds in the office and inspect the parcel addressed to 'Mrs M. Abernathy, Poste Restante, Wanderrie Creek.' Her breaths came as shallow as a mouse's and her hands had a fine tremor as she undid the brown paper. She grabbed the paperknife to slit the envelope inside it, and felt a dull pain in her chest at the sight of a pro forma document, with her name typed in at the top.

2nd September 1969

Dear Mrs Abernathy,

Thank you for your letter on behalf of Miss Myrtle Keenan. *As I am sure you will understand, we have a strict policy of confidentiality, not only as regards the young mothers who entrust their babies to us, but also for the couples who provide them with homes, and the babies themselves.*

Adoption is a fresh start for mother and baby, and it is generally acknowledged to be unwise to do anything that would jeopardise the integrity of Baby's new home. We therefore strongly encourage former mothers to devote their energy to their fresh start, knowing that the children are loved and cared for by families who desperately want them.

Thank you in anticipation of
your co-operation.

After this, the 'Yours sincerely' was typed through with a line of 'x's, and further typing added:

In the specific case of Miss Keenan, so much time has passed since the adoption that we can see no benefit to the now adult adoptee, her mother, or indeed to Miss Keenan herself, in disturbing what is most likely a very happy arrangement.

I therefore enclose her letter and parcel. I believe that, upon reflection, Miss Keenan will see the wisdom of this approach.

I wish her well in the fruitful life she has no doubt fashioned for herself after the unfortunate experience of her younger years.

Yours sincerely,
Dr. P Trethowen,
Director,
Harbourside Adoption Service
(Formerly Camperdown
Nursing Home)

Myrtle read it again and again, occasionally gulping a deep lungful of air after forgetting to breathe. Eventually, she rose unsteadily from her stool and carried the letter and parcel to the kitchen. She checked the clock. Clive's meeting would last until eight thirty.

As she went outside, the sun had just set, and the sandgropers were starting their croaking chorus in the faded evening air. She extracted her own letter from the doll's box and laid it on the garden table, before picking up the shovel and digging vigorously behind the Lorraine Lee rose bush: close, but far enough not to disturb her roots. Once she had dug a sizeable hole, she lowered the box in, the doll blinking through the cellophane at the sudden change in angle. Then she took her garden shears and cut the letters into fine confetti, which she mixed in with the soil she replaced over the box, and spread some loam over it.

She went inside and made herself a Vegemite sandwich for dinner, chewing as she scanned the funeral notices in that morning's paper. Tomorrow: 'Lycett: Stanley George, Requiem Mass at Our Lady Queen of Heaven Church, 10 a.m. No flowers please.' Tomorrow. She would let herself cry then. For now, she would tidy up her little records; update any notes with information she may have come across. And she would look again at her notes about Rose MacBride and her boy; follow that thread which hovered somewhere at the back of her mind.

As it happened, she wasn't the only person in Wanderrie Creek pondering the story of Rose MacBride that evening.

The following day, Sergeant Rundle nodded as he passed Myrtle on her walk back to the post office from the funeral. Then, to her surprise, he stopped and turned back.

'Excuse me, Mrs Eedle' – he steadfastly resisted her invitations to use her Christian name – 'I wonder if you could help me with a question.'

'Of course.'

He looked about, but there was no one within earshot. 'The MacBrides, out at Meredith Downs. What can you tell me about them?'

A flush came to her cheeks at being trusted with such a question. She considered her words. 'Quite a prominent family. Very sad history.'

'So I see from the records,' the policeman said. 'On an even keel now, though?'

'Oh yes.'

'The daughter, Rose . . . decent girl, was she?'

'She died before my time here . . .'

Rundle rattled the change in his trouser pockets, and asked in a lower voice, 'Had an illegitimate child, I gather . . .'

Myrtle, too, lowered her voice. 'Little Andrew.'

'And the father?'

'I can't say I've ever heard a name.' She pursed her lips briefly. 'What makes you ask?'

'Just checking my facts.'

'I see.' But Myrtle wondered if she really did see. That ungraspable instinct about Rose fluttered just beyond her awareness. 'Well, if I do hear anything about the father, I'll let you know.'

59

MATT SHONE THE light at the cave roof, where Bonnie had been chipping small pieces away every yard or so, slipping them into the calico bag. She marked the latest tag with the felt-tipped pen: '#774 – 16 Oct 1969', then dropped the sample into the bag Matt held out.

'I know you don't want to talk about it. That's sort of the problem,' she said, hooking her rock hammer onto her belt.

'Can we *please* change the subject?' His tone had an edge, and Bonnie hesitated.

'Just hear me out.' She wiped some grit from her eye.

Matt let out a slow breath. 'Go on then.'

'Things are changing, Matt. *Times* are changing. What used to be a big dark scandal ten years ago just *isn't* any more. I know at least two couples in Dalkeith who are living together who aren't married – and everyone knows!' She slipped her notebook into her breast pocket. 'I want to tell you about my cousin – Bernice. My Uncle Cyril's daughter.'

Matt leaned against the wall of the cave to wait out the lecture.

'I had no idea she existed until a few years ago. *No one* had any idea. Not even Uncle Cyril . . . Cyril always was a ladies' man – everyone turned a blind eye. Turns out he'd had a fling with a barmaid at one of the pubs in Avonmore, twenty-something years ago. Once the gold ran out, he upped sticks, leaving this barmaid pregnant.' Bonnie ran her fingers along the rock to select the next spot, then went on, her words punctuated by the *clink, clink* of the sharp hammer.

'Then about five years ago, a girl turned up at the office asking to see "Mr Hollamby". Cyril's dead, so the receptionist just assumed she meant Uncle Reg, and because the girl said she was family, showed her in. She handed Reg a letter from her mother, which said how she'd never told a soul and never wanted a penny, but that now she was dying, and her daughter was going to be alone in the world, so it seemed right to appeal to her father. If Cyril decided to disown her, there was nothing she could do, but she wanted to give him a chance to show the child that there was "goodness in the world, and kindness still".' She stopped. She knew she had Matt's attention.

'And?'

'And that girl became my cousin Bernice!' Bonnie inspected the latest sample, labelled it, and gestured to Matt for the calico bag. 'She's a secretary at the Commonwealth Bank in Forrest Place now.'

There was a silence. 'That the end?'

'Yes.' At his expression, she said, 'Well, no, it's not the end. Or it's not the point, anyway. If Cyril had known about the pregnancy back then, he'd have run a mile, or tried to make her get rid of it. I think that's why the mother didn't tell him. And yes, everyone in Hollamby circles would have wagged their tongues and gone on about the shame and the scandal. But not these days. People don't go around asking Bernice to produce her birth certificate every time they meet her.'

'So your point is?'

'My point is' – she leant over and shook the dust out of her hair – 'that your assumption that Andy's dad doesn't want anything to do with him might be wrong . . . It may never have been right, or it may not be right *any more*. Times change, and rules change. And most of all, *people* change, Matt.'

Matt was silhouetted against the mouth of the cave. His voice wasn't loud, but his tone was flint hard. 'This isn't Dalkeith, Bonnie. This isn't your world and it certainly isn't your family. You don't know a thing about my sister. The sooner poor Andy forgets the whole bloody thing the better. Just *let it alone*.'

He strode into the dazzling light, leaving Bonnie to stare after him.

In the nights that followed, Matt found himself back in shadowy dreamscapes he thought he had left behind for good. The fragments faded from his waking grasp: Andy bitten by a snake, lips blue and mouth foaming as Matt carried him back to the homestead to tell Lorna; Andy falling from the top of a mill and landing in a bloodless heap below, or succumbing to scarlet fever. Each dream would usher the same sequence of emotions: grief; overwhelming relief at the lifting of a monstrous burden; and, on waking, icy shame at that relief.

When he couldn't get back to sleep, Matt would go out to the verandah to smoke, listening to the crickets' relentless rhythm scraping the night sky. What did Bonnie know already? What else could she be allowed to know, about how Rose died at least? But how could knowing about that possibly help Bonnie? How could it help Andy? That was up to his mother. If she wanted anyone else to know how her daughter died, then he'd have to accept it. But he wouldn't be the one to rip that protective innocence from the boy, like a layer of skin.

He blinked a curl of smoke from his eye and looked up at the sickle moon that stared back at him out of the cloudless night. A sandgroper crawled up onto the verandah, trailing its loud chirrup on its way to find a better shelter. Its call was as loud as a frog, but it was just a tiny insect that preferred to stay buried under ground. Ants would make short work of it if it didn't burrow down again quickly. Matt nudged it back over the edge, back to cover.

60

ON THE DAY Charlie Knapp came to buy some of Lorna's pigs that October – a lengthy process, what with choosing them and catching them and loading them onto his truck – Andy had more time than usual to investigate the Fruit Crates.

He began, as he often did, with Rose's blue velveteen knitting bag. He inspected its thickest pair of needles; weighed them; held one like a pen, then a sword. He stuck the blunt ends up his nostrils to make tusks; wiped them on his shorts and put them back. Digging further, he pulled out a single, tiny yellow bootee from a ball of the fluffiest wool Andy had ever felt.

Next, there were the familiar pamphlets with sketches of girls looking dumb and staring into the distance, and inside, lots of mysterious numbers and letters. Andy knew these were knitting patterns because Nanna Lorna had some. About to put them back, he glimpsed a corner of something poking out.

He winkled out an envelope with a small gold crest. Inside was a thick white piece of paper, with the same crest.

27th April 1958

Dear Rose,

I am writing to apologise for my poor behaviour. I am so sorry to have hurt you. It was certainly not my intention.

Rest assured I shall never do such a thing again, nor speak of what happened, to you or anyone else.

I hope no harm has been done, and that you can forgive me.

With fondest regards, and sincere apologies,

Miles

The handwriting was perfect, like in school books. Below it in green ink, in writing he recognised as his mother's, were the words 'Touch has a memory', followed by a little sketch of a rose.

Andy gasped. This was definitely a secret. It was *his mother's* secret. And now it was *his*, too. Perhaps it belonged to the *three* of them, because the letter *might* be from his father.

He slid his hands around his shoulders and gave himself a hug, like the embrace of this little family he was kindling. This little family, this *true* family, that he would discover. If he just tried hard enough.

He slipped the envelope inside his shirt and put everything else back. He showed no interest in the bootee. It wouldn't have occurred to him that it was the only thing his mother ever made for him.

Names had floated about Andy in a grown-ups' mist since he was little. He'd grab at them like butterflies, not always grasping them fully. He liked it when he understood that Neil Tinnett knew Grandpa Phil in the war, for example. Or that Maudie Knapp was one of the first people to wheel him in his pram in town. It was like identifying new rock formations.

Where did the letter fit into his landscape? After some days, he decided to take a risk. He waited until he was alone with Matt, in Monty's shed, where his uncle was applying varnish to the deck.

'Matt, have you ever heard of anyone called Miles? Around here, I mean.'

Matt was absorbed in his task. 'You mean Miles Beaumont?'

'Miles who?'

'Beaumont. Worked as a trainee manager here, years back.'

'Oh,' said Andy, tapping the rudder from side to side.

'Great bloke, Miles. English. Practically royalty or something. Fantastic cricketer.'

Andy looked astonished. 'So there were *two* of them?'

'No.' Matt stopped his brushwork to look at Andy.

'But wasn't *Omo* really rich and good at cricket too?'

'His name wasn't *actually* Omo, you nitwit! It's the same bloke. "Omo" was a nickname.' He laughed again, a real belly laugh – what went on in that kid's mind? 'His father was Lord Beaumont. In fact *he* could be Lord Beaumont by now, if he's inherited the title.'

'What was he like? Was he handsome?'

Matt gave him a look. 'Funny sort of question . . . Looked like a film star, as it happens. Rosie had such a—' He stopped himself.

'Such a what?'

'Nothing. She just liked him. Why all the questions?'

'I thought I heard the name somewhere.'

'Uh-huh.'

'Did he die?'

'Not as far as I know. He's probably back in England playing cricket and drinking port in the bosom of his family.'

'Maybe we could visit him one day . . .'

'We could sail there,' said Matt, and brushed a dot of varnish on Andy's nose. He wondered where Miles was, these days. Not dead, he hoped. But he doubted he was in the bosom of his family, either.

61

SINCE SERGEANT RUNDLE'S questions about Rose MacBride and her boy, Myrtle's thoughts have returned to the pair like a tongue explores a broken tooth. It's not until Pete Peachey himself comes to the post office that she sees an opportunity to gather more information on events at Meredith Downs.

Since long before Myrtle's time, Pete Peachey's been sending these money orders. The amounts have risen steadily over the years, and these days they're in dollars, not pounds.

Myrtle enters them in the ledger for 31st October 1969.

'There you are, Mr Peachey.' She hands him the first order for a hundred dollars. 'Payable to P. D. Peachey, as usual.'

'Thank you.'

'Should I write "Peter" in full?'

'No. Thank you.'

'Right you are. And here's the fifty-dollar one – to the Methodist Mission of Nagasaki. Have I spelt that correctly?'

'Yes.'

'I always mean to ask you . . .' Myrtle began, and Pete's eyes flicked up to hers. 'What is it, the Nagasaki thing?'

He folded the money orders into his pocket. 'A charity. Orphans.'

'I suppose you can't blame the kiddies for what the Japanese did in the war, can you?'

'I don't.'

Pete was turning to leave when Myrtle said, 'Speaking of orphans . . . young Andrew MacBride . . .'

Peachey waited.

'I was trying to remember – a fall, was it, that took his mother?'

'Why?'

'Oh, Sergeant Rundle was asking. It was all before my time, but it occurred to me that of course you'd know . . .'

'Most people know about it – the fall.'

'Old mineshaft, wasn't it?'

'Very old.'

Myrtle straightened the papers in front of her. 'What was she like, Rose MacBride?'

'She was—a fine girl.'

'That poor little boy . . .' She closed the ledger book. 'Was the father ever in the picture?'

Peachey hoisted up his strides from the back of his belt. 'Mrs Eedle, if you're looking for gossip, you've got the wrong person.' He read the handwritten sign on the bowl of toffees: 'For kiddies only!' 'It's all old news. Lord knows why Sergeant Rundle would care. There have got to be better ways to spend his time . . .' He strode out, leaving Myrtle wondering yet again about what shame can do to a girl.

As Andy waited to be served at the post office a few days later, he surveyed the various posters: the calendar bearing the Commonwealth coat of arms; an advertisement for a bus trip around Australia; extracts from the Dangerous Goods Act 1938 prohibiting the posting of explosive materials without a permit. He imagined Harry Badger sending him some dynamite from his dad's mine . . . or would gelignite make a better bang?

'Next.' Mrs Eedle's voice pierced the daydream, and he heaved his box up off the floor.

'Pop it on the scale,' said Myrtle. 'Seven pounds five and a half ounces. For your friend in Mount Halcyon again, I see . . .' She ran her pencil down the price chart. 'That's thirty-five cents. Don't tell Mr Eedle, but I nudged the weight down to seven pounds. The next rate's forty cents.'

As Andy turned to go, she held up the toffee bowl. 'Don't forget!' He slipped one into his pocket.

'Actually, dear, while you're here, you might be able to help me . . .'. Is Mr Peachey shooting on your property at the moment, by any chance?'

'I think so,' said Andy, then wondered whether he might have given away something he shouldn't.

'A parcel came for him. Just missed the mail truck today. Seeing you're here, I wonder if you could do me a kindness and pass it on?'

She disappeared, and returned with a large flat box. 'Paris!' she exclaimed in a whisper. 'Say what you like about their food, but they *do* know how to do a stamp, the French.'

Andy reached for the parcel, but Myrtle said, 'I'll just pop some string around it.' With no apparent haste, as she wound the cord about the box she said, 'Remind me, what's his wife's name?'

'He hasn't got a wife.'

She tied a bow. 'Does he have a girlfriend? A lady companion?'

'No.' Then, less certainly, 'Don't think so . . .'

'Well, thanks again for taking this.'

Andy blushed as he walked down the street. His mind had fallen through a trapdoor. Pete Peachey *married*? The roo shooter *with a girlfriend*? It then skipped to the appalling and irresistible: Pete *smooching* a girl? The gears kept turning, until his heart started to thump wildly – his own *mum* was a *girl*. And Pete Peachey *knew* her. And her Fruit Crate had a target he'd made for her, with a .22 hole right through the middle.

Andy was almost running by the time he reached the car, and he very nearly cried aloud, 'Pete Peachey has to go on the List!' But as he saw Matt sitting behind the steering wheel – arm hanging out of the window, cigarette between his fingers – Andy willed himself to calm down. He would talk it over with Rascal when he got home, and together they would make a plan.

'What you got there, Soot?'

'Parcel for Pete. Mrs Eedle asked us to give it to him. It's from Paris!'

'Is that so?'

'Matt,' asked Andy. 'Does Pete have a – a girlfriend?'

'How old do you reckon Pete is?' Andy asked Matt the next day.

Matt leaned closer to the rain gauge to read it. 'No idea.'

'Did he really win the King's Medal?'

'Apparently.' Matt jotted: '6 Nov. 1969. Home Shed 8 a.m. 10 pts', and gave a nod of approval.

Andy inspected the note and nodded too. 'How long have you known him?'

'Since I was a kid. He came over from Queensland.' Matt handed back the notebook and pencil, and they headed to the car.

'Was he here when . . .' The boy paused for a run-up. '. . . when my mum died?'

Alert now, Matt said, 'Yes.'

'And before that?'

'He came just after the war.'

Feeling he'd made a successful raid on the information bunker,

Andy decided to make a tactical retreat, and changed course as he got into the front seat. 'How come he never talks much?'

'He talks when he's got something to say.' The engine rumbled into life and Matt put the car in gear.

'But not about his life and stuff.'

'We're not all chatterboxes like you.'

'Do I talk too much?'

'Nah. But you like your questions . . .'

They stopped for Andy to open the gate, then close it. Picking up as though there had been no pause, Andy said, 'But questions are how you learn, aren't they?'

'He spent a few years in a Japanese prisoner-of-war camp. If he doesn't want to talk about stuff, that's up to him. Lots of POWs don't.'

Matt's mention of POW camps did nothing to dampen Andy's curiosity: in fact, it had the opposite effect. He took to observing Peachey closely whenever he could, watching out for scars or other prisonerish signs. He also started to look for any family resemblance.

62

LATE ON THE same November afternoon that Wanderrie Creek is holding a small parade to send its latest batch of young men off to the latest war in Asia, Pete Peachey's .303 from the Second World War rests against a crate. His tent is warm from the spring sun, and he leaves the flaps open, guarded with insect netting. The narrow camp bed is neat, as is the folding table, served by an empty Castrol tin as a seat. Propped on the tabletop, beside his battered copy of *The Odyssey* and a volume of Shelley, is a mirror.

From under the bed he pulls a slim, crocodile-skin case. He settles onto the oil tin and flips open the case's catch. His leathery fingers hover over the contents: heavy crystal jars with silver tops holding face power, ointments, cold cream. The lids are frosted with red dust. He touches each piece reverently, the sensation on his fingertips taking him back to long-ago scenes lit by flames from rancid cooking fat – to a moment of respite.

Outside, a few flies buzz about probing the defences of the netting. The only other sound is the metallic creaking of the Jeep's engine as it cools. Peachey breathes in the expanse of thousands of acres, then turns to the task at hand.

First, he applies a rose-scented cream, light and buttery, his fingertips working it into his newly shaven skin and chapped lips. Next, he picks up the pot of rouge and dabs it along each cheekbone. He blinks and stares, blinks again, then opens a dainty compact cocooning a cake of mascara. He pours a few drops of water onto the black square and works it with the brush. Opening his eyes wide, he coats his lashes, first the top row, then the bottom. At a stroke they are longer, thicker; his eyes bluer. A dab of grey eyeshadow makes them almost violet, his long fingers surprisingly accurate at this delicate task. From another compartment he draws a lipstick, barely a stub now. With one coat, then a second, brilliant scarlet lights up his mouth

Putting on a play had been considered good for morale by the higher-ups, and harmless enough by the Japs, as long as they didn't have to supply anything. There had been much debate and negotiation about the choice. Nothing with swords or other combat, which ruled out half of Shakespeare. Nothing with a hidden political message, which ruled out the other half. At length, they settled on *The Importance of Being Earnest*, with roles allocated by a draw of twigs. And so it was that, against all probability, Captain Peter Peachey of the 2/26th Battalion found himself making his stage debut at the age of thirty-six in the role of Cecily Cardew, perhaps the first man over six foot tall ever to tackle the role.

As he enacts the ritual now, all his muscles relax. His heartbeat slows, just as it did when he stumbled upon it at the first dress rehearsal. There, amid the ribbing and the ribaldry, some sort of miracle unfolded itself in him. He was no longer a starving prisoner, no longer an officer, a soldier – not even a man, but a beautiful, bubbly girl, armed with some of the wittiest lines in English literature.

He found he could preserve that peaceful state deep within for hours afterwards: squatting over a putrid pit not fit to be called a latrine; squeezing nits between what was left of his thumbnails; holding up a companion too ill to stand at roll call. All the while his mind lingered somewhere in that perfectly civilized place.

Lady Bracknell ('A *kit*bag?' – liberties were taken with the text, which had been reconstructed from memory by a professor of

English literature) was a Welsh gunner barely respectably over five foot. Ernest and Jack were twins from Gundagai who'd joined up on the same day. Gwendolen was a notoriously dour quartermaster from Dundee with a previously undetected flair for comedy, and the Reverend Chasuble was an atheist Marxist who had once scored three tries for England. The play had been a triumph.

None of the others ever made it home.

It is almost done. Though he does not know it, he is beautiful like this – features fine and strong, mouth vivid, eyes glimmering with old sorrow. From the kitbag he draws the crimson satin – a lace-edged slip with straps so fine he has to be careful not to tear them away from the bodice. It slithers easily over his thin frame, transforming him inch by inch with its cool caresses. The touch of silk soothed him then, and soothes him now.

After the final performance, before the costumes had to be surrendered to the guards, he cut two inches off the hem of Cecily's dress. He kept the strip of pale green silk rolled up tightly, thinner than a cigarette. It fitted easily inside the hollow leg of his bed, and he had perfected the art of retrieving it and restoring it to its place unseen. A relic of the feminine – the touch of the women he loved and missed – the feel of this token, neither harsh nor threatening, sustained him. It became a secret talisman of tenderness in a place in which all tenderness was punished, and expressed only *in extremis* – smuggling an egg for a fellow who was nearing blindness from starvation; murmuring a prayer with another as you held him on his way to death in your arms.

He performs the ritual now by way of offering: to those who didn't make it; to the self that survived, and the self that died in the camp.

He makes his way out into the evening and straightens up, scanning the sky for the first glimmer of the Southern Cross, triangulating the then and the now by fixing his eyes on the constellation that has witnessed both.

63

BONNIE PASSED ANDY another pebble. 'Come on. As hard as you can.'

Andy hurled it with all his strength, making barely a dent in the red dirt. He was trying again as Matt pulled up in the ute and came to join them.

'What are you two up to?'

'We're seeing how hard you have to throw something to bury it in the ground like tektites are,' said Andy.

'Any luck?'

'It's hardly fair,' said Bonnie. 'I was just explaining how they hit the earth so hard you can find them a foot or more under the ground. It can take thousands of years for them to surface – by erosion, floods, wind.' She tousled Andy's hair: 'Luckily for geologists, nothing stays buried forever.'

'Bonnie brought me a new one. And some chrysocolla, and malachite. And azurite. Come and look!' Andy pointed to the verandah table. 'See the beautiful blues and greens? That's from copper.'

Matt picked up a slice of rock, one side polished to a glassy sheen. There were swirls of blue and turquoise, ultramarine and navy, with an occasional vein of brown. Other samples had been planed into random shapes, with an explosion of brilliant hues.

Andy handed Matt a magnifying glass to examine the minuscule crystal caves pitting the surface.

'You found this here?' Matt asked Bonnie.

'No. One of our copper mines, further north.' She stroked a sample with a thumb. 'Strange, isn't it? All these dazzling colours are caused by light, but they were never meant to see light at all . . . You have to defy nature to discover their beauty.'

'I'd never thought of it like that before,' said Matt, picking up a small black pellet. 'Tektite?' he asked Andy.

'Yeah.'

'Sure it's not a sheep dag?' Matt rolled the sphere between his fingers. 'Pretty boring, compared to the coloured ones . . .'

'No!' exclaimed Bonnie. 'They're the best of all.'

Matt looked dubious.

'Imagine what they've been through! People used to think they were meteor fragments, or even bits of the moon, but the latest theory is that they're terrestrial. Picture it – you're a bit of dirt, just sitting around, minding your own business, when *bam*! a meteorite slams into you, and you're flung hundreds of miles above the earth's atmosphere. Then you hurtle back down so fast that the friction melts you, completely re-forms you, and you hit the ground so hard that you bore down into it, knowing you'll probably never surface again . . . Changed forever in an instant.'

Andy reclaimed the tektite from Matt, who seemed to blink away a thought before asking, 'Are you going to peg a claim up near the lake?'

Bonnie hesitated. 'You know – sensitive information. Not mine to pass on.'

'I don't want to know anything you don't want to tell me,' Matt said. He eyed the progress of the sun. 'I'd better get going. Just came back for some more wire. Promised Bob Sowerby I'd help fix a bit of boundary fence with Maundy Creek that's come down.'

Andy gave him a quick 'Bye', and turned to Bonnie. 'Will you help me catalogue the new samples?'

Matt laughed. 'I'll miss you, too, Soot!'

In Andy's room, instead of getting out his collection, the boy handed Bonnie a letter, and pointed. 'How do you say this word?'

Dear Andy,

My dad can't work now. He has a thing called 'mesothelioma'. Some of the union say it is because of asbestos, but the company say it is because he did not wear the proper clothes they gave him and the mask. But it is too hot for the clothes, so they just wear shorts and they say they can not breathe properly with the masks.

He plays chequers with me and a card game called Briscola. My mum cries a lot. I am saying prayers for him so he will get better.

My mum bought a camera. I am enclosing a photo of my family. If you have one of you and your dog Rascal please send it.

Yours sincerely,
Harry Badger.

Bonnie took in the photo. A smiling, deeply tanned little boy with long, dark eyelashes and higgledy-piggledy teeth; a baby girl in his lap; and, on either side of him, a woman with short dark hair and pain in her eyes despite her smile, and a man with a gaunt, lined face. His hand grips his wife's on the baby's blanket.

A chill ran through her.

Andy folded the letter into its envelope, then turned to Bonnie, on the verge of a question.

'What?' she prompted.

'Nothing.'

'Go on.'

He didn't look up. 'You're looking for asbestos here, aren't you?'

'Amongst other things.'

'So do you reckon the union's right, or the company's right?'

'Not sure, Andy. There are different opinions.'

'But . . . if there's a crocidolite mine on Meredith Downs, will I get sick?'

'We're a very long way from putting in an actual mine, kiddo. I wouldn't start worrying just yet.'

It was one thing to see numbers on a page. It was another to see the face of a man who's almost certainly going to die. The medicos seemed to think it was probably safe enough, with protective gear and filtered air. Still, thought Bonnie as she drove back to camp, she'd raise it with Uncle Reggie; maybe ask around at the big mining conference she was due to attend in Sydney in January. And she'd get them to run the numbers again on the return on investment for this project.

64

UNLIKE THE EXAMPLE in the post office, there were no fly specks on the Annigoni portrait of the Queen in the Wanderrie Creek Police Station. It hung prominently behind the counter, where, on this November morning, Pete Peachey was applying to add a new .25/20 to his gun licence.

'Nice gun,' said Constable Stidworthy. He looked through the sight. 'Just between you and me, I'd make sure all the details on your licence are correct – all your guns listed.' There was a nervous edge to his voice as he added, 'Things have changed since Wisheart's time.'

'So I gather,' said Peachey.

As he completed his inspection, the young constable enquired about the stock, the gunmaker, whether Peachey thought it was good value, then ticked the box on the form to confirm that it appeared to be in safe working order. His hand automatically added another neat tick to the section confirming that the licence holder was a 'fit and proper person to possess a firearm'.

'Right,' the constable said. 'Just need to pop out the back to get the Big Boss to sign it.'

'Don't you usually sign it yourself?'

'New rules. Likes to know what's going on. All part of his campaign to "clear the moral sewer".'

'That'll keep him busy.'

While Peachey waited, he took the rifle from the counter, and moved the bolt back and forth a few times, testing the smoothness of its glide. When the constable re-emerged a few minutes later, he was not alone.

'Mr Peachey, is it?' asked Rundle.

The sergeant was examining the licence, with its list of registered firearms, and Pete asked, 'All in order?'

Rundle read on for a moment. 'Satisfactory.'

Peachey put out his hand for the licence, which now listed the new gun, but as the sergeant returned the paper booklet, he said, 'Actually, I'd like a word with you about something else, while you're here. Mind stepping into my office?'

The sergeant disappeared through the door, leaving Stidworthy to give Peachey a wary shrug.

'Have a seat,' said Rundle, sitting down at a desk with a few manila folders.

'Anything wrong?' asked Peachey.

'Just a general query. Help with a bit of local background.'

Peachey gave a nod.

'You've lived in the district a long time,' said Rundle.

'A while. Came after the war.'

'Know the locals well, I suppose.'

'Not especially.'

Rundle tapped the point of his pencil slowly on the open folder in front of him. 'Bit of a loner then . . .'

'I keep myself to myself.'

Pete considered. It was no skin off his nose what sort of a bloke Rundle was, except in one respect: they both knew the sergeant could take away his gun licence if he decided he wasn't 'fit and proper'. Under the Firearms and Guns Act, the local policeman could make his life hard: search his camp, his ute; call time on his shooting days altogether if he wanted.

'Know the MacBrides pretty well, though, do you? I hear you were friendly with the father, Philip? When the constable brought in the form, I thought I recognised your name.' He gave another few taps to the file. 'You were the one who found her.'

'Found who?' Pete's mind had raced ahead, but he still couldn't work out where this was going.

'The MacBride girl. Rose.'

'Ah. I did, yes. Long time ago now.' He settled back in his chair, and offered no more.

Rundle was studying the documents. 'I'm a tidy man, Mr Peachey. Tidy habits. Tidy mind. So you know what makes me unhappy? Untidy files.'

Pete raised his jaw a fraction.

'And a few of Sergeant Wisheart's files are a dog's bloody breakfast, I can tell you.'

'I see.'

'You may have heard of some of the irregularities I've come across? The Ashbrook case, for example?'

'Not really.'

Rundle steepled his fingers. 'So . . . Rose MacBride. You found the girl. Tell me about that.'

The question took Peachey by surprise – the bluntness, the directness. 'What – you mean—Well, she was dead.'

'Yes, yes, but what were the details? The *details*, man? What time did you find her, exactly? What was she wearing?' He brushed a dead moth from the file. 'What state were her clothes in? File's very vague. Did you make a statement at the time?'

Pete took a breath. 'I told Sergeant Wisheart everything. Took him to see where she fell.'

'Only, there's nothing in the file from you. And no autopsy. No inquest.'

Peachey thought back to that time, and to the agreed story which, by the sounds of things, Wisheart had kept to. But could he be sure? He decided to take a risk. 'Sergeant Wisheart looked into it thoroughly, as I recall. I wouldn't know about the formalities. It was a fall.'

'So . . . I'll just have to take Sergeant Wisheart's word for that? Unless you'd care to fill in some of the missing details?'

'Not much I can tell you after all these years. The MacBrides are a good family, and Rosie was a fine girl.'

'*Rosie*,' remarked Rundle. 'Not Rose. Close to her, were you?'

'I'd known her since she was a tot.' Pete saw a muscle twitch in the policeman's jaw. 'Lots of people called her Rosie.'

'And the boy's father?'

'The father?'

'You said you were very close to her. No idea who the father of her child was?'

Peachey ignored the subtle twisting of the words. 'Not sure she ever told anyone.' He took a deep breath, and tilted his head towards the tower of files. 'You're going to have your work cut out if you're going back over all Sergeant Wisheart's cases.'

'Not all. Just a few anomalous ones. It's never too late to investigate, and to right a wrong. That's why it's called "the long arm of the law".'

'You might need to bring in reinforcements if you're going to start policing the past as well as the present.'

Rundle was about to say something, but stopped. 'Well. Shame you couldn't shed more light.'

When Pete got back to his ute, Strife was waiting eagerly in the passenger seat, and he scratched the dog's neck. 'We've got a doozy there, mate. *You* wouldn't give him the bloody time of day.' The old dog, sensing something in his master's bearing, nudged up beside him until they were shoulder to shoulder against the world.

65

A FEW WEEKS after her fruitless questioning of Pete Peachey, Myrtle's magnifying glass hovered above a photograph in the back of the Wanderrie Creek Observer in the 'Remember When?' section. Every month it reprinted an old article – about a cyclone, an official visit, a sporting event – from a back number of the paper. Myrtle raised the magnifier, and then lowered it for better focus. Yes! It *was* her. Rose MacBride, with other named members of the Young Pastoralists' Committee, all pointing at a map of the route the Queen Mother's car would take during her visit to Perth the following March.

This was the first time Myrtle had seen a photograph of Rose. As well as looking like his uncle, the little boy looked like his mother. She checked the date. December 1957 . . . A tingling at the back of her neck made Myrtle put down the magnifying glass. She shuddered, and pulled the sides of her collar together as inky shame surged through her veins.

Hunching her shoulders, she hugged her arms, almost dizzy with the speed with which she was seventeen again, soon to give birth. Nurses scurried about the ward, muttering sternly to one another about Shirley, the girl missing from the bed two spaces down, whose baby boy had already been collected by his new parents. '*Have you checked the grounds? Looked in the bathroom?*' She pictured them all flowing like a tide out of the door, then eventually trailing back in, ashen-faced and tight-lipped, dispensing, under duress, pinched phrases: *'Fall from the balcony. Fatal. So unfortunate.'*

Shirley and her 'fall' . . . Myrtle examined Rose's picture again. Perhaps she was just jumbling stories. But the evening of Shirley's death was the first time she had been aware of the murkiness within herself – beneath the fear and the shame. And it had been the first time she could call it by a name: rage.

She remembered looking along the ward – there were ten beds, all but Shirley's occupied, by girls from twelve to twenty-five, coming to pay a price. *Where are the men?* she had wanted to scream. *None of us did this by ourselves!*

Now, Myrtle went to the Drawers of Death and tiptoed her fingers across the notebooks, opening the one in which she'd jotted down details of all those MacBride deaths. 'Rose MacBride. January 1959. Fall at mine on Meredith Downs, family property.' After a moment's hesitation, she added the asterisk that had been hovering about in her thoughts since the day she'd first heard the story.

Where are the men? Where was the man who was living happily now, years after Rosie MacBride had disappeared like Shirley had, after her 'fall'? And that little boy, Andrew, who would never know his mother's love? There was a man strolling around, possibly right here in Wanderrie Creek, who'd fathered a child and got off scot-free, while a girl had paid with her life.

She pictured the men who came into the post office, and wondered, *Was it you?* She wasn't at all sure what she might do if she ever found out. Confront the fellow? Slap him? Denounce him? Or perhaps just murmur, 'I know,' as she passed him his stamps . . .

As she took up the scissors to cut out the article, a vision of silk and chiffon came back to her. Pete Peachey . . . He'd been hanging around the MacBrides for years. And who was he buttering up now with his fancy satin nighties?

66

When Humpty Dumpton visited Meredith Downs for lunch that December, Lorna asked Matt to invite Bonnie. The dark dining room held the fierce heat at bay as Lorna passed around platters of cold meat and salads. As people began to eat, Coral glanced at her husband, then tapped her glass with a fork. 'Everyone? We're going to have a baby!'

A ripple of surprise crossed people's faces, and she added, 'We've been given the OK to adopt!'

Matt clapped Humpty on the shoulder. 'Good on you, mate!'

As Lorna put her glass down after the toast, a thought drew her gaze to Andy, methodically picking out pieces of gherkin and quarantining them on the side of his plate. Funny little beetle. Would he have been doing that in another family, had Mrs Blencombe found him another home? Would he have become a different person? Every adopted baby comes from a cradle of sadness for someone. She said a silent prayer for the child who would be given to Hughie and Coral, and for its other parents.

After lunch, Andy disappeared on an adventure with Rascal involving a home-made bow and arrow, and a head-dress of old chook feathers for the dog, while the women went to inspect Lorna's roses, leaving Matt and Humpty in the shade of the verandah.

'You've certainly cheered up since I saw you last time,' said Humpty, grinning. 'I can see why.'

'Oh bugger off.'

'You're not going to let her get away are you, you spastic?'

'Spastic yourself,' Matt replied, and began to roll a cigarette. 'But the adoption – that's fantastic. You'll make a beaut dad.'

'I reckon you would too. Hence my previous remark.'

Matt's lit match halted a moment before reaching the cigarette.

'Seriously, what are you waiting for?' Humpty took a sip of his beer. 'The bird's obviously crazy about you, you dimwit.'

Three days after Humpty's lunch, Bonnie takes in the spectacle of a flock of budgies – tens of thousands of them in a starburst around the claypan lake that's formed after recent unseasonal rain. They'd begun to arrive just after dawn, hundreds at a time, building up to this vast, noisy storm of wings in green and gold. The joy of it, the limitlessness of this place, makes her feel physically – just *more*. She's felt so alive since coming to Meredith Downs.

Though she's not from this country, it speaks to her, just like rocks anywhere tell you things if you know how to read them. She's captivated by the creatures that are so at home here: the thorny devil she sees scuttling away, its spikes and stripes of ochres and browns providing life-saving camouflage. A few feet away lies the dried-up carcass of an emu savaged by a dingo, the deep teal eggshells emptied of their treasure. The intricate war of survival. The lives left behind.

Breathing in deeply triggers a memory – of the evening, over two years ago now, that Stewart proposed. The way her heart had seemed actually to wobble, and her head spin: *chosen* by a man who was everything her parents could hope for, everything her friends would want. She remembers trying so hard to *deserve* him: getting her hair cut exactly the way he said to; endlessly standing on the sidelines of rugby pitches in muddy drizzle or of cricket ovals in withering heat; always dressing so that she was 'a credit' to him. As for the pressure he'd put on her to sleep with him before they got married . . . She shivered.

Here, in this expanse of sky and land and time, she could hardly believe what a *small* life she'd been living, trying to squish herself into an existence as dainty as the high heels he liked her to wear. Bonnie laughed: Matt MacBride probably didn't notice if she was wearing shoes at all, unless there were snakes or thorns around. Never told her what to do, what to think. '*Quiz*'. She liked that he'd christened her that. She tried to make a survey of the reasons he made her heart beat faster: she was drawn to the mystery of him, the puzzle. She wanted to belong, not *to* him, like Stewart had wanted, but *with* him.

Sometimes, though, she wished he would hold her a little more tightly. She burrowed under that thought to find its root . . . She wasn't sure whether . . . whether she had his *permission* to love him – that was it. Couldn't be sure she made him feel the same way he made her feel whenever she saw him.

There were times she felt so sure he loved her, even though he'd never let those words pass his lips. He treated her so gently, attentively, when they were together, always waiting to follow her lead, saying not to rush things. But there were times – times he was a million miles away: as though he barely knew who she was. Perhaps there was something in him that was simply . . . broken.

She took in the whirlwind of birds again, fewer now. Was she just imagining things, with Matt? Maybe it was all just her own wishful thinking. She'd got it wrong once before, after all. She burned at the memory of the deadening humiliation after breaking off the engagement. The awkward, pitying looks. At least she'd had the guts to do it. Stewart truly didn't see what she was so upset about; had called her hysterical, and lectured her about mountains and molehills and bad form and spinsters ending up on the shelf.

The budgies had flown off, invisible now as they foraged for seeds in the wild grasses, leaving the air still, quiet.

She was running out of excuses to be at Meredith Downs. On her last visit to Perth, Uncle Reggie had said, 'The results there aren't sounding too promising, are they, Bonbon? We'll give it a bit longer, but it's starting to look like a wild goose chase. I could do with your help on that bauxite project when you come back from the Sydney conference.'

The fact was, she couldn't bear the thought of leaving. Bugger bloody surveys of reasons. She loved Matt, broken or not. She loved him and not the next guy, just like she liked the colour blue and not yellow, or liked the taste of watermelon and not plantain. It was sort of chemical. Like copper, always wanting to bond with oxygen molecules, because it just bloody did.

The light was changing, a dusty pink washing into the blue as the sun splashed droplets of light on leaves and an occasional glinting quartz fragment. She could only stall Reggie for so long. But hell might freeze over before she worked out whether Matt really wanted to be with her. If only he were a sample she could shove into a mass spectrometer to get certainty.

'Come on, Edquist,' she said aloud. 'You're a long time dead.' And she wished Matt had been there to see the wondrous flock of birds with her; looked forward to telling him about it. She turned her attention to the map in her hands, working out the distance back to camp.

Ever since Hughie and Coral had announced their adoption news, Lorna had been wrestling with a thought. Of course she wanted happiness for Matt, but it hadn't been until that moment that she realised how desperately she wanted it, and she realised some things were going to have to change. Could she find the courage, though?

When Bonnie had dropped in a report that afternoon, Lorna had quizzed her subtly about her work and her family and what she made of life in Wanderrie Creek. Last time Lorna was at the post office, she had only half minded when Myrtle Eedle had made some knowing remark about Matt and Bonnie 'getting along very well' – seen them at the pictures together, apparently. Even Neil Tinnett had made a comment about Matt seeming like a new man since 'that mining girl' had come on the scene.

The nights she'd lain awake worrying about her son . . . The number of times he'd come back from social outings she'd engineered, always answering her question of 'Anyone special there?' with an embarrassed frown. Something about that lunch with Humpty had given Lorna a sense of urgency. So, when Lorna had mentioned to Bonnie that Matt seemed so happy these days, she was gratified that the girl blushed. 'Don't want to jinx things,' Bonnie had said.

Now, as Bonnie followed Lorna up and down the rows of beans, the older woman occasionally stooped to snip a few and drop them into the wicker basket on Bonnie's arm, to join the apple cucumbers and sweetcorn.

'It's so nice of you, Mrs MacBride. We're not exactly spoilt for fresh vegetables at camp.'

'Got to get your vitamins. And do call me Lorna, dear.' Though it still didn't sit entirely comfortably with Lorna, she had to admit that she liked Bonnie Edquist, for all that she was digging up the place left, right and centre.

Bonnie flicked a money spider off the corn. 'No Andy today?'

'He's wrapped up in that blessed family tree project. It's a wonder he hasn't bent your ear about it.'

Bonnie shifted the vegetables in the basket, thinking back to her promise of secrecy to the boy. 'He – ah, he mentioned something . . .

Come to think of it, I could probably give him a hand.' She mentioned her experience with her own family tree; with research.

Lorna had 'talked things over' with Phil a great deal of late, and they both agreed that Bonnie was good for Matt. She was even good for Andy. Now, as she bent down again, Lorna consulted Phil about the whole business of Rose: what to say to Bonnie, and when.

She thought back on her marriage. It had been *one* life, not two: what Phil knew, she knew, and vice versa.

Lorna could wait years for another suitable girl to come along. 'There is a tide in the affairs of men . . .' If she wanted Matt to have what she and Phil had had, then whoever he ended up with was going to have to be told about Rose at some stage, if only to know to keep Andy away from the topic.

Lorna dropped some silver beet into the basket and put both hands to the base of her aching spine. 'It's very kind of you to offer to help with the project. But . . . there's something about Andy you need to know.'

'You mean Rose not . . . not being married to his father. Yes, of course, I understand that that's, well, delicate.'

'It's – it's not that, dear. Though you're right, that *is* delicate.' She slipped her garden fork into the pocket of her apron. 'Andy . . . doesn't know the whole story of how his mother died. Only a handful of people do.'

'The fall?'

'Yes.' Lorna hadn't told another human since she'd confessed it to Maudie Knapp, after Sergeant Wisheart had left that day in 1959. She consulted Phil again: there could be no un-telling. Could this girl be trusted? To which Phil's silent response was, *You're a good judge of character, love. You decide.*

Slowly, Lorna wiped dirt from her palm. 'If I tell you something . . . can I trust you to treat it in the *strictest* confidence?'

'Of course.'

'I'm telling you so that—so that Matt doesn't have to hide it from you, and so that you'll promise to keep Andy safe from it, if you help him with his project.'

The muscles in Bonnie's jaw were tight as wire, her anxiety growing. 'I promise.'

'Rosie did die in a fall at the mine . . . but it – it wasn't an accident. She . . . took her own life.' Lorna gazed in the direction of the Proserpine ruins. 'And she – tried to end Andy's life with hers – he was in her arms. That's how he got the little scar near his eye.'

Bonnie didn't breathe. 'And Andy has no idea?'

Lorna's eyes glistened. 'He's a little boy!'

Bonnie couldn't reply.

'So, if you do help him with the project, you'll wear kid gloves if he asks about his parents. Don't go putting questions in his head or encouraging ones whose answers would ruin his life.'

Still, Bonnie had no words. Her heart raced as she thought back to her conversation with Matt about her cousin Bernice: it felt so fatuous.

'I'll let Matt know we've spoken,' said Lorna. She eyed the angle of the sun. 'Better get this into a box for you and get you on your way. Not much light left.'

When Bonnie told Matt about the conversation a few days later, she said, 'I won't mention it again . . . I can't begin to imagine how you've coped.' She stroked a small blister on his thumb. 'I wish I could change it for you.'

12th December 1969

Dear Harry,

Thank you for your letter of the tenth inst. I hope your dad is better.

This is a secret so please don't tell a sole. I might find my father soon. It is hard because there are two people it probably is. One is our roo shooter Mr Peachey who is old but nice. He is good at shooting and I am too so we are alike. I am doing surveylance on him. The other person is called Miles. He is royal or something and good at cricket and probably lives in England.

Does your dad like you and what should I do so that my dad likes me when I discover him?

Yours sincerely,
Andy MacBride

P.S. *Remember it is* TOP SECRET.

67

THE WIND HAS been dancing over this land forever: gentle breezes, mischievous willy-willies, fierce storms – all have shaped and reshaped the place now called Meredith Downs. Whispering through grass and whistling through flywire, it tells its timeless story. Once in a while it roars through in a terrifying vortex, like the cyclone that hit nearly two weeks after Humpty Dumpton's visit, and was as violent as it was unforeseen. The warnings from the Bureau of Meteorology were for districts further west, but, as cyclones sometimes do, this one – Linda – had changed her mind at the last minute and rampaged inland. She might have been almost welcomed had she brought blessed rain to make the ancient rivers run and the frogs spring up from underground and the earth sprout green. Instead, she was the rarer kind that brought only winds – solid air that flattens all before it, hurling trees and buildings and mills like a raging giant.

But first came the dead calm.

The strange red-grey sky, heavy and still, was the earliest signal that something was coming. The air felt charged with electricity; the birds fell silent. Matt and the station hands did their best to tie down equipment near the homestead that would otherwise become missiles; closed shed doors and tin shutters; then headed to their respective quarters to hunker down. Lorna had filled the bath with water, along with the sinks and basins and as many jugs and buckets as she could find – the homestead rainwater tanks were old and might not hold. She got Andy to fill all the oil lamps and gather the boxes of candles and matches. By 3 p.m. the sun was a pallid glow that had burrowed to safety behind the clouds, to watch just what the approaching wind was going to do.

What it did was destroy: blast, shatter, lash. It hurled itself at everything that stood above the ground, twisting mills, peeling tin off the roofs of some of the sheds, while Matt, Lorna and Andy sat in the kitchen listening as it strained to get at them. When the aerial mast crashed to the ground, they were completely cut off from the outside world. There was nothing to do but wait. And hope.

Now and then, a thump or a clang would punctuate the buffeting of the wind, but if Andy tried to peer outside, Lorna would warn him away from the windows, knowing each pane of glass could become lethal. Matt and Lorna had been through countless cyclones, but – as their silent looks to one another acknowledged – never one as savage as this. Though to Andy, Lorna would say, 'It'll pass, Beetle. Things'll be all right by tomorrow.' And Matt would go back to testing him on minerals with the help of that bible, *Junior Geology*. When the boy finally went to sleep on a mattress under the table, they sat up all night, taking it in turns to doze, Lorna knitting and Matt browsing *The Countryman*, while his thoughts were dragged constantly to Bonnie, and to her crew. There had been no means to contact them when the storm hit. Though the caravans were sturdy, they were hardly built to weather this.

But Hollamby Mining had deep pockets, and years of experience in the outback. Best case was that head office would have taken no chances about the cyclone's path, and sent instructions in advance to shut down the site and head into town until it had blown over. Worst case was that Bonnie had decided she wouldn't be beaten by a stupid cyclone, and that every drill bit and core sample and pipe had been turned into weapons against her.

As the world swirled around Matt, so it tumbled within him. His thoughts kept oscillating between Andy, at least safe for now, and Bonnie, who was somewhere either in harm's way or out of it: he had no way of knowing. When he told his mother he had to go and check on the miners, she said, 'You'll never reach them in this. You won't be much good to Bonnie dead.' Then her face had softened. 'She will have gone to safety. She's sensible, that one.'

As the night wore on, sensations within him grew and merged and formed a clear realisation – he couldn't bear the thought of anything happening to Bonnie. He couldn't bear the thought of life without her.

* * *

The night had passed somehow, and eventually the wind feathered to an innocent breeze.

By morning, the inside of the house had undergone a transformation: grit had blasted down chimneys and swirled under doors, found the slightest gap in any window frame, and insinuated its way into every cupboard, even between stacked plates, which now rasped to the touch. Every surface was caked in dust and fine sand, like an emery board: the collars of Matt's shirts, the pockets of his jackets in the wardrobes, the socks in the drawers, the pillows, the lampshades, the keys of the piano. Even the face of Old Wally glistened with fine silica, though somehow he managed to chime the hour just the same.

When Matt ventured outside in the bruised early light, he was struck by a change in the colour of his car. A finger traced through the dust on the bonnet revealed bare metal: the cyclone had sandblasted the windward side of all the vehicles, stripping away the paint.

Most of the sheds were intact, though with sheets of metal missing here and there. The old tank stands for the homestead had survived. But when Matt tried to get the generator going, it had seized up, completely filled with grit.

The first job was to get the wireless aerial back up, which with the help of a couple of the boys was achieved by mid-morning. Lorna used the whistle to send the emergency transmission tone to make contact outside their usual time slot, to let the Flying Doctor know they were safe. She in turn listened to the reports of who'd been hit by the cyclone and who'd been spared. There had been deaths – a couple of well-sinkers whose truck had been crushed by a falling tree; one of the jackaroos on Termite Plains who'd had an artery severed by a sheet of flying tin. Just as Matt was pushing a note in front of Lorna to get her to ask about the Hollamby crew, the operator said, 'Hang on. Telegram for you. "All safe in town STOP Bonnie STOP You? STOP".'

The relief that had flooded through Matt at hearing the telegram was banished by the sight that greeted him when he drove with Lorna and Andy to inspect the damage beyond the homestead. The wind had corrugated the roads like claws scraped through flesh. Every trough was clogged with sand. Some of the mills were down, a few completely flat or folded in half as if bowing. The rain gauges were full, not of water, but of earth: there had been barely a drop of rain. It took Matt a while to work out the other impact – so big it was hard to take in. About five inches of topsoil had simply disappeared. For decades, sheep, with their sharp teeth, had been chewing down vegetation much lower than cattle could, uprooting plants altogether. Their small hooves had broken the delicate ground that had been naturally webbed by a million fine invisible roots. Now, the earth had been carried off as if by a thief, smuggled to the claypans or the cliff sides, piled up against fences and the sides of sheds, or carried hundreds of miles to descend as a gossamer mist in the desert. Those plants in the path of the wind that had not been wrenched out completely were now exposed to the ends of their roots, at the mercy of the desiccating air.

When the family finally pulled up back at the homestead hours later, Matt gave a deep sigh, and leaned his head on the steering wheel, defeated, bewildered.

'We'll get through it, Mattie,' said Lorna. 'We've got through worse than this.'

Late that afternoon, as Matt approached the Hollamby campsite, it took him a moment to work out what he was seeing. One of the caravans had been upended, and leaned against a collapsed drilling rig like a drunk propping up a bar. The tubular core samples strewn about reminded him of the coloured sprinkles Lorna put on cakes. Then, as though someone had drawn a line, the other side of the camp, including the caravans and a Land Rover, was utterly untouched.

He got out of the car to inspect the damage. Hands on hips, the wing of his sunglasses in his mouth, he righted a tin of powdered milk with his toe, took in the smashed mugs and sauce bottles that the wind had flung about. Hell. This was going to take some putting back together.

As he reached the corner of the mangled caravan, he saw the silhouette of someone sitting on an oil drum, unlacing a boot. Then came a roar. 'Argh! Come on you bastard bloody stone! Get out of my bloody shoe! I haven't got time for your crap today. Bugger off!' Bonnie shouted, and hurled it over her shoulder in disgust.

When her eyes alighted on Matt, she ran to him. He hoisted her up onto his waist and locked her in his arms, squeezed almost as tightly by her.

He gave her a long, urgent kiss, then lowered her to her feet and pulled her in to him.

'How's the homestead? Lorna and Andy OK?' asked Bonnie eventually. She took in the smashed core samples, the mangled equipment. 'Bloody hell . . .'

'Your crew'll be able to put things back together. I'll get some of the boys to help, if you like,' said Matt.

Bonnie looked at him, then looked away. 'Too late.'

'That's not the Bonnie Edquist I know. Where's that bloody-minded determination?'

'I . . . The search results haven't been as promising as we'd hoped.' Matt's eyebrows arced in a question, and Bonnie said, 'I – I shouldn't really be telling you. We haven't made any announcement to the stock exchange or our investors yet . . .'

'About what?'

'We would have been packing up anyway . . . This is just the last straw. I've been called back to Perth: that's why we were all in the meeting in Wanderrie Creek. The company's made a big bauxite find near the border. Uncle Reg wants me to go and have a look, as soon as I get back from the Sydney conference.'

Matt's body was reliving last night: the terror at the possibility of harm coming to Bonnie. Now, the tide of relief that had swept over him at seeing her surged out again just as quickly. As if he'd had any right to feel like that. To imagine she might stay.

His gaze was fixed on the drill rig. 'How long have you been planning on leaving?'

'It's more a question of how long I've been trying to stay . . .'

'What?'

'For a smart bloke you can be pretty slow on the uptake, Matt . . .' Bonnie picked up a dented Thermos, gave it a shake, then let it drop as she heard the broken glass inside it. 'I think you . . . just don't like taking risks.'

'I've honestly got no idea what you're talking about,' said Matt, but his heart had picked up pace.

'Well, you work it out. Why would I have tried to stay here?'

'For your work.'

She slapped her forehead. 'Agghh! There you go again. Always leaving it to me to make the running . . .' Taking in the uprooted trees, the sand banked up against a row of toppled oil drums, she said, 'If I stayed here longer, it wouldn't be for my job . . . It'd be because someone had been silly enough to ask me to.' She turned to him. 'Brave enough to ask me . . .'

Matt took a few steps away but she clasped his arm. 'Stop. Don't pretend you don't know what I mean.' She looked into his eyes. 'Just for once, can you let your guard down, Matthew MacBride?'

Matt felt the sudden heat in his cheeks. 'I – I've got no right to ask you to stay . . .' He watched a single wisp of cloud, evaporating before his eyes. 'I couldn't make you happy in the long run.'

'And here's me thinking we already *were* happy.'

Matt picked up a mug that was still in one piece, and put it on an upturned crate. 'I haven't had a . . . a straightforward life, Bonnie.'

Bonnie took the mug and brushed the dust off with a thumb as she spoke. 'I understand that people you've . . . you've loved . . . have just disappeared without warning. Maybe you think I'll disappear too, but I won't. I understand that you've been through more than anyone should have to . . .'

'There's stuff about me you don't know, Bonnie. And if you knew it, you'd run a mile.'

'"Stuff". We've all got *stuff*! I know you're a good person,' she said. 'I know you love your family . . . And even though it'd kill you to say it, I think maybe you . . . sort of love me.'

Something in Matt collapsed at the truth of it – hearing it aloud. Then he turned away as images flashed through his mind – hospitals and cradles and coffins . . . and rain – rain hammering on a tin roof.

Bonnie said, 'I'm willing to risk it if you are . . .'

So vulnerable, but so bloody fearless, this girl. If she had the guts to jump then maybe he could find them too. 'Quiz . . . Stay. Stay for—for always.' He forced himself to press on. 'Marry me?'

68

For Sergeant Rundle, the only consolation in the approach of another Wanderrie Creek summer was the knowledge that it brought him closer to his return to the city, with a lawn he could mow and a choice of wireless stations and no damned goannas wandering into the kitchen.

When he entered the post office that December afternoon, having spent days dealing with the aftermath of the cyclone – assessing damage to roads, putting up 'Danger' signs where sheets of tin had blown off the hospital roof, passing on reports of stranded travellers – his mind was on posting his Christmas parcels (unavoidably late) to family in Melbourne. He was full of envy of the cooler day they'd be having, perhaps even with gentle rain; the choice of productions of Handel's *Messiah* they could attend . . . Blinking, he realised that Myrtle Eedle had asked him a question as she weighed the packages.

'I've been giving more thought to your question about Rose MacBride and her boy.'

Instantly, he was back in this post office, alert.

As he watched, the rage that had been simmering just below the surface for so long in Myrtle Eedle found its way out, not in an explosion, but in a leak through a crack. 'On a strictly confidential basis,

I wonder if Mr Peachey, their roo shooter, might be able to help you with your inquiries . . .'

Rundle eyed her obliquely. 'If you've got specific information . . .'

'Call it women's intuition.'

'You're saying, what? That Peachey's the boy's father?'

'It would explain why he's always stayed at Meredith Downs. And I suspect she's not the only girl he's carried on with around here.'

'Why's that?'

'Let's just say some of his parcels are expensive gifts for women.'

'To be clear, Mrs Eedle, you think he could have something to do with the girl's death?'

'You don't always have to lay a finger on someone to take their life away.'

Rundle wondered about this woman, with her perm and her locket and her 'intuition'. 'Are you making an accusation?'

Her tone was suddenly light again. 'Heavens, no. Just trying to be helpful. Tragic that a child should never know its own mother.' She proffered the bowl of toffees. 'Butterscotch? For Gavin and Pam?'

The policeman took his hand from his pocket, then stopped. 'It'll only rot their teeth.'

Bloody mosquitos. Rundle slapped at the one on his neck, but his elbow knocked the radiogram and scratched the record, making it stick. He gently raised the arm, blowing dust off the needle, then lowered it to the beginning of Tosca's final moments, setting up Puccini's soprano once more to throw herself off the parapet. Her last notes came almost like a wild scream, and he imagined her plummeting, as the orchestra brought back the soaring theme about the stars shining.

The howling of a neighbour's dog dragged him back from the

shimmering Rome sky to Wanderrie Creek. To the heat. To the dust. He switched off the lamp and let the moon drape itself over his lap as the record player arm lifted with its familiar series of clicks, the opera done, the woman dead, justice evaded. She had, after all, killed a man. Even so, the music never failed to get to him.

He tapped his fingers on his knee as he considered the file on Rose MacBride. The last one in that wretched filing cabinet. He would bet Wisheart hadn't given it a second thought since the day he'd dumped it there. No good wondering what Wisheart thought about it, though – he and his wife had sold up and 'gone travelling' after her cancer diagnosis. Rundle hadn't been able to trace him. That Dr Rafferty hadn't been much help, either. Said he'd signed the death certificate and left the rest up to the sergeant. Nothing to suggest it wasn't just a fall, but *how* she came to fall he couldn't say. No, she hadn't wanted to go back to Meredith Downs after the baby: probably post-partum depression. No, he couldn't speculate about the father. Yes, Pete Peachey had been a fairly regular presence at the station – had been since the war.

Then he thought of probabilities: the numbers never lie. The father of that baby probably was someone local. Likely not a type who could have waltzed off to church with her when she found out she was expecting, otherwise he would have. The chances of the girl falling accidentally, carrying a baby with her – well, they weren't high. The chances she was killed intentionally by someone else and that Wisheart turned a blind eye – well, they weren't high either. That wasn't the sort of thing Wisheart had let through to the keeper in the other cases. Suicide itself was a crime, of course, but the penalty for succeeding was academic.

One more full moon before his time here finished. One more case before he could make a clean sweep of the Misc. (Defunct) s. The frustration that was never far below the surface bubbled up again: this place, these people, this cosy approach of picking and choosing which laws to obey.

Call it a gut feeling. Call it a theory. Pete Peachey definitely knew more than he was letting on. Rundle tapped his fingers again. *Misc. (Defunct)* . . . The words pulled at a thread, and he wandered to the record shelf. By the milky light he picked out an album – Palestrina's *Missa pro defunctis*. Mass for the dead.

69

BONNIE SAT ON the grass beside the river in Peppermint Grove, watching the ivory sails of the boats in the twilight race cruising sedately in the absence of the usual stiff sea breeze. She'd walked the few blocks from her parents' house – the family Christmas celebrations felt so cooped up, after Meredith Downs. In a couple of days, she'd leave for the mining conference in Sydney. Then back – to Matt, and announcing their secret news.

She thought again of her drive back from the station four days ago. As she had watched the passing trees and fences and mills – some wrecked, others untouched – she imagined looking at Meredith Downs one day like Lorna must see it – layered over and over with memory, with belonging.

She had come to the river to think. Not about Matt, but Andy. She had taken to heart Lorna's warning about the family tree. Kid gloves. She'd given the boy some pages about Brinleys and Quorties, some of which information he already had, some not. He was particularly pleased to get copies of a few grainy photographs of men with starched collars and bushy beards. She'd hoped that might satisfy him.

But then, after she'd said goodbye to Matt, just as she was driving off, Andy had chased after her on his bicycle, and caught up as she was closing the first gate. He presented her with a sizeable dumbbell tektite – one of his most prized, she knew, that he'd found on the station himself. After making her cross her heart and hope to die if she told, he'd handed her the envelope she now held in her hands. A note, from that Miles fellow to Rose MacBride.

Bonnie traced her fingers over the thick paper. It was hardly a smoking gun . . . but it was something. She thought back to their argument in the cave – Matt warning her not to encourage Andy's hunt for his father; how he didn't want the boy upset or let down. But surely it could only *help* Andy to know who his father was? Imagine having just a question mark there all your life. Poor kid.

If she'd got this note when the boy had first asked for her help, she'd have felt differently – it wasn't her place or her problem then. But now, Andy was going to be family. And, as crazy about Matt as she was, she thought his approach to the whole father question was plain wrong.

With this note, maybe . . . maybe there was a middle ground: maybe Andy wasn't looking for a needle in a haystack, after all? Lord Miles Whatsit could be back in England hunting, shooting and fishing, now with a wife in twinset and pearls. Not the worst father a boy could have.

Andy's pleading face hovered in her memory, then Matt's frown . . . But if all she did was find out whether this Miles was still around, and where . . . She'd probably turn up a blank anyway . . . No point even mentioning it yet. 'Cross that bridge when you come to it,' as Uncle Reggie would say. If she *did* find something, well, then she could tell Matt, and leave it entirely up to him to decide what to do.

In Andy's position, would she rather know, or not know? She'd choose knowledge, every time.

But there was another reason. Maybe it would lift the burden Matt carried. She loved this man. She loved him so much that the idea of being away from him for the next few weeks made her chest hurt, like holding her breath for too long. And if there was anything she could do to bring him happiness, even if it was in spite of himself, she'd do it.

70

As Pete's car neared Proserpine Mine, Strife gave a bark. Something was different. Pete squeezed his eyes tight shut for a moment, but there was still a police car parked beside the low wire fence. 'What in God's name's *he* doing here?' Pete muttered to the dog.

Pulling up, he saw Sergeant Rundle pacing about the entrance to the mine; squinting down it with a torch; taking in the slant of the bleaching sun. Peachey left his engine running – the chiller van was full of carcasses. The dog followed him out, sounding a low growl at the stranger who now approached, wiping sweat from his forehead and slipping his hat back on to rectify his uniform.

'Morning,' the policeman said.

Pete looked about. 'What brings you out this way?'

As if he'd heard nothing, Rundle eyed Peachey's trailer, took in the rhythmic *tap-tapping* of blood into the dirt below it. 'Messy, your line of work . . .'

Pete angled his hat brim against the glare, and sized up the cop, as Strife sat alert at his flank.

'All that killing,' Rundle said quietly as he began a circuit of the vehicle, inspecting the tread on the tyres, the registration plates, the licensing transfer on the windscreen. Pete breathed slowly: the man would find nothing out of order, but still, he was wary.

Inspection completed, Rundle flicked his head in the direction of the mineshaft. 'So, this is where it happened?'

'Ah. That what this is about . . .' said Pete.

Rundle pushed down on the wire, and headed to the mine opening. 'Mind coming here a minute?'

Pete looked at Strife. 'You stay here, fella,' he said, and strode to join the policeman at the mineshaft's edge.

'I wonder if you were as helpful as you might have been, when we spoke at the station . . .'

'About what, in particular?'

'About the MacBride boy's father, for a start.'

'What the hell's that got to do with anything?' asked Pete, with genuine surprise.

'He's the key to the jigsaw.'

'Jigsaw? Rose's death wasn't some game.'

'Far from it . . .' Rundle examined the mine edge again. 'Maybe the girl did fall. But maybe . . . she jumped.' He fixed Pete with a direct gaze, alert for any flicker. 'Or *maybe* the boy's father didn't want to be unmasked, and gave her a nudge.'

Pete asked steadily, 'You got any evidence for that?'

Rundle peered into the void. 'Down there, was she?'

'Yes.'

'And you just happened to be passing, after she fell?'

'Yes. Saw the car.'

'Passing the middle of bloody nowhere . . .'

'This is one of the best roads on the property – from the days of the old mine. Still better driving than most of the other tracks. I'd taken a shortcut across the paddock; came out here. Nothing unusual about that.'

'No one else around? The brother? The mother?'

Pete lowered an eyebrow, and Rundle went on, 'Just you, and just your word for it – that you weren't with the girl when she died.'

Pete stayed silent, weighing up what was coming next.

'How do I know you didn't kill her?'

There was real concern in Pete's voice as he asked, 'Are you feeling all right?' The policeman's expression pressed the question, and Pete said, 'What, so I'd push her and the baby down the mine and then be stupid enough to pretend to find her? And rescue the baby I'd apparently just tried to bump off? What a lot of rot!'

'Is it?'

Rundle thought of the neatly stacked files on his desk; of the notes he'd started writing for his successor; of the planned holiday in Melbourne before taking up his new post in Perth: a test match at the MCG with Gavin. Then, like a piece of lint on his parade uniform, he pictured the one remaining Misc. (Defunct) file: 'MacBride: Rose Annabel', and that familiar, intangible itch returned. 'Let's see about that, once I've questioned the MacBrides.'

The muscles in Pete's neck tensed. 'You'd really drag them through that girl's death again?'

'If I have to.'

'You don't *have* to do any of this. I hear you're moving on soon.'

Rundle barked at him, 'You don't get to tell me my duty, Peachey,' and strode toward the fence, then turned. 'Which way is it?'

'Which way is what?'

'The damned homestead!'

Pete took his time joining the policeman at his car.

'Well?' Rundle demanded.

Strife gave a whine. The only other sound was the compressor of the chiller van, struggling against the rising heat. A large red pool now scabbed beneath the trailer, flies glittering like beads.

Pete kept his eyes on the blood. 'What do you want, sergeant? *Really?*'

'*Really?*' Rundle hurled his hat through the car window, then sank to his haunches, back against the door. 'I want a fair go. A fair society. Fairly bloody exercised laws.'

'And how is interrogating the MacBrides going to achieve that? You call it justice to drag that poor family back to the worst time of their life?'

'I call it the law.'

Pete glanced towards his ute, and Strife took it as permission to join him, lolloping to sit at his feet, chin up, ready to be patted.

Rundle put out a hand to the old dog, and after a nod from Pete, Strife approached cautiously, letting the policeman pat him. 'My daughter's allergic. We can't have a dog.' He rubbed behind the animal's ears, under his chin, as he considered his next move.

Questioning Peachey was about as much bloody use as questioning a cloud. If he'd made it out of Changi alive, you wouldn't get anything out of him he didn't want to tell you. Bastard. He sighed, his resolve sapping away, and there was a thin undertone of desperation in his voice as he said, 'Look. I'm not a vindictive man. I'm not a violent man. Hell, I'm not even an unreasonable man. But I *need* to know the truth.'

Strife had returned to his master, and licked the hand that came down reflexively to pat him. 'Sounds like you're making a rod for your own back raking all this up,' said Pete.

'If I have to, I'll get the information out of the MacBrides. But if you really do want to save them that upset . . .' Rundle stood up. 'Cards on the table: I've got a theory. *I* know I can't prove it, and *you* know I can't prove it. My theory is that the MacBride girl killed herself from shame, maybe from post-natal depression. My theory is that the father of her boy was right here on Meredith Downs – still is. I think . . . the reason you're still here is that it's you.'

A bungarra rustled through the dirt to get at the flies on the blood.

'Tell me if I'm wrong about that.'

Pete thought as he watched the lizard flick at the flies with its long tongue. Rundle was many things, but he was, Pete judged, a man who would keep a promise. 'And that'll be the end of it? No more questions? No further action? You give me your word you'll destroy that file and leave the MacBrides alone?'

'I give you my word.'

Pete eyed the mineshaft and its 'Danger' sign; eyed Rundle. 'Then I won't say you're wrong. And you won't get another word out of me about it, whatever you do.'

When the policeman's car had disappeared from view, Pete met Strife's upward gaze. 'Don't give me that look. You don't want that nitwit giving Matt and Lorna the third degree either. If his stupid theory lets him close his bloody file, then let him believe it.' He scratched the dog's neck. 'Come on, mate. Let's get this lot to town.'

71

THE YEAR STUMBLES to a close, and 1970 begins, as Meredith Downs gradually emerges from the wreckage of the cyclone. Both Andy and Matt miss Bonnie, though neither mentions it. Each awaits news that will follow her return, though their pictures of what will be announced vary dramatically.

Lorna has been on a campaign, washing every article of clothing, scrubbing out every cupboard in a quest of almost religious fervour. She will take dominion over her home again, and banish the dreaded sand that has invaded it. Matt and the hands are still restoring fences, digging earth out of water troughs, stripping and greasing engines until they roar into life again.

And Andy? He feels invisible; useless – not tall enough, not strong enough, not experienced enough to be in charge of any of the work. But as it's Christmas holidays, there's no school work either. Instead, he practises on Caramel for the gymkhana coming up on Maundy Creek, where he'll be playing polocrosse.

Secretly, he still devotes his energy to the List. The names always firmly at the top are Pete Peachey (Esquire) and (The Honourable) Miles Beaumont. Some days he swaps their order, depending on his mood.

*

This afternoon, Lorna didn't bat an eyelid when he announced his plan to go out stargazing. The sky is gin-clear and will afford a perfect view of the passing constellations, and Lorna, happy to see him perk up after all the turmoil, waves him off from the verandah.

He cycles the first two miles along the gravel track, then leaves his bike at the gatepost and crosses on foot, down towards the creek. It'll be too dark to bring the bike back cross-country, but with the generator-light on the handlebars he'll be all right on the road. The light is leeching from the sky, but Andy keeps his torch in the bag slung across his back. As he walks, he does a mental check of his equipment: binoculars, compass, ground sheet, waterbag, plus a box of matches, just in case. He's left Rascal at home: Strife, Pete's dog, would smell him a mile off.

He slows his pace as he nears Pete's camp. Andy knows he's been here for a couple of days, and that today he took the chiller trailer into town to hand over his kill. Now it's back, but empty, so the compressor's off, and the only sound is the insects starting their night's work.

If you'd asked Andy what he was looking for tonight, what he hoped to find, he really couldn't have told you. He just wanted to *know* something: it didn't really matter what. He couldn't observe Miles at first hand – he was relying on Bonnie to follow up that clue. But Pete – Pete was right under his nose.

A creamy glow revealed the tent, and as he crept nearer, Andy could make out a billy on the fire beside it. A few hundred yards away, he stopped and soundlessly put down his things. He laid out the ground sheet and sat cross-legged, raising the binoculars to his eyes. It took him several sweeps of the area to find his target, guided by the sound of Strife, who had started to growl, possibly at the scent of Andy on the breeze.

'Settle down, old fella,' came Pete Peachey's voice. As Andy watched, he emerged from the creek, and reached for the towel draped over the pole at the tent's entrance.

You never saw Pete with his shirt off, no matter how hot he got, or how dirty. Nanna Lorna often told him he was welcome to use the bath at the homestead, but he would reply that he preferred the creeks. Now, as Peachey turned his wiry body away from the fire to hang the towel to dry, Andy could see great slashes, dark tiger stripes that crossed his back, his bottom, and the tops of his thighs. He twiddled the binoculars' focus: the fire made the marks glow so red that they almost seemed to bleed.

Naked but for his boots, Pete Peachey made himself a mug of tea from the billy and sat down on an upturned crate. Beside him on another crate was a gramophone. Andy quietly shifted onto his tummy, elbows propping up his hands – the binoculars were getting heavy. Pete put on a record: a man singing: 'My love is like a red, red rose that's newly sprung in June . . .'

Strife joined in with a whine, and Pete stroked his head gently. Andy knew the song from the old shellac disc in Rose's Fruit Crate. He had heard Lorna singing it. 'I will love thee still, my dear, while the sands of life shall run . . .' Then she'd sighed, 'I can't think why it came into my head.'

Andy contemplated Pete's scars, and how they would feel to touch. He thought about the List, and Mrs Eedle's question about Pete Peachey's girlfriend; tried to imagine Pete with a lady . . . with a baby . . . With Mum. Appalling. Thrilling. He wanted desperately for it to be true, and to know absolutely that it was not true. He'd played this game before with candidates at the graveyard, but that was different: they'd been lying under slabs of cracked concrete with angels carved above their heads.

Andy gave a start as Pete rose and entered his tent. The lamp hanging inside splashed shadows all around, like a magic lantern show. He put his field glasses down, trying to imagine what Pete might be up to. Checking again a few moments later, he was shocked to see a lady in a dress emerge from the canvas. Tall and straight and thin. So he *did* have a girlfriend! The idea made Andy feel peculiar: excited, but a bit scared. He grabbed the binoculars: she had no bosoms . . . and not much hair . . . He fiddled with the focus, but it didn't need correcting. There, in front of the fire, accompanied by the moonlight and the man singing about his love like a red, red rose, was Pete Peachey, dressed in a lady's silk nightie.

The boy's heart raced as he watched the man stroke the fabric, dancing slowly around, back and forward in a waltz, turning occasionally. The singer's voice was tinny, and the crackles on the record blended in with the clicking of the crickets and the croaks of the sandgropers. Peachey moved awkwardly, not with the grace you saw when he went for a shot – at those times it was like his body was liquid and just became one with his rifle. As Andy inspected his face, he saw that Pete was smiling. Tears shimmering on his cheeks, and smiling at the moon.

Andy's face burned, and he wiped snot from his nose, then used his thumbs to clear his eyes of their furious tears. What the hell was Pete Peachey *doing*? And what the hell for? He felt stupid, like *he* was the one who'd been caught dressing up as a girl. He was aware of a sick feeling of being way out of his depth in the ocean of stuff grown-ups did.

Andy needed not to be here. Not to have seen this. Not to have ever had Pete Peachey on the List at all.

* * *

By the time he's reached his bicycle, Andy has stopped crying. By the time he's made it home, he's composed himself enough to tell Lorna that stargazing was all right, and that next time he will take Rascal after all.

In bed, his mind is all chopped up. He knows what he's seen but also knows he hasn't understood it. He knows he can't ask anyone about it without giving away the secret.

He can still feel the anger. Pete's not how he's supposed to be;

how Andy wants him to be. He's only nice on the *outside*. On the inside he's weird. Andy is newly indignant. In fact, what he is, is shocked: as shocked as a nun in a brothel.

By morning, his feeling of disgust has mutated into something else: excitement, at having a proper, gigantic *new* secret – something *only* he knows. Not even Pete Peachey knows he knows.

For days, he carries the secret around, and takes it out of its hiding place to consider it, polish it. He practises telling Rascal, working out different versions to see how they sound out loud. The dog seems quite happy with all of them. Ultimately, Andy decides it will be a *funny* story. The roo shooter is ridiculous. Andy is not *afraid* of whatever this is: he is above it, and can look down on it, like Johnno looked down on him for not knowing what 'bastard' meant. He writes his List again from scratch. Pete Peachey's name is expunged.

A Queenslander by birth, when things fell apart after the war, Pete Peachey had made his way to the opposite side of the country. Thousands of miles; hundreds of days.

'You're not right in the head, Pete!' The look on his wife's face – disgust wrestling despair – had been burnt into memory. 'I don't know what the Japs did to you . . .'

Coming home early from a shopping trip with their daughters, Pearl had discovered him sitting at her dressing table, putting on her lipstick, hip bones showing through the silk nightgown he'd bought for her, above his malnourished, hairy legs.

The younger child, a mere babe in arms when Peachey had gone off to fight, had giggled and said, 'What are you doing, Daddy?' Then she'd turned to her mother. 'Mummy, what's he doing?'

Pete could find no words.

There had been no words for any of it. How could anyone else even begin to understand, when he himself couldn't make sense of all he'd been through? And the aftermath: the homecoming, the relief that wasn't; the reunion with 'his girls' that was supposed to put everything to rights but didn't. Pearl had taught the girls to sing 'My Love Is Like a Red, Red Rose', and on his first night back they had lisped their way through it with their mother's help, but before they'd finished, he said he had to go outside.

'I've got to think of the girls, Pete,' Pearl said a few weeks after walking in on him. 'I've tried to help, tried to understand . . . But' – and here she twisted her wedding ring – 'I can't have you doing this around the kids.'

'It's not . . .' he stumbled, 'I wouldn't ever . . .'

But Pearl would hear no more. 'I can live with the fact that you won't talk about it. I can live with the fact that you can't . . . well, that nothing happens . . . down there . . . any more. But I can't have a p—' She tried to smother the word, but it would be held in no longer: 'a *pervert* in the house . . . no matter what you've been through.' She walked soundlessly to the wardrobe and took down the suitcase she'd bought for her honeymoon eight years earlier. Only ever used that once. She placed it on the bed. 'It doesn't mean I don't love you, Pete.' She touched the inner edge of her eye to arrest a tear. 'It just means – Oh, I don't know. Maybe the Japs won our corner of the war after all.'

He hadn't moved since she'd come into the room. Stay still. Do nothing to attract further punishment. Above all, never try to tell them they're wrong.

She waited a moment to make sure there was no reply coming, no last-minute reprieve, but he hung his head and stared at his lap, so she said, 'I'll let you get on with packing, then. I'll leave some money for a train fare on the table.'

There were times, when he first came over to the West, picking up jobs boundary riding on stations here and there, out for days at a time in open country, that he'd camp by the railway line, just to hear the sound of a train if it passed at night; just to know there were people going about their business, heading to welcoming homes somewhere, perhaps. A safe distance was all he could bear back then.

When Phil MacBride bumped into him at the post office in Wanderrie Creek, he recognised Pete from Officer Training Camp, where they'd been in different battalions and had gone off to very different wars. Peachey had turned down Phil's offer of a job as overseer, so Phil had proposed he do some roo shooting at the property instead. 'We can't move for the bloody things – eating the feed, drinking the troughs dry . . . You were the best shot I ever saw,' he'd said, taking in the gaunt look of the man, the brokenness he'd seen in plenty of others from the POW camps.

And so it was that Pete Peachey had been loosely stitched back, a day at a time, into a family, albeit not his own. It had suited him – the freedom; the privacy; the space; and over the years a deep, respectful affection seeped into the bedrock of all the lives concerned on Meredith Downs.

72

THE GET-TOGETHER AT Maundy Creek, the station next door to Meredith Downs, is officially a gymkhana, arranged by the Wanderrie Creek Horsemen's Association. Bob Sowerby from Maundy is on the committee, so it's his turn to host the event on the ninth of January, on a bit of cleared ground in a paddock on his boundary with Meredith Downs. He's damned if he's going to let a bloody cyclone get the better of him, and insists everything carry on as normal. The damage is done. It'll do people good to take a break from the slog of putting sheds back together and locating sheep that've wandered over flattened fences. That work'll be going on for a long time. Christ, he still hasn't got around to fixing the machinery shed that got washed away in the flood twenty years ago.

Whilst there's a good forty miles between the homesteads, here the properties touch. 'It's only next door,' Andy assures Lorna as he sets off with Matt.

'See you on Monday, Beetle,' she says, and to Matt, 'See you later tonight.' She gives a thump to the car roof to launch them. 'You be a good boy, now,' she calls through the rising dust behind the car.

People start arriving at these events from Friday afternoon onwards, and usually retreat somewhat the worse for wear on the Monday morning. Contestants think nothing of loading their horses into floats and trucks and travelling for days at the snail's pace the animals can tolerate. Entrants come from across the state, and even one or two from over the border. Some people bring caravans; a few, like Matt, drive the fifty or hundred miles home to sleep in their own beds at the end of each day, but most just pitch a tent.

As well as dressage, there are the typical novelty races: tent pegging, bending races, keyhole and the like. A big draw, however, is the polocrosse competition, played this weekend on a field that's more dirt than grass, and only just about marked up with chalk lines. In a blend of polo, lacrosse and netball, two teams of six riders with long lacrosse-type sticks scoop up the ball at a gallop and pass it down the field to hurl between two tall goalposts.

Matt and Andy arrive in time for the welcome barbecue on Friday evening. Dead trees have been cut down and carried whole to the campsite to build fires for cooking and for boiling billies. The grog flows freely as people compare notes on cyclone damage, catch up on gossip. A couple of folks have brought guitars and are singing country and western, though not everyone's thrilled about that.

Andy's staying in one of the tents for the junior boys, pitched a respectable distance from those of the junior girls. It's exciting but daunting to be with so many kids his own age. Some he knows from School of the Air, recognising not their faces but their voices. One or two he's seen in town. For the beginners, they lump the girls and boys in together, and a lot of the girls, pony-mad since they were knee high, are streets ahead, as are the kids from the properties that still muster entirely on horseback.

The juniors are allowed to cook their sausages on their own campfire. Glancing over from the adults' gathering fifty yards away, Matt watches Andy share the occasional word with another boy, and even once or twice a girl. He's aware of a warmth at seeing the kid swimming on his own like that, then a thought occurs to him: tomorrow will be the tenth of January. This is the first time in all these years that he hasn't noticed its approach. Maybe that's because of Bonnie. The idea makes him miss her even more. It's a foreign feeling – strange, but good.

After dinner, the kids sat in a circle around their fire to tell scary stories about ghosts or people having their heads chopped off when they opened the front door to a stranger, or murderers perving on sweethearts at the drive-in. Andy thought it was pretty stupid, but couldn't help checking the darkness around him, just in case.

When Kelly, the girl beside him, grabbed his arm with a squeal at the mention of a severed head in a box, he froze. When she withdrew her hand, he stayed very still, feeling into the sensation on his arm, the faster beating of his heart. He'd noticed her on the polocrosse field earlier, practising with some of the grown-ups: tackling, passing; turning her pony like a spinning top. He'd learned her name when a clique of girls had whispered admiringly about how good she was.

The skin on Andy's bare arm still buzzed from her touch, and made him think of Elizabeth Taylor in *National Velvet* – which showed in Wanderrie Creek every year, the older boys whistling and calling out sexy comments from the back. He thought about all the kisses he'd seen at the pictures (hardly any, in fact). There was one with a lady in her undies. He couldn't remember the rest of the film, just the undies. He thought back to Bonnie swimming in the dam. Then an image ambushed him – Pete Peachey in the nightie. He wiped a hand over his face.

The scary story session had been Kelly's brainwave, and after a few more kids had had a turn, she announced, 'I've got another idea.' Then, in a stage whisper, 'Let's play "secret or dare"!'

There was a general wide-eyed burble of 'Yeah!' from the girls, who leaned in with scrawny, hunched shoulders. The boys were less keen, but didn't have any better suggestions. 'We'll take it in turns,' Kelly commanded. 'It has to be a proper, juicy secret. And if you don't tell one, we can dare you *anything*.'

Kelly set the bar high with a story about kissing a boy at the gymkhana at Mount Boyd last month. As his turn approached, Andy racked his brains. His rock collection was the first thing that came to mind. Where he'd found the sample of tantalite, maybe?

Kelly poked his ribs. 'Your turn!'

'Well, I've got a piece of tantalite in my rock collection. And the way I got it was a big secret. I said I found it on the ground, but really I climbed down the old abandoned mine on our place, where I'm not allowed to go.'

One of the girls had begun tickling the girl next to her; a few of the boys were poking the fire with sticks.

'Is that it?' someone asked.

'Yeah,' said Andy.

There was a ripple of laughter. 'Big deal,' said one of the girls, but Kelly intervened, delighting in wielding mercy. 'You haven't played before, I can tell . . . You can have another go later. Debbie! Your turn.'

Old Ma Sowerby made them all jump as she materialised from the shadows with a loud clap of her hands. 'Right, kidlets! Nine o'clock. Lights out. Early start tomorrow, so bed, now, the lot of you.'

On the way to his tent, Andy caught sight of Matt, approaching with a wave. 'You right, mate?'

'Yeah.'

'I'm heading home now. Back in the morning. Got everything?'

Andy raised his bottom lip. 'Forgot my toothbrush . . .'

'Your teeth probably won't fall out just this once. I'll bring it tomorrow. Have a good night.' Giving a squeeze to the boy's shoulder, a strange feeling went through him. Ah . . . He'd never left Andy anywhere by himself for a night. Then a second wave washed through him: the knowing that he wasn't entitled to the feeling; could never tell anyone about it.

The next day, Matt was surprised to find a downcast and hesitant Andy.

'I don't feel well. Maybe I should go home . . .'

'What's the matter?' He inspected the boy's face. Seemed OK. 'Did something happen?'

'No. I just – Maybe I'm coming down with something,' Andy said, using Lorna's favourite diagnostic phrase.

Matt felt his cool forehead. 'Worried about the scratch match? You're a great little rider. You'll be fine.'

Andy's eyes drifted to the playing field, and Matt followed his gaze. 'Oh . . .' Making their way onto the polocrosse field for the first chukka of the morning were Johnno MacBride and his arsehole mates from the Royal Show. 'I get it.'

'I'm coming down with something. Really.'

'Worried they'll pick on you?'

'No,' Andy insisted; then, 'Sort of . . .'

Matt bobbed down and put a hand on Andy's shoulder. 'Johnno MacBride wouldn't know if his bum was on fire. Greg Crimp's a drop-kick. Don't let some idiots spoil your day.' The boy was looking at the ground, face red, and Matt knew Andy's fears couldn't be dismissed as nothing. 'There's family stuff – goes back a long way. The cousins have had their fights about things over the years. Johnno's got a chip on his shoulder, that's all.'

'OK . . .'

Andy's effort to be brave got Matt in the guts. How long could he protect him? How long could he stave off the unkind and the nosy and the downright cruel?

Johnno MacBride is indeed accompanied by those older teammates from the Royal Show. As well as Greg Crimp, whom Matt had put in his place, there are Snake and Dunce. The former is actually Tobias Yenning, who earned his nickname after surviving a run-in with a Brown snake during an episode of acute intoxication. He had lost two fingers from the venom, but escaped with his life and the new soubriquet. Dunce, on the other hand, was Bradley Waghorn, an unfortunate Christian name for someone who had never been able to pronounce his 'r's, and had to go through life as 'Bwadley', so he actually preferred Dunce. His shooting abilities made him, he had been convinced, a shoo-in for the army, but when he applied to enlist two months ago he'd failed the medical due to a heart murmur, and was still disguising his humiliation by talking up the Nashos and taking every opportunity to describe what he'd do to the *slant-eyes* if only he had a machine gun and a few grenades.

In fact, Johnno and his mates didn't give Andy a moment's thought that day.

73

PETE PEACHEY, CAMPED a few miles away in a paddock bordering Maundy Creek Station, had been persuaded to be a judge at the gymkhana shooting competition, having declined to compete himself. When he disqualified Dunce on Saturday for putting his shots on the wrong target, there was much laughter, but not from Peachey himself. 'It can happen,' he said, though he remained utterly unyielding to the youth's protests and appeals and then threats.

Finally, Dunce stormed off. 'You can shove this! I'm gonna go and do some weal bloody shooting! Let's go!' he called to Johnno and Snake, sitting beside Greg Crimp on the sidelines with an Emu Bitter in each hand. 'This is a bloody joke!' and the four of them collected the rest of their carton of beer and headed for their car.

* * *

The shooting competition comes to an end, not a moment too soon for Pete Peachey, who's had enough of people for one day. He heads off down the dirt road, and turns onto a sandy track that will take him to a gate between the properties. A mile or so along it, he hears the unmistakeable crack of a rifle shot, and a *ping* as a bullet hits the front of his Land Rover. He brakes. Looks around. Hears laughter.

Sitting on the bonnet of their station wagon in the scrub, Johnno and his mates are firing pot shots at anything and nothing. At their feet are the carcasses of three emu chicks, blood oozing into the dirt below.

'Sowwy!' shouts Dunce, giving a dismissive wave with his rifle.

Johnno is handing him another can, freshly spiked, foam pouring out. 'Here you go, Ned Kelly!'

Pete Peachey gets out and strides towards them; takes in the dead birds. 'What in God's name do you think you're doing?'

'Keep your hair on! Just having some fun,' says Dunce.

'You're all half bloody cut!'

'Stwong words!' Dunce raises the rifle and ostentatiously takes aim at Peachey.

The roo shooter seizes it mid barrel and points it at the sky before wrenching it from the boy, who staggers off balance. 'Don't be so bloody wet! Damned thing's still loaded.'

Johnno gives an idiot grin.

'There are people around! Kids, for God's sake! Those bullets go for miles.' Pete calculates the distance back to the gymkhana, and to the Maundy homestead. He's closer to his own camp. 'You know you can get locked up for a year for handling a gun when you're drunk? You can have this back when the gymkhana's over and you've sobered up. Bloody halfwits!'

'Hey!' Dunce cries. 'That's my gun!'

'Monday morning,' says Pete.

Johnno steps forward. 'Who the hell do you think you are? Give him back his gun! Would have served you right if he *had* hit you.'

Pete shakes his head. 'Call yourself a MacBride . . . Hard to believe you're even related.'

As Pete walks away, Johnno turns to Snake. 'You're not going to let him treat us like that, are you?'

Snake slides down the side of the car. 'Oh, who cares. Stupid bastard.'

'I care!'

But Dunce has closed his eyes to stop the world spinning. Snake's head is lolling, and a streak of spit dribbles from his mouth, as his remaining fingers clutch the beak he's cut from an emu, to claim the bonus.

On the Sunday, Andy did a decent job of his beginner's polocrosse match. When Bob Sowerby said he showed 'real promise', Andy accepted the compliment with a serious shyness, and Matt felt a surge of pride for him, though habit instantly suppressed it. In the evening, he again joined the grown-ups' barbecue. Johnno's mob were back, drinking and cackling around another campfire, a way off.

Around the kids' fire, the secrets game started again under the instruction of Kelly, who had made a great show of sitting next to Andy, so close that he could feel her warmth. Watching her 'Young Champion' trophy glistening silver and gold in the flames' glow, he was increasingly nervous as his turn threatened. Again he racked his brains, his face hot with the humiliation of his last attempt. He didn't know anything that was a proper secret.

And then he remembered that he did.

* * *

Later that night, before lights out, Kelly goes to the grown-ups' camp area to see her older brother; show him her trophy. She tells him about the campfire tales; tells him about the really funny secret the boy next to her told her.

'Ha!' he says. 'That's a good secwet.'

74

'GRAB THE GUNS!'

These are the first words Pete Peachey hears as he startles awake in the starlit night. A metallic clatter confirms that his rifle, always beside him while he sleeps, has been moved, together with the one he took from the young bloke on Saturday. The air is hot and he's been lying naked under a mosquito net on top of his swag, outside his tent. Normally alert at the slightest sound, tonight he has been filtering out the vague, distant noises that have drifted over from cars coming and going to the gymkhana. What he had thought was a dream of Strife making a terrible racket is real: somewhere out of sight his dog is snarling and barking savagely and being sworn at.

'Get up, you mongrel!' comes a shout, not at the dog, but its owner. Peachey recognises the voice as Bradley Waghorn's because he's actually being called a 'munggwel'.

All this has taken only seconds. There's enough light from the last of his campfire to decipher three, no, four men around him. They reek of beer.

'What in God's name—' A foot in his ribs winds him.

'We told you to get up, pervert!'

Peachey doesn't move. Instead he squints, working out who else is in the mob. A couple have torches, and shine them in his eyes. Bradley has seized back his own rifle. Snake is holding Peachey's .22.

Greg Crimp returns from rummaging in the tent and holds something up. 'Get a load of this!' he says, and waves around a crimson silk petticoat. 'So the little MacBride bastard wasn't bullshitting!'

The others erupt in a cackling as the petticoat gets passed around.

'Get up, you poofter!' barks Dunce.

'Bradley?' Pete looks at him. 'Why the hell are you doing this?'

Snake and Crimp each grab an arm and hoist Pete Peachey to his feet.

'What do you call this then?' says Dunce, throwing the garment at him.

Peachey doesn't answer.

Snake pokes Peachey with the rifle butt.

'Well? What is it?' asks Dunce again.

'Nothing you'd understand,' Pete says.

'What the hell do you get up to out here, you – you perv? Pretending to be Mister Bloody Respectable. When all the time you were just waiting to – to root us or – or something,' says Johnno.

'Look what I found!' Greg Crimp is crowing over a book of verse by Shelley. 'Poems!' says Crimp. 'He reads fucken' poems!'

Pete reaches for the book, but hears the click of a rifle being cocked. Dunce has the gun trained on him as Crimp throws the book onto the fire.

'Get a load of the marks on his back!' says Johnno. 'You like kinky stuff, I bet. Whips and chains!'

The curdled smile on Dunce's face is reflected on Snake's as an idea arcs between them, and Snake stoops to pick up the petticoat at Peachey's feet. He grins to the others, holds it out to Peachey: 'Put it on!'

'Come on, you deadshit!' demands Snake. 'I said put it on.'

'No thanks.'

'Yeah, put it on and we'll all give you a woot.'

'Bet you'd love that!' says Johnno.

'Sounds like *you* might,' replies Pete, looking him in the eye, his breathing still even.

There's a place Pete Peachey created for himself, all those years ago in the camps: a mental watchtower, to which he could withdraw. He built it plank by plank; knows every join and nail. It's high up, far above the action around him, and he learned how to retreat into it so that he's entirely beyond reach, beyond harm. From the watchtower now, he sees the absurdity of these men waving around French silk underwear and burning Shelley. His ears register voices: someone has put on a gramophone record, which is now playing the strains of Nellie Melba singing Mozart.

When the blow to his guts comes, he's half expecting it, so isn't completely winded. Then he's on the ground and there's a kick to his mouth from a boot that tastes of dust and sheep dags. There's another in his back, in his kidneys, and pain races though every nerve. The blows rain down and he's in a ball on the ground, waiting it out.

Suddenly there's a wild growl as Strife, who has broken free from the rope they tied him with, hurls himself at his master's attackers, going straight for Dunce's throat.

'No! Strife, down!' Peachey calls, but it's too late. Dunce has turned by reflex and shot the dog – a dirty shot through shoulder and down through the hip, splintering bones and tearing muscle. The howl rips through the last of the darkness.

'You bastard! You rotten bloody swine!' Pete yells, and with a vigour that shocks his assailants, launches himself at Dunce, whose gun is still pointed toward the wounded dog. Pete slams a fist into his temple and Dunce goes down in a heap. Snake and Johnno are quick to grab Peachey again, and Greg Crimp now grasps the slip and starts trying to force it over Pete's head as Dunce lurches to his feet, gathering up his rifle. Johnno has got hold of the makeup set from the tent and is flinging its contents on the ground as he rummages through it, the powder clouding the air, its scent now smothering the reek of alcohol. He seizes a scarlet lipstick and smears it on Peachey's mouth. It spreads to his teeth, his cheeks, as he struggles against their grip.

Pete is on his knees, being held up by Johnno and Greg Crimp, and Snake gives him a kick in the groin.

'Hold him still,' orders Dunce, unzipping his flies. But as he nears Peachey, the air is rent by the crack of a gunshot, and all heads spin around to its source.

Matthew MacBride is fifty yards away and striding fast, aiming while he moves. No one notices Andy, invisible behind a torch and running to keep up. Matt's .44 is pointed at Dunce. 'Let him go!'

Dunce starts to raise his rifle and Matt blows it out of his hands.

'I said let him bloody go!'

Dunce goes to move again, but Matt has lined up a shot just near his foot, where the dust explodes in the half-light. 'I've got enough rounds for the lot of you.' He puts his eye to the sight again as he walks. By now he's only feet from them, and they've all frozen.

Andy runs in and snatches up Pete's rifle, and aims it squarely at Johnno, while Nellie Melba sings on behind them.

'We were just sorting something out,' says Dunce.

'He's a poof, Matt!' says Johnno. 'A bloody queer!' At Matt's silence, he goes on, 'Ask the kid, if you don't believe us. Probably been fiddling with him.'

'Never!' shouts Andy. 'He never!'

Matt's voice is steadier than he feels, his mind racing to make sense of the scene while his eye takes aim. 'I'm giving you one chance.' The record comes to an end, revealing a silence punctuated by the whimpering of the dog, and the first of the butcherbirds waking up. 'Get your hands off him,' he says, 'and get the hell off my property.'

'You a poof as well or something? He been rooting you, too, eh, Matt?'

A bullet pings the ground an inch in front of Johnno's boot. It's Andy who's fired this one, and Matt flicks him a warning glance before turning to the others.

'Get going. Clear out, the lot of you.'

The men look at one another, suddenly too tired and hungover to defy him.

'He bloody deserves it,' mutters Johnno. He shuffles past Matt, followed by the others. Matt watches, rifle at the ready, until they've poured themselves back into their ute and revved the engine, before receding into the horizon.

Andy stands beside Pete, who's kneeling on his haunches. The boy is embarrassed by the man's nakedness, but transfixed to see so close up the vivid scars on his back. He offers him the rifle, which Pete takes without a word.

'Pete?' says Matt, but he takes no notice. Oblivious to his own nakedness, Peachey rises and shuffles over to Strife, who is barely managing to whimper now, drawing quick, shallow breaths. He crouches down, inspects the wounds; puts a hand on the animal's heart. The dog looks up, and a silent knowing passes between them. Pete takes a few steps back, nods to the dog, and with surgical accuracy shoots first the heart, then the head. Instantly, the ribs cease their jerky efforts. The eyes are closed. The stillness around the animal sets, almost solid.

Andy stares at the dog, then the shooter – back and forth, still in shock. Trails of snot dribble from the boy's nose.

Matt is taking in the meaning of it all. He catches himself wondering about the silk petticoat on the ground. Whatever this good, mysterious man's secret was, it's desecrated now.

It's minutes before anyone moves.

'Pete?' Matt ventures again, and hands him the towel that's hanging off the back of the canvas chair. 'You want me to have a look at . . .' He lifts a hand vaguely towards him, and the blood drying on various wounds – a split lip, a swollen eye, blossoming bruises and abrasions on his back and knees. But the most violent red comes from the lipstick smeared all over his mouth and chin. Pete looks at Matt, not understanding at first, then gazes absent-mindedly at his body and its injuries. As he wraps the towel around his waist, he gives a tiny shake of the head, like flicking away a fly.

'Shall I – bury Strife for you?'

'I'll do it,' says Pete.

'Come with us, back to the homestead. Get you cleaned up. Get the police . . .'

'I'll be right.' Pete glances at Strife. 'It's over now.'

Matt breaches his gun to empty the magazine, as Peachey himself drummed into him years ago, then snaps it shut. He wipes his forehead with the back of a hand, and watches the sun just edging above the horizon as he considers trying to get him to change his mind. Pointless.

On the way back to the ute, out of Peachey's earshot, Matt puts a hand on Andy's shoulder. 'You all right?'

Andy gives a slow nod.

Matt stops, and turns the boy towards him. 'That was—It was really ugly. You shouldn't have had to see it. I told you to stay in the car. I didn't know – I would never have let you come if I'd even thought—'

Andy's response was a gasp of air that collapsed into sobs.

'Hey, hey, Sooty. Come on . . .' He squatted down to the boy's level. 'You did the right thing.'

'No, I did the *wrong* thing.'

'You came and got me; warned me they were going after Pete. You saved him.'

'But . . . it was *me*! *I* was the one who told about Pete, Matt! It's my fault.'

'What do you mean?'

'I saw him, dressing up and that.'

The boy recounted the story, the secret.

'Why'd you tell, Andy?'

'Dressing up in ladies' stuff . . .' He turned his head away. 'Well blokes aren't supposed to. It made me – really cross.' He couldn't begin to explain about the List, and his disgust at the thought of Pete Peachey and his mother. He tried to get more words out, but the sobs cracked his speech. 'I only whispered it to Kelly. I only told one person.'

'It only takes one person,' Matt murmured. He rested his hands on top of the child's head, then pulled him in to his shoulder, where Andy buried his face. Eventually he said, 'Soot, mate, sometimes our secrets aren't ours to tell. Saying them will just hurt the people they're about, and it'll do bugger all good to anyone else.'

'But that stuff he does. That's wrong, isn't it?'

Matt held the boy a little away to look him in the eye. 'It's private is what it is, mate. It's not your business and it's not mine, and it's sure as hell not Bradley bloody Waghorn's, or those other cretins'.'

'But Kelly reckoned—'

'Bugger what Kelly reckoned. It's our Old Pete you're talking about . . .' He took in the scrubby bush around him. 'He risked his life in the war, and he – well, he went through things you and I can't even begin to imagine . . . So if he wants to dress up as the Queen of bloody Sheba in his own time it doesn't make any difference to me, and it shouldn't to you, either.'

'But why would he wear ladies' clothes?'

'Beats me . . . Why do *ladies* wear ladies' clothes? It's a mystery.'

Standing up, he put an arm around Andy's shoulder, and they started off again. 'By the way, Soot. What have I told you about pointing guns at anything you didn't want to kill?'

'But *you* did.'

'I'm a lot older than you are, mate. When you're big enough to live with the consequences, you can point it at whatever you like. Until then, *never*, *ever* do that again. Understand?' Andy nodded, and Matt gave him a sideways glance. 'Bloody good shot, though.'

75

When Pete's Land Rover pulled up, it took Matt a minute to work out what was different: the silence. Usually, Strife would have been in the back, tongue hanging out, surfing the bumps in the road and revelling in the whoosh of the wind.

It had been three days. Pete's face was blotched purple and yellow; a cut on his bottom lip had formed a shiny black crust. Overnight, he had become an old man.

'Over here, Pete.'

Peachey shielded his eyes from the sun, and located the voice inside the machinery shed. 'Afternoon,' he said, his sure, brisk stride replaced with a slow limp.

'Gedday.' Matt gestured to one of the small school chairs left over from the days of correspondence classes. 'Have a seat.' He fetched another for himself, and the two men perched on the stunted but sturdy chairs, Matt leaning forward, elbows on his knees, Peachey upright against the backrest. He pulled his hat off and wiped his brow.

'How are you?' Matt asked.

Pete gave a short nod, and turned his attention to a scab on his knuckle.

'You're going to report it, aren't you, Pete? To Trundle?'

Peachey shook his head.

'I'll back you up . . . be a witness . . . You can't let them just get away with it.'

Pete gave him a look.

'What? They should get what's coming to them.'

'Have a bit of sense, son.'

'I don't get you.'

'Think it through . . . Word'll have got around. And you know what Trundle's like.'

'But that doesn't mean he shouldn't charge them—'

'He'd probably want to charge *me* instead.'

'What for?' asked Matt; then, 'Oh . . .'

'There are things . . . things that are just no one else's business . . . I don't need all that codswallop – police and courts . . . And newspaper reporters. None of it can change what happened anyway. Except to make it worse.'

Matt studied the bruises on the man's cheekbones, the lines on his forehead. It was dear to him, this face: familiar and dependable and timeless. Pete Peachey had lived a peaceful life here, and one careless word had torn it apart. 'I'm sorry, Pete. And Andy's sorry. He's ashamed of himself.'

'He's just a kid.'

Pete cast his eyes around the shed: over branding irons; storm lanterns; an ancient wool press, rusting into oblivion. His glance was drawn to a corner, to where some relics from the homestead had been relegated: a battered bookcase; a primitive washing machine. A dented tricycle – Peachey recognised it as Andy's, long retired.

'As for the others . . . Some people just like to know anything they're not allowed to know – can't bear to be kept out of it. Then they turn it into tittle-tattle, and half-truths and downright lies . . .'

Matt's heart tripped as the words pierced some sort of defence within him.

'It brings out a cruel streak. A dangerous one.' Pete paused. 'Maybe some things need to . . .' He frowned, searching for the words, eyes now trained on a blade of sunlight on the floor. '. . . to wait for kinder times.' His fingertips wandered to a livid bruise on his jaw. 'Guard your secrets well – that's my advice. Forget they even exist.'

There was something in his tone . . . Matt's pulse was racing now, and he was about to ask a question, when Pete stood up. 'Anyway, I just called in to say goodbye.'

Matt jumped up, sending his little chair tumbling, but before he could speak, Peachey had wiped his hand on his shirt and was offering it to him to shake.

'Where are you going? How long for?'

'Time for somewhere else, I reckon.' Pete's finger traced the rim of the hat in his hands. 'Besides, what's a roo shooter without a dog? I'm too old to train a new one.'

'But – You can't just—' Matt couldn't keep the shock from his face, or the distress from his voice. 'Well, stay on here then, at the station. There's plenty of work. Come and help manage the place . . .'

'Thanks all the same.'

'But you'll . . . you'll come back and visit soon? Check up on us?'

Peachey shook his head, and turned to leave.

Matt followed him out. 'Hang on. Let me get Mum, and Andy.'

Peachey turned, managing the slightest shadow of a smile. 'Nah. Give them my . . . my best. They've been good friends, too.' He put on his hat. 'Don't want any fuss.'

'But—what are you going to do?' Matt couldn't tell whether the sick, desperate feeling that washed through him was for Pete or for himself.

'Don't worry about me. I'll be all right.' He gave Matt an iron handshake. 'But I won't be back . . . Take good care of them.' He limped slowly towards the car, then looked back. 'And . . . keep Andy safe from mongrels like that.'

Watching Pete's car drive off, Matt stood, abandoned by someone who, he realised now, was never his. As the wake of dust plumed up, just for a moment he imagined Strife standing officiously on the back, barking.

'Keep Andy safe': the phrase burned into him. He went to shoo a fly from his cheek but his fingers found tears. He covered his head with his hands. When he looked up, car and man and absent dog had disappeared into the melting end of day.

Saturday, 29th March 1958

Despite its size, there are only so many places on Meredith Downs you can shelter from a storm. Pete Peachey knows every last one, and as the rain starts savaging the dirt, he runs through them in his mind: the homestead and its outbuildings; the overseer's cottage; the outcamps; the Home shearing shed and its shearers' quarters. All of these are well beyond reach and there's no sign of a let-up in the deluge, which could be setting in. He won't make it back to his own camp. Normally he wouldn't think twice about sleeping in or beside his ute, but if this turns into a flood, the car could be swept away in the night.

The old shearers' quarters at the Top Shed, on slightly higher ground, will be the nearest safe point.

Strife is alert but quiet as they arrive in darkness via the back track, the engine's noise drowned by the rain. Once it's day, he can survey what damage there is. He pulls a ground sheet over his shoulders and, by the light of his torch, hoicks his swag into one of the tiny rooms. He gives it a once-over with the beam and squashes a redback with the heel of his sodden boot.

Strife has followed him in and, after a quick shake of his body to fling off the water, is already stretched out beside the swag by the time Peachey lies down in his clothes and switches off the torch. The man closes his eyes, but opens them after a minute or so, about to roll over. There's something not quite right. He blinks a few times, but he's not imagining the very faintest of lights coming from what must be the shearing shed.

'Stay put,' he says to his dog, and, picking up his rifle, he makes his way to the shed. The doors are closed, but some of the tin windows are propped open, leaking light. If there's a car, it'll be on the other side of the shed, out of sight. He makes his way noiselessly up the steps at the side, and, back flat against the wall, slowly turns his head to look in at the window space. By the glow of a hurricane lamp hanging from the wool press he sees one – no, two – two sleeping figures, one almost naked, entwined on a wool bale. As his eyes adjust to the scene, he recognises them.

'Christ almighty,' he breathes to himself, and slips soundlessly from the window. Long before dawn he sets off into the drying day, his tyre tracks soaked up by the puddles.

76

THE SCOTCH COLLEGE boatshed sat snugly below the cliff of Devil's Elbow in Peppermint Grove. The place where Matt had learned to row as a schoolboy lay in the same crescent bay as the yacht club where he'd learnt to sail. It was a few blocks from Bonnie's family home, and before she left Meredith Downs for her trip over East, this was where they'd agreed they would meet.

Matt had just had time to have a shower, and change into what he still thought of as Warren's funeral suit, at the Weld Club in Perth. All through the long, hot drive from the station, he'd pictured what would follow. Tonight he would meet Bonnie's parents. Ask her father's permission. Slip the ring on her finger. Tonight, it would all become official, public. When Matt had caught his reflection in the rear-view mirror, his smile had taken him by surprise.

The shady bench on which he sat now was protected from the stiff sea breeze. Matt contemplated the old weatherboard boatshed – unchanged since schooldays. A memory appeared, of the Head of the River race in his final year at school: at the time, losing to Christ Church was the worst fate he could imagine. This world . . . this world had a way of taking things away from you; slamming you a knock-out blow from nowhere. Turned out that that young schoolboy was standing on ground that would disappear from under him just months later. Something in Matt's belly warned it could again. Everything had changed, since Pete.

In his jacket pocket, the tiny shagreen box nestled safely, but somehow, touching it brought home how the hope he'd had just weeks ago when he bought the ring was drying up like a creek bed.

He saw Bonnie approaching, dressed in a blue silk cocktail frock, hair swept up into a clasp that sparkled as she walked. He scanned the surroundings before kissing her lightly on the lips, but Bonnie pulled him to her, cupping the back of his head to give him a long, tender kiss.

'I missed you,' she said, pressing her head against his chest.

He circled her with his arms, lips touching her hair. 'Me too, Quiz.'

They stood in silence, soaking in the feel of each other, familiar and new. At last, Matt took her hands and held her away to see her better. 'You look . . . I don't know – like Miss Australia material! Bit of a change from your shorts and Kodiaks.'

They sat on the bench, Bonnie resting her head on his shoulder as she slipped off the back of one of her high heels to inspect a scarlet blister. 'Are you nervous? About meeting Mum and Dad?'

'Terrified.'

'Don't be. They're softies, really. Dad can seem a bit fierce, but as long as you talk about cricket you'll be in like Flynn.'

They were almost shy now – on the brink of this enormous undertaking – and took refuge in small talk, tiptoeing their way back to one another. When she asked whether they'd had any rain, Matt's answer was distracted. He had discreetly slipped his hand into his coat pocket to check on the ring. He kept trying to find the right moment to present it. Then, he realised what Bonnie had just said, 'Actually . . . I used some of my time there to look into that thing for Andy.'

He stroked her arm. 'Which thing?'

'His project.'

'*What?*'

'Just that family tree thing. I promised I'd help him . . .' She touched his hand. 'Don't be cross, but he – he showed me a note, just before I left. Something from that fellow Miles, to Rose.'

'What are you talking about?'

'Andy said he found it hidden somewhere. It was barely more than a few words, to be honest. Miles was apologising to her for hurting her somehow.'

'Does it—What—' Finally he managed a complete thought. 'When was it written?'

'April 1958. From what Lorna had said about Miles, and from the date . . . Well, I – I thought it was worth just following up.' Matt took his arm away. 'Andy has no idea yet, of course. I promised your mum I'd treat the whole family tree thing with kid gloves.'

'But . . . Why would—' Matt had the sense of being dragged along in a flooded river, heading for rapids. 'Why would you not tell me?'

'I *am* telling you. This is the first time I've laid eyes on you since I got the note. I just thought . . . It would make such a difference to the poor kid if it turned out to be, well, relevant. Andy's going to be family for me, Matt. I want him to be happy. I want us *all* to be happy.'

Matt fixed his eyes on the boatshed.

'It was actually pretty easy to track Miles down to Sydney,' Bonnie said. 'So I thought, since I was there . . .'

As Matt stood up, a flotilla of black swans glided past, beaks glowing red like navigation lights against the shadowed water. 'And?'

'Turns out I was barking up completely the wrong tree. He's got – a *boy*friend. I *met* him!'

Matt gave the lightest of nods.

'So – you knew?' Bonnie absorbed this. 'Well, it means Andy can definitely rule him out of his family tree, anyway.'

'Not sure that follows biologically.'

'I realise that. But he denied any knowledge . . . And I believe him.'

At the sound of voices, they both turned and fell silent. While a couple with an elderly Labrador slowly made their way past, Matt took in the news from Bonnie, and its implications. What could Miles be apologising for? A desperate, illogical hope that it could change the truth arose and evaporated within the same thought.

When the dogwalkers had gone, Bonnie stood and put a hand on Matt's arm. 'We'll find Andy's father eventually. I'll help you. It's just a question of digging and patience and deduction. I spend most of my life hunting stuff you can't see on the surface.'

Matt's shoe crushed his cigarette butt until it was unrecognisable. He breathed in the salty river air. 'How did your boys get on without you?'

'I saw Merv at our office yesterday. He said they've nearly finished packing up. I'll have to go back for a last sign-off. Then the sheep can have it all to themselves again.' She hesitated. 'Merv . . . well, he told me what happened . . . to Pete Peachey.'

Matt gave her a sharp look, and she went on, 'I'm *so* sorry. I can't begin to imagine . . . How is he?'

'How do you think?'

'Are *you* OK?'

'Pete Peachey's a better man than those mongrels'll ever be, and they've crucified the poor bastard for something that was – that was none of their damned business. Anyway, he's gone.'

'Gone where?'

'Who knows?' Matt's voice thickened. 'Just said it was time to move on.'

He turned and considered Bonnie's face, caught a deeper question in her eyes.

'Matt, you know . . . you know you can talk to me, don't you? Always.'

At her words, a desperate sadness washed through him. His thoughts connected with each other in a tangle, each connection shutting down something in him like unplugging a string of lights at the end of a party.

'You all right?' Bonnie asked.

Matt nodded.

'Did I say something wrong?'

'No. It's not you. It's . . . God, it's the whole bloody world. I can't put it into words.'

Reaching to touch Matt's hand, Bonnie caught sight of her watch. 'Better not be late.'

'I'm parked over at the yacht club. I'll get the car for you. Back in a sec.'

Matt walked, his instincts at war: the feel of Bonnie's arms around him, the way she slotted into his side like another limb; his sense that things could work out – all somehow tainted now. He thought of Pete, bruised, broken, and his words rang in his ears: *keep Andy safe from mongrels like that*'.

By the time he reached Bonnie and opened the car door for her, a knowledge emerged, like the signal on the shortwave radio when it finally found its wavelength – there was no mistaking the thin, clear note, and it ripped through his guts.

Climbing into the seat, Bonnie's hand brushed something square and small in Matt's jacket pocket, and she raised her eyebrows with a quick smile, then smoothed her skirt and gave directions.

Matt made vague responses to Bonnie's questions about wedding dates and venues. The more excited she sounded, the more desperate he felt; the more the little box seemed to burn his side. Finally she gave him a long look. 'There's no need to be scared, Matt. As far as I'm concerned, we can get married in Timbuktu with just you and me there. Or in a damned shearing shed. Nothing else matters.'

He kept his eyes on the road. 'I couldn't hope to find a better woman, Quiz. Ever.'

She kissed his fingertips, and pointed out the right driveway.

Matt got out and opened her door, taking her hand. She looked at him with shining eyes. 'Ready?' Her voice was relaxed and confident, and Matt felt it in his chest. Saw in a single glimpse the pleasure of arriving with her at parties and weddings and field days for years to come. Though he'd never before in his life used the word, he knew he loved her. He opened his mouth but found he couldn't speak.

Bonnie kissed him. 'Come on, Mr MacBride.'

He loosened his tie and wrestled his collar button. 'Bonnie, I'm – I'm not coming in. I can't.'

She stared at him, as though he'd suddenly started talking another language.

'I can't explain why. And I don't expect you ever to forgive me. But I . . . I can't—'

'Don't be nervous.'

'That's not what I mean. I can't—'

Bonnie took his hand. 'You *can*, Matt. Just follow me. I'll protect you.'

'Please, Bonnie – let me get the words out.' Matt let go of her fingers. 'I can't marry you.'

77

A FEW DAYS later, Lorna sat at the kitchen table as Andy stood on it. She looped the tape measure around his skinny calf, then laid it against the garter elastic on the table and snipped. 'Boarding school's not a punishment, Beetle, it's a privilege. Not everyone gets to go. Down you pop.'

Andy climbed off the table. 'So you're not sending me away because of . . .'

Lorna looked at him.

'. . . you know, cos I told on Pete.' The boy didn't look up, and Lorna put aside her needle and thread to lay a hand on his shoulder.

'We're not "sending you away" at all, dear. You're starting real school, like you were always going to: Matt did, and Warren. And Grandpa Phil, and *his* dad. You're just going a bit earlier. You'll get used to it quicker than you think. You'll make friends there. Like Matt and Hughie did.'

Andy weighed this, and folded his arms in a hug. 'Can I take my rock collection?'

'Better leave it here, safe and sound.'

The decision had been taken after Pete Peachey's departure. 'It'll be good for him,' Lorna had said to Matt. 'Let him put, well – *all that* – behind him. And it'll do him good to make more friends his own age.'

She felt a stab at the thought of life without him around the place. Oh, it always cut deep, this sending a child off on the first step towards adulthood. She'd forgotten how hard it had been, letting her own kids out of her reach, a lifetime ago now. But this little chap . . . he'd have a harder road ahead. He would come through it, eventually: she prayed for that every day. She had to let him have the same opportunities as the others: he deserved a chance at a normal life. 'You'll end up loving it. The others all did.'

When he sniffed back a tear, she drew him into her arms.

The next day, Andy went to the post office to send a letter to Harry Badger while Lorna visited the bank manager.

Coming through the door, Andy caught sight of the familiar silhouette of a woman, her back to him as she wrote on a parcel at a bench. Quietly, he stepped nearer, and reached up to touch her shoulder with a 'Boo!' Bonnie Edquist spun around, looking first into mid-air, then lowering her gaze to find the grinning Andy. 'Scared you, didn't I?'

Bonnie gave a weak laugh. 'Sure did . . .' She scanned the room. 'On your own?'

'Yeah,' said Andy; then, screwing up his face a little, 'What's wrong with your eyes?'

Bonnie drew a handkerchief from her pocket to blow her nose. 'Just the dust.'

'Oh.' He stuffed his hands in his pockets. 'Did you find anything out? About the letter?'

Bonnie's face clouded. 'Drew a blank, I'm afraid.'

'That's OK. We can look again, when you're properly back.'

'I . . . Didn't they tell you? Andy, I'm not coming back.'

His freckles took on a sherry colour as his cheeks flushed. 'Huh?'

'Sweetie, we're pulling out.' She gave her nose another wipe. 'Didn't find what we were looking for after all.'

'But – you're going round with Matt . . .'

'We – ah – we split up.'

Andy looked astonished. 'How come?'

'It's – a long story . . . But you'll be fine finishing your project. You've got lots of olden days stuff.'

'Oh . . . Probably doesn't matter now anyway.' He found his deepest register to say, 'I'm leaving, too. I'm going to Scotch, to board.'

Bonnie took in his slight frame, his freckles, his spindly body that was trying so hard not to give away his feelings. Something in her broke, and her sob came out as a strangled hiccup. 'Damned eyes!' she said, wiping them with her knuckles.

She looked down at her parcel. 'Actually, you've saved me a stamp,' she said, forcing herself back to a conversational tone. 'I was about to post this.' She handed him the small package.

'Why didn't you just bring it? Aren't you coming to say goodbye to Rascal? And Nanna Lorna?'

'You say goodbye for me . . .' She took a deep breath. 'So, you going to open it?'

Andy undid the string and paper, then opened the box. Beneath a layer of cotton wool lay a piece of arsenopyrite in the middle of a quartz crystal. He gasped. 'Are you . . . are you dying or something? This is your *Prime Sample*! Why would you give it away?'

She considered the rock for a moment. 'It's more like passing on the baton. I know you'll treasure it. I know you really *get* it.'

Andy frowned intently at the object, then replaced the lid. He tucked the box under one arm and extended his other to shake Bonnie's hand with the tightest, most grown-up grip he could manage. 'Thanks, Bonnie.'

She put a hand on his head. 'My absolute pleasure, Andy. It's been – it's been a real privilege to know you.'

He gave a single nod, mouth clamped shut.

'Study hard, and if you ever want a job when you've finished school, you just come and see me. I could do with a smart bloke like you around the place.' After a moment, eyes glistening, she said, 'Well, better let you post your letter . . . You take care,' and she turned and left the post office at something approaching a run.

As soon as he got home Andy curled up on his bed and cried, snot seeping into the pillow as he clutched Bonnie's gift to his chest.

Eventually, he sat up and blew his nose, then slotted the Prime Sample into his rock collection. He was just closing the lid when Matt appeared at his door.

'Gedday.' Matt ran a finger along the chest of drawers until he reached the cricket ball that always resided there. He tossed it from one hand to the other. 'Mum says you're down in the dumps.'

'Am not.'

Matt replaced the ball. 'Fair enough.'

Andy leapt off his bed and launched himself at Matt, punching him with furious fists.

'Hey!' said Matt, trying to get hold of his hands. 'What the hell's got into you?'

The boy kept hitting Matt as hard as he could. 'Why didn't you tell me, you – you *arsehole*?'

Matt finally got an arm around both of the boy's, and held him with his back against his stomach. 'Tell you what?'

'About Bonnie! That she's never coming back.'

'Oh, God, Andy!' This was the punch that landed.

The boy tried to struggle free but Matt held him easily.

'Well?'

'If I let you go, are you going to hit me again?'

'Yes I bloody well am!'

'Soot . . . Come on,' said Matt, and turned him around.

'She's my friend!'

'I know, mate.'

'What did you do to her?'

Matt pulled the boy down to sit beside him on the bed, and drew him into his side. 'Soot, there are things . . .' He looked at the family tree on the wall, much enlarged with Bonnie's help. 'Things that won't make much sense until you're older.'

'I'm not a baby!' spat Andy, tears wetting his cheeks. 'I understand about girls!'

'You're one up on me then,' murmured Matt.

'You don't care about me! You only ever do what *you* want to do.'

'If that's how it seems to you, then I'm sorry, Soot. Sorrier than you can know.'

'Then make her stay!'

'I can't *make* her do anything, mate. She's not a bloody ewe.'

'It's not funny!'

'You're right. It's not funny at all. But it's not kids' stuff either.'

Andy spoke into Matt's ribs. 'It's my fault, isn't it?'

'How could it be *your* fault?'

'Because you have to look after me, and she'd be stuck with me too if you got – you know, married.'

'Oh, Sooty . . . Nothing about this is your fault.' He leaned down and masked wiping his eye by picking up the blazer. '. . . Come on. Try it on. And I'll tell you a bit more about Scotch.'

78

Up on Wallaby Ridge, Bonnie froze, and let out an 'Oh God!' at the sight of Matt. All week she had rehearsed her fury, her demands for explanation. She'd gone to sleep comforted by the feeling of slapping him, of smashing his car with a sledgehammer – then woken to the sick reality: the pity in her parents' eyes, the scarlet humiliation of this second jilting, and the ache of loss. But between falling asleep and waking, her dreams were about happy, sun-bleached days with him: the tautness of his skin and the sinews beneath it; the smell of him; the shy curve of his smile, as elusive as a butterfly.

Facing Matt now, all her rage, all her caustic retorts deserted her, their energy as dead as earthed lightning: 'Just . . . came to see this view . . . one last time.'

The untouched world of Wallaby Ridge stretched below them. The scent of eucalypts drenched the bone-dry air, and the light that searched every rock and leaf disclosed no other living creature.

Each day since Matt's return from Perth, he had found himself pulled, like in an ocean rip, back to this spot. Just now, when he caught sight of Bonnie, he'd hesitated, but she'd already seen him. He thrust his hands in his pockets.

A breeze raised a whisper from the leaves. Bonnie murmured, 'Don't want to forget Jemima's trees.'

'You never saw them in flower . . .' He was about to reach for the tobacco in his shirt pocket, but dropped his hand. 'Bonnie' – he eyed the horizon – 'if . . . there's anything about me that's worth a damn, it's – well, that I try to do what's right. Make up for stuff I've messed up.'

She listened, eyes on the ground.

'But some things can't be fixed . . . And I've got no right to drag you into them. I—Well, I can't give you any explanation beyond that. Not one that would make any sense.'

Bonnie was aware of a toughening within her – a protective layer that hadn't been there before, and she found a flinty voice. 'Oh, it makes sense,' she said. 'I'm just not the one for you.' She attempted a smile. 'There's no reason why I should be, even if . . . even if you're the one for me.'

He searched the cloudless blue. 'I'm damaged goods, Quiz. I have to live with that, but you don't.'

The sorrow in his eyes melted something in Bonnie; called forth not just a need to understand, but an instinct to rescue. 'Nothing can be that bad!'

He looked away, and Bonnie felt she was in some new territory – neither hurt nor angry – just in some sort of 'now' that was the very end of something. She took Matt's hand in both of hers. 'Maybe next lifetime it'll work out for us.' She stayed like that a long moment, before leaning in to kiss his cheek. 'Goodbye.'

Then her lips were gone, leaving a wound.

From a few paces, Bonnie turned back. 'Look after yourself, Matt. And look after that lovely kid. I hope . . .' She breathed in the heat and drew herself up a little taller. 'Well, I hope you have a happy life, truly. You deserve some happiness.'

Matt watched as her car gradually lost its shape and colour and shrank to a barely perceptible dot.

The losing of her spread through his body like a cramp, and he was seized by an urge to run after her. But he heard her demand: *'No secrets.'* Matt could bear the knowledge alone. But to thrust that weight on another person . . . It wasn't his to share. His muscles stilled, and he buckled under the truth of it.

'Take good care, Quiz,' he murmured. 'You deserve better than me.'

PART III

Image To Come

79

AGE CREEPS UP on you a day at a time; sits so quietly on your shoulder that you hardly feel it getting heavier. Things change slowly. You get used to the shape your life has taken, even though you never meant it to, just like you get used to the lines on your face you never thought you'd have. For Matthew MacBride, the years after Bonnie left passed steadily enough, according to the station diaries that recorded them. They brought the usual share of droughts and floods; wool prices that crashed, then rallied a little, but never saw their heyday again. The diaries hinted at leaner years, with fewer stock, fewer staff, smaller wool clips, and land that was struggling.

In December 1975, they noted, 'AM won Commonwealth Scholarship for Leaving results', and in February 1976, 'AM started at Muresk'. Andy's studies at Muresk Agricultural College stood him in good stead – a degree in Agriculture rounded out the knowledge he'd absorbed from birth on Meredith Downs with new methods, new science, and he came back champing at the bit to put new ideas into practice, doing things his way. He was popular in the district, known for keeping the stock healthy, and the books, too.

Before long, Andy was the father of three kids with a girl who'd married him without a second thought, because what girl wouldn't want a husband as sunny as Andy MacBride? He'd met Jane at

Muresk – they'd graduated on the same day, though she was from cattle people, not sheep. When they married in 1983, Matt moved into the old manager's house, ceding the homestead to Lorna and the newlyweds. 'You need the space more than I do,' he said. 'Besides, you'll take it over eventually. Might as well start now.' Jane had a whole tribe of brothers and sisters, with parents and grandparents filling out the ranks, so the homestead was always welcoming some relative or other of hers.

Once in a while over the years, Andy or Lorna – or worse, both of them – angled to set Matt up with a suitable wife, but nothing much ever came of it. And once in a while, like a spinifex barb under the skin, he felt the sharp missing of Bonnie Edquist.

There was a day – a specific day – on which, like the elephant that Andy had told him about as a boy, Matt finally felt able to break the string that had held him as tightly as a chain to Meredith Downs. It was the day Andy brought home his third child, a little girl called Rosie. Andy flew himself to Perth and back in the station's Cessna, and the baby's arrival at the 'drome reminded Matt of Andy's own homecoming with Rose and Fin Rafferty in the Flying Doctor Hawker de Havilland.

On that evening, as they were sitting around the fire, the infant asleep, the little ones snuggled beside their mother, and Andy sitting on the sofa with an arm around Lorna's shoulder, Matt had a clear thought: if time could stop just here, just at this moment. *This* was what he'd done it for; lived his life the way he had. *This* was worth it. Because anyone observing the scene would say with complete certainty that the MacBrides had healed and re-formed, the scars faded and the dread banished. Andy finally had enough experience under his belt to run the place himself now. And clear as day, Matt remembered Miles Beaumont coming to him to ask for his Nunc Dimittis thirty years earlier. 'You'll be all right from here on in, I know,' Miles had said. And though Matt had doubted it, Miles had been right. He had come to terms with the fact that the thing that hurt his heart the most – Andy – also healed it the most.

Matt had made a solemn promise that he would not walk away from this boy. He would stay for as long as it took. And on this evening, the boy was now a man, toe-wrestling his own eldest son, a cheeky four-year old, while the two-year-old brother tried his best to disrupt the game.

Matthew MacBride was looking down the barrel of nearly fifty by the time he finally left Meredith Downs in 1988. It didn't need him any more. In fact, what it needed was his absence.

80

BOOM AND BUST. THAT'S always been the way in Western Australia. The gold rush of the 1890s came in like a tidal wave and went out just as dramatically, leaving once-thriving towns high and dry, dwindling to a few piles of bricks stranded in a wilderness of spinifex and sun-baked earth. The nickel scramble of 1969 that saw shares in mining companies rocket soon petered out, too, burning a lot of fingers in the process. And just like after the wool boom of the 1950s, there was a hell of a hangover. As markets plummeted, mines were mothballed and exploration budgets slashed.

As for asbestos, it took a while to reach the consensus that there's pretty much no safe place for it except under the ground: some things are best left undisturbed. Andy MacBride reckoned they dodged a bullet when Bonnie's lot left Meredith Downs empty-handed in 1970. Harry Badger's father died later that year. Litigation over his case, then later over the whole industry, rumbled on for decades, as the extent of the damage done by the 'wonder mineral' slowly revealed itself.

As for the land, years of carrying thousands of sheep had flogged most of the sheep stations in WA. Gone were the days of the twenty-stand shearing sheds, as the country was gradually eaten out, and left vulnerable to drought. Meredith Downs, always steadily managed, got off better than most. And the land around Wallaby Ridge, in particular, managed to escape the fate of some areas, which were now all spinifex and poverty bush.

When Andy's oldest boy did a project on Jemima's trees in 1996, he dug out the old letters between Jemima and Kew Gardens. He got his mother to help him write to London, to ask what name they'd officially given to the tree Jemima had described in such detail and had shown Mr Sampson, the botanist, when he was passing through, all those years back. The upshot was that the location details furnished by Sampson were so vague as to be untraceable, and the species, *Eucalyptus sampsonii*, had been presumed extinct, hit by grazing and roads and land clearance in the few other places it had ever been officially recorded. Wallaby Ridge, fenced off from stock and protected all those years, was therefore promptly listed and gazetted and declared a Site of Special Scientific Interest, being the only remaining habitat of this tree that had, against the odds, survived the jaws of evolution and the teeth of sheep.

When miners in the area packed up after the latest downturn, their claims were mostly surrendered or allowed to lapse. Which placed Andy MacBride, who knew just about every rock on Meredith Downs, in good stead when markets eventually picked up again towards the end of the nineties.

He'd talked it over with Jane, with Lorna. He'd explained on a crackly and shockingly expensive line to Matt, a hemisphere away. 'Your decision now,' Matt had said. 'You and Jane decide what feels right, and I'll go along with it. Just – don't change anything until Mum's . . . ready.' Andy had learned young that you can't stop someone coming to dig up your land if they want what's underneath it. So, as he told his wife, 'If you can't beat 'em, join 'em': he pegged claims himself, then negotiated to bring in partners who could develop them.

So it was that in 1999 Andy sat in the Perth office of a mining company, and talked terms. The Meredith Downs pastoral lease would be transferred to a new company in which the MacBrides would own shares and of which Andy would be a director, and Andy and his family would stay on in the homestead. There would be a joint-venture arrangement for the mineral rights, with any areas mined to be restored once mined out. With all this, the station would be destocked, and for the most part converted to a nature reserve, allowing the land to revert to its wild state, while introduced species – the feral cats and dogs and goats and the like – would be eradicated, to give the surviving native animals a chance to escape extinction. There was still no shortage of roos, however.

Jemima's trees, with their long elliptical leaves and feathery yellow flowers, found nowhere else in Australia these days, had been classified as Declared Rare Flora, and protected by legislation. Andy wanted to make it a term of the agreement that not only would the company not mine near Wallaby Ridge, it would also exclude a wider area, to protect the birds and insects vital for pollination. This last issue had been a sticking point, with the mining company's lawyers digging in their heels. Andy had therefore come to this final meeting armed with lawyers of his own, and facts and figures about Jemima's trees (which he had to remind himself to call *E. sampsonii*), ready to fight his corner.

Negotiations that day dragged on. From the company's boardroom on the twenty-fifth floor, Andy could see all the way to the ocean seven miles away and out to Rottnest Island, behind which the sun was nearly set by now. The sky was scorched a deep burnt orange, and the city was disappearing outside the windows, leaving a skeleton of lights. So different from the sunset at Wallaby Ridge, and the way it drew its blanket of utter darkness over Meredith Downs for the night ahead, with just the shimmering stars left to keep watch. Taking in the polished wood and sleek modern furniture of the boardroom, Andy suddenly felt a long way from home.

Against one wall was a large display cabinet of mineral samples, which had caught Andy's eye when he arrived. Now, while both sets of lawyers chewed over Clause 135 (2) (a) for the umpteenth time, arguing about the position of a comma which could radically affect liability, he felt an overwhelming urge to touch the rock specimens, feel something real, familiar. He asked the junior mining company lawyer opposite him if he could open the cabinet. When she looked doubtful, he assured her he knew how to handle samples properly.

'Well . . . I suppose . . .' she said. 'But be careful. They belong to our MD. *Personally*. She knows exactly where each one belongs. But she lets people handle them sometimes.'

Andy knew that the 'MD' the girl mentioned was Bonnie Edquist, who had taken over the reins of Hollamby Mining a while back: it was the main reason he'd chosen to approach them. He figured he could trust any outfit run by Bonnie, even though he wouldn't actually meet her – she was a real high-flyer these days. In fact, she probably had no idea the deal was being done – it wasn't worth nearly enough money to get onto her personal radar: he realised that.

Opening the cabinet, Andy felt ten years old again, excited finally to see the collection – or at least part of it – that he'd heard so much about from 'Bonnie Head Quiz'. He was mesmerised by the brilliant blue of some azurite; by the neat natural cubes of limonite known as Devil's Dice; the fine, intricate tendrils of natural copper; a large chunk of orbicular granite, with its mysterious rings formed by nature and time. Beside each item was a small map showing its source.

Lying on a white chamois cushion was a decent-sized dumbbell tektite. Surely he was imagining things . . . He read the card. 'From Meredith Downs Station, near Wanderrie Creek, WA. A generous gift from Andrew MacBride, noted local geologist.' A lump came to his throat as he remembered those days with Bonnie – her smile, her way of making him feel grown up. It occurred to him now that she was probably the first true friend he'd ever had.

'So, if we add a rider,' one of the lawyers was saying.

Andy cut in. 'Is she here? Your MD? Can you let her know what we're arguing about?'

This caused some controversy, and prompted puzzled looks and mutterings of 'busy' and 'travelling' and other general fobbing-off.

Andy turned to the junior lawyer. 'Is she here today?'

'She could be anywhere. She travels a lot.'

He stepped towards the cabinet and carefully picked up the tektite, while the collective gathering watched in consternation. 'Can you just – well, can you just see if she's here, and if she is, give her this? Tell her the geologist who found it is here, and needs to talk to her about *E. samp*—about Jemima's trees.'

The girl departed, and after twenty minutes, the door to the boardroom opened as an elegant grey-haired woman in a pale linen suit appeared. She was unmistakeably Bonnie. Older; *tidier*, but definitely the woman Andy remembered.

As for Bonnie, seeing the man in front of her almost took her breath away: the absolute image of Matt, though with some lines; more weathered skin – he was years older than Matt himself had been when she last saw him.

'Andy!' She was about to hug him, but checked herself, and instead took his hand in both of hers.

'Bon—Mrs Gracechurch,' said Andy, using the name on the documents he'd seen.

'"Bonnie", please. Now, let's sort this business out.' She sat down gracefully at the head of the table. 'I've been briefed on the deal. And on the sticking point.'

'Let me explain why we want it,' said Andy. 'I—'

Bonnie raised a hand to silence him. 'Save your breath, kiddo.'

Andy's face fell, but Bonnie went on, 'One of the perks of being the head of Hollamby Mining is that I get to say what goes.' She smiled. '*Of course* I understand what's so special about Jemima's trees, Andy. You're knocking on an open door as far as I'm concerned.' To the advisors on her own side who demurred, she said, 'Yes, I know it's your job to talk me out of it. And I respect your advice. But not everything's about money, or winning every point. We can make this work.'

When the details had been wrapped up, instead of leaving with the lawyers, Bonnie stayed behind, alone with Andy. 'You know I have to say it: "Look at you, all grown up!"'

'I've still got your Prime Sample.'

'I should hope so too!' She stroked a gold bracelet on her wrist. 'Funny how life turns out . . . I remember once saying I'd give you a job. Didn't quite picture it like this, though.'

'Neither did I. It'll be like old times.'

'If only . . . Hard to know where the years have gone, but I'm actually retiring soon . . . I'll make sure we stick to our promises, though, even once I've gone.' She straightened a blotter on the table. 'So, will Matt be coming? For the signing?'

'Oh! No . . . I got power of attorney from him – I'll be signing for all of us. He's seen the paperwork, though. All done via the Australian Consulate in Athens – he's in Greece at the moment. He left the station years ago.'

'Ah.' Bonnie gave a slight nod as she absorbed the information, then glanced at her watch. 'Well, I've got a plane to catch, I'm afraid.' As they stood up, she put a hand on Andy's shoulder and kissed him on the cheek. 'Safe trip back. And good luck with the project.'

The draft papers had indeed been sent to Matt via the consulate. When he read to the end and saw the reference to the Managing Director of Hollamby Mining, his heart skipped a beat at 'Bonnie'. His first conscious thought was, 'Well done, Quiz . . . I knew you'd go far.' It took another second for him to notice the surname – *Gracechurch*. Ah. So that was that. No need to go back to sign. Andy could do it for him.

81

Monday, 10th January 2000

WALKING THROUGH THE corridors of Wanderrie Creek Hospital, Matt was assailed by wisps of memory of his time there, inhaling them with the disinfectant. In the newly opened Fairchild Wing, he entered a room and approached the bed.

'Hello, stranger,' he said, and swallowed hard as he bent to kiss the forehead of the woman in it. Her face, unseen by him for so many years, was old, the skin papery, the hair silky white.

She opened her eyes, and a sparkle came into them as she recognised her son. 'Mattie!'

He sat down, and took her bony, sun-mottled hand. And just as they had decades ago, the cold metal sensation of her wedding ring, the way her palm fitted with his, built a bridge of recognition between them – a bridge to the Lorna who was beyond the reach and the measure of time. 'Mum,' he said, and lifted her hand to his cheek.

They sat like that for a good while. Finally, Lorna said, 'Mattie darling, not long now, I think.'

He squeezed her hand and gave a nod. The cancer had been discovered only weeks ago, much too late for help.

'I'll be sorry to leave you, though,' she said, 'and Andy and his little ones . . . And the station, of course. I've loved that place.' She smiled. 'I'm not afraid, though . . .' She raised her other hand to clasp his, and Matt stroked her hair.

They talked about his journey back, his life abroad. They spoke about the old days; fell quiet again. Then Lorna said, 'I hope Rose will forgive me.'

Matt looked at her with a question, and she said, 'I've always felt what happened to her was my fault, somehow.'

'It wasn't your fault, Mum. And it wasn't her fault either.'

'Was I a good mother to you, Mattie?'

'The best.'

'I'm proud of how you turned out. After such a hard start. And I'm proud of all you did for Andy, when you could have just walked away. You didn't have to.'

Matt said, 'I did have to, Mum.'

She smiled. 'You always were the kind one.'

'And have you forgiven me, for leaving?'

'I'm glad you got to live your great adventure, eventually. I'd always hoped you would . . . Oh, the hours you used to spend spinning the globe on Phil's desk. "*There*," you'd say. "I'll visit *there*," wherever your finger landed on the map.'

She tried to cough but couldn't manage. Matt plumped her pillows and lifted her up – as light as a wren. Eighty-nine, and dwindled to bones and feather-soft wrinkles. What weight those bones had carried, though, one way and another. He held a tissue to her mouth as she coughed up some mucus; then he wiped her lips.

'Want some water?'

'Just you, love,' she said, and took his hand again.

As they listened together to the wild melody of a butcherbird outside, Matt recalled that favourite phrase of Pete Peachey's: '*A bird has many different songs.*'

A grimace of pain crossed Lorna's face, and she opened her eyes, letting out a low moan.

'Shall I get the nurse?'

She shook her head. 'It'll pass in a minute. The morphine will only muddle me, and I need to tell you something . . .' She bit her bottom lip and winced as she changed position. '. . . about Rose,' she said, then stopped to draw breath.

Matt's heart quickened, and he worried she could feel his palm sweat.

'I'm going to tell you a secret,' the old woman faltered, her voice using her in-breath as well as the out-breath. She grasped his hand. 'I know who Andy's father was.'

The butcherbird fell silent, as though to hear better. Matt sat motionless, sick fear flooding through him.

'It was . . . Miles Beaumont,' she said, and gave a single nod, as though having put down an enormous burden, then closed her eyes. 'It's not so bad . . . He was a fine young man.' Then, after a few more breaths, 'You can tell Andy, if you want. I'll leave it to you to decide what's best.' Her face darkened. 'But I don't think there's any reason to tell him about Rosie's death . . . or about his fall. That could only hurt him.'

Matt desperately weighed something in the balance. His mother had perhaps hours, at most days, left . . . What right had he to correct her, and desecrate her last minutes? How could it bring her anything but suffering, then or now?

Lorna opened her eyes to find him crying. 'Mattie . . . There, there, Mattie darling. Don't be sad. Eighty-nine's pretty good going. I've had a good run. And I've had so much love along the way . . . That's all you can ask, isn't it?'

The butcherbird started a new melody, and Matt laid his head on his mother's chest, listening to her unsteady heartbeat threading with the birdsong, and feeling the sun streaming gently through the window, melting into a moment of peace.

At Lorna's wake in the church hall a week after Matt's return, it took him a moment to recognise the frail old lady who greeted him. Only when he saw the ever-friendly Clive, still with his psoriasis, did he work out it was Myrtle Eedle.

'So good to see you after all this time,' she said.

'Thanks, Mrs Eedle,' Matt said. 'Good to see you, too.'

'A fine woman, your mother. She'll be sorely missed around here,' said Myrtle. Matt just gave a nod, so she added, 'Lovely service.'

'Thanks.'

'Were we still running the post office when you left in – when was it – 1986?'

''Eighty-eight,' said Matt. 'I think so, yes.'

'Clive retired years ago, of course, but I still like to keep my finger on the pulse.' This was true. Her Drawers of Death now filled an entire filing cabinet, and she had already jotted notes onto Lorna's order of service: 'Excellent turnout. First MacBride to die of old age in living memory. Matthew returned for occasion.' She went on, 'I hear there are changes afoot on Meredith Downs?'

'One or two.'

Myrtle waited, eyebrows raised to invite further details, but Matt just said, as another guest approached, 'If you'll excuse me, Mrs Eedle . . .'

'Of course,' she said, and tottered to a corner to update her notes in a spidery hand.

It was a big gathering. Humpty Dumpton had come with Coral, armed with snaps of kids and grandkids; Harry Badger, who'd flown from Perth and the mining-equipment company he owned; Maudie Knapp, widowed now, but as energetic as ever, helping out with the spread. Finally Matt greeted Sneaky Snook, still as round, still as florid, but now with a shock of white hair, and a walking frame to supplement his 'dancing shoes'.

'How long are you here for?' the old man asked.

'Not long. Just came back when I heard how sick Mum was. A few things to tie up, then I'll be off.'

'We miss you! Shame you're not staying.' Sneaky nabbed a small sausage roll from a passing tray and popped the whole thing into his mouth, dispatching it rapidly. 'Not a patch on your mother's.' He wiped his fingers on the hanky he produced from his pocket. 'Now, you went off to do something with boats, am I right?'

'Yeah. Joined a boatbuilder's in Queensland. He took me on as a fairly geriatric apprentice. Since then I've travelled about a bit, sailing mostly. Crewing on yachts in England. The Caribbean. Greece . . .'

'How's your Greek?'

'Non-existent. But boats are boats, and water's water.'

They reminisced about Lightning, about the old days on Meredith Downs.

Sneaky leaned his head to one side. 'Ever hear anything from Pete Peachey, after he left?'

Matt shook his head, and felt a deep pang at the memory of the man who'd meant so much to him.

'Well, I'll tell you a funny thing,' said Sneaky. 'Not long after you left, two women came to town, trying to track him down. Traced him to Wanderrie Creek through some old money orders – he'd sent them from various places, apparently.'

Matt raised his eyebrows a little. 'That's a turn-up for the books.'

'That's not the funny part. The *funny* part,' said Sneaky with a grin, 'was that the two birds were the spitting image of Pete! Both tall, and as skinny as a yard of pump water. They said Myrtle had tried her best to help them – bent over backwards, apparently, but drew a blank, so she sent them to me.'

A smile came to Matt's lips. 'And?'

'Oh, I never knew where he went, after . . . that business. Anyway, I told them to keep their ear to the ground, and if they heard about a place where the roos were losing the fight, try looking for him there.' He put his hands in his pockets and chuckled to himself. 'Full of surprises, that one.' Wiping a rheumy eye with a knuckle, he asked, 'And is it true? That you're selling Meredith?'

'It's a bit more complicated than that,' replied Matt. 'Came to an arrangement with a mining mob, and with the government conservation people. Andy'll keep the homestead, but the place'll be destocked.'

'Wouldn't be the first place round these parts to get out of sheep,' said Sneaky. 'Pretty hard to make a living out of wool now.'

'Yeah.' Matt looked around at the old faces. 'Everything comes to an end, eventually.'

Matt and Andy sat on either side of Old Wally, the clock still steadfastly ticking away the MacBride minutes after Lorna's funeral and wake. The early evening light came soft and coppery through the windows.

'You all right?' Andy asked.

'Fine,' said Matt quietly. 'Nice that so many people came to the funeral.'

'All the great and the good. I reckon she'd have been happy enough with it. A few old hymns, and not too much nonsense.' Andy topped up Matt's beer and settled down in his chair again, raising his glass. 'To Nanna Lorna.'

'To Mum,' said Matt. As he drank, his gaze was drawn by the shouts of the kids he saw messing about outside. 'How old are they all now? I lose track.'

Andy looked to the ceiling to calculate. 'Nick's . . . sixteen, so Dom's . . . nearly fourteen, Rosie's twelve next birthday and Sam's – God, nearly three already.' He laughed. 'Our little surprise . . .'

'You look happy,' said Matt. 'Really happy.'

'I am.'

'No regrets? About handing over the station?'

Andy looked out at his children on the lawn, where Jane had dragooned them all into a game of croquet, to give Matt and Andy a moment alone. 'No. Time for a new chapter. What about you?'

Matt shrugged a shoulder and took another sip. 'I'm doing all right. Sound in wind and limb, as they say.'

'The kids always love the postcards. Though I'm not sure they really get what a "great-uncle" is.'

They fell into a comfortable silence, Andy trying to undo some fiendish knots in the string of Rosie's kite, Matt taking in the changes to the room: all sorts of additions thanks to the kids – a wonky clay fruit bowl; a sheep made of pipe-cleaners and bits of old fleece; a Mother's Day card with a stick figure of Jane, still on the mantelpiece long after its season. All these lives – thriving and healthy and knitted together in such an ordinary way . . .

A new millennium. Matt pondered all that had changed over the years – all the old secrets that these days might have earned a shrug at best. Miles could be with Sandy, or any bloke he wanted, for that matter, without getting thrown in gaol. Pete Peachey could wear what he liked and no one would bat an eyelid. But nothing had changed for Matt. Nothing had changed for Andy's position: they were still in Rundle's 'moral sewer'. That was never going to change: there was no statute of limitations on *that* particular sin.

Matt thought of Lorna, and her last words to him. He'd be gone again soon enough. Who knew whether he'd ever see Andy again? 'Funny question, Soot, I know, but . . .'

'Go on.'

'Do you think you'd have been happier, if you'd found out who your father was?'

Andy was thrown: Matt, of all people, touching on the topic he'd avoided all Andy's life. Funerals sure had strange effects on people . . . Then, to his own surprise, Andy found himself laughing. 'God! I remember when I was obsessed by that! That bloody family tree project and everything.' He scratched his head. 'To be honest, it's been – boy – donkeys' years since I've even thought about it.'

'Would you want to know, if you could?'

'Why?' Andy gave Matt a look. 'Did Nanna Lorna say something? Before she died?'

'Nothing like that. I was just wondering.'

'No time for much else when you've got four kids careering around. That and running this place doesn't leave me much time for contemplating my navel. And soon there'll be all the changes . . . Nah. I suppose – I'd put it this way: I don't know who I might have been, but I know who I've become. I reckon what matters most now isn't who *my* father was, but that I'm *their* dad.' He nodded toward the window. 'Jane knows who I really am; my kids know.'

He smiled as he remembered something. 'Pete Peachey once said a forgetment was a free pass: I could make things the way I wanted them to be.' He gave a laugh. 'What if my father had turned out to be an arsehole? Or if he wanted to muscle in on our lives? He could be dead by now, anyway . . . I reckon finding out could only make me *less* happy, not more. I'm happier that he's a forgetment.' He shrugged. 'Besides, I always had you.'

Old Wally chimed the hour, and each chime soaked into Matt, dissolving something within. 'Is he still getting his fair share of booze?' he asked with a glance at the clock.

'My oath!' said Andy. 'And the kids cottoned on pretty quickly that they could make that tradition apply to lollies. You'd be amazed how much chocolate that bloody clock can eat.'

As Matt turned his eyes to the swing set on the back lawn, he did a double take at the sight of himself, or perhaps of Andy, sailing up on the seat, pushed by a girl. In the split second it took to remember that it must be Sam, Andy's youngest, his body had already retrieved the feeling of playing with Andy on it. The touch of those tiny hands that reached for him with such trust; that taught him it was all right to reach back.

82

A CHIRRUP LIKE a squeaky toy drew Matt's attention to the long blue tail of a splendid fairy wren coming and going to his nest with food for his chicks: once the mother, feathers a dull fawn, has hatched the eggs in the little dome of grass, the male helps with the feeding. Pretty rare to see one this late in January, though: the brilliant cobalt of his mating season plumage was already surrendering to its usual mousey brown.

Three days had passed since Lorna's funeral. As Matt surveyed Jemima's trees, the strong, dry waft of eucalyptus carried him back to all he'd been through in this place – times he'd believed he would never survive. Somehow, being back here erased the intervening years – travelling; working; the occasional stab at romance that always ended with one or the other of them retreating. In this place, the memory of Bonnie washed everything else away like a wave. He hadn't seen her since the day they'd said goodbye at this spot . . . the day she had joined the ranks of all the people he'd lost.

And now, those ranks included Lorna. He had lived away from his mother for years, but it was different, this missing her that had settled into his bones since her death. One of his hands moved to embrace the other, as if to prolong her last clasping of it. From Lorna, his mind drifted to his father; to Warren; to his sister. With a lurch, he pictured Rose, body laid out under a sheet on the kitchen table, just an elbow of her polka-dot pyjamas peeping out. He took a gulp of air and shook his head. *Oh, Rosie . . .*

A fragment of music had been playing over and over in his mind since Lorna's funeral – '*Dear Lord and Father of Mankind, forgive our foolish ways. Reclothe us in our rightful minds . . .*' His memory of Lorna's coffin shaded itself into the image of Rosie's. He calculated: yes, Andy's oldest – the youngster with bad skin and a fairly poor go at a shave, who he'd last seen as a small child, and who had greeted him gawkily a few days ago – that kid was almost the same age he'd been himself at the time of the crash . . . and of all that came after. The thought hit him like a body blow: so young. *Oh, Bliss. We were just bloody kids!* So ridiculously young to have to deal with—with all that.

But it was in Rose's voice that he heard the next words: *And we paid for it, Bubba . . . Enough, now . . .*

He breathed deeply. *Maybe you're right . . .* '*Yawa, yawa, yawa,*' he whispered. '*Yawa,* Rosie love.'

He pictured her with Andy as he was now, together. He had grown up sane, happy. Matt couldn't have hoped for more. Now, Andy had answered his question, and his answer had been certain. The secret was not Matt's any more, but forever Andy's: it must be allowed to become a *forgetment*.

Matt gazed out into the distance, watching the shadows grow and bend the trees earthwards: storing up the view as a treasure he could carry with him, just as he'd done as a little boy. He heard a car. Andy was due to meet him here, maybe with the kids. Matt hoped this place was special for them, too.

When Matt turned he saw not a man, but a woman with straight grey hair pulled into a ponytail, who appeared as utterly startled to see him as he did her. In shorts and T-shirt, she still had that unmistakeable, rangy physique.

'Quiz?'

'No one's called me that in a while,' said Bonnie when she could finally find words. 'But . . . Where's Andy? He asked me to meet him here.'

'Asked me, too,' said Matt.

'I had no idea. Truly. I heard you were on a Greek island or somewhere.' She glanced at her watch. 'I'm sure this was the time he—'

She stopped, as the truth dawned on them.

'Bloody Andy . . .' said Matt.

Eventually, Bonnie said, 'It's – it's good to see you.'

'How long has it been?'

She put her hands in her pockets. 'Thirtieth of January 1970. It was a Friday.'

The precision of her reply loosened something in Matt. His breathing slowed, his body stilled, not wanting to frighten the moment away, not wanting to rush through it.

'Is that so?' He motioned with his head to the flat ledge, and they made their way to sit down.

'I was sorry to hear about your mum,' said Bonnie. 'I understand why you and Andy didn't want to change anything while she was alive.' She paused. 'The company'll take good care of the place. And you're welcome here any time.'

'I won't be back, actually,' Matt said. 'Just came to say one last goodbye.'

'Ah.' Bonnie raised her chin as she took in the news. 'Me too . . . I'm retiring. I'm just on a farewell tour of our sites – got here today. I'd told Andy I'd be in the neighbourhood.'

Matt's eyes were fixed on the view without seeing it, his thoughts racing, his skin alive with the charge that seemed to come from the narrow gap between them. 'In the paperwork Andy sent you're Bonnie Gracechurch. You – got married, then?'

'I did,' said Bonnie, 'eventually.'

It took Matt a moment to recover from the stab of it. 'Good for you.' He paused. 'Any kids?'

'No . . . Don't know that I was ever going to be the type to sit at home and knit and make school lunches.'

'I can't see you doing that either.'

'Bob wanted it – the knitting and the kids. So we only lasted a couple of years.'

'Sorry to hear that,' said Matt, his scalp beginning to tingle.

'Don't be,' said Bonnie. 'And you?'

A shadow of pink crept over Matt's face. 'Never married.'

The wren had returned to its nest, and they watched it together, the narrow opening in the grassy dome occasionally revealing the gaping mouth of one of the featherless chicks.

'I never thought I'd see you again,' Bonnie said.

'Neither did I.'

She brushed some red dirt from beside her, clearing a small circle of bedrock with her finger. 'There have been so many times, over the years, I wished I *could* see you – because I wanted to tell you something. Never thought I'd get the chance.' She tapped her temple with the heel of her hand. 'Now that I have, the words feel all jumbled.'

Matt fixed his attention on her.

'I wanted to tell you,' she said, 'that . . . I know what it's like to have things you don't want to talk about . . . and to have someone try to drag them out of you. Bob didn't want me to have any corner of myself that he couldn't get into. He'd get jealous if he thought there were things he didn't know about me. It took me a long time to understand how you—how it could have felt for you,' she said. 'But now I do. There are bits of me that are—well, just mine.' She shrugged. 'And that's all right.'

Matt held his silence, every sinew taut, alert . . . Maybe she'd want nothing more to do with him. He could hardly blame her: he knew how terribly he'd wounded her.

She kept watching the nest, the wren darting in and out with a grub or a cricket. 'I know none of it matters now, but for what it's worth, it took me a long time to work out that I . . .' There was a long pause. '. . . well – *loved* – you because of how you were, mysteries and all. If I'd turned you into someone else, maybe I'd have stopped loving you.'

The tingling in Matt's scalp washed through his whole body. Against all odds, here was Quiz, sitting so close he could feel the heat of her body, smell her hair, one last time. Who could say how much longer either of them would be on this earth? Regret had hummed beneath every one of his days for as long as he could remember, and if he didn't speak now, it would stay that way forever. He eyed the wren. 'And have you?' he murmured. 'Stopped?'

'You . . . pegged a prior claim on my heart. No one else could ever quite get in. I don't know whether you knew that.'

Matt reached for her hand. 'I knew, Quiz. I knew. Because it was the same for me.'

A black beetle had been making its way along a rock just below them, and without warning, the wren dropped down from the tree to a spot just beside Matt's boot. They both froze so as not to disturb it. The bird jumped onto Matt's foot, then swooped on the beetle, seizing it in its beak and staring at the two of them briefly, head to one side, before flitting back up to its nest.

'Is it—oh, I don't know – too late, Matt?' Bonnie turned to him. 'Did we miss our chance?'

'Depends . . .' Matt said; then, quietly, 'Is your heart still beating?'

Bonnie took his hand and rested it on her ribs to feel its beat, strong and rapid.

'Then maybe we're not too late.' He turned to face her, and drew his fingers along the grooves beside her eyes, his thumb along the furrows time had etched into her forehead, and dared to look into those turquoise eyes, searching for the woman he had lost years ago. There she was, looking out, searching for him, too.

He pulled her to him, tucking her head beneath his chin. As he kissed the top of her hair, the last traces of an ancient pain lifted, and his body recalled a childhood sensation – of jigsaw pieces, clicking back into place as though they'd never been apart, their belonging inevitable, more powerful than time.

It took a week or so to dismantle the shed. It took a few more days for the transport crew from Hollamby Mining to rig up and secure the special sling. This first part of the journey would be only sixty miles, just as far as the rendezvous at a rail siding.

Goodbyes had been said at the homestead, but Andy, Jane and all four kids bid one last round of farewells to Matt and Bonnie as they all gathered together in the sharp morning light that was already baking the earth.

'You need your head read, you mad bastard,' said Andy, grabbing Matt in a bear hug and slapping his back.

'A promise is a promise, Soot. And between us MacBrides, we've been promising Uncle Monty for years that we'd scatter his ashes in the ocean.'

'I can think of easier ways of doing it,' Bonnie said.

'But not a more fitting one,' Matt replied. 'And I distinctly remember you volunteered to crew. Though that was a while back.'

Andy nudged Sam, his youngest, forward. 'Go on. Remember what to say . . .'

The boy produced a bottle of beer and held it up to Matt with a solemn frown. 'For the Monty boat!'

'We reckoned Monty deserved one last beer,' said Andy.

'I'll make sure he gets it,' Matt said, clearing his throat to cover the crack in his voice. He ran a knuckle down Sam's cheek, then squeezed Andy's shoulder and gave him a final nod.

Matt and Bonnie climbed aboard the big Hollamby helicopter, which began its slow ascent, hoisting the slack steel cables until they became taut with the weight of their cargo. Andy gave Matt a salute which turned into a wave that shrank with distance.

Bonnie turned to Matt, her voice raised through the headphones against the racket of the rotor. 'Matthew MacBride! What the hell are we doing?'

'Haven't got a bloody clue, Quiz.' He took her hand. 'But we'll work it out.'

Generations before, people and kangaroos and bungarras and God knew what else had looked on, astonished, as a camel team had painstakingly hauled Monty's pearling lugger onto Meredith Downs. Now, their respective descendants watched in wonder as the boat made its way skywards, finally heading home to the water by a means their forebears could never have imagined. The boat under them climbed steadily – swaying a little – and below, Matt could see the sheds, the windmills; make out the ancient skeleton of the wrecked truck. Gradually, trees turned to patterns and then to dots; rocks blurred into sandy patches, and the homestead of Meredith Downs, together with the lives of all the people who had lived and loved there, grew more and more distant, until they were barely a smudge on that timeless red landscape, their deeds, good and bad, destined to join the vast ocean of human forgetments.

Acknowledgements

1 Page To Come